FAL THORNS

The awakening is only the beginning.

It has been nearly two months since the events of the Summer Solstice, but for Misha Briar, it's been an endless stream of dreams and nightmares. Unsure of what is true, Misha grapples with waking to a reality in which she's lost her home and nearly all her family. Not to mention what she's done to Julian Warin, her best friend and love of her life, and if he can ever forgive her.

If she can ever forgive herself.

When Misha was poisoned, cast into the cursed sleep, something was awoken deep within her. Something that demands to be set free, to seek retribution for all she's lost.

Can Misha hold the darkness at bay, or will it become her?

In the sequel to Summer's Snow, Misha Briar struggles with new and unfamiliar magic, stopping at nothing to save her sister, her love, and her kingdom.

FALL'S THORNS

Carly H. Mannon

FALL'S THORNS

Carly H. Mannon

For those who struggle with darkness.
When even standing feels too great a task,
know that no matter how
the shadows bind you,
to someone
you are the sun.

Rise.

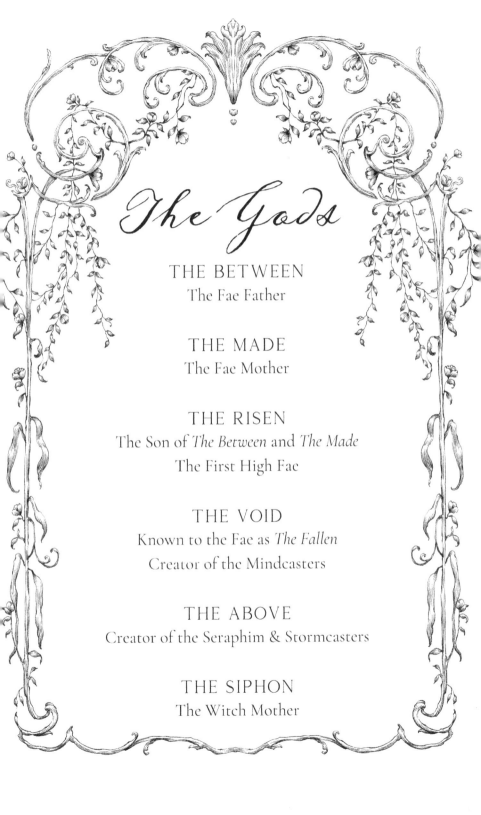

The Gods

THE BETWEEN
The Fae Father

THE MADE
The Fae Mother

THE RISEN
The Son of *The Between* and *The Made*
The First High Fae

THE VOID
Known to the Fae as *The Fallen*
Creator of the Mindcasters

THE ABOVE
Creator of the Seraphim & Stormcasters

THE SIPHON
The Witch Mother

PROLOGUE
Diana

M etal clinked softly as I opened the velvet pouch, spilling the contents into my hand: two pendants, one silver and one gold, twisted into a four-cornered witch's knot. Through the open library windows, sunlight hit the ruby and emerald, casting them aglow with an ethereal light.

The witch promised me even the fine chains would withstand any force or magic. Water and ice, the tug of thorns and claws, fire—nothing should harm the necklaces. And the pendants themselves, with the magic resting within, would protect my daughters.

I had one chance to save my daughters' lives. One opportunity to prevent a sure death that would suspend them in everlasting sleep until they could be awoken by the one they trusted with their entire being.

I would never know if the witch was true to her word. The magic in the pendants would be tested only long after I was gone.

My fingertips swiped beneath my eyes, catching the tears before they spilled. I reached my hand deeper into the pouch and pulled out the gold bands, plain except for the inner inscription: *One evermore.*

Alesia and Eve's chosen words from their mating ceremony.

My breath caught in a laugh, remembering how such stubborn hatred between them had turned into ferocious love. My twin might have denied that my meddling swayed her into pursuing her mate—and maybe she was right—but I would never stop gloating over it. Alesia and Eve were perfect complements to each other. I would love my sister-in-oath for the peace she'd brought Alé during a lifetime of violence.

The rings had gone to the witch as well, so she could strengthen them to persist against the same forces, just in case. My anniversary gift to them both.

I placed the rings back in the velvet pouch. There was only an hour before Alé and Eve's anniversary celebration began, and I still needed to bathe and dress.

Outside, the gardens flourished in the May warmth—nine months since I'd had the vision that had changed everything. The stars had only shown me one vision since: my daughters each holding the swords, blades of wrath and mercy in their hands. The words on the blades had been spoken to me by the stars during their forging, the language ancient and long forgotten.

It had taken me months to find someone capable of translating the words and another to discover how to reach her discreetly. With the help of a hawk, I'd sent her a letter asking for her expertise and silence—no one else could know what I had requested. To my relief, she'd agreed. Now, I awaited her response and prayed it would not come too late.

I had three months until the twins arrived. Three months until I was out of time.

As I placed my hands on the arms of my chair, readying myself to stand, the hair on my neck prickled to attention, and I knew I was no longer alone. My head snapped to the human woman standing in the wisteria-covered doorway. I'd never seen her before, but there was recognition in her dark brown eyes.

"Who are you?"

"Alesia . . ." the woman whispered, ignoring my question. "But she watched you—" Her words cut off as I stood from behind the desk. Her eyes grew wide with disbelief as they landed on my belly, swollen late in my pregnancy. "You're Diana."

My head tilted. "Was my sister expecting you?" The woman must have been someone working with her in the guard, a new one I had yet to meet. But she was surprised to see me—utterly bewildered even—when she thought I was my twin.

The woman shook her head. "No. I'm sorry, I am just trying to understand." Her eyes were haunted, as if she'd seen a ghost—

"Oh." My heartbeats grew slow but forceful, pounding against my ribs. "Our paths are crossing in different times. Aren't they, Seer?" The hands of the towering clock between us sat unmoving, stilled in a moment caught between.

To me, it was the future. To her, the past.

"When are you here?"

The woman's eyes flicked down to my belly again. "Twenty-two years from now, giving a few months."

My hands tightened over where I cradled them protectively. "You've come from my daughters," I whispered, my eyes drifting down to the twin lives growing inside me. The ones I would happily give my own for.

She nodded.

"You know them?" The question poured from my lips before I could stop it. "You've met my daughters?" My hand shifted on my belly, right to where one of the twins kicked at her mention: Misha. I could always tell when it was her—my little lion. The lively being hardly gave me any rest these months. She further squirmed as if making a point.

"Just one. Nicole."

"Nicole," I whispered her name, savoring how it fell from my lips. Dominic and I had only decided on the twins' names a few days ago.

Nicole, too, stirred at her mention, seemingly reaching for her sister, and Misha's movements calmed.

"And Misha?" I asked.

"Not yet." Her head shook. "Nic is going to her now. It's why we're here."

"Has she survived it then? The poisoning?" I held my breath as I awaited her answer, clutching the velvet pouch. "The necklace kept Nicole safe until he came for her?"

Over seven decades ago, the Fates showed me a vision of a man kneeling before a shrouded figure trapped in ice—the one who would turn the tide of the war. I'd thought it had been our current one, except the vision never came to pass.

Only when I'd learned I was pregnant did I realize the war I'd seen was one yet to come.

And August Warin, son of the man I so vehemently hated, was destined to protect her—my daughter. The love I'd seen on August's face—I'd seen it before, in Dom's eyes for me and in Alé's for Eve.

As wary as I'd been of him, August had proven himself during the war. Ruthless but fair. We knew little of him personally, but Eve vouched for August time and time again. She'd never said why, but she was adamant he was nothing like the monster his father was.

"Yes," the woman nodded, confirming. "Nicole is safe."

My breath shook as I exhaled. "They worked," I whispered, clutching the velvet pouch, my daughter's salvation, tighter.

One daughter had survived the vision I'd had during the late August snow. One was safe, but the other was still in danger. Though if the pendant had saved one . . .

"Misha?" I asked, unable to keep the hope from my voice.

"The roses blooming on the ruins lead us to believe Misha is still alive," the human Seer said, her voice sure. "Nic is freeing her while we evacuate the palace."

"They worked," I whispered again, joyful tears welling in my eyes.

Thank the Gods. The stars wouldn't show me who poisoned them or how, my daughters' betrayer little more than a vague malevolence that remained shrouded in darkness. And it would do little good to ask about it now. I already knew that part of the future couldn't be changed—their betrayer would find some way to get to them, regardless. But it was enough to know that my daughters were kept safe, thanks partly to the gifts I would leave behind.

"The necklaces worked," the Seer confirmed. "The witch's knot cast their protection over her."

"So, Nicole knows what she is?"

In my collection of books containing the knowledge my daughters would need, I'd discovered the witch heritage through mine and Alé's mother, Marisela. Misha and Nicole discovering this power would be vital, but they could not learn of it until the right moment. If found out too soon, it would put them further at risk, and they'd be hunted even more greatly.

The woman inclined her head. "We made the connection after Nicole woke. When I saw the pendant, and when she described how her magic had come from the water itself—much like mine—their heritage became clear."

"You are a Seer and witch." A small smile tilted my lips. "Just like . . ." My thoughts drifted to this morning when I'd retrieved the jewelry. In the apothecary, there had been a human girl with brown skin and thick black curls.

Firebringer, she'd whispered, pointing to my belly hidden beneath my cloak, before her mother shooed her back behind the curtains. *¡Miranda! Ve a tu cuarto.*

"Miranda." The woman gasped as I said her name. "Your mother made these." I pulled the pendants from the pouch, their gemstones flickering in the late morning light.

Her eyes widened in recognition. "I didn't realize—many women came to my mother for help. The fates would show me visions of how their futures would change after coming to her. But I was so young and didn't recall until now . . . we've been intertwined all along."

"It seems we have—all of us." My smile fell. "All pieces in this game of Fate."

Were the stars helpful or harmful with the pieces they chose to share and those they shrouded in darkness?

For months, I'd been trying to decipher the best way to tell my daughters what they would need to do—what they would need in order to fight what was coming for them, for our continent. Nothing had yet seemed right. No solution a clear way to keep the information safe until it was time for them to know.

I locked gazes with Miranda again. This—*she*—was the answer.

"There is more." I slid the pendants back into the velvet pouch, tucking them into the pocket of my skirt as I walked toward her. "There is much I need my daughters to know. And you've been brought here to tell them. Come, while we still have time." I reached out my hand. Miranda hesitated only briefly before setting her palm in mine.

We needed to go; the stars wouldn't give us much more time, but there was one more question I needed to ask.

"Do they know?" My throat grew thick. I swallowed, forcing out the words. "Do they know how much I love them?"

Miranda squeezed my hand. "They do, but I will tell them again. *Both* of them," she promised.

"Thank you." I nodded, releasing my grip.

She fell into step beside me as we left the library, heading toward the gallery as quickly as I was able, this far along in my pregnancy.

"My daughters will need both swords."

PART I:
The Awakening

CHAPTER 1

Nic

T hick clouds obscured the rise of the sun, only the shift from black to grey denoting the passing dawn.

I loved the forest like this: the heavy weight of the air before a storm, the dark emerald green of the trees' leaves, and how their trunks were threaded with silvery mist. Lifting my chin, I reveled in the prickle of fog, the humidity singing against my skin. August's magic clung to me, shrouding me where I knelt among the shadows. Its headiness filled my lungs as I breathed him in. I could almost taste the electricity coursing through it, impatiently waiting to be set loose.

The vial of antidote Miranda was confident would awaken my sister rested heavily in a pocket of my leathers, crafted from the same apple that had thrust me into a deep sleep. Its weight accentuated every beat of my pounding heart.

Lowering my chin, I took a deep breath and willed the beats to slow, to settle into the calm before a fight—just like Alé had taught me.

Only five guards ahead, Teale's airy voice sounded in my head from where she remained hidden in the forest west of the ruins, where Misha and I would emerge if everything went according to plan.

I kept a sliver of my mental shields cracked for her mindcasting ability. The essence of her magic felt like the demi-Dryad, earthy and ethereal.

So few is an insult.

A chime of laughter followed my words. I imagined Teale shrugging, her blue-green eyes shining with delight.

Each of the Seven had their roles to play this morning. Damian was hidden with Teale, joining us in case the antidote didn't work or to mend unexpected injuries. He was young for the High Fae, but his healing ability far surpassed his years. Celeste and Jophiel were with August, ready to lead the Montevallan soldiers in a blockade against any that would prevent us, the palace staff, and Hahnaleyan civilians from escaping. Simon remained on the ships, ready to greet them, his human face meant to ease any fear or worry.

Miranda and Shai had taken the most dangerous task, sneaking into the palace through a hidden seaside entrance to gather the staff for evacuation. Shai, with his bone-white hair denoting him as Reynian, would blend in perfectly, and with his mindcasting magic, he could unravel any hold Adrienne had cast over the staff and urge them to leave to safety. Miranda, as a human, would not attract much attention, falling in with the other staff Adrienne had ordered hidden from her and the High Fae's sight.

Hatred curled deep in my gut as I thought of how the staff and guards had been treated under Adrienne's—my former stepmother's—rule following the coup that had stolen the throne from my sister and me.

But by noon, they would be free of her. They would be safe.

I waited a few more minutes, the sky brightening only infinitesimally. Then, with footsteps silent on the damp earth, I stalked out of the forest toward the ruins of the former High King's castle.

Five faces snapped toward me. "Princess?" a guard stammered as I came into view.

I recognized him as one of our former stablemen: Tobias, a High Fae with the ability to winnow, a gift that allowed him to jump through space. He'd exchanged his fern green Hahnaleyan uniform for deep Reynian purple. Had he only done what he needed to survive, or had his loyalty to the Briar line ceased with a simple change of clothes?

Regardless, Adrienne believed in his loyalty well enough to entrust him with the task of guarding these ruins. As a Hahnaleyan, he knew what the Briar roses meant and who had cast them.

The four others, also High Fae, I did not recognize. They were from Reyna then.

"Stand down and let me pass."

Their backs were to the thick flora covering the single gap in the crumbling stone wall, the thorny vines extending well above three times their height. The guards looked at one another, unsure of what to do.

"You may have thought me dead, understandably, but as I stand before you, that was clearly a lie," I went on. "So, if you respect the Briar crown—and the Blood Treaty—you will move aside."

"The Blood Treaty is null." One of the Reynian guards stepped forward, an earthcaster by the way the ground trembled as he readied his power. His force was insignificant compared to the majesty of snarling thorns behind him.

I sneered. "And *who* nulled it?"

The Reynian ignored the question. "The queen gave her orders. No one passes."

"My sister and I are the rightful heirs to the throne." I called to my magic, the ice and fire that burned through my veins. Flames flickered to life, coating one palm, while frost blossomed on the other. "Adrienne Deimos is a traitor. She is queen of nothing."

Their gazes went to my hands, pupils widening a fraction, but looked otherwise unsurprised. So, they'd heard of the return of fire—yet the guards still didn't step aside. They remained between me and the ruins, even the Hahnaleyan.

One of them is a mindcaster, Teale's voice whispered. *I feel the tendrils of his power reaching out to warn others. Hurry, they're coming.*

"Step aside." My flame flared brighter. "I won't ask again."

The earthcaster gathered magic into his palms, earth levitating from the ground beneath him. "We have our orders." The others' hands went to the hilts of their swords, all made of Galorian silver. The metal was undoubtedly bonded to rowan wood ash. One cut would make the Fae as vulnerable as a human. Only Tobias's grip was weak, hesitating.

The air grew thick as they called to their magic, their choice made. One guard raised his chin defiantly. "Long live the Queen."

A crown of fire and ice formed upon my head. "Long live the Queen."

The earthcaster lifted his hands, and hundreds of sharp rocks hurtled toward me. I shielded with a wall of fire between us, turning the stone to dust. Another, a watercaster, pulled from the stream to counter my flame, but my control over the element was stronger. I seized it from him, the water whipping back and wrapping around his throat. The force of it snapped his neck.

Both water and flames danced through my fingers. "You should have just let me pass."

The guards braced themselves with whatever magic they had, two winnowing into the fold of space. But the fire had only been a distraction.

Thin daggers of ice flew for the two remaining guards, nearly invisible as they sliced through the air. They fell to the ground with a thud as the shards struck the guards through the heart.

The earthcaster materialized behind me, the blade of his sword aiming for my neck. I ducked, rolling as I drew the Iradelmar from my back, unflinching as I blocked his next strike with my aunt's Galorian silver blade.

The last guard, the Hahnaleyan, appeared at my back and hesitated, making no move toward me.

Keeping a sliver of awareness trained on him, I kicked the other guard away with a foot to the chest. Before he could right himself, the Iradelmar's blade sliced across his throat. He fell, clutching his neck as he died.

I turned on Tobias, sword ready to defend another strike.

He dropped his blade. "Princess." Tobias bowed, taking a knee with his hands raised in surrender. "Mercy. It was I who sent the word to the spies, telling them of the roses. Please."

The way he asked for mercy, as if he wasn't sure I would grant it, startled me. The blood that was slashed across my face seared into me. My composure nearly faltered.

How monstrous had I become since my aunts had died? How far was I willing to go to rescue my family and seek vengeance for what Adrienne had done to them?

To save my sister's life, I would go much farther.

But not today. Not now.

Swallowing the lump in my throat and my guilt along with it, I sheathed the Iradelmar across my back. "Stand." Tobias did as I commanded, head still bowed. "Ships are arriving outside the cove nearest the palace. If you truly remain loyal, you and your family can seek refuge in the North. Bring only what you must. Montevalle will provide all else."

"Montevalle?" He balked at the mention of the mountainous kingdom to the north, known for its ruthless king and vast armies. It was home to the same man who'd given me refuge in the Redwood, in more ways than one. The man I'd fallen irrevocably in love with.

"Montevalle," I confirmed.

A light rain began to fall—August's signal. Within minutes, he would bring the storm to its full height, drawing Adrienne and Evander's attention to him, a diversion from me and those fleeing Sanserria.

"If you think you can use that information to keep you in Adrienne's good graces, you are too late," I warned. "The King is here."

Thunder boomed, shaking the stone around us.

Tobias, face stricken, nodded before dashing southward toward the city.

Now alone, I examined the wall before me. The mossy stone was wreathed in dark thorns, so tangled it would be impossible for anything larger than a rabbit to scurry through. The vines were marred in some places, where axes and blades had tried—and failed—to pierce through. Roses grew upon them, masking some of the brutality.

Stepping forward, I ran a fingertip over the pink petals to gently brush the golden center. They weren't natural blooms. Only two Fae had ever cultivated them.

Briar roses.

The thick vines twisted back on themselves to create a small path. As I climbed through, careful of the rubble and thorns—which, knowing Misha, would be severely poisonous—the sentient vines shifted and coiled, seemingly excited by my arrival. The petals of a rose reached out, brushing my shoulder. A blooming but thornless vine twirled around my wrist, breaking off to twine around my forearm. New buds unfurled as it clung to me, and the magic pulsing through the blooms sighed at my presence, as if Misha's essence was reaching for me.

Sister.

Once past the thick stone wall, I stepped into the courtyard. The smell of decay slammed into me. With the crook of my elbow, I covered my mouth and nose, my eyes watering. Celeste hadn't downplayed the carnage she'd seen through Aetos, her golden eagle's, eyes. Bodies of fallen guards were strewn across the ground. They hadn't even made it within twenty meters of the ruined castle. Moss, mushrooms, and wildflowers sprouted from the remains as if Misha's magic had meant to bury them. Thick mist hung heavily over the gore.

I held back a retch at the smell of the corpses, breathing through my covered nose and focusing on the leather smell of my sleeve. I didn't dare open my mouth. The roses covering the castle ruins did little to mask the stench, even with their sweetness cloying the air.

I hurried past them, taking care to keep from stepping through a ribcage wound with ivy, and bounded up the steps that would take me into the former High King's throne room. Once inside, I stepped through the stream running through the center, slowly approaching the once-grand stone dais. The room was untouched except for the mass of thorny vines draped over nearly every surface. They wound up the walls and into the beams high above.

Once we'd learned where Misha was, the dreams of my sister had shifted, and I imagined her laid before the ruined throne on a bed of moss and lotus blossoms. There, she slept peacefully in the gauzy turquoise gown she'd worn on the Summer Solstice—our birthday and the last time I'd seen her.

I should have known it wouldn't be that easy to find her, but my heart still clenched at my sister's absence.

I paused, considering where I'd search first. Misha loved every nook of this place equally. Turning to the right, I decided to head toward the halls that would take me to what had once been an atrium of exotic plants, one of the places where Misha had often written her letters to Julian, the boy she'd secretly written to until they were both no longer children.

The sound of rock shifted outside, and I froze. The silence returned, heavier than before.

"Julian?" I called. He had to be here with her; they'd both gone missing that night.

Nothing, only more silence. Then I heard the sound again, like rock scraping against itself—no.

Claws.

"Rasalas?" My voice softened as I called for my sister's pet, the jaguar that had rarely left her side.

The sound came again, louder now and close enough that I could pinpoint it.

The massive arched window behind the dais, its stone panes long since broken away, framed the trees outside. The nearest branches came through the window, heavily laden with ruby-red apples. Some had fallen to the stone floor, fermented and rotten.

My heart pounded as I waited for any sound in these unnaturally quiet ruins. A rustle moved through its leaves, followed by the screech of claws on rock.

Rasalas never made that much noise.

I crouched, drawing the Iradelmar, still praying my sister's jaguar would climb through the window. But when the beast finally emerged, the claws gripping the window's edge were too large to belong to the great cat. Each talon was longer than my arm. I gasped as its scaled head crested above the stone.

The creature that rose hadn't existed in a hundred years—not since the Great War, when the Warins slayed them all with their lightning.

The thorns hadn't ripped the guards apart.

The *dragon* had.

The beast pulled itself through the grand window, its serpentine eyes locked on mine. Its scales were the exact silvery blue of the storming sky behind it. Horns framed its massive head, gleaming like iron. Ridges of spikes ran down its long back to the tail, where the spines turned into venomous, knife-sharp barbs. A low, rumbling growl thrummed in its chest as the creature took me in.

What was that? Teale's mind reached out. *I thought I heard—*

Dragon. I opened my mind further, allowing her to see through my eyes.

Fuck— Teale's mind stuttered. *How—nope, doesn't matter.* Run. *Don't try to fight it. You won't win, Nic.*

The dragon shifted, stepping a taloned foot onto the stone floor, followed by another. Its neck stretched upward until the dragon's height reached over half the distance to the fifty-foot ceiling. The rumbling grew deeper in its chest. Its great mouth, filled with curved fangs for shredding apart flesh, began to part.

I wasn't going to wait for what I knew would come next.

Breaking out of my frozen shock, I sprinted toward one of the hall-ways off the throne room, the stone doorway too narrow for the beast to fit through. Fire erupted from the beast's mouth, blocking my path. I slid to a stop before the flames, hitting the ground hard on my side. My palms scraped against the rough stone.

Remember, Nic, you are impervious to fire.

Right. Firecasters couldn't burn. I should have run through it. I regained my footing and ran as hard as I could for the passage on the opposite side of the room.

Teale, do not *tell August about this.*

If he knew, he would come, and he was needed at the ships. I leapt over a toppled statue of the former High King and sprinted for the arched stone door ahead.

The dragon roared as it swept around, its momentum slamming the beast into the stone wall at my back. Dust and small stones rained down from the ceiling.

I readied myself to run through the dragon's flame, but it never came. Instead, I heard the scrape of its talons as it followed after me.

I didn't dare look back.

Teale grunted, disagreeing. *Then you better run faster. If you die, and I didn't tell him about this, I'm next.*

I smacked hard into the wall past the arched doorway, and pain shot through my shoulder and side. The dragon let out a roar as I scrambled up the stone steps out of its path. Chancing a glance back, I saw its snout following me through the arch—it let out a huff, the rest of its head unable to fit into the narrow hall. The beast slowly pulled away, but I knew better than to think it was deterred.

This passage had only one destination, a curving set of stairs that led into its highest tower: the High King's chambers. Clutching my side—a few ribs were definitely cracked—I flew up the steps, pain slicing through me with each breath. At the top, I reached a thick, wooden door reinforced with iron. I leaned into it and pushed.

Locked.

Calling to my magic, flame erupted and quickly ate through the wood. Once it was gone, I climbed between the glowing iron bands.

The grand suite took up the entire level, the only one this high. The balcony to my right was worse for the wear; much of it and the surrounding wall were torn away, giving an unimpeded view of the forest canopy. The room, despite the century of disuse, was elegantly decorated. Golden sconces and painted tapestries of forest scenes hung from the stone walls. The once fine furniture was strewn about, although most of it was smashed or toppled over.

Against the far wall, resting on a bed made entirely of Briar rose blossoms, lay my sister.

Misha looked serene, her golden blonde hair fanned out around her and blue eyes closed. The turquoise gown she'd worn on the Summer Solstice was intact, although the lotus blossoms had long since faded away.

"Sister." I ran to her, putting my ear to her chest and my fingers to her neck, desperate to hear or feel a pulse.

It was soft, but it was there. As were her slow breaths, gently brushing against my hair.

Alive.

A relieved sob erupted from my mouth as I sat up and pulled the antidote from my breast pocket. Tipping her head back, I poured the vial's contents onto her tongue. Her cheeks seemed to pinken ever so slightly, her pulse quickening, yet still, she laid unmoving.

"Misha," I murmured, hoping to rouse her.

My sister remained in her slumber.

The scrape of talons returned outside the tower. The dragon was climbing.

I spun to the open balcony, torn enough away that it would be large enough for the beast to crawl through. The dragon's scales were impenetrable to nearly all things: metal, stone, and even fire. It was what made them so difficult to kill and why the former High King once prized them so greatly. His family line, the Etherii, were animaglia, High Fae with magic over all creatures. Their magic had been strong enough to control even dragons, using them to terrorize any who might challenge them. The edges of dragons' soft bellies were the only place they were vulnerable—and their throats.

That was how August had killed so many, with lightning down their throats. Was how my mother had killed one, turning water to ice from inside its lungs.

When the creature opened its mouth to breathe fire, I'd have to be faster.

Standing between the gaping balcony and my sleeping sister, water flecked with ice began to wreath around my arms. Familiar, long talons gripped the edge of the crumbling balcony, scales the exact color of the now-raging storm in full force. A perfect camouflage. It would be nearly impossible to spot flying in the clouds above.

As the dragon continued to climb, bits of the remaining railing tumbled to the ground below. My heart pounded beneath my ribs. Lightning cracked across the sky, followed by booming thunder.

The horns appeared next. I lifted my arms. My magic pulsed through the air, readying to command rainwater from the storm into the beast's lungs.

The metallic, serpentine eyes rose past the stone floor.

I exhaled slowly, and the rain stilled around the dragon. Now or never.

"Nicky, stop!"

CHAPTER 2
Misha

My sister froze, and the rain with her. Prisms of ice were suspended, glittering in the air.

"Misha?" Nic's voice broke as she remained between me and the dragon, still pulling himself onto the balcony. Her neck was rigid, clearly wanting to turn to me but unable to pull her eyes away from the threat.

I winced as my feet touched the cold stone floor, and I stood. My head spun, my vision nearly going black as blood rushed to my toes. My heart pounded in an attempt to right it, my body long unused to standing upright.

Is this real?

Forcing one foot after the other, pins and needles prickling my soles, I staggered between them. "Nic, you can't—" My arms spread wide to block her. "—you can't hurt him."

My sister looked ready to lunge or pull me behind her, her dark eyes contemplating the effectiveness of striking at the dragon now, where he was hanging partially onto the balcony.

"Misha, it's a dragon." Nic's eyes flew between each of us.

But she'd hesitated, and that was all I needed.

"It's him, Nicky. It's Julian." I backed away, moving toward him. With all my attention on my sister, I stumbled.

Julian's foreleg reached out to pull me into him, steadying me. My body relaxed into his touch, and I could have sworn he did the same.

"Look at his eyes, Nic. They're grey—Warin grey." I turned, resting my hands on his face.

A deep rumble came from Julian's scaled chest. Those grey eyes gleamed with relief, his attention only focused on me. I remembered the night I'd been poisoned, the horror of watching him become this and knowing it was *my* magic that had done it. I wondered how long he'd watched me sleep—unsure if I was dead or alive all this time.

Shame flooded my veins. *I'm so sorry, Julian.*

Julian bumped his nose—snout—into me, a reassuring gesture. His head was nearly as large as I was tall.

When I looked back at Nic, she was still rigid as she assessed the dragon and me. Finally, she lowered her arms, though they remained tense at her sides. "How?"

My hands tightened on Julian's face, my cheek falling to rest against his cool scales. "I was poisoned from the comb—that damned rose gold comb someone left in my room with a note saying it was from Julian. After we left, it pricked my skin, drawing blood. And as I went under—" I shook my head. "I don't know. Everything went hazy, but my magic pulled from the earth, and the vines and thorns sprouted from beneath

31

us, scattering everywhere. Julian was holding me, but then he wasn't because he was becoming *this*." I ran my hand along his massive jaw. The rumbling in his chest deepened. "After that, I blacked out. It's been—" The words caught in my throat. This wasn't the time. "It's been nothing until now when you woke me," I lied.

Nic went still, wary as she focused on Julian's deep rumble. I could see how it might sound as if he were growling. With his lips spread, showing nearly all of those curved teeth . . . his attempt at a pacifying smile instead looked utterly ferocious.

"But you found me, sister." I pushed on Julian's arm. He moved away, freeing me to return to my sister.

I threw myself upon her, breathing in Nicole's scent—more familiar to me than my own. As we embraced, my head fell to her shoulder, and Nic's arms wrapped around me tightly. She smelled like amber and snow and nights spent braiding each other's hair.

Real.

My sister pulled back, her voice thick. "I can explain everything that's happened later, but right now, we need to leave. Can you—" Nic seemed to be searching for the words, waving her hand vaguely at Julian's new form as she pulled away. "—Put him back?"

"I don't know," I said, dread flooding me. "I don't even know how I did this."

Julian dropped his head, bumping my waist as if to say, *We'll figure it out, love.*

"I should've known I wouldn't be the only one to manifest new magic on the Solstice," Nic murmured before growing quiet, considering our next steps.

My mind, still in a haze from the sleep, tumbled over her words. "What new magic? What else—"

Nic's eyes lit up, and she strode toward Julian, cutting me off. "This might be better, actually. Two Fae are in the forest waiting for us. But August needs to be informed before he sees us, lest he strike down his own brother."

The infamous dragon killer . . . and the brother I'd accidentally turned into one. I cringed.

"One is a mindcaster," Nic said before going quiet, moving toward the balcony as she communicated silently with the Fae while keeping Julian in her peripheral—hardly a difficult task. She was growing more comfortable but still seemed wary of him, even though he'd done nothing but sit still, listening to our debate, unable to contribute. "I relayed the news to her about Julian. Do you think he can fl—"

Nic's words were cut off as Julian bellowed out in pain. He slid backward across the balcony, his talons screeching across the stone floor. Nic dove, rolling out of the way. Julian whipped his head toward the forest floor, the ruins trembling with his roar before he fell from sight.

I screamed, reaching as if I could stop him from falling. The guards' shouts sounded from below. "Reload the harpoon!"

No.

I burst forward, but Nic grabbed my waist, holding me back. "Reynian guards," she spat, looking down on the soldiers of the southernmost country, Adrienne's home.

"What?" I pushed against her, ready to go over the ledge myself to get to Julian, nearly mad with my need to help him. "Why are they here, and where are *our* guards?" We could talk to them, order them to stand down.

Two dozen guards in steel armor surrounded him, more pouring in every moment through a crack in the stone wall surrounding the grounds. The archer's arrows bounced off his scales, but another guard reloaded a giant harpoon—what had struck true and pulled him from the tower.

"A lucky shot. It's not fatal," my sister assured me.

It might have been a lucky shot, but they wouldn't get another. The vines on the wall behind the guard surged, wrapping around him. They snapped the harpoon, its mount, and then the High Fae's neck.

Julian roared again, slicing his great tail through the air. The guards, too slow to escape, were slammed into the wall, impaled by the thorns. I watched as his head reared, fire collecting in his throat. With a sweep of his head, the dragon's flames devoured the others, burning them alive in their scalding metal armor.

I've never wanted my first reaction to be violence. I want—I need *to be better than my father.* Words I remembered from Julian's letters.

Bile rose in my throat as I watched the carnage unfold. The Reynian guards were still coming, blindly running toward their certain doom. *This is all my fault.*

"*Misha,*" my sister hissed, pulling me back, so much stronger than me now that I'd been sedentary for the gods knew how long. "But we have got to go. We'll help him finish the guards and get out of here."

My gaze still on Julian, I turned to follow her only to run into Nic's still form. She'd frozen before the doorway, utter fury on her face.

"Hello, girls."

Adrienne, our stepmother, blocked the only path out. Her pale hair, nearly the same shade as her white gown, fluttered in the breeze. A mark gleamed on her forehead: a red scythe's blade tipped onto its side.

Nic stepped to the right, sliding in front of me. "Not bothering to cover your blood mark, traitor?"

I had never heard such violence in Nic's voice.

Adrienne laughed. The sound was wrong, mocking. "It is a symbol of power now, Nicky."

"Power?" Nic spat. "You only have what you steal. And instead of facing us, you used poison like the coward you are."

The pieces fell together. Reyna's Guards . . . traitor . . . blood mark . . . the treaty.

The comb had come from Adrienne.

Nic looked ready to lunge. "You *murderer*—"

Adrienne's tone dropped low, deadly. "Then what does that make you, Nic?"

My sister went utterly still, her voice as sharp as the blades at her sides. "I've done what you made me do."

What had my sister done? My gut clenched, guilt coursing through me. *What had she been forced to do because I wasn't there?*

Nic went on. "Everything I've done since the Solstice has been for my family. Vengeance for what *you* began."

"Family," Adrienne choked out, her pale blue eyes clouding with rage as her stoic facade started to crack. "My only family is dead. My brother is *dead* because of you."

Nic's hands curled at her sides, ready to rip our stepmother to shreds. Flame licked down her arms. I remembered my dreams—or had they been dreams? Had all of that been real, too?

My head spun. *Firecaster.*

"And how many brothers have you killed?" Nic accused. "How many fathers and au—"

"No," I whispered, my voice soft but enough to silence them both. "You killed our father."

It wasn't a question. Part of me had always known there was no possible way Dominic Briar, hundreds of years old but still in his prime, could be taken by a simple blood disease. I'd blamed myself. I'd believed it had to have been the plants and flowers we'd been growing—the poisons we cultivated from their leaves and blossoms with Eve as she worked to make antidotes for them. It was my aunt's—my godmother's—life's work to create the Panacea, the cure for all things.

Surely, I'd thought, working with that much poison had affected him. The toxic magic had lowered his immunity just enough for a blood disease to slip in and take root.

"You killed him," I repeated. The thorned vines around me began to shift, coiling, readying to strike. To wrap around my stepmother and choke the life from her.

Instead, a vise wrapped around my own throat. I tried to cough, to force my lungs to fill, but the air in them was frozen. My hands went to my neck, clawing as if I could free the hold over it. I heaved, my magic stilling as every focus went to trying to breathe.

Adrienne watched me choke with feral delight, but the mindcaster shouldn't have possessed an air elemental's magic. Nic's words to Adrienne clanged through me: *you only have what you steal.*

Nic struck, air and ice colliding as my sister attacked the shield of wind Adrienne had formed in front of herself. Flame followed, rushing from my sister's palms. Adrienne smothered the flames, stealing their air, but couldn't fight it all at once, not while maintaining her hold on the air in my lungs. Her shield faltered, and slices from ice shards bled red from Adrienne's tan skin and slashed the white silk of her gown.

But our stepmother only needed to hold out for a bit longer. If she killed me before her shield was torn apart, my sister lost.

The unexpected loss of breath made me weak. I wanted to launch myself at Adrienne, tear out her throat with my own hands, but I lacked the strength. I sank to my hands and knees as black spots formed in my vision, my head light and dizzy. Surrounding vines rushed for me, supporting me in a strangling embrace.

Lifting my head, my gaze met a familiar set of gold eyes, shining from deep within the thorns and roses covering the open door behind Adrienne. Both Nic and Adrienne were too immersed in their deadlock to notice as Rasalas stalked forward on silent, padded feet.

Adrienne hadn't thought to shield her back.

As the jaguar prowled, his black spots bled outward, covering him until the gold from his coat was gone—all except for thin, shimmering lines. He grew larger, his torso and legs stretching and becoming thicker as his claws and fangs elongated.

I could only watch and not understand what was happening—what was becoming of the jaguar I'd raised from a cub.

In a second, the transition was done, my sweet cub now a monstrous version of himself.

Rasalas dove onto Adrienne, knocking her to the stone floor.

Sweet, cool air filled my lungs.

Nic halted her assault, reaching down to pull me up. "He's buying us time. We need to go now."

"No." I pulled my arm away from her just as Adrienne pulled out a dagger of dark metal and stabbed it into Rasalas's side. His roar of pain ripped through my soul. Air blasted him back, and the jaguar's body hit the stone wall with a sickening crunch. *"No!"* I cried, reaching for him.

Thorny vines slithered from me to Adrienne, wrapping around her. She cut through them, blade never faltering, but ten more sprouted for every one she cut, overwhelming her.

I ran to Rasalas, and he shifted. Not back into his adult jaguar form, but into the small cub I'd rescued years ago.

I scooped him into my arms, placing a hand on his abdomen to staunch the bleeding. Swallowing, I held back a retch at the feeling of his blood sliding through my fingers.

Nic hesitated, watching Adrienne as she was overtaken by the rose vines and thorns. Hatred flashed in her eyes.

"I want to kill her too, Nic." I grasped my sister's arm. "But we need to go, yes?" Julian roared again from outside the window, the sound pained as it pierced through me. He needed us.

Nic stiffly nodded, understanding—we would leave Adrienne for another day.

We sprinted down the steps and out of the ruined castle, my legs wobbly as a fawn's, the muscles burning from disuse. When we emerged into the courtyard, we found Julian had killed many of the guards, but he was becoming exhausted, his movements sluggish. The remaining few drowned as Nic stalked toward them, rainwater tunneling into their lungs.

Julian slumped, relieved, before coming toward us. One back leg dragged, bloody from where he'd been struck in the crease of his hip. It was thankfully a non-fatal wound, but it needed to be healed.

"Nicky, we need Ev—" The words died on my lips as two unfamiliar Fae sprinted toward us from the woods.

The female was tiny, her head not even cresting the shoulder of the male beside her. Both were identically dressed in black leather armor. Her short blonde curls and his brown hair were plastered to their foreheads from the rain. Their eyes darted between us and the sheer carnage of the fallen guards.

They must have been the ones my sister mentioned. Nic said she'd warned them of Julian's state via whichever was the mindcaster, but they still froze when they saw the dragon.

My sister walked toward them, snapping them from their shock. "Misha, this is Damian and Teale. Part of August's council."

"Nice to finally meet you." The petite female—Teale—bowed her head. Her eyes were a striking blue-green, her skin pale but tinted the green of summer leaves—*a nymph?*

"He's injured." The Fae male's—Damian's—light brown eyes dropped to Julian's back leg where the harpoon still protruded from the vulnerable area between the scales at his hip crease. His blood stained the soil red beneath him.

"Can you help him?" I pleaded, going to my knees beside the male as he knelt, examining the wound.

Rasalas squirmed in my arms, twisting to get a better look. His own wound had closed already, only a faint scar remaining beneath my hand. His gold eyes met mine as I thought, *What* are *you, little one?*

Yours.

Damian nodded, his tan hands emitting a soft, golden glow as he assessed Julian's injury. "Sorry about this, Jules." He gripped the harpoon's shaft, pulling it swiftly. Blood poured from the wound anew as Damian tossed the weapon to the ground.

Julian hissed, steam rising from his lips as they pulled back over the curved fangs.

Damian's hands glowed brighter as he covered the wound, staunching the bleeding. Slowly, the dragon's leathery skin began to mend together.

"It *is* him." The nymph's face went slack with awe as she looked up at the dragon towering over her. "I can hear his thoughts. It's Julian."

"I can't imagine the curses you heard just now," Damian murmured, his eyebrows furrowed in concentration.

Julian dipped his head and bumped Teale with his snout, sending the petite Fae stumbling backward as she laughed in disbelief.

"Does he think he can fly?" Nic asked Teale, her eyes on Julian.

The nymph stood silently for a moment, all her attention focused on speaking mind to mind with him. Then she nodded.

"He's flown?" I asked, wondering how he could have without being discovered.

"No," Teale shook her head. "But he's convinced he can." She shrugged.

"And we're going to test it *now*?" Damian stood. Julian's bleeding was staunched. His leg looked as if he'd never been injured at all.

"We have no other options," Nic snapped. "Climb onto his back. Now."

Julian stretched out his foreleg, easing the climb up his daunting height.

I climbed Julian's arm to his back, with Nic just behind. I settled myself between spines. Rasalas clung to me as I leaned forward, keeping him securely tucked between me and Julian as I gripped two protruding, rough scales.

"Can he carry us all?" He hesitated as he climbed, looking back to Teale.

The nymph smiled. "He said your lack of confidence wounds him." She unfurled her wings, translucent and gold-veined like dragonflies'. They fluttered as she flew, coming to sit behind Nic. "Have a little faith."

Damian grunted but followed, taking a seat behind her.

Nic's arms came past my waist to grip another of the spines. "Teale, make sure no one shoots us with anything—especially lightning—when we get to the coast."

"What should I tell him?"

Nic loosed a breath. "The truth."

Julian's wings spread, their length magnificent. His muscles shifted and bunched beneath us as he tested them, beating the air. Then, he began to run.

We each held on fast to the spines on his back. I leaned forward, praying my grip would be enough. Nic's arms tightened against my sides, securing Rasalas and me further.

Julian ran for a clear path between the trees, his great wings beating as he picked up speed. My loose hair whipped around me, and Nic sputtered as she caught a mouthful. Before I could apologize, my stomach dropped, stealing my breath. We lifted, sailing into the air before the tree line. The forest canopy shrank beneath us.

And we were flying.

CHAPTER 3
Misha

J ulian skimmed the belly of the heavy, low-hanging clouds. The mist obscured us, the steel blue of his scales melding into the storm. Thunder rumbled, shaking me down to my bones.

Between gaps in the fog, I saw as the forest began to thin, yielding to the palace grounds. The plain abruptly dropped off into the sea, where foaming white waves crashed against the base of the white stone cliffs. Further out, over a dozen ships floated, silver sails billowing. Dinghies ferried citizens from where they spilled onto the beach from the open mouth of the tunnel connected to the palace. A watercaster stood at the helm of each small boat, guiding and protecting them from the thrashing waves.

The white stone spires of our palace came into view. On the plain before the gardens, Reynian and Montevallan soldiers clashed with Hahnaleyans split on each side. Most fought along the Montevallans, but some—at least a third—had defected to the Reynians.

Their betrayal stung, and I found myself straining to catch their faces. I recognized far too many fighting along with Reyna, choosing Adrienne over my sister and me. I clung to the hope that they hadn't chosen this and that they had instead been coerced by Adrienne's mindcasting—but naïveté had gotten me into this mess in the first place.

Winged Seraphim battled from the air, holding the line between fleeing civilians and those who would stop them. The fiercest among them was a tall female, her silver helmet adorned with golden upswept wings—their commander. Light glinted across her sword and round shield, shining as if it had been pulled from the sun itself, gleaming despite the heavy rainfall. Where she struck, opponents did not rise.

Nic's arms tightened around me. I turned my head as much as I dared, ready to ask what was wrong, but my sister was wholly focused on the stormcaster in the center of the plain—on August Warin.

In the thickest part of the fighting, the King of Montevalle rained down lightning, unlike anything I'd ever seen. The storm wholly surrendered to him, its eye swirling above where he stood. Crackling bolts struck into his hands before he cast them back out.

Julian roared, diving for his brother. The soldiers halted on both sides as they saw him—the first dragon in a hundred years.

As we neared, those on the ground saw us clinging to his back. "They're alive! Both princesses are alive!" Some shouted in rejoicing, others in warning.

August's eyes glowed silver with storm magic as we approached. "Pull back!" he commanded of his Montevallan forces.

They immediately obeyed, retreating to the cliff's edge behind the line held by the Seraphim.

Rowan wood arrows shot at us as we descended. My stomach lurched as Julian abruptly dove and weaved, tipping to shield us with his wing. The arrows bounced off him unharmed.

As the Montevallans pulled back, the Reynians took the opportunity to charge. August stood his ground as the sky itself descended in a funnel of raging lightning and wind, holding the line alone with the tempest of his magic.

Julian circled back, descending until we came to a shuttering landing on the grassy plain behind August. We dismounted, quickly sliding down Julian's side. Nic went first, catching me around the waist as I hit the ground, unable to steady myself with Rasalas in my arms.

When we were clear, Julian crept forward until he stood beside his brother. Eyes on the enemy, he roared, the sound shaking the earth between them and Adrienne's forces.

The Reynians halted their charge and began retreating, but not fast enough to escape the fire gathering in Julian's throat. He lowered his head, sweeping flames across their front lines.

Soldiers that could winnow did so. The others broke formation and ran, shrieking back to the safety of the palace.

A trail of fire remained, snaking through the plain between us unimpeded by the rain. As we watched the grass burn before our home, August walked toward us.

The tempest lifted, the rain slowing to a drizzle.

August's grey eyes still pulsed with lightning as they met Nic's, the magic not quite reined back into himself.

"It's really him?" the king asked, turning to watch the dragon. His face softened, not daring to hope but unable to stop himself.

Deeming the fleeing guards no longer a threat, Julian pivoted back to us.

My sister nodded, taking August's hand and gently squeezing. "It's really him."

August tightened his hand on hers, hesitating only briefly before striding over to his brother. Julian lowered his head so they were eye to eye.

The king took a moment, surveying him, the horns and teeth, before meeting his eyes—the eyes they shared. Warin grey.

The last crack in August's hard mask broke free. His eyes gleamed with tears of relief as he lifted a hand to Julian's face. "Brother."

Julian's eyes closed. The slitted pupils of his grey eyes glassed, brimming with emotion for the brother who had protected and raised him.

Rasalas lifted his head from my shoulder, assessing the others. I felt his small body pulse with magic as he considered shifting back into the beast form he'd used while attacking Adrienne.

I cupped his head, gently rubbing behind his ears. *No. You were just injured.*

Ras's magic settled, eyes meeting mine with understanding.

"What are you?" I whispered to the jaguar, running a hand down his damp fur.

"A familiar." The answer came from Nic. "I'll explain later."

"Like a witch's fam—" My question was cut off by the arrival of the Seraphim Commander. She was nearly as tall as August, only an inch or two shorter, but was just as intimidating.

"Everyone has been accounted for?" She removed her helmet, revealing golden-blonde hair cropped short in the traditional warrior style. Her blue eyes scanned the plain, taking in every detail, including the soldiers, who were loading onto the ships now that all the civilians had been evacuated.

"Jophiel. Montevalle's War Commander," Nic whispered to me.

August nodded, his hand never parting from Julian. "Everyone who has been confirmed loyal by Shai. The palace is clear. Everyone is waiting for us on the ships."

"Then it's time to go. Additional Reynian troops are ascending from the south and will be here within the quarter hour." The Seraph—Jophiel—nodded to my sister and me. "We've got to get them out of here."

Dread dropped in my gut with the thought of having to abandon my home. But I knew it was impossible to stay. Remaining to fight would endanger everyone who'd been evacuated, and getting those we cared for to safety was more important.

"What about the rest of the city?" I asked.

Nic was the one to answer. "August's spymaster sent people to spread rumors amongst the humans and faeries from each of the cardinal markets over the past few days. They started in the south and reached the north this morning. Civilians were led to believe that Adrienne Deimos was planning to seize their property as part of a martial lockdown and that it was best to leave now."

"To go where?"

"North through the Redwood."

I frowned. "Half will be picked off by beasts before they can make it." Shuddering, I thought of the tales of skinwalkers and shadowhounds that dwelled in the Redwood's darkest parts.

Teale stepped closer. "My relationship with the Dryads and other earth-bound nymphs is tenuous at best, but they all hate Adrienne.

They've promised to help guide travelers north to Montevalle through the Redwood. They've sworn to protect them as best they can."

"It's better than staying," Nic said softly, assuring me.

"And if the Reynians follow?" I pushed. "If Adrienne orders them hunted down?"

Teale's blue-green eyes flashed with malice. "They will find that the Redwood is not kind to those loyal to the magic thief. They won't make it more than a few hours, much less catch up to those fleeing."

I nodded, the knowledge easing some of the vise around my chest. Silently, I looked back at our home, the white stone spiraling into the sky more than a mile off, covered in part by climbing roses, ivy, and bougainvillea. My heart lurched with everything we were leaving behind.

"Nic, the horses." I whipped my head to my sister. "I can't leave without Hyacinth." The mare was the last gift I'd received from our father before he died. My grip tightened on Rasalas. I would leave neither.

Nic's face blanched. "*Shit*. I was so focused on getting you, I didn't think—"

"They're on the ship." August stepped forward, cutting her off. Nic's head whipped to him as he continued. "Shai ensured they were loaded with the stable staff. All of the horses were accounted for."

Nic turned, walking back to August until they were only a foot apart. Tipping her head up, she whispered, "You thought of the horses?"

August stepped closer, narrowing the space to inches as the corner of his mouth lifted. "Luthíen is an excellent judge of character. Couldn't leave her behind." His eyes laughed at some joke between them.

Nic's face softened, and she closed the space between them. Her hands went to his face, pulling his mouth down to hers. She kissed August swiftly but urgently—and certainly not for the first time.

My eyebrows shot nearly to my hairline. "*Sister* . . . what have I missed?"

Nic's face flushed as she stepped guilty away from him. "I—"

"—will tell me all about it later." I winked, grinning as I locked my arm with hers. "We have a ship to get to, yes?" And family I couldn't wait to see and hold.

Before August could answer, Jophiel gave me a quick nod. "Teale and I will fly with the other Seraphim, scanning the perimeter for anyone left behind. You four—August, Damian, and the princesses—will winnow directly onto the Yuki's deck," she said, indicating the largest of the Montevallan ships.

The sky began to part as August loosened his hold on the storm, and sunlight came down in beams between the clouds. The light reflected off Jophiel's white feathered wings as they rustled, shaking off the rain.

"And Julian?" I asked.

"The Yuki's deck is large enough to hold him," August said firmly as if trying to convince himself as much as us. "Five minutes," he ordered.

Teale and Jophiel nodded before launching into the air.

"Sister." Nic grasped the elbow of the arm holding Rasalas. Damian grasped my other hand, and August completed our circle across from me. A moment later, we were winnowing.

We landed in the center of the warship's deck. The woodgrain was stained a deep blue, and the silvery sails, the same color as sea foam, shimmered in the breeze, growing stronger as the ship's aircasters readied us to sail.

I ran to the railing, hair whipping about my face as I searched the horizon for him.

Julian sailed into view, wings spread wide as he crested over the cliffs.

My heart surged. He was beautiful.

The dragon flew toward us, wings stilling as he glided downward. He flew over us, the ship rocking in his wake, before curving back around in preparation to land.

"Move off the deck!" August shouted. "Clear the way!"

The Fae and humans scattered, rushing onto the quarter deck or climbing below. As he neared, Julian's great wings slowed his descent, beating in the air. His legs reached down, preparing to land.

"Nicole!" August called to her over the roar of the wind.

Nic held her arms out over the rail, calling to the ocean water as ice formed around the ship, steadying it should Julian's weight throw the boat off balance.

Julian's hind legs hit first, then the forelegs, as he landed, tucking his wings into his sides. Some who'd remained on the quarter-deck were gaping. Others—the Fae who had been alive during the High King's reign—went pale, either with fear or rage. They didn't know who he was or that he was their prince. All they could remember was the Etherii's dragons slaughtering so many of their own during the Great War and the centuries before.

Passing Rasalas to Nic, I went to Julian and placed my hands protectively over his neck. He pulled me into him, wrapping his long body around me. I called to my magic, wanting to shield him, but no earth or plants sprang up with us so far from the shore. I only felt the tug between Julian and me: what we had assumed—hoped—was the thread of our mating bond, yet to be confirmed. Whatever it was, it tethered us.

Pressing my forehead to his silvery scales, I closed my eyes. *Julian.*

My magic reached out, searching, until I felt him reaching back. The invisible threads between us sprouted like vines beneath my fingers. They began to unravel, pulling and tugging until the core of him was revealed. In my mind's eye, I could see it, the petals around him unfurling to reveal his heart and soul.

Come back to me.

In a flash, Julian was human again, toppling onto the wooden deck. The scales had peeled away to reveal long limbs and golden brown skin—very naked golden brown skin.

"Julian!" I stumbled forward, kneeling where he was. My hands flew to his face, skimming over the features I would know with touch alone: the broad plane of his nose, the thick lashes, the short stubble of his beard, and full lips. My hands tangled in his tightly coiled black hair, needing to feel all of him. *He's real. This is real.*

He pulled me onto his lap, my skirt covering him as his arms wrapped around me.

"I'm sorry," I said, tears welling then overflowing. "I'm so sorry." *For turning you into a monster. For making you the killer you never wanted to be.*

"Shh, love." Julian's hands clasped my face, then pushed back my lank and snarled hair. "It's all right. I'm all right."

"Are you?" The words stuck in my throat.

Julian smiled, but the light didn't reach his eyes. "I will be."

My grasp tightened around his neck at his lie.

August, coming to stand behind his brother, draped a cloak over his shoulders. Remembering we were not alone, I scrambled back and climbed to my feet so Julian could rise.

Clasping hands, August helped Julian to his feet.

"Brother." Julian embraced him, so hard August nearly staggered back.

"Let's go home." August's voice was thick with emotion as he clapped his brother on the shoulder. The king stepped away reluctantly, turning to command his sailors to prepare to sail.

I tried to step back so the others could greet Julian, people who I knew were on August's council, and the brothers' longtime friends. But Julian's hand shot out, clasping my wrist.

He brought my knuckles to his mouth, his lips hot against my skin as his other arm wrapped around my waist. I hadn't realized how cold I was until I was pressed against him. "Stay, love. Please."

I nodded, unable to step away from him if I wanted to. Julian held me for a few moments before turning to greet the others, his hand never leaving mine.

The first to approach was Damian and a human woman with rich tawny skin, the two wearing matching mating bands. The pair brought Julian pants he laughingly accepted, though they were a bit too snug and short in length. The friends embraced for a long moment. "Miranda, my wife and mate." Damian introduced her. She wore a loose-fitting gown over her curves, her curly black hair tied back in a thick braid. I only had the chance to nod to her before they were stepping back, allowing the rest to approach Julian.

Shai, whom I'd met with August at the Summer Solstice, stepped forward. His features deemed him from the South, as did his tan skin and short white hair. His black eyes stood stark against them. Though born in Reyna, I knew he'd been August's confidant for over a century, thanks to Julian's letters. Another High Fae approached behind Shai, her black skin and finely box-braided hair adorned with small gold rings. Her sharp face softened as she and Julian embraced. "Celeste," Julian said as he introduced us. Finally, an older human man, his brown skin

51

lightly crinkled about the eyes, embraced Julian tightly in the kind of hug one might give a son. They were unrelated, though they shared a similar coiled texture to their hair.

The man, Simon, also greeted me, telling me what good things he'd heard from Julian and how well he'd gotten to know my sister. I smiled back as he spoke. But the entire time he spoke, my eyes roamed the deck, searching.

Were they on another boat? But why wouldn't Alé—

Nic wrapped a cloak like Julian's around my shoulders. I hadn't noticed I'd begun to shiver from the wind, my tattered gown still soaked from the rain.

The human woman, Damian's wife, held Rasalas. She murmured to him, stroking down his back.

"Miranda is a witch," Nic explained. "Her own familiar, Ker, is somewhere around here."

Miranda set the small cub on the deck, and Rasalas transformed back into his full-grown form. The jaguar padded over to us and brushed his head under my hand.

Julian knelt, hands scratching the great cat's ears, his only companion as we'd been trapped in the ruins. "Hello, my friend."

Rasalas lowered his head, butting against Julian's shoulder affectionately.

I turned to my sister. "Nicky, where—"

"To the South!" one of the sailors shouted.

Reynian ships, at least a dozen, crested around the cliffs. They were a few hundred meters behind and approaching fast.

The Council around us scattered, and Jophiel and August shouted instructions to prepare for defense against the oncoming ships. The other

Montevallan ships' sails pulled taut, taking advantage of the enchanted wind cast from the air elementals on each of their decks.

Our sails slackened as the others shot past us. I noted ours was the only ship without civilians. Instead, it was filled with soldiers who now manned their posts: archers on the elevated quarter deck, aircasters erecting shields of air and wind, and watercasters churning the sea behind us.

The Yuki was *the* warship of the North, and she hummed with eagerness for battle.

For a moment—or several, it was getting harder to tell—I did not see a ship preparing for attack. I saw thorns and fangs shredding flesh. I saw arrows flying. Chests pierced. I saw a spattering of blood on a forest floor and my sister's face as she screamed.

"Misha?"

Nic's voice broke through my daze. I saw the question in her eyes: should we go below to safety or stay on deck to fight? I knew where she would be; her hands were already shimmering with frost.

Julian looked down at me, waiting for my answer. Lightning had begun to flicker in his grey eyes, and he was prepared to defend the ship.

If they were staying, so was I.

Julian nodded, seeing my resolution. "Where to, brother?" He shouted, turning to where August stood at the stern.

Before August could answer, something vibrated across the water, creating tiny ripples across the surface of the sea. The call—a humming somewhere between horn and song—floated up to us from beneath the waves themselves.

I grasped Julian's arm. "Do you hear that?"

"Hear what?" he answered, brow furrowing.

"Nic?" I turned to my sister.

She was looking out over the waves, utterly still. Her eyes were wide as they met mine.

"What was that?" One of the High Fae soldiers neared, having overheard us. She stood at the rail, hands set downward as if steadying the waves—a watercaster.

"Cover your ears!" Nic shouted, spinning away from the rail. The humming grew louder, more forceful. A final warning.

Some listened immediately while others hesitated, wavering between her command and continuing their preparation for the approaching Reynian ships.

"Sirens!" my sister cried, her voice shattering like glass across the ship. No one hesitated now.

"Aircasters, shield the sound!" August commanded.

Four High Fae followed his order. They willed the air to still around us, the sails falling slack. Everyone else dropped whatever they had, archer's bows and other weapons clattering to the ground as everyone covered their ears.

The ship stilled completely as it fell into silence.

The other Montevallan ships sailed ahead, thankfully pulling out of range. Safe.

Taking advantage of our stillness but not knowing the reason, the Reynian ships gained on us quickly. In moments, we would be in range of their archers. Magic would strike first, attacking our air shields until they cracked, yet not one person moved.

The humming grew, turning into a full song. It was muted but strong enough for the whisper to reach us. Nic cast ice skittering over every surface, freezing every foot onto the deck.

The lore said that Sirens only hunted males. Others said they only hunted specific males: those who had harmed a female, forcing from them what wasn't theirs to take. But I sensed somehow—as did Nic—that this song would be different.

It was indiscriminating.

A death ballad.

The Sirens emerged between our ship and the Reynians, their beautiful faces rising as if born of the sea foam. Their ears were delicately finned, and jewel-like scales lined their collarbones. Silken hair floated around them in hues of deep greens, blues, purples, and reds as they surrounded the ships. They swam toward them, smiling coquettishly as if greeting long-lost lovers. All the while, they sang.

The Sirens' ballad was a call captivating enough to entice you to fall into a watery grave with open arms. Each haunting verse made the soldiers more willing to present their throats to the Sirens' fangs.

No one from our deck moved. The air shields and Nic's ice held everyone steady.

The Reynian ships did not fare so well.

Soldier after soldier jumped from the deck into the dark, churning water, where the Sirens greeted them with open arms before taloned hands and fangs sliced into their prey. They dragged the soldiers beneath, leaving behind bloody trails in the blue sea.

Then, the screams began.

Some of the Reynians had realized in time and covered their ears, but even they were not safe. The Sirens came for them, climbing up the sides with talons that dug into the ships' hulls. They carried weapons carved from coral and shells, the edges razor-sharp. Several had tridents crafted of oxidized metal, turned green from so long under the sea.

The Reynians fought back, cutting down Sirens as they pulled themselves up to the rail, but were swiftly overpowered. The Sirens tore through them, all while their sisters in the water kept singing their deadly ballad.

We all watched, entranced and horrified. A series of large cracks speared through the air, and the ship nearest to us began to tilt.

Julian's mouth formed soundless words. "Gods. They're sinking it."

August lifted one arm, signaling a command for wind, and we began to sail once more, watching as the last Reynian ship was swarmed. The other ships had stilled, bobbing abandoned like forgotten toys tossed between the waves. Not a single soul upon them was left alive.

As we sailed away, the Sirens' song dimmed until it faded away into nothing. The sea rocked and waved as it always had, brutally indifferent to the lives it had claimed.

August and Julian slowly dropped their hands from their ears once Nic and I nodded to them that it was safe. The other soldiers hesitantly followed suit before moving to resume their duties. Many continued glancing to the water's surface with fear-stricken eyes.

The humming over the water returned, gentler now as it thrummed over the starboard side.

Nic met me at the railing. We peered over, spying an emerald-haired Siren bobbing alone in the water, swimming pace with the ship. My sister found a ladder, secured it to the railing, and tossed it over the side for her.

The Siren climbed up until she reached the top, supporting herself on the railing with her forearms, the skin a pale sea-green. "Sisters," she smiled, revealing her pointed teeth and fangs, but neither felt threatening.

August and Julian joined us, standing just behind. The others on the deck gave us a wide berth, pointedly finding anything to do that far away from the Siren.

"Thank you for the warning," Nic said, stepping closer.

August's hand clenched as if stopping himself from pulling her back.

The Siren nodded. "Of course."

"It was you," my sister said, recognizing the Siren as the one that had pulled her under on the beach, showing her the vision of what would come. "You've helped us twice, yet I don't know your name."

"Niniane of House Muir, clan of those first blessed by the Mother. Queen of the Western Sea."

The four of us bowed, paying her the respect due to her title.

The Siren looked between my sister and me to where August and Julian stood. Her dark green eyes, wider-set and larger than human or Fae, surveyed them. "Bloody hands . . . but both pure of heart."

Something about her words seemed to soothe August. But Julian blinked, flinching.

I'm so sorry, my love.

"Why did you help us?" Nic asked. "The matters of Fae have never swayed your kind before."

The Sirens had always remained impartial, if not malevolent, toward the Fae. Nowhere in recent history had they intervened in such a way.

"What is to come is more than just Fae dealings," Niniane answered. "Before long, we all must come together. *Resurge et ardere,*" she repeated the words she'd spoken to Nic beneath the waves.

"What does that mean?" my sister asked, needing to make sense of them.

"For what has happened already and what is to come. *Arise and burn.*" Before Nic could ask any other questions, Niniane leaned back. "Until midnight." The Siren pushed off the railing, diving back under the waves.

"Why does she always have to be so cryptic?" I murmured, turning to Julian.

The sea cascaded behind our ship, taking us into the openness of the ocean. On this ship and surrounded by my loved ones, I could go anywhere—except home. Not anymore.

As my arms wrapped around him, Julian took my face in his hands, letting out a slow breath. His touch eased me, the vise steadily slipping from my chest.

"You have no idea how it feels to see that you are all right, Misha, and standing before me. Most days, I tortured myself, convinced I was guarding a corpse."

My hand went to his chest, his brown skin hot beneath my palm. "I thought I was half the time. Everything and nothing felt real. And the things I dreamed . . ."

His lips met my forehead. "This is real, love."

Julian's arm slid around my shoulders, mine encircling his waist beneath the cloak as we turned to face our siblings.

August stood before my sister, his eyes dark, conveying more than his words.

"The Yuki? For your mother?" Nic whispered, seeing no one but him.

August nodded. "You found them, Snow. Brought them back." He reached out, planting a tender kiss onto her rain and sea-soaked black hair.

My sister's face went soft, soft as it had been only around our family. "We found them."

Julian and I exchanged a look, full of shared disbelief at how close our siblings had grown in the time we'd been gone.

We stepped closer to them, and I laid a hand on August's arm. "We were all rooting for you, you know. At the end of the celebrations. Eve and I, but even Alé, too."

August went rigid, surely from the shock. My aunts' approval was hard won.

His eyes went to Julian's, the brothers silently communicating. Julian's brow furrowed, and then he paled, looking like he would be sick.

I pushed out a smile through the dread sinking into my gut.

"Speaking of, where are our aunts? They've missed everything. It's unlike them. Are they on another ship helping the others?" I turned to my sister, who had gone utterly still. August's arms tightened around her, steadying her. "Nic?"

My sister pushed back from August. He reluctantly loosened his hold but kept one hand pressed to her lower back. When she looked up, I saw the tears welling on her lashes.

My sister didn't cry. I'd only seen it twice. Once with Callum, and when—

No.

"Nicky . . ." The words were hardly a rasp as my face fell. "Where are they?"

Julian held me up as my knees began to buckle. I hardly felt it.

My sister's mouth opened, but no words came out.

"*Where. Are. They?!*" I screamed, my voice drowned out by the roaring in my ears.

59

That had been a persistent nightmare, one I'd dreamed more than most as I'd slept. I'd told myself my mind was conjuring my worst fear: that my aunts had been struck down as I watched from the canopy, one with an arrow through the chest and the other by a blade across the throat.

But it wasn't real—it couldn't be real.

Nic shook her head, tears streaming down her face. "We were attacked. Adrienne's guards ambushed us, and I . . . I didn't see until it was too late."

"No . . ." I shook my head. "No, no, no." My legs crumpled from beneath me, Julian's arms the only thing keeping me from crashing into the deck.

My sister's arms came around me. "I'm so sorry, Misha. I tried—I tried." The words broke in her throat. She had a gold ring on each middle finger. She took one off and handed it to me. I knew the inner inscription by heart, knew the matching set.

One evermore.

After reading the words, I could no longer see through the tears pouring from my eyes; I couldn't speak for the sobs ripping out of my lungs. My chest heaved, knowing it was true before my sister said it:

"Alesia and Eve are gone."

CHAPTER 4
Adrienne

I entered my chambers and screamed.

Air coiled around me, knocking crystal vases, jewelry, and trinkets from every surface. The pillows on the bed ripped from the force of it, sending white swan feathers swirling.

Fourteen ships were destroyed, and countless soldiers lost, their corpses rotting on the plain or bones being picked clean by the fish at the bottom of the sea.

I had neither twin's heart to show for it.

And my brother—my *brother*—was dead. Because of *her.*

I'd gone two hundred years in this life without love. It was too dangerous for a mindcaster, as susceptible to the feelings and emotions of others as we influenced theirs. Love was a weakness—a choice to be avoided at all costs.

Once you love one person, you could lose everything.

But then I'd held him. That tiny infant in my arms.

After a century of my mother's hope for a son, there he was, come too early from the womb. Underweight and frail, his skin was a greyish pallor over a spiderweb of blue veins. His underdeveloped lungs rasped as he struggled to obtain the air he needed. Yet he fought obstinately, wielding every gasp like a sword, battling for every breath. A warrior.

My mother had left him with the nurses, having done her part in providing my father a son—an heir—and returned to her parties and frivolousness. Father had not spared him a glance, his son too sickly and frail to be of any notice. Already a disappointment, they hadn't even bothered to name him.

So, I had. I named him for his warrior spirit: my Alexander.

After that, Alexander was mine in all the ways that mattered. I'd bottle-fed him, raised him, and loved him as my own. I trained him to be strong and formidable, teaching him to fight for everything he desired. The entire world could be his; he had only to reach out and take it.

And he did. Alexander grew into a powerful High Fae male, the sickly infant he'd once been left long in the past.

Only then did my father recognize him as a son and see the worth I'd always known he had.

I exterminated any possible threat to him or us, including other High Fae like the remaining firecasters. Feeding the High King's paranoia over them was simple. After centuries of ruling, it only took a few well-placed whispers to set his mind upon it. Once the fire elementals were gone, only the High King would be able to control the devastating element through his dragons.

Yet his paranoia had grown too great until he was questioning even his most loyal advisors—including me and my brother. He was right to, of course. With their combined forces, the rebels had much more power, and siding with the obvious victors seemed simple.

I'd been so close to removing them, the only ones with the power to challenge my brother and me. The Shaws were now dead, and their son was in my debt. Only the Warins and Briars were left.

I knew total control of the continent was soon to be in our grasp.

Until I'd found my brother's body scorched from the inside out.

I should have never left him at that lake. I should have never returned to Sanserria, to my mirrors for a way to break through the ice. I should have stayed with him so that when Nicole Briar rose, I'd have been there to kill her once and for all.

Instead, she'd killed my brother.

Another scream of agony broke free. Glass shattered, blowing out the windows and splintering the ornate ivory mirror above the bed. With a sharp crack, the magic ceased, the air settling as if it hadn't just been raging around me. In its wake, utter silence fell. The room went unnaturally still.

Smoothing back my platinum hair, I took a deep breath, steeling myself.

Nicole manifested fire, and Misha revealed herself to be an animaglia—no small magic. The High King had ruled over the entire continent with his power to control animals, lording the dragons over us. And Misha Briar had brought one to life within her lover.

No wonder *he* wanted their hearts.

I needed more allies. Now, this was about more than taking the continent and solidifying my brother's and my place as the new High Rulers—

I needed revenge.

And I would start with killing everyone my brother's murderer loved.

Nic Briar was many things, but she was careless with her love. There were many pieces of her heart she'd given away in her short years, and not just to her sister. I would find a way to end them all as she watched until she was the only one left. Left alone with nothing—like me.

Brushing the swan's feathers from my skirt, I opened the door to my chambers to address the guard standing outside. "Find six guards. None of the high-ranking Reynians, but ones who are fresh from training. I don't care which country they hail from. I need one elemental each, one animaglia, and two healers."

"Of course, my Queen." The guard bowed and began to turn away.

"And guard—" My words halted his steps. "—Have them meet me at the entrances of the gardens."

He nodded silently before leaving to fulfill my wishes.

A quarter of an hour later, I descended the terrace steps to find the guard and six others waiting. I was impressed with his haste and clear eagerness to please.

"Water, earth, and air." The guard indicated the three to his right. "And the animaglia and healers." He nodded to the ones on his left before stepping back.

The six were aligned before me, set against the backdrop of early autumn roses. Five wore Reyian purple and one who had chosen to remain—or had been left behind, but I didn't care—after this morning was in Hahnaleyan green.

I smiled before clasping my hands together. "Guards, I appreciate you coming to me. You were all very brave this morning, defending your chosen queen as the defectors attacked." The six guards stood straighter, the compliment boosting their confidence. "Your allegiance and sacrifice to your queen will be honored."

They stiffened at the word. *Sacrifice.*

Several of their eyes widened in understanding. But I had their minds in my grip by then, and they could not escape. One by one, their eyes rolled back as I crushed their consciousness. I walked toward them as they fell, pulling the dagger from my belt.

"Guard," I said as I leaned over the nearest fallen soldier. "I require a tray to collect the hearts. Silver."

"Of course." The guard swallowed as he left to do as I asked. He might fear me after this, but I was done with hiding. Everyone would see my power and know I was not to be challenged.

I pulled back the first fallen guard's jacket and began to carve out his heart.

In my chambers, I set the six hearts on the table laid out before my seven mirrors. Using that same dagger, a gold alloy inlaid with moonstones and onyx, I pierced each one and recited the words: *Quondam tua, nunc mea.*

Once yours, now mine.

The magic of the hearts floated up from the cut in shimmering, effervescent streams. I wafted them into the coiled shell hanging from my throat, binding the magic to its new vessel—to me—all except one.

I saved the second healer's magic for last, guiding its essence into a separate pendant, a simple golden locket—a gift.

When I finished, my hands and forearms were covered in blood, and the white silk of my gown was stained a deep maroon, but I felt the magic thrum through me as I held the shell.

The earth and watercasters' power wasn't what the Briars' had, but it was not insignificant. This magic wouldn't allow me to create as they did—a uniquely Briar skill, creating water and life from nothing—but I imagined that, after I collected enough faeries' power, my manipulation might rival theirs.

To assess, I called to the water sitting in a basin at the end of the table. It slid through the air to me, cleansing my skin and gown, although it seemed to do so begrudgingly and required a large amount of concentration to keep from slipping away. The magic always fought me most when it was fresh, but it would break after a while, as the air from Orelia Shaw's heart had.

Once clean, I stepped back and looked at the mirror on my left. Tall and rectangular, its mahogany frame was vividly painted with forest, mountainous, desert, and ocean scenes.

The Mirror to Travel.

Closing my eyes, I clasped the shell, imagining where I needed to go. The mirror's surface began to warp, waving like the sea. I stepped through, emerging in the entry hall of Reyna's castle.

The guards stationed there were momentarily stunned but quickly recovered. They bowed to me as I passed. "Our queen."

I walked on without a glance. The castle was crafted of sandstone, stripes of it leading down the halls in the colors of a sunset: pale cream, ochre, sienna, and umber. The light of the early afternoon sun streaming through arched, glassless windows caught on the sand's crystals, sparkling in the waning light. The sea stretched beyond it, a cool aqua-marine compared to the sapphire in the Hahnaley.

I walked down passageways and stairs, heading to the dungeons on the lowest level of our castle. This far underground, the stones wept with condensation, clogging my nose with the dank musk as I passed cell after cell. The prisoners stilled, quieting as I strode past. They knew better than to plead for release. To draw attention to themselves was to ask for death.

At the end, I reached a door barred with Galorian silver. The guards standing on each side inclined their heads before using leather-gloved hands to unlock the mechanism. Behind the door was one last set of steps.

I reached for a lantern hanging by the passage. "Leave the door open," I ordered, "and leave us."

Worry crossed the guards' faces, but with silent bows, they obeyed. I waited until their footsteps receded before descending into the chamber.

Here, only one prisoner resided.

Behind the Galorian silver bars—wrapped with thick, leaf-covered rowan wood and berries that were replenished daily by human ser-vants—a figure sat on a threadbare cot, elbows resting on his knees. His tan skin had lost its golden sheen, so long cut off from sunlight. Even his once-gleaming silver hair was long and matted. But what hadn't changed were the magnificent white wings spread out behind him, glowing softly in the torchlight.

"Hello, General Zarr."

"Hello, traitor." His voice was coated in sand, gruff from disuse.

A laugh escaped me. "Come now. It's been a century. Surely, your anger has cooled by now."

Bright amber eyes slowly rose to meet mine. "A century of rotting in this cell. A century since I was stripped of everything. A century with only the company of my memories, my mistakes, and the vows I pledged."

The anger in his tone lifted my lips. "Wonderful, I was hoping you hadn't changed." The lantern clanged as I set it on the iron hook beside the cell. "I've come to strike a deal."

"So you can betray me as you did our High King?" Zarr stood. He was so tall my eyes only reached his collarbones. The Seraph was undoubtedly magnificent. "You and your brother turned your back on the High Fae by siding with those half-breeds and other sympathizers." He spat, turning his back to me. "Leave."

He faced the far wall, covered in Seraphim glyphs. For a few moments, I observed him, looking over his drawings. After all this time, he was still crafting war plans.

There was hope yet.

"That I cannot do." I sighed. "You see, I am in need of a new War Commander."

"No."

I continued undeterred, having expected his refusal. "I only went to the rebels' side to survive, Zarr. They had all the power. You might be too prideful to admit it, but you aren't stupid. No one could have predicted the Sancristas to be what they were, stained by half-human blood. Once the dragons began to dwindle, we all knew it was a lost cause. I won't apologize because you were too blinded by your loyalty to see it. I am and have always been dedicated to the future we once spoke of," I partially lied. "My beliefs have never wavered. I still want what you want."

Zarr snorted.

"You and I were close once," I purred, stepping closer to the cell; the weight of the Galorian silver and Rowan wood pulsed against me. I gripped my pendant, and the sensation dulled. "We accomplished such incredible things together: the expansion of the High King's armies, the hunting of the firecasters . . . you did love to set them ablaze once they were ashed and no longer immune to the flames. Destroyed by the very thing they loved. The symmetry of it thrilled you. Tell me you don't want that back. That you don't want to retake the continent. That you don't want to rule it all . . . together."

Zarr turned to face me again, his amber eyes heating at the memory. There was nothing he loved more than bloodshed.

I reached a hand through the bars, brushing his skin. "We could be what we once were."

His hand brushed over mine, the palm callused from centuries of war. A spark ran through me as I remembered the other things we used to do together. The sleepless nights with him above me, beneath, behind. Of all the lovers I'd taken, Rainier Zarr was among the best.

His fingers clamped over mine—hard.

Zarr's face broke into a cruel smile as a bone in my hand snapped.

I hissed as I pulled the hand back. "Not even to seek revenge against the Sancristas?"

Zarr's rage at their mention gave him away. "You and your brother can't handle them yourself?" he lashed out. "Still?"

Pain lanced my chest, but I held in the flinch.

"Ah, not those Sancristas. Diana is dead—killed in childbirth. And I poisoned Dominic Briar after beguiling him into marrying me and giving me his country. Then I ordered Alesia Sancrista and her healer mate executed. Though I guess you wouldn't have heard, being stuck in this damp, forgotten hole."

"The hole *you* put me in," Zarr snarled.

"After I had that healer save your *life*," I snapped. "After Alesia Sancrista severed your wings and ran you through with her sword so thoroughly, you were a whisper away from death. The healer slowed your bleeding and your heartbeats, passing you for dead and reviving you upon *my* command. I hid you here for this moment, for when it would be safe to set you free again. If any of them had known I'd kept you alive all these years, they'd have killed you themselves. And me with you."

Zarr began to pace. He remained silent for a few moments until his curiosity got the better of him. "If the Sancrista twins are dead, what do you need me for?"

"Diana and Dominic's daughters—more twins—survive them. They've grown more powerful than their parents and have each manifested two gifts. One is an earthcaster like her father but is also an animaglia. The other of water, like her mother, and fire."

His eyes blazed on the last word. "So, fire returns . . . and they are challenging the throne you stole?" Zarr inferred.

"Their throne, the West, is mine already, along with the South. And I control the heir to the East—the king now that Orelia and Cedric Shaw are also dead."

Zarr's brows raised, impressed. "By you as well?"

"Betrayed by their own son, can you believe it?" I gasped in mock horror.

Zarr laughed, throwing his head back. "Vicious. I didn't know they had it in them to raise such a child. They were so softhearted."

"Sometimes ferocity is simply born, Zarr."

His chuckle faded as he looked at me again. "So, you want me to help you gain the last throne? Take the North away from Josiah Warin?"

"Not Josiah." I shook my head. "August Warin is the king now. It's rumored he killed Josiah himself to claim it."

"The Dragon Killer . . . August always was the greater threat." Zarr's eyes gleamed, no doubt wishing he'd had the opportunity to face the stormcaster in battle.

"You can get your chance, Zarr—your opportunity to face him yourself as well as Diana's daughters. Alesia raised them. She became their mother in the wake of her sister's death. Join me and seek your revenge."

Zarr returned to his cot, sitting as he leaned back on his elbows and shrugged. "It may be more amusing to watch you and your brother try and fail a second time."

This time, I couldn't hold in the flinch.

"Ah." Zarr's eyes gleamed in understanding. "There is a reason you've come to me alone. Tell me, which one of them killed Alexander?"

"He was found burned from the inside out."

"The firecaster, then." His answering smile was cruel. "So, the Briar's daughter killed your brother, and now you want me to help exact revenge?"

"What is that saying? The enemy of my enemy is my friend?" I rolled my shoulders back, standing taller. "Except we were once more than friends, Zarr, and they have always been our enemies."

He shrugged. "I suppose . . . though I still haven't heard enough to join you, traitor."

I paused, then gave Zarr the information I knew would sway him to agree. "Speaking of enemies and traitors, I saw your former second today. She led the Seraphim against us."

Every pretense dropped. "*Mikaela*," Zarr snarled, hatred lacing every syllable.

"Yes," I affirmed. "Jophiel Mikaela is August Warin's War Commander now. She turned the Seraphim against you and now leads them in your stead."

Zarr stood, coming as close as he could to the Galorian silver bars. "Swear it in blood. Swear that if I join you, you will not betray me."

"Nor you me." I pulled the gold knife from my belt. "What shall the terms of the blood bond be?"

Zarr passed a hand, palm up through the bars. "Death."

I smiled. *Clever male.*

I took his hand in mine and pressed the dagger to the fleshy part of his palm beneath the thumb. I made a small cut, drawing just enough blood, before doing the same to my own. Our hands pressed together as we made the blood vow.

Neither could betray the other, or the fault would be death.

When it was done, and we were bound, I whispered the words only my brother and I had known, never trusting anyone else with the key to the ancient warrior's keeping. The Galorian silver bars lifted, freeing General Rainier Zarr.

The Seraph stepped out of his cell for the first time in a century, closing his eyes and breathing in deeply. The smell of freedom.

"I have something for you—a gift," I said, drawing his attention back. Zarr's eyebrow lifted in question. "It will assist in our mission." I presented the small, golden locket.

Zarr took it hesitantly. "What need have I for—"

His words cut off as he felt the power within it, his mouth curving into a truly delighted smile. "This certainly changes things."

72

"I thought you might like it," I said, turning toward the steps. He followed closely behind, wings tucked in tight. "Now that we are re-aligned—" I turned, smiling. "—let's hunt the last firecaster."

CHAPTER 5
Misha

The sea rocked beneath me as I laid on the bed facing the windows. The curtains were pulled shut, but the early morning light still managed to sneak in through the crevices. The slivers of beaming gold taunted me, slicing through the shadows I hid within.

After learning of my aunts' deaths on the deck, Julian carried me here, his arms holding me together as I broke apart.

My tears had slowed as I fell into a daze, every emotion draining until I was nothing but a husk. I laid across Nic's lap, clinging to her legs as her fingers ran through my hair, slowly untangling the snarls. She spoke to fill the silence, but her words came through a haze as if I were listening from underwater.

Still, I heard everything.

Nic told me everything that had happened since that night. The attack, the death of our aunts, and her travel northward. How she'd arrived in the north and how the Seven had saved her. In more ways than one, I deduced.

Her tears dripped onto my skin as she spoke, telling me how she and August had desperately awaited any news of us, praying for any clue to Julian's and my whereabouts. How she'd put together my location based on the Briar roses. Nic left out how she'd fallen in love with August, focusing instead on what she'd learned of our stepmother's betrayal. Adrienne had planned to carve out our hearts, stealing our magic for herself—as she'd done to Cedric and Orelia Shaw.

Adrienne eventually found Nic, sending skinwalkers and then Evander to try to retrieve her. Both attempts were unsuccessful, but the third time, she had disguised herself as Julian. Adrienne succeeded in drawing Nic out, poisoning an entire grove of apples with the hope that my sister would take a single bite. The poison was something stronger than the rowan wood ash, and it had incapacitated my sister completely.

I remembered exactly what it had felt like to be poisoned by the comb as it pricked my skin: the rush and darkness, the sudden fatigue and loss of control in my limbs. How my grasp on the magic deep in my chest had emptied to nothing.

The same had happened to Nic as the apple lodged in her throat.

My sister explained how our mother's pendants—the emerald and knotted gold still pressed against my chest—had protected us from the poison, keeping us alive. The spelled necklaces each held one opportunity to save us from death, putting us into suspended sleep instead. Slumber that could only be broken by one our heart trusted absolutely. August had saved her, and she'd saved me.

Witch magic.

The spell had worked because our mother had been half witch—*we* were part witch.

That's why Nic had been able to connect to the lake after being poisoned, drawing energy from it to incase herself in ice and shield herself from Adrienne.

As I'd laid dying—or so I'd thought—I'd felt the energy of the earth pulsing beneath me. The magic had siphoned through me, sprouting vines and thorns to protect Julian and myself. But it had also transformed him, turning him into the dragon.

Animaglia.

I was no longer only an earth elemental. As Nic had manifested fire on our twenty-second birthday, I'd manifested magic connected to animal life. Hers had been let out in rage—a need to destroy. Mine, by the need to protect.

No earthcaster—outside of my father and I—could create plant life from nothing, Nic explained. No other could cast beings into plants like I'd done to those who had once tormented my sister. My magic had done the same to Julian, turning him into a dragon as a means of protection. It had turned him into a nearly indestructible being, one only threatened by the most powerful of Fae: those like August Warin.

Like our mother.

I glanced at Julian as he listened, taking in my sister's words from where he sat beside the bed. His gaze trailed down to his hands. The skin was red and cracked—scrubbed raw.

When Nic finished, he stood.

Julian kissed my forehead, whispering, "We're safe, love. Because of you."

But what was the cost? I silently asked him, begging him to meet my eyes. His spoke the same language and could read everything they yearned to know.

He didn't. Only a kiss on the forehead, his eyes blank, before he turned away.

I was losing him.

Rasalas prowled to the bed, gracefully leaping up to join Nic and me. I knew now that he was no normal jaguar but a familiar. Our meeting hadn't been accidental; he'd been meant to find me. We were bonded, our life threads bound, as all witches and their familiars were.

Before my sister and I, he once again shifted into that monstrous form. His true body, I realized. It felt like a hallucination, like the dreams I'd had in the tower. My breath raced, panicking. *Is this real?*

Nic's arms tightened around me, her scent of winter and amber coals soothing me.

Real.

I took Rasalas's new form in: the great fangs and body the size of a horse. Rasalas may have been monstrous now, but his black nose was the same—cold and wet as it brushed against my fingertips. He spoke to me with no words, but I understood.

You're safe.

This was part of the bonding between a witch and her familiar: the reveal of the creature's true form. It had been halted because I hadn't been aware of that part of my heritage, but when bonded to a witch, familiars grew more powerful, and their abilities heightened. In exchange, they protected their bonded.

It was a symbiotic pact, as Miranda explained.

Hours later, I stoked a hand down his back as he slept beside me, having shifted back to his jaguar form. Julian, however, hadn't returned.

Rasalas's gold eyes slowly opened, glistening in the dark. Nic's arms were wrapped around me, and I clung tighter to her, questioning my reality. Waking blurred the line between dreams and reality in my mind, and I was half convinced I was still stuck in the tower.

A slender vine covered in thorns slid toward me on the bed, much like the ones that had shielded me when I'd been poisoned. I reached out and pricked my finger on the nearest one. A drop of blood fell onto the sheets, and a rush of pain filled me.

Real. This is real.

My head spun, breath slowing.

Another thorn grew, replacing the first. I pricked myself once more. The rush dulled on the second sting but was not quite gone.

I knew I needed to rise. I imagined growing fangs and claws, then sinking them into Adrienne and Evander and all those who had hurt everyone I'd ever loved.

Instead, my teeth were blunted, and my fingernails were bitten down to the quick, raw and bleeding. My ribcage had turned to lead, pressing down on my lungs and dragging me down and down.

Father. Mother. Alesia. Eve. Orelia. Cedric. All gone.

I still had my sister.

I wasn't so sure if I still had Julian.

Nic's arms were wrapped around me, her breath soft in sleep as she held me.

I loved them—and I'd failed them. If I had been more wary, like Nic, I would have never been poisoned. I could have been there with my aunts and twin. Could've acted as another variable to see the attack coming and protect them.

But because I'd been much too trusting and blinded by love, I hadn't been there.

And for the love I'd been consumed by . . . I'd made him into a monster.

I couldn't fail them again, but I couldn't seem to find the energy to rise. They deserved better than me. My love would only hurt them more.

The darker the shadows, the brighter the sun.

There was no sun.

They died, blood soaking the forest floor, and blew away as ash in the wind.

Get up.

Turning from the morning light and pulling away from my sister, the shadows wrapped tighter around me, pulling me deeper.

Get up.

I can't.

CHAPTER 6
Julian

I stepped out onto the deck, nearly stumbling in my need for air.

My elbows hit the deck railing, and I ran my palms over my face. I pulled them back, staring down at my hands. They clenched, and the urge to return to the bathing room to wash them struck again. I wanted to scour them with the brush until they ached.

I knew they were clean. And yet, all I could see was the blood, my palms utterly soaked from the lives I'd taken in the past weeks.

When I realized Misha had been poisoned, I'd run, carrying her. I'd felt her magic thrashing wildly as it was drained away. Convinced her heart would stop once it did, I'd dropped the barriers between us, ready to give her mine. I would have done anything to keep her heart beating until we could reach Eve.

Instead, Misha's magic had hurdled into me, overpowering everything. I'd stumbled, dropping her as she went sprawling across the ground, weak from the poison and unable to move. The magic had raged through me, shifting and changing.

But her magic hadn't chosen the form I'd become.

As soon as I'd seen Misha's hand coated in blood, I'd gone wild with rage, feral in my need to save her and rip apart whoever had done this to her. The next thing I knew, the shift had overcome me, pushed forth as Misha's magic pounded through my veins. My fingers became talons, and scales erupted from my skin as I grew and grew.

When it was done, Misha was so small beneath me, lying still and broken.

Sure she was dead, I'd laid there, curling myself around her in the dragon's body as my heart broke and bled.

But then I'd felt the pulse of her magic around me in the thorns and roses, gently glowing from their golden centers. I felt that same magic still coursing through me, like it had broken away—as if part of her was living in my chest next to the heart that would only ever be hers. I saw the slow rise and fall of her chest as she breathed.

She was alive.

That night I swore I'd do anything to keep her that way, even if I lost everything she loved about me in the process.

August came to stand next to me on the rail, looking out over the sea.

Even at twenty-four, sometimes I still felt like a child next to him. Like a nine-year-old boy running into the arms of someone you trusted implicitly. There was something comforting about being held by arms you knew would do anything for you, even kill to protect you.

I'd known what I was doing that day, even as a child. I'd hugged my brother, knowing he'd see my flinch as he held me. That he'd see what our father had done—his cruel punishment taken out on my back. The whip's lacerations my father ordered go unhealed the day before.

I could still feel those few lashes on my back, though it'd only been half a dozen that one time. A tremor skated down my back at the thought. How August had endured it as many times as he had, I couldn't imagine.

My mother had sat with me the entire night, applying salve on my open back, the wounds too painful to allow any bandage, sheet, or clothing to brush against them. She cried more than I had, unable to do anything to stop it—or to prevent it from happening again.

Only one person could.

I knew what August would do.

I'd made my brother murder our father—what kind of child does that? I'd let the rage and pain overcome my better judgment. I'd just been so *angry*. When it was done, there was only regret. Not for our father being dead, but for what I'd schemed my brother into doing. The blood on his hands should have been on mine.

After I'd truly realized what I'd done, I had sworn never again to take a life.

A promise broken.

"You did what you had to, brother," August said, piercing my thoughts. He'd always been able to see me, reading my mind as if the thoughts flittered across my forehead in scrawled lines.

A choked laugh escaped me—it wasn't really a laugh at all. "Did I?"

Listening from the shadows of the ruins, I'd known the guards who had found us weren't there to help. They'd come for Misha, to carve out her heart and take it to Adrienne. They spoke so freely of it, never considering who might overhear. I didn't know if they chose to do it of their own free will or if Adrienne had poisoned their minds, but I didn't care—all that mattered was that they were there to hurt her.

"The guards at the ruins attacked you first," August said. "You were protecting her and yourself."

The guards that survived the thorns due to the twice-thickened armor . . . I thought of how they'd come through the split in the wall. How they'd frozen when they saw me, unable to believe their own eyes.

"And if they didn't?" I murmured. "Attack first?"

I hadn't given them the chance. Metal armor didn't stop fire. It was probably the worst thing they could have been wearing, actually. I'd watched as the metal had heated, burning hot red and gold until it seared their skin, and they had roasted alive inside it.

August shrugged. "They made their choice."

Of course, he would see it that simply. August had never quite been able to shed the brutality our father had forced into him. Anyone who threatened him or those he loved would be met with unrelenting violence.

Growing up, I admired my brother greatly. He'd done what needed to be done in the war and against our father. But I'd never wanted to be him, never wanted to be the warrior he was. I saw the toll it took on him to do those things. How they'd scarred him mentally and physically.

For nearly three hundred years, August had been bred and trained to fight, first by our father and then by years on the front in the Great War, slaying dragons and the High King's soldiers. August was a warrior down to his soul. To defend what he loved, he acted swiftly and decisively.

But I'd never wanted my gut reaction to be violence. I'd wanted—needed to be more than our father.

And I'd failed. I hadn't needed to lift a single finger to end the lives of those guards.

I pushed up from my elbows, standing and nearly coming eye-to-eye with my brother. "So, what happens when we return home and reconvene? Are we going to war?"

August nodded. "The sisters deserve vengeance for what Adrienne has done to them, their father, their aunts, and their kingdom."

"Is that why you killed Adrienne's brother?" Nic had recanted the story to Misha, telling how August had slain him with a bolt of lightning down the throat until Alexander was scorched from the inside out.

I knew brother wasn't the right word to describe their relationship. Adrienne was to Alexander more like what August was to me: a confidant, guardian . . . a parent. She had raised him, more of a mother to him than their own.

August's face remained unchanged, eyes like stone. Unflinching. "No, but taking from Adrienne what she's taken from them does ring with some sense of justice."

He didn't regret it—would do it again in a moment.

I turned to him. "Did you not think to take him prisoner? Or to use him to negotiate with Adrienne?"

August's face pinched—ah, there was the regret. Until now, he had never considered that there could have been any other way than killing him.

"He had her," my brother whispered, his eyes remembering as he looked back over the sea. He was seeing that day once more—seeing Nic under the ice. "Alexander had her. And what he spoke of doing to her—" August's hand rubbed across his mouth, as if even the thought of speaking the words sickened him.

Had Misha been in Nic's position, would I have stopped to consider negotiation?

I exhaled, rubbing at my eyes. *No, I wouldn't. Not for a moment.*

"I would have done the same," I said. I *had* done the same to the guards at the ruins. "But how much death is enough, brother? How far are we going to take this?"

How far, indeed. I was beginning to spiral. I knew what my brother had done when I was hurt—but what if I'd been *killed*? What would Adrienne do now that Alexander was gone?

August took a moment, considering. "Some people cannot be reasoned with, Julian. Diplomacy can only go so far when greed for power overtakes all reason. Those people—our father, Adrienne—must be stopped before the devastation is too great."

But when would it end?

August's jaw set as he went on. "I forgave our father for what he'd done to me. For how he'd raised me. But I should have killed him for what I suspect he did to my mother, but . . . I didn't want to become the killer he was and act without reason or proof. And look what good my hesitance did. He hurt you and Sena just the same—because I did nothing for so long."

Yuki Saitō, August's mother. My brother had always suspected that our father had killed her in the war but could never prove it. Josiah was supposed to be stationed on the opposite war front, and multiple generals had confirmed it. That had halted August from acting upon his vengeance, but still—I knew it was one of the few things he regretted.

"So, war it is?" I asked again.

August nodded, looking to the door to the cabins where the twins were resting as if he could see Nic through the wood.

I thought of all the lives lost since the Solstice: Orelia and Cedric Shaw, Alexander Deimos, Eve and Alesia. I thought of the last two with a stab of pain through my chest.

August believed war would be the only outcome.

But if this kept going back and forth, would *any* of us be left standing?

Nic left when I returned, giving us space.

Misha still slept, curled in on herself, the duvet pulled tight to her face. I knelt beside her, my hand hovering over her hair, her skin.

I was terrified to touch her. Dying not to.

Withholding myself from Misha felt like strangling myself from within. Every time I pulled back, the noose pulled tighter at my throat. To be without her was to be without breath.

There was only so much I could take.

Crawling onto the bed, I took Misha into my arms. I sat propped up against the headboard and cradled her head against my chest. She hadn't stirred in the transition, lost so deeply in her sleep.

Selfish bastard. She deserves better than you.

Looking down at Misha, as gold light danced across her face and hair from the candle on the nightstand, I thought about that night and the tiny velvet box that had been in my pocket. After gaining approval from Eve and Alesia as we danced on the Summer Solstice, I'd planned to give it to Misha in the ruins—the place where she'd written her letters. The place where we'd first made love.

The question had lingered on my tongue the entire week: to marry me, complete the mating bond—anything, so long as she would agree to spend her life with me.

Whether it was for a millennium or only a year—I wanted to spend every moment with Misha Briar.

I remember the ring and how I'd designed it for her: a marquise emerald, green as her magic, surrounded by glittering diamonds and pearls, set in gold—the same shade as her hair—and wound like vines.

When Misha was poisoned and her magic transformed me, it was lost. I thought she had been lost with it.

When I realized she was alive, I took her in one taloned claw, holding her close to my chest as I scaled the tower wall. I was terrified the entire time I held her—that even though she'd somehow survived the poison, I would be the one to kill her, accidentally crushing her in my grip. I'd placed her up high where she'd be safe and where I could protect her.

Now, I was afraid to touch her for a different reason.

Looking down at her, I wondered how I could ever ask her to bind herself to me now—after all I'd done. After all the blood now on my hands.

The worst thing was that I didn't regret it. I'd tear apart the guards again and again to keep her safe. No remorse flitted through me from what I'd done.

This was the root of my ambivalence—my guilt laid bare: how monstrous did I have to be not to regret the lives I'd taken, even if it was to protect hers?

I looked down at her again, breathing softly.

My heart constricted in my chest.

Misha's magic might have made me the beast, but I was the monster alone.

CHAPTER 7
Nic

T he maps laid out before me blurred and warped.

Misha only had enough energy to eat small spoonfuls of broth before falling back to sleep. An hour later, she'd woken in a panic from a nightmare, clinging to me as her tears wet my hair and neck.

They're gone, Nicky. Everyone is gone.

It was all my sister could say, choking between sobs.

I sent Julian for Shai and Miranda, hoping they'd help to calm her. When they arrived, I warned Shai not to use his magic to steal her grief—instead, the mindcaster calmed her racing heart, settling her into a softer devastation. Miranda gave my sister a tonic that she readily accepted, letting her fall into a dreamless sleep. Only then did Julian and I step out.

Dread sat heavily in my gut. The poison had kept Misha in a suspended sleep for almost two months. She shouldn't have so easily slept again after being awoken.

She shouldn't have wanted to.

I looked to Julian on my right, his silver eyes dark and distant. He worried the same.

On my other side, August's hand brushed the back of my neck, bringing me back to our present, our reason for convening in the Yuki's war room with the rest of the Seven.

Julian already knew what had happened since the Solstice, having listened to me tell Misha. He spoke first, his face hard as he turned to his brother and Simon. "We have so many spies. How did we not see what Adrienne planned to do?"

Julian's eyes flickered to Miranda, who had crept back into the room carrying a large bundle, but he knew better than to say anything. The Seer set down her object at the far end of the table before turning to look out the porthole, her eyes distant and regretful.

Simon answered softly, eyes trained on the table before slowly lifting to meet Julian's gaze. "Adrienne chose her confidants well."

"And we—I—" My words were choked. I should have seen it. All that time, Adrienne was right there. Living in our home, sitting upon my father's throne. The throne she'd *murdered* him to take.

My chest felt like it was about to cave in, my ribs turning in on themselves. I couldn't get in enough air.

Then August was standing behind me, arm hooking around my shoulders and pulling me into him until my back met his chest. His breaths steadied mine. His head tipped as he nodded to someone.

Her blue eyes softer than I'd ever seen them, Jophiel changed the subject and asked, "Did you notice what we didn't see in Sanserria?"

"Desdemonian soldiers," August answered.

"Nor Evander," Shai said. "He wasn't in the palace either."

Breaths finally even, I said, "We know he promised Adrienne soldiers and Desdemon's backing in exchange for . . . what he did."

What he did—three words that hardly encapsulated his murder of his parents by his own hand, followed by stealing their air magic for his own. That's all Orelia and Cedric were to Evander—not a mother and father but a source of more power.

"So why weren't they there?" Julian asked.

"He could be having difficulty rousing them. Easterners, particularly from Sossulla—" I flinched at as I spoke of Eve's birthplace. "—Follow a specific mourning ritual. No food to be eaten during the daylight hours, specific mourning attire, and prayers to the Father for the deceased morning and evening."

Celeste spoke up, also being from the region. "That is correct. This happens for a full moon cycle following the loved one's passing."

"So, what happens when an entire country mourns their king and queen?" Julian asked.

"Then the entire country mourns for one month," Celeste said simply.

"But Desdemon has been sending supplies to the West and Adrienne," Simon said. "We received those notes from our spies."

"Evander must have found a way to do that while in mourning, likely rousing the Desdemonians to his call for vengeance," I mused. "The Desdemonians could have collected and departed from Valora. With that many soldiers traveling through the Daire Hills, they would arrive in Hahnaley in about two months, even with the full cavalry."

The Desdemonian Cavalry had more Areion horses than any other country. The horses were a special breed; myth said they were blessed by the Father to be swifter and lighter of foot than any other. The first had supposedly been the Mother's horse, gifted with magic before she'd ascended to godhood.

The East had two thousand of them.

"If they are crossing, they will most likely take the Cailleach Pass. It's the widest and has the least elevation gain." August drew his finger across the map. "When we land in the North, Simon can reach out and confirm with the spies in the neighboring villages." The spymaster nodded his agreement. "And Teale—" August called, looking to the demi-Dryad.

She sat taller, hair even more curly in the sea air. The roots were tinged a pale orange as autumn neared, shifting with the seasons. "Yes?"

"How will the Aurae feel about an army crossing their hills led by a Fae male with stolen air magic?"

"I would guess they wouldn't like that much at all." Teale smiled impishly. "I will try to speak to them. They're . . . difficult to talk to." Her aquatic blue eyes went distant, already planning how to reach the Aurae, nymphs of the breeze.

We didn't see many in Sanserria, being too close to the Redwood and far from the wide open spaces they loved to roam. I'd only caught glimpses of them in Chiaran, dancing in the fields among spring's first wildflowers. They looked like silver and gold spirits of air, wafting to and fro in the sunlight. Aurae thrived in the wind, and in the stillness, they dissipated. Could they even hold form long enough to speak to one of us?

Then again, if anyone could manage it, it would be Teale.

I leaned forward, my finger going to the capital of the East. "The infantry will slow them down, and even Areion horses need to rest. Travel from Valora across the continent and northwest to Sanserria will take significant time. Not to mention that they had to mobilize and call in whatever reserves Evander wants. And not every soldier would have been in their post, not when we've had peace for a hundred years, and there's been no reason to think that would change."

Especially when the peace that was broken had been when their king and queen were murdered.

Orelia and Cedric had been the best of us, kind and trusting—the fatal flaw that led to their slaughter at the hands of their own son.

Jophiel leaned forward, resting her hands on the thick mahogany table. "The last count of their army was thirty thousand strong, with two thousand on Areion horseback. We need to stop them before they reach Adrienne."

"Agreed," August said before turning to me. "Do you think Gemma could sway them?"

The Desdemonians would listen to no one but their own, especially if Evander had coerced them with lies. Only Gemma could tell them the truth.

But Gemma's health was still . . . delicate. Orelia and Dominic's youngest daughter had been abused by Evander for years behind their parents' backs, manipulated into forgetting by her mindcasting sister, Lorraine. She'd only learned the truth two weeks ago and was still processing it all in the North under the watchful care of Sena, Julian's mother. I didn't know how she'd fare against her brother, in words or in magic. Evander was charismatic, born with the ease of charm.

My cheeks heated as I remembered falling for it.

Gemma's magic was more promising, and her power had been on course to surpass her elder brother's—until he'd stolen his father's, adding it to his own.

I shook my head. "I don't know."

"We'll have to try," Julian said. If Adrienne adds the East's forces, her army will equal ours."

I scanned the map, doing the math in my head. Montevalle had the largest army of any country on the Continent. The Hahnaleyans were unknown. Many had been boarded onto the ships we sailed with, but not nearly enough. We'd have to wait and see how many crossed the northern border to Montevalle. I counted that about half would side with Misha and me as the true Briar heirs—optimistically speaking. It shrank to a quarter when I was pessimistic and assumed most were swayed by Adrienne's lies or her magic forcing them to stay.

And if Adrienne kept all of Desdemon, the Reynians, and half of Hahnaley, it would be too even a match for me to feel comfortable.

We needed to find a way to stop Adrienne before this came to a full-out war.

"Once we return to Ankaa, we can assess Gemma's state and her capacity to assist," August said. "It will be easier to convince the Desdemonians to defect with her, but we must prepare to do this without her."

Everyone understood. Stepping back, the Seven began to file from the room slowly.

"Nic." Miranda drew my attention as the others passed through the door. "I saw something. In the palace." She led me over to the bundle she'd brought, her hands hesitating over the cloth. "I wanted to show you with Misha, but . . ."

I understood. In her current state, my sister wasn't in any place to take any more news. "You don't think this should wait," I finished for her.

"No." Miranda sighed.

August hesitated in the doorway, eyes asking: *Do you want me to stay?*

I shook my head. Something in my gut told me I wanted to be alone for this.

Miranda opened the bundle with only us in the room. Two swords—Luxien and the Mercedelmar—lay before us.

My parents' swords.

"How did you get these?" I whispered, gently running a hand over my mother's blade. The Mercedelmar's gold-and-sapphire-embedded hilt was twin to the Iradelmar at my side. My father's, Luxien, had a golden hilt etched with intricate roses and thorns—briars.

I'd wanted the swords, of course, but hadn't asked Miranda or Shai to stop to find them. Evacuating the palace had been too important. I'd told myself they were safe because Adrienne couldn't enter the library, gallery, throne room, or West Wing, where my family resided, thanks to the magic of the palace.

"I saw her," Miranda breathed. "It was a vision, but unlike any other I'd ever had. It led me to the library, where I saw Diana. I talked to her."

The Seer's words gripped my heart as she explained. The vision had taken her back over twenty-two years as my mother was nearing the end of her year-long gestation with my sister and me. As Miranda saw the past, my mother saw the future.

"What did she say?"

"Your mother said the swords would be important but did not elaborate, just that you needed both," Miranda said as I ran my fingers along their blades again, "and that everything you need to know is here." Miranda held out a book, the leather cover worn and aged, the gold-leafed florals flaking and peeling away.

I opened to the first page. I didn't recognize the handwriting but knew it immediately; we curved our F's in the same way.

August 22

I don't think my hands will ever stop shaking.

I knew the fates would send a message soon; the lightning storm followed by a late snow in August was too unusual. A sign if there ever was one.

As I sat upon the windowsill, the world outside blanketed in sparkling white, and the trees burned to raven-black husks, the needle pricked my finger. As my blood fell upon the snow, I saw it.

I was in a room with walls black as night and seven mirrors of various shapes and sizes. They were all dreadful, whispering of malicious intent, but in the center was the worst: framed by obsidian and inlaid with moonstones and stardust with a large crystal at its peak. It called to me, the glass shimmering and warping my reflection as I approached.

In its surface, I saw broken castles covered in ash and thorns. A drop of poison muddied clear water as it rippled outward. A dragon roared as thunder erupted. The earth cracked and broke apart as a piercing scream of agony rang. Then, out of the fractured, snow-covered ground, a being of nightmares rose. One of fury and wrath sharp enough to consume the world.

Then it showed me them.

Two children, little Fae girls about five years old, one with hair dark as night, the other golden like the sun—my daughters.

I watched them grow. Dominic, Alesia, and Eve, raising and tending to them. In a flash of twenty-two years, I saw everything. They would be surrounded by so much love, experiencing the hardships and heartbreaks we all do while becoming the daughters I had always dreamed of.

But I never saw myself. And now I know that I never will.

As their life begins, mine will end.

Even as I write, I cradle my stomach, not yet swollen with them, these tiny sparks of hope in the darkness to come. I will do everything I can to protect them and to give them every advantage in the years to come.

I hope they will know how much I love them, how devastated I am to never meet them. But they will have the best father and the best godmothers in my sister and her mate.

My sweet girls, I hope one day you will read this and know I love you so much.

Diana

Tears streamed down my face. I was careful not to let them fall on the journal lest they blur my mother's words. Silently, I flipped through the rest of the pages.

My mother wrote about her plans—how she'd obtained the necklaces that protected my sister and me, keeping us alive after we'd been poisoned. She included what she'd told Alé and Dominic, our father, in the letters left after her death. What she knew of what was to come, vague as it was, and how important it was that Misha and I be prepared for the coming challenges.

Taking a deep breath, I closed the journal, holding it tight to my chest. Shaking, a sob ripped out of me. My knees hit the ground.

Miranda wrapped me in her arms. "She wanted me to tell you—to tell both of you—how much she loved you."

She held me as I cried, mourning the mother I'd only ever know as stories from my father and aunts—all now dead as well—and the words in this journal.

Jealously pierced me that Miranda had gotten to see her—to talk to her. A chance I would never get. The unfairness of it all was overwhelming.

After minutes—or hours—I stood, brushing away the tears. I imagined building a stone pillar within myself, one too strong to be knocked down. Too steadfast to be washed away again.

"I need to show my sister," I said, wiping away the last falling tears.

No matter how deep Misha was in her grief, she would never forgive me for keeping this from her.

CHAPTER 8
Misha

Outside the window, the full moon's reflection stretched across the sea, rocking and swaying with the waves. I sat propped against the headboard, clutching my mother's journal to my chest.

When Nic had explained to me what it was and who had written in it, she'd stood tall, her voice unwavering. Only a glint of tears shimmered in her eyes as she shoved down her emotions.

Scream, Nicky. Show me how you're hurting, too.

She wouldn't.

Nic and I browsed the journal together, taking in our mother's words. Diana Sancrista's handwriting. She curved her A's like Nic. Flicked her Y's like mine.

We knew there was more information in here about her visions and the future she'd seen and wanted to prepare us for. But for now, my sister and I just savored having this piece of her.

Our mother touched these pages, I thought reverently, running a hand down the parchment as I felt the ridges left by the ink. Candlelight danced across the journal, the words basking in it. The memory of my mother was more alive than ever.

Nic had drifted into sleep a while ago. An hour or so, maybe more. She slept on her side, facing me. My sister always looked softer when she slept, all her hard edges soothed.

I'd been reading the journal since, unable to get enough of my mother's inner thoughts and how she'd seen the world.

I flipped toward a passage in the back and fell once again into my mother's psyche.

May 19.

Dominic and I named our daughters today: Misha and Nicole.

I'm desperate to know what their relationship will be like. Will it be like mine and Alé's, where sometimes we fight like alley cats, sick to death of each other, and in the next moment are inseparable, laughing in a world of our own making? But always—always—each other's favorite person, the one we'd die to defend? Alesia would sooner take a spear through the heart than see me harmed, and I am the same.

As I'm writing this, she's dancing in my belly. Misha, my little lion. She is so restless, like me. Dominic and I haven't discussed second names, but I want her to have mine, Camila, and Alesia's second name, Maria, for Nicole. Sisters to sisters. Just like my mother and her twin's had been. A piece of us that will always live on in them.

But only if I can help them.

The pendants will be ready soon. It's their one chance against death, sustaining them in life. It has to work—it must. I cannot bear the thought of my daughters living only 22 years.

If they fall, I will ensure they rise again.

Diana

My breath caught on Alesia's name, snagging on a shard of my shattered heart.

It was unfair, somehow. My mother never stood a chance, though she'd done everything for us—*given* everything for us. She grew us in her womb, loved Nic and me with her entire heart, and protected us from the evils to come. And yet, no matter how much I mourned her, it felt like mourning an idea. A, "*What could have been.*"

But Alesia was the mother we knew. In every part of our lives, she'd been there. I remembered how she had washed and combed mine and Nic's hair, applying warmed jasmine oil to the ends to smooth the flyaways. She'd done this from my earliest memories to my last. Even when I could do it myself, I'd begged her to, wanting to feel her touch.

They were each our mothers, but missing Alé and Eve was not the same as missing Diana.

I held the journal against my chest, tears silently cascading down my face as I looked toward my sister. Nic looked so much like Alé with her black hair and deep brown eyes. I felt a pang of jealousy for this part of our aunt and mother she had gotten and that I hadn't. By all accounts, Diana and Alesia were identical, only differentiated by their mannerisms by those who knew them best. With my blonde hair and blue eyes, I felt left out. Omitted.

Immediate regret lanced through me as if the thought were a betrayal of our father and his blue eyes that matched mine. Then I was missing him too, and my head was fuzzy, my thoughts spiraling. I couldn't find a ray of light in the swirling of my mind—nothing was good enough.

One more entry, and then I would sleep.

I flipped back through the journal, searching for my father's name. My eyes landed on the curved D—the flourish my mother liked to add only to her mate's name—and I halted.

April 25.

Sena agreed to do the translation on the swords. She's the only person I could find with such expertise in the old Fae language.

I worry that Josiah will find out. He's always held a certain disdain for my sister and me—nearly as much as we do for him. But Sena agreed to secrecy and seems confident she can do this discretely, her pen strokes strong and firm in the letters we pass between us via the hawk. So, I'm trusting her.

The bird calmly waited for my reply, black as night as it rustled in the window. It looked at me with eerie intelligence, as if pledging the letter would be delivered safely.

I hate that I have to keep this from Dominic. From Alesia and Eve. But they can't know about the vision, or about the tools I'm collecting for our daughters, because then they'll ask why, and they can't know I won't be here to help.

Keeping things from my mate, my sister, and Eve—the friend and sister I never knew I needed—is agonizing. But it's the only way.

Diana

"Sister," I hissed, shaking Nicole's shoulder.

Nic jerked awake, blinking her eyes against sleep. "Meesh?" She sat up quickly, shifting to peer around the room, assessing for threats. Seeing none, her eyes settled back on me.

I handed her the journal. "Read this one."

She squinted, willing exhaustion away as she read. Her eyes went wide as she realized what I'd discovered. "Sena knows what's on the swords."

Because of Miranda, we knew the Iradelmar and Mercedelmar were important, but not how. This was it. If we could translate the messages, we might know more about the prophecy of what was to come. It might help us stop Adrienne's plans.

My sister kept reading, her eyes shining at the mention of our father and aunts, but she swallowed down the grief before it could grow further. "We can ask her when we reach Ankaa."

I nodded. My sister set the journal on the table by the bed and blew out the candle. We laid facing each other, hands interlaced. Dawn was rising, soft light illuminating her face.

I took her in, one of the few people I had left to lose. "What are we going to do?" I whispered.

Nic knew what I meant—she always knew.

"Live, sister." Nic pushed my hair back from my face, wiping an errant tear away. "Live for them. Because of all they gave."

Our parents. Our aunts. Everyone we've lost.

"What if I can't?" I choked out. "What if I can't live like I used to?"

"Then don't, Meesh. Live in whatever way you can. No matter what, I am here with you, sister. I will lay beside you until you are ready to stand." She held my hands tighter, anchoring me.

I hated that I might let her down.

CHAPTER 9
August

Cool water splashed against my face, sweat-drenched from a night in which I'd barely slept, plagued by familiar nightmares.

My eyes were haunted as I looked in the mirror—all of the ones on the ship had been warded with Miranda's magic to keep Adrienne's prying magic at bay, but the thought did little to soothe me.

My brother had returned. Safe . . . and yet not.

Any time we'd spoken, Julian's eyes were tormented in a way I'd never seen, flooded with equal parts guilt and ambivalence. I knew that look—I had started seeing it in my reflection over two hundred years ago, when I took a life for the first time at my father's demand. I'd been fourteen.

Over the years, I had come to terms with what my father made me do—what I felt I had to do to escape Josiah Warin's wrath. Still, the weight of the lives I'd taken was a burden that rested heavily on my shoulders.

Now, Julian was struggling under that same weight. I'd failed to protect him from it.

My hands flexed on the water basin, empty.

As if my need summoned her, Nicole entered our room with silent footsteps. She pressed her cheek to my bare back, her arms winding around my chest.

"Did you learn anything new from the journal?"

The skin along the edges of her nails was ragged, close to bleeding on some fingers. She was picking again. I took her hands in mine, kissing each one.

"There was one thing I wanted to tell you, actually," she answered, snuggling closer to me, cheek pressed between my shoulder blades. "It involves Julian's mother."

I crooked a brow, turning to face her. I leaned against the vanity and stroked a hand down her back.

Nicole's nose was a bit red at the tip, and her lips were swollen. She'd cried after leaving her sister's room and tried to hide it before coming here—not from me but from anyone else she might have seen in the hall.

At the cabin, she would come downstairs in the morning, and you could never tell she'd cried herself to sleep. Nicole used her ice magic to clear the puffiness in her eyes away before she faced anyone, not wanting them to see how badly she was fracturing when no one watched. She never realized her nose and mouth swelled, too, every time she cried.

I did. I always saw her. I never could look away.

Reaching out, my fingers pushed back the raven-black hair curling around her face in the briny air of the sea. My thumb traced the moon-pale skin of her cheek as she went on.

"I can explain it later, but for now, can you hold me?" she asked.

I shifted my hand to her head, cupping it as I pulled her into me. Nicole remained quiet for a few moments, taking deep breaths to steady herself. My chest grew damp with her silent tears, unable to hold it back any longer.

"You found her, Snow. We have them back. They're both safe and unharmed."

"Safe, yes," she murmured. "But unharmed . . ." Nicole shook her head. "They each told us what happened, but we don't know what they went through. Not really."

With my fingers, I tilted her chin up. The shadows beneath her eyes were dark with exhaustion and worry. "They will tell us when they're ready."

Nicole was having trouble sleeping since Adrienne poisoned her with the apple; she now found it difficult to make it through the night without waking several times. She would jolt back to consciousness, gasping for breath as if still under the water. The magic had protected her, but it wasn't without a cost.

Her arms tightened around me as if nothing could pull her away. "I just worry that—"

"You can't take her grief, sweetheart. You can't fix this heartache." But I knew how she felt. If I could, I would carry the entire burden of Nicole's pain—my brother's, too. I would suffer for an eternity to know they didn't have to. "She has to feel it."

Nicole nodded, pressing her lips to my chest as she relaxed against me.

Love for her overwhelmed me. I never thought I would find someone I could be this open with, who could see so many parts of me and not think them hideous.

But someone had, I remembered. It was so long ago, but the memory was undimmed by time. She had seen my scars and told me that I was a better man than I believed myself to be—than I let others think I was.

It was one story I hadn't yet shared with Nicole. One she needed to hear.

I brought her hand to my chest and pressed it over the scars my father had carved. *Failure.*

Gently, Nicole ran her fingertips over the raised edges. "Have you ever thought about—"

I nodded. It crossed my mind often. "Damian could remove them. He's skilled enough. I trust him—all of them—and yet . . . I've found I am not yet ready to bare this piece of my history to the Seven."

Her brow creased. "They don't know?"

I shook my head. "Only my mother, you, and one other have seen the marks my father left. I've only been injured badly enough to uncover them once."

"During the war . . ." Her voice drifted, thinking. "You said you were severely injured when you fought the last dragon—the one my mother killed, saving your life."

I nodded. Taking her hand, I pressed it to my side, just beneath my heart, where the wound from the dragon had been. Nearly every rib had been shattered, the lung on that side had collapsed, and the internal bleeding was so severe I'd scarcely survived winnowing into the healer's tent before I'd passed out. "The healer did their work well."

Nicole's hand went still, her eyes going distant. When she spoke, her voice was thick with sorrow as she remembered. "Eve healed you . . . she saw. She knew."

"She did. She promised never to tell anyone, and she didn't. Eve kept my secret for over a hundred years. Not even Alesia knew."

Tears trickled from Nicole's eyes as she thought of her aunt. "I *knew* she had a soft spot for you."

I chuckled softly, remembering. Eve had gone out of her way during the Solstice to be welcoming to my brother and me. While Alesia and the Shaws regarded us warily—not that I could blame them—she'd been nothing but open.

This world had lost a light when it lost Eve Kamati.

"But what about during—" Nicole's brows furrowed as she struggled to find the right words. "—I mean, you're so old—"

I laughed again. The sound was more of a surprise, breaking free unexpectedly.

Nicole's lips turned up. "I didn't mean it like that—well, sort of. What I am trying to say is that you must have been intimate with others before me. But they never saw . . ." She ran her hands over the scars again, possessively now, and, gods above, if that didn't stir something in my chest.

I shook my head. "You're the only one who's seen me like this. The others . . ." My words drifted. I swallowed before continuing. "The others I was only with in a very specific way, a way in which they would never see what had been done to me. It was always clothed and facing away and never more than once. Those couplings were only a mutual need being met, but with you, it's different. Everything with you is different, Nicole."

"You always want me to look at you," Nicole whispered, cheeks heating. Red as a June rose against the snow.

"You are the only one who sees me," I whispered back.

108

"When I think I can't love you more, you say something like this. It cracks my heart open, and you fill the spaces."

"I've waited so long for you." I cradled her face in my hands. "For someone who could see my scars and understand. You said once that you loved me because I saw you—all of you—and did not shy away. You did the same for me."

Nicole saw every ugly and hideous part of me, every scar, and through every mask. She didn't look past it but stared straight through. She saw each blemish as something beautiful, as something worthy to be loved. No matter how much I resembled my father and no matter how terrible he'd tried to make me, I couldn't be such a wretched being if *she* were mine.

My mate. My salvation.

This beautiful person who had somehow been linked to me through the stars, their threads of fate binding us and pulling me to her since the moment our eyes first met. Those same eyes were pleading with me now.

Fuck, I would give her anything—*everything*—to take that look from her eyes. The pain that laced through her irises, the dark brown flecked with amber.

I knew what would, what she was asking for. It's what I needed, too.

Grasping her hips, I walked Nicole back into the wall. "Do you remember the moment we met, sweetheart?"

I placed my hands on either side of her head, her scent of amber and freshly fallen snow filling my nose. My mind ran over that day, the memory crystal clear. She'd burst through the door, hiding from the males she'd picked a fight with. Then she'd fought with me after I tried to keep her there—desperate even then to be near her, to learn her name.

"How could I forget? You were being a domineering prick," Nicole teased, but the breathlessness with which she said it betrayed her.

I grinned. "You aren't wrong."

My hand lifted, tucking a strand of black hair behind her ear, more rounded than other High Fae due to her part-human heritage—the witch heritage, as it turned out. Nicole's skin prickled at the contact. Her tiny moon and star earrings glittered in the morning light.

"You had fire dancing in your eyes even then, and I couldn't bear to part with you just yet. I was fascinated. Enchanted." I leaned into her, running my nose up the column of her neck. "I might have even loved you."

"Liar." Her fingers trailed down my chest. My stomach. Lower. "You beautiful, godsdamned *liar*."

I chuckled against her throat before planting a kiss on her pulse. It wasn't a lie, but it didn't matter if she believed it. Nicole knew how I felt now.

"Too beautiful." She shivered as my lips dragged across her collarbone and ran her fingertips along the inside of my waistband, torturing me. "You were too beautiful. It made me hate you more than I should have."

I placed an open-mouthed kiss on the base of her throat, running my tongue along her skin as her grip tightened. "Who's the liar now, sweetheart?"

Nicole's fist swung out, hitting me lightly in the arm. "Ass."

"You hit harder the first time." I caught her wrist, planting kisses down her forearm to her elbow. "You were magnificent. There was so much fight in you. Mesmerizing . . ." I whispered along her skin, softer than any silk. It made me want to seek out more, to run my fingertips over every part of it. Every part of her—again.

"Even after I knocked you on your ass?"

"Especially after you knocked me on my ass." I caught her face in my hands. "Had you given me the chance, I might have begged you to stay with me. Possibly even knelt before you to convince you and show you just how enthralled I was." I kissed her, our lips molding together. My tongue ran along the seam of her lips, and she opened, giving me more access.

I broke away, kneeling before her. "Will you let me now, Snow?" My hands reached for the waist of her linen pants, toying with the drawstring as I awaited her answer.

Nicole shivered, but not from the chill in the air. Her fingers tangled in my hair as she answered breathlessly, "Yes."

I tugged her pants down as she stepped out of them and ran my hands up her thighs. "Thank fuck."

Lifting one of her legs onto my shoulder, I pulled her lacy undergarments to the side. I ran my fingers over where she was already glistening with anticipation.

"So perfect, Nicole." I spread her with my thumbs, then leaned in to taste her.

She moaned, gripping my hair harder as I licked and kissed and worshiped her until she was breathing my name like it was the air she needed to survive.

Like how I'd come to need her.

Her leg buckled as she came, only my arms supporting her against the wall. I continued to make love to her with my mouth, drinking in her arousal until her shaking ceased.

Only when she came down from her high did I relent, placing her foot back on the ground. Her hands came to my shoulders, steadying herself as I pulled her undergarments the rest of the way down her legs.

As I stood, Nicole's hands went to my pants, pushing them down my hips and freeing my almost painfully hard cock from its confinement. I kicked them away as she gave it a gentle stroke, and I shuddered.

"My turn, sweetheart. Arms up."

Nicole sighed at my command, letting go of me reluctantly as I stripped her of her remaining clothes until she was bare before me. Tossing them aside, my hands gripped her ass, lifting as her legs wrapped around my waist.

Nicole's back arched, pushing forth those small, perfect breasts. I boosted her higher so they were level with my face. I took one fawn brown nipple into my mouth, then the other, sucking and nipping until she was pleading, her thighs tightening around me.

"August, *please*. I need you."

I lowered her, aligning Nicole just above my cock. Pressed against the wall, she ran her hands up my ribs and chest, over the scars covering them, and finally to my face. Her fingertips grazed over my cheekbones, the touch lighter than falling snow as her gaze stripped me somehow barer.

"You are so beautiful. Every part." Her lips tenderly grazed mine.

"I love you," I whispered against her mouth as I pushed into her.

Nicole's hands tightened around my neck. Her nails dug in, leaving little crescent-shaped marks I hoped never healed. She gasped as I sank in fully, my lips softly brushing her cheek.

Fuck, every moment with her was ecstasy, but this—this was everything.

I began to thrust into her slowly, savoring every movement. "I cannot wait to take you to my home, Nicole," I panted against her ear, laying my heart bare. "As soon as you let me, I will call a Priestess to seal this mating bond between us and make you my queen before I take you under the stars. Then we can show all the heavens that there has never been a love like ours."

I kissed her in that spot between her neck and shoulder, the one that made her arch into me—every fucking time. I groaned as she tightened around me.

Her hands moved to my hair, tightening against my scalp before she pulled my mouth back to hers, and Nicole devoured me, body and soul.

"Yes," she breathed against my lips. "Gods, I love you, August. *Yes.* Always yes."

Her agreement ruined any self-control I had, and I drove into her, harder and deeper against the wall, until we were lost to anything but each other.

She panted my name so beautifully as she broke apart. To stifle her moans, her mouth went to the soft spot between my neck and shoulder, her teeth biting hard enough they would undoubtedly leave a mark.

The feeling of her climaxing around me, mixed with the pain of her marking—her claiming—took me over the edge with her.

I slowed as the euphoria faded, and we stood there, her legs still wrapped around me, still connected as I kissed her once more. Softly. Gently. "I meant every word, sweetheart. "

Nicole's eyes met mine as she pulled back, heavy-lidded. Her thumbs grazed across my lips as she held my face between her hands. "As do I." The vehemence in her words spoke of her devotion, a love I never thought I could have. Could never deserve. "Beyond titles and mating bonds, you are mine, and I am yours."

Carrying her to our bed, I laid her down gently. Nicole's body sank into the pillows. The toll from our lovemaking had the intended effect of relieving some of her tension. For a moment, the worry we shared over our siblings had eased.

I went back to the water basin, wetting a cloth before returning to her.

Since our first night together, we'd each taken contraceptive tonics, negating any unintended effects of our lovemaking. Even if I might have wished for something to take root, we hadn't had that conversation. It wasn't the right time. With the state of our countries—our families—there was no place for a pregnancy.

But one day . . . gods, I hoped.

I kissed Nicole's stomach, lips brushing just below her navel, as I wiped the cool cloth between her legs, soothing the after-effects of our lovemaking.

Nicole stroked her hands through my hair, and her eyes fluttered closed. When they opened, her eyes went to my shoulder. "I might have gotten carried away."

Tossing the cloth away by our discarded clothing, I leaned forward, bracing myself over her as I once again brought my lips to hers. I kissed one corner of her mouth, then the other. "My goal is always to make you come harder than the last. If that means you leave some marks, even better." I grinned against her.

Nicole gave a short laugh, her hand swiping at my chest. "*You* are incorrigible."

My teeth nipped her bottom lip before standing again, and I took some of the rowan wood ash from our weapons table. It stung as it met the marks where she'd claimed me.

Nicole's eyes fluttered, her voice thick as she watched me. "It will scar."

"And everyone will know I am yours."

She smiled softly as I lay next to her, pulling her away from those damned pillows she loved—my greatest rivals—and curling her into me instead. It was still early in the morning, meaning no one would miss us for a couple more hours.

Exhaustion hit me like a battering ram. Without Nicole next to me, rest was nearly impossible.

I murmured against her hair, "If I could cover myself in memories of you, I would, Snow. So that, when this is over, hundreds of years from now, you can touch them and know how much I have always loved you."

"How could I ever resist you when you say such things?" She rested her cheek against my chest. Eventually, her breathing began to slow as she finally drifted off into sleep.

I ran a finger over her lips, slightly parted and swollen. "Rest, Nicole. I've got you," I breathed into her ear, settling into sleep myself. "Today and every day after," I pledged my soul to her.

No matter what happened with our family, no matter what came next, Nicole and I would weather it together.

CHAPTER 10
Misha

The deck of the ship was empty as the sky began to lighten into the violet before dawn.

I leaned on the railing, my chin on my hands as I stared at the churning water beneath. My stomach roiled with it, but whether it was from hunger or nausea, I could no longer tell. After long enough, they felt the same.

My mind whirled like a top, trying to determine how many days we'd been on the ship. I was sleeping so often that I couldn't tell the sunrises from the sunsets.

This morning, I'd crept out of the bed, leaving Julian to sleep. With each passing moment, I more strongly believed he would never be able to forgive me for that night and my stupidity with the damned poisoned comb. He would eventually regret what my magic had forced him to become. But he was so good that he'd stand by me regardless, especially in this state.

It was only a matter of time, though.

I couldn't stand it, having him watch me as I fell apart. He would grow to resent me—the one who'd made him a murderer—soon enough.

The sky slowly turned lavender, then peach in the distance, readying for the sun's arrival.

Footsteps approached, heavy and sure, warning me of their approach. Nearly everyone on this ship was Fae, and even the humans had a certain lightness of foot after being around us for so long. If their footsteps made a sound, it was because they wanted to be heard.

Jophiel came to stand beside me at the rail, taking a deep breath of the early morning air. It smelled best at this time, full of the possibilities a new day could hold.

I watched her. She was tall, possibly even taller than Julian. The white feathered wings added to her domineering posture, but more than that, the Seraph held her head high, like she didn't know what it was to bow. Or that she did and had sworn to never do so again.

For a moment, it was familiar. No longer was the Seraph standing beside me but instead, it was my father. Their postures were so similar. The image was jolting, like a plunge into frigid water.

Their ghosts wouldn't leave me, the family I'd lost. No, not lost—that alluded to a chance of finding them again. My parents and aunts were irrevocably gone, torn away from me.

During the poisoned sleep, I'd been gifted with memories and dreams of my family. Only upon the news of Alesia and Eve's deaths did I realize it hadn't been a gift—it had been a haunting. The ghosts of everyone I'd lost and of those I still had left to lose.

117

I pushed up onto my elbows, shaking the memories away. I inhaled deeply through my nose, willing the tears not to fall, clasping my hands to hide their shaking.

"It's remarkable," Jophiel said, breaking the silence. "How much you two favor each other."

I knew exactly what she meant. Nic and I had our differences, her hair black to my gold. My skin was the tan of our mother's, where Nic had gotten our father's paleness. Even our bodies were different: I had curves, whereas Nic was all lithe muscle—or I used to. My body had grown weak since the Solstice. But our faces were the same, perfect mirrors of the other.

I knew Nic had spent weeks with the Seven in the Redwood, just north of the border, but how well did Jophiel know my sister? How well did she know *them*?

Nic and I had never been separated before—ever. And the time she'd had without me was a festering thing deep in my gut. Because I didn't know who I was without her, and now Nic had all of these memories and relationships she'd built without me.

I realized I hadn't spoken, spinning around in my thoughts. How much time had gone by as I just stared at her?

Jophiel remained patient, seemingly unbothered by my silence.

"Yes. We get that a lot." I didn't know what else to say.

Jophiel, thankfully, didn't seem to mind, nor feel pressured to say more. We fell into silence once more, and it wasn't awkward. It was almost peaceful.

Something scraped on the deck behind us, and we turned to see.

Rasalas had followed me out here. The other sailors eyed him warily, but the jaguar stood aloof, watching as they went about their duties. A small black cat silently crept up behind him, flattened herself against the deck, then pounced. Rasalas leaped out of her way playfully, pretending to be surprised in the way he often did with me.

Ker—I believed that was the name of Miranda's cat—stumbled over her paws, an expression of comical shock dawning on her face. As I watched the two familiars tumble about like kittens, a smile almost surfaced on my lips—almost. Until I remembered what Rasalas's blood had felt like, and I recalled the dagger Adrienne had plunged into him.

The sun rose, pulling my attention from the cats. The warmth seeped into my skin, caressing every place it touched. A shimmer caught my eye as Jophiel slightly spread her wings. The golden light danced along the Seraph's feathers, brightening her pale skin. Jophiel closed her eyes, basking in it.

"Our magic is derived from the sun and starlight," Jophiel opened her blue eyes to meet mine. Explaining, though I hadn't asked.

My cheeks flamed, having been caught staring.

Blessedly, Jophiel went on, pretending not to notice. "It is but a flicker of what it once was, far weaker than the legends of the old Seraphim blessed directly by the Goddess Above. But the magic feeds our weapons, guiding them. It acts as a barrier in battle."

I remembered the golden aura around her the day I'd awoken—the shield against other magic. "What does it feel like?"

She paused, considering. "It feels . . . warm. Like a second coating of skin but more. It is difficult to explain."

Jophiel pointed out across the horizon, drawing my eye to the strip of land beginning to emerge. Montevalle.

"Another couple hours or so, and we will dock."

Another couple of hours away from Sanserria, where all my best memories lived. Where my family had lived—and died. My home and the one place I could not return.

I stood tall despite my legs beginning to wobble. I needed to lie down, the darkness of my room beckoning to me.

I turned and caught Jophiel watching me. However, *she* seemed unabashed in her staring, eyes piercing straight through me.

"What you are feeling is normal, Misha," she said unblinkingly. It is okay to want to hide from it all."

Any response caught in my throat, unable to break through the knot of regret stuck there.

She went on. "Sometimes, we need the darkness to better see the light. And the darkness within us—" Jophiel looked back out upon the sea, her face clouding in memory. "—is necessary. It makes us who we are."

But my darkness hurt the ones I loved. It broke them. I was drowning in it and couldn't find a way back to the surface.

And if the darkness was part of who I was, then I could only be a monster.

I looked out upon the horizon again at the distant snowcapped mountains just coming into view. Julian and I had written so much of what it would be like for me to visit his home.

But now I thought of the stiffness with which he'd held himself since arriving on the ship, even when holding me. He only relaxed in sleep. I thought of the bleakness in his eyes and how hesitant he was to touch me.

Arriving in the North with Julian shouldn't have been like this. It was wrong—all of it.

I'd ruined it. Like I ruined everything.

Pushing away from the railing, I stepped away from Jophiel without a word or a backward glance and headed to the cabin door. Not back to Julian or Nic, but to some hidden corner where I could drown in solitude.

There, my darkness would smother no one but me.

CHAPTER 11
Nic

The trees in the north towered above us on the path between the mountains, and the Redwood forest was just south of our path. It whispered to me with its dark familiarity, something within seeping out, reaching toward me with dark, spindling fingers to draw me back in. But the forest didn't feel entirely malicious. It just *was*.

Misha remained more spirit than flesh.

After we disembarked from the ship, she rode on horseback with Julian, his arms wrapped around my sister as he guided Hyacinth's reins and spoke softly into her ear. He pointed out every tree and plant, all things he knew would interest my sister—or that had before.

Misha said nothing as she looked at the forest, her eyes blank and unseeing. But sometimes, I saw a flicker as Julian spoke. She leaned back against his chest, head between his neck and shoulder. Her fingers traced the cuffs of his cloak, wrapping herself in him.

Our journey would take us through the mountains for three weeks until we reached the Montevallan capital. As we passed through the small towns and villages, different faces, human and Fae both, paused in the street and peeked out from doors and windows as we traveled past. They whispered about us, the two princesses from Hahnaley.

Simon rode to my left, Miranda on his other side. Shai was on my right, quietly scanning the minds of those we passed.

"They're only curious," Simon murmured as he smiled and waved, receiving the same in return. The spymaster, it seemed, was immensely popular.

Miranda leaned closer. "You are a watercaster that manifested fire after the element had been dead for centuries," she explained. "And your sister turned out to be an earthcaster and animaglia—an animaglia with the strength to turn *another* Fae into a dragon. This is power heard of only in the old tales. Of course, they're curious."

I remained silent, eyes fixed on the dirt road ahead of us. The villagers were looking to Misha and me for answers, as if staring at us for long enough would explain how we'd manifested this variance in magic. But all they would see were two High Fae with a spattering of human features. No answers to be had.

Simon changed the subject, nodding to where August rode with Jophiel at the front. "The August with us, who he was in the cabin, is not always who he will be here. He won't always be the person you know."

I turned to him. "How so?"

"It's only been fifteen years since August took over the kingdom from his father," Simon said. "He has rid the Montevallan court of the more . . . unsavory characters, but there was no way to get rid of them all. Removing each of them would have stripped him too bare, leaving the kingdom open to a coup. The ones who remain are the most palatable of his father's former court—the ones who will do anything to keep their power, even if it means bending to August's rule. But they wait and watch for any sign of weakness."

"Like allying with two exiled princesses?"

"Maybe," Simon answered. "But August will not allow any talk of such. Just . . . you should prepare yourself for how he handles it."

I nodded understanding. As much as I could defend myself and my sister, this was his kingdom—his rule. Here, August would have to handle any slights against us, showing himself to be as ruthless as the rumors claimed. Prove that he was the king no one dared challenge.

"Josiah should have never been king," Shai said, piquing my curiosity.

"What do you mean?"

"The Blood Treaty chose *him*," Shai said, nodding to August. He spoke louder now that we were clear of the village.

"Chose?" My father had never explained it to Misha and me, though being so young, we'd never thought to ask. We just assumed it had been verbally worked out between the rebel leaders.

"When the rebel leaders came together—your parents, Orelia and Cedric, Adrienne and Alexander, and August and his father—there was much fighting over who would govern which land," Shai explained. "The east, Desdemon, is rich in land and its soil fruitful. Both farming and livestock flourish there. The North is rich in minerals and metal ores—iron, silver, gold, and copper. The West, as you well know, has each of these."

"And the South is barren," I said. The Deimos had traditionally governed it under the High King, but I could understand their play for a territory with more resources.

"It wasn't always so," Shai said. "Salt mining there has uncovered various things suggesting the land was once as plentiful as the West. A land of many lakes and springs."

Now, all that remained were the beaches and sand dunes—beautiful but worthless, especially now that the fish had fled their seas. It did not seem a coincidence that Alexander's admitted murder of the Sirens along their coasts led to the disappearance of other sea life.

"So, the four argued over who would receive which territory?"

"Yes, ineffectually so." Shai nodded. "Josiah suggested they duel for it."

I clicked my tongue. "Of course, he did."

Shai chuckled. "In the end, the treaty decided. They cast their blood once into a bowl, binding them to the terms. Another onto a map. The magic moved the blood to cover an area, staining it with the land the blood giver would receive."

"So, what happened to indicate the magic chose August?"

"August's blood traveled to the north. Josiah's remained still."

"August told you this?" I pressed. It didn't seem like something he would share. My own parents had been rather tight-lipped about the Blood Treaty arrangements with Alesia and Eve.

"In a way," he answered evasively. I gave him a sharp look, waiting. Eventually, Shai went on. "August wanted someone on the outside to know what happened during the treaty's creation in case something went wrong. He let me into his mind."

"The Deimos didn't sense it?" Adrienne and Alexander were the best of the mindcasters, only rivaled by the Oscuri.

Shai smiled, a rare expression of arrogance from the mindcaster. "No."

"So why hasn't August been the king all this time?"

"Josiah argued that because August was his heir and he himself had agreed to the treaty, this meant the North was *his* to rule. That it would pass to August one day but currently, and as his father, the land was his by right. August, still reeling from the death of his mother, did not argue, and truthfully, he neither wanted nor was capable of leading the country then. Not in his state." Shai looked to where August rode ahead of us, softness in his eyes for the male he'd befriended over a century ago.

"But August has changed much in the past hundred years," Shai went on. "Though who he was in the war, and even the decades after—" Shai swallowed. "Simon spoke true. There are parts of August you have yet to see."

"August was never as Josiah was." I remembered the pain in his eyes the night I'd discovered those scars. August might have been crafted of that cruelty, but he wasn't born of it.

"No, never," Shai agreed. "Did he tell you how we met?"

I shook my head.

"I was assigned to his battalion at the beginning of the war. It was mostly northerners already familiar with August. I didn't understand the dynamic at first—whether he commanded their obedience by respect or fear."

"Which was it?"

"Both," Shai answered simply. "He had the same capacity for cruelty as his father except . . . August was fair. It didn't take long until I witnessed it myself. In the first village we conquered, a small one to the east of Haldrin on the border of the Redwood, August discovered several of his High Fae soldiers had—" Shai paused, swallowing. "—*taken* some of the human women."

I went still, the sound of blood rushing through my ears.

Shai went on, "The rumors reached him at dusk, and August found the four of them that night. Knowing of my gifts, he brought me along to confirm in their memories what they'd done." His tan skin paled at the memory of whatever he'd seen in their minds. "August didn't just want my verbal confirmation—he wanted to *see* it. He wanted to feel what they had at the moment, how much they'd enjoyed it. The utter lack of remorse. I'd never felt rage as deep as when he watched. When it was done, August sent me away. He took his time with each one. Hours later, at dawn, he crucified them, still alive but just barely, in the village square to set an example. August wouldn't only slaughter our enemies but would punish *anyone* who defied his utmost commands—that the civilians were to remain untouched and that enemies be given a quick death unless he deemed otherwise. And if an unclean death was necessary, August would do it himself."

I crafted the images in my mind as Shai spoke them: August, like a wrathful avenging god. Peeling back the layers, I looked deeper into his heart, my own cracking with what I saw. August only knew how to hurt them because of what he'd endured himself—what he'd survived at his father's hand.

"I respected him for it," Shai said reverently. "Though there were times it felt like his mother's kindness was the only thing keeping him in check. After her death, I worried what would come to pass. Luckily, the grief morphed him. It made August more determined than ever to be nothing like his father, especially as he always assumed he was the one who'd killed her."

Shai's story should have scared me as I learned what August was capable of. But I remembered what I'd done to Adrienne's guards as they'd joked of such things, how they laughed as they planned to do the same to Misha and me.

I remembered how I'd sliced until I hit bone.

Sometimes, I still dreamt of it: how I'd carved through those guards, especially the commander. I knew it was the difference between me and them, this feeling of remorse I couldn't shake, yet I still couldn't bring myself to truly regret what I'd done to them.

August was the same. We shared the same beliefs, skirted that edge of brutality, and suffered the same nightmares. No one else could understand but him. My perfect match.

I watched August ride ahead of us, posture tall and confident—every bit the king, once War Commander—and thought of the tender moments we shared. On the cabin's roof and after the nightmares. In the quiet moments, when he brewed tea. August had many facets and many faces. Each one I treasured, and I loved discovering more of him.

August looked back as if sensing my thoughts of him. Lifting a hand, he beckoned me to join him at the front.

Gently coaxing Luthíen, I rode to him, taking his side and his hand in mine. A hand scarred by battle that was as gentle with a teacup as when he held me. Powerful enough to bring a storm to heel.

Forever mine.

After two weeks of traveling through the Mountains of Rei, the towns and villages grew farther and fewer between.

I rode beside August, flanked by Simon and Jophiel. The trees seemed to shift toward us, leaning in as if to get a closer look. To catch a glimpse of our words and carry them away.

When we saw them, I knew it wasn't in my head. Wisps of Dryads and Oreads—nymphs that only dwelled in the mountains—whipped between the pines, spruces, and firs. Tiny palm-sized pixies darted overhead in the canopy. We only saw them in our periphery, disappearing before our eyes could settle on them.

I glanced around, looking for Marle, the tiny librarian pixie who'd escaped the palace with us. She normally flitted around Teale, but I couldn't spot her pink hair or hummingbird-fast wings. I wondered if she was flitting above with the others, regaling in flying with old friends.

My mind reached for Teale's, where she was riding a few meters behind me with Celeste. *What do the nymphs want?*

The word she relayed stopped my heart for a moment. *Misha.*

I glanced back at my sister, riding near the rear of our party with Julian, quite a ways behind. Shai was just behind them with Damian and Miranda.

Not in that way, Nic. Listen. Try to hear them.

I heard nothing at first, only the leaves rustling in the wind. The soft patter of small animals hidden in the brush. Then, after a few moments, words drifted along the breeze, nearly indistinguishable from the sounds of the forest. *Awakened. Lifebringer.*

Misha is connected to the earth and its creatures more than ever, Teale explained. *She is both the flora and the fauna. They speak with awe. They have come to see.*

Julian's arms had grown taut around my sister, on alert with Misha's new observers. My sister's eyes remained unseeing, but her ears were pricked. She was listening, too.

The northern wind rustled through the canopy, sending a chill down my spine.

Run.

Fear lanced through me. This wasn't the airy voices of the nymphs, half-breeze and song. This was a feeling, clear in my mind. Luthíen whinnied nervously beneath me.

August turned to me with concern. "What is it?"

"I don't know." My ears strained, searching the forest for the sounds of animals. "Teale, do you hear the nymphs anymore?" I said aloud.

I looked back at the demi-Dryad, as her face went pale. "No. They've fled."

I pulled on Luthíen's reins, bringing her to a stop. The feeling tore through me again, clearer this time.

Hurry.

"Nicky?" Misha roused, sitting up as she sensed my distress in the way only twins can.

Defend.

No one could winnow in or out of our caravan, a safety precaution we'd long established. Knowing it would take longer to unravel the wards, I shifted my weight, pulling Luthíen's reins, and we spun around.

"Nicole!" August shouted, halting his own horse to follow.

"Misha!" My heels dug into the mare, urging her to a gallop. My sister was about a hundred meters away.

From that distance, I saw three black snakes wind through the grass coming onto the road near Misha and Julian. Miranda, Damian, and the escort guard's horses skittered back in fright as the serpents sped toward my sister.

Hyacinth reared, feet lashing at the snakes. The motion knocked my sister and Julian to the ground. He held her tight, bracing her from the fall, grunting when his back hit the hard earth.

I leaned into Luthíen, urging her faster. "Celeste!" I screamed, begging the animaglia to intervene.

"They're not animals!" she cried.

The black snakes reared, doubling, then tripling in size until the serpents were as thick as a human torso. *Familiars.*

The monsters coiled upon themselves, preparing to strike. Lightning crackled from Julian's hands, striking at the creatures, but they passed through his magic unharmed.

Still at a gallop, I lifted my hands from Luthíen's reins, casting a shield of fire between them and my sister. The serpents passed through, utterly unscathed, as they continued racing toward her.

"Fae magic won't work!" Miranda's hands were moving before her. The witch's lips murmured swiftly as she tried to craft a ward between them and the snakes I wasn't sure would erect in time.

Rasalas and Ker appeared from nowhere, winnowing themselves between the serpents and my sister and Julian, fangs bared and snarling as they shifted into their true, monstrous forms. The cats each leaped toward a serpent, agilely dodging their fangs.

But there were only two of them.

While the cats fought its siblings, the third serpent slithered between them, rearing as it prepared to strike. Shai ran between them, drawing his sword, a toothpick compared to the snake's bared fangs.

Julian turned, shielding Misha with his body. "Do it," he begged Misha, taking her hand and pressing it to his bare chest.

"I can't." Misha shook her head as she struggled against Julian, pulling away, trying to push past him.

As I neared, I felt magic pulse around my twin and blast out from her, but the earth remained still. Julian did not become a dragon.

The serpent coiled, head raised.

I was almost there.

"No!" I shouted, jumping from Luthíen's back. I rolled, tumbling to the earth as I found my feet again and began to run.

The serpent turned its head toward me instead, hissing. Fae magic wouldn't work, so I tried to pull from the witch part of me instead, willing it to take shape. But the power was new to me, and there were no great bodies of water nearby, unlike the lake where I'd been poisoned. The unfamiliar magic slid through my fingers.

The snake eyed me hungrily as it pulled back. I drew the Iradelmar as it lunged.

Protect.

A black blur shot down from the sky, crashing into the serpent's head and knocking the snake off its path. Its fangs slammed into the ground, and I crouched, covering my face to avoid the spray of dirt.

The bird, a hawk with feathers of all black, tumbled across the ground—and shifted.

Righting itself, the hawk's wings spread to well over the length of the road and its body grew to the size of Rasalas in his beast form. Its feathers seemed to grow harder, almost metallic, and two more limbs grew from beneath its wings so it stood on all fours, each foot ending in three curved talons the length of a hand.

The serpent, having recovered, faced the hawk—the familiar.

Rasalas and Ker took the arrival of the bird and the momentary hesitation of the other serpents as their opportunity. With their claws and teeth, they made short work of the snakes. Ker crushed the head of one, her talons smashing it into the earth over and over, while Rasalas ripped out the throat of the other. His fangs gleamed with blood as he tossed the beast aside.

The hawk stood tall, spreading its wings wide as it let out a piercing screech in challenge.

The last serpent lunged.

Shooting into the air, the great bird flexed its talons, piercing the serpent through both eyes. The snake thrashed, blind as it struck at empty air, the hawk scarcely avoiding its fangs. Sensing where the other familiar was from the beat of the air, the serpent's tail whipped upward, slamming into the hawk's right wing. The monstrous bird screeched in pain and fury as it dove.

Grasping the serpent's neck in its beak, the hawk's talons pierced its body. Shaking and tearing, the hawk cried its victory as the snake's head was torn from its body, head tumbling to the ground. Its body still writhed, flailing and churning before it finally fell still in death beside its brethren.

"Misha." I scrambled over the dead serpents to reach my sister. Rasalas was already at her side in his jaguar form, his mouth and paws slick with blood.

Julian reached her first and clasped my sister's face in his hands. "You should have changed me, Misha. Why didn't you?"

"I couldn't." She shook her head, hands grasped in his shirt. "Not again. I won't do that to you again."

"I don't *care*, Misha. It would have killed you!" Julian's voice was desperate, his face pale with fear. "And you wouldn't let me help." His eyes spoke of his hurt as Julian searched her face, trying to make sense of it.

"I won't be the reason you become the thing you hate," my sister whispered. Julian's gaze softened as she gently lifted a hand to his cheek. "There was another way."

Julian only stared at her, all at once hurt and confused and yet so damned relieved. He opened his mouth to ask for more as I reached them, but Misha turned out of his embrace, flinging her arms around me.

"Sister," she said as I embraced her, soothing a hand down her back as she shook, coming down from the adrenaline. "There was another way. They were coming, Nicky—they were here."

"I know, Meesh. I felt the warning, too." As she and I had heard the Sirens, we must have both heard the familiar's warning.

"No." Misha pulled back, shaking her head. "Not the serpents. Them." She turned toward the woods.

None of us had noticed, enthralled by the battle between the familiars. But now, glancing around, I saw them: wolves, foxes, badgers, mountain cougars, and more had gathered at the forest's edge.

Celeste's hand flew to her mouth. "Gods above."

From between the shadowy trees stalked Nemean lionesses, at least ten of them, each the size of a horse. They moved forward, stepping out of the brush and to the edge of the road. Behind Misha, a male lion approached. Scars littered his golden hide. His dark mane shook as he walked, brown eyes settling on me.

I'd seen him before.

"They were here," Misha repeated. She'd called them—all of them—with her magic.

The familiars might have been unphased by mine and Julian's Fae magic, but Misha's was different. The serpents could not pass through fangs and claws. And though she refused to turn Julian into the dragon, she had instead willed every predator in the vicinity to come to our aid—including a pride of Nemean lions.

Even if the familiar hadn't come, Misha would have saved us.

With the threat settled and my sister's magic calmed, most of the animals backed away, returning to the woods. All except the lions.

"In the Redwood," I whispered, searching my sister's face for answers. "The shadowhounds . . . that was you?"

Misha's brow furrowed in confusion, but slowly, recognition lightened her blue eyes. "The nightmare. I saw you surrounded by shadowhounds in the woods—saw you carving through them. I watched, desperately wishing I could help, but I couldn't. Then one bit you, and I knew you were going to die if you didn't escape soon." My sister's eyes shined with tears as she remembered how helpless she'd felt. Her jaw hardened. "So, I grew fangs and claws, and I *ripped* them apart."

Her magic had reached out all those miles through the Redwood, summoning the lion and rescuing me when I needed it most.

I hugged my twin again. "The lion saved me—*you* saved me."

Misha's face broke apart as she clung to me. "But I couldn't save *them*," she whispered, devolving into sobs. "I saw them, too. I watched from the canopy like I was in a terrible dream. I watched Alesia and Eve die, Nicky. But I didn't know it was true until the ship." She grew frantic, reseeing the death of our aunts across her mind's eye.

I soothed a hand down her loosely braided hair. "Shh, Misha. Breathe—just breathe."

I couldn't tell her it was okay. It wasn't. And I knew better than to promise that it would get better. So, I held my sister and let her cry.

When Misha wore herself out, crashing from the adrenaline and use of so much power, Julian took her. He lifted them onto Hyacinth's back, Misha curled against his chest in sleep. Hyacinth and the other horses had calmed after Celeste cast her animaglia influence on them, no longer spooked by the serpents' lifeless bodies strewn between them.

"We need to put distance between us and the corpses," August said as he approached, head inclining toward the dead serpents. "We don't want to be near when other creatures sense the blood and come to feast."

Jophiel wrinkled her nose in disgust. "Agreed." Her weapons were still drawn, shield softly glowing with light.

As I walked beside August toward our horses, a soft screech pulled at my attention. The familiar, returned to its hawk form, limped toward me, the one wing askew. Broken.

Reaching down, I picked it up, cradling it to my chest, careful of the wing.

Safe.

I felt the wordless sentiment through my chest, just like I'd felt the warning before the serpents arrived.

"I think you've found your familiar." Miranda came to my other side, Ker perched across her shoulders. "Or rather, she found you."

"She's hurt," I said, gently stroking the hawk's night-black feathers.

"They heal themselves. She just needs a bit of your magic—should you accept the bond."

The familiar's magic reached out for me, offering a bond like I'd only felt with my family and August during our power-sharing drills. The familiar's essence was like mine: a burning sort of cold, sharp and biting.

"A night hawk." August lifted a finger for the bird's inspection. "They're common in the mountains." The hawk assessed him carefully before bowing her head, allowing August to stroke her crown.

I moved closer to Miranda, my voice low. "How can we know if the familiars acted on their own? Or were they sent by other witches?"

"An attack like this could only have been ordered by the familiar's master. Unbonded familiars seek out witches, sensing for compatibility. They would never hurt one," Miranda answered, stroking Ker. Dread settled in my gut.

"So why is a witch attacking us?" Julian asked, holding Misha more tightly against him.

"*Witches*," Miranda corrected. "None of us have spoken about you and Misha being part witch, but if they knew—"

"How could they have known?" August said, his voice low as he and Julian's eyes met. "Only the Seven, Julian, and I are aware."

"Maybe we passed them on the way, and they sensed it?" Miranda guessed. "One may have been a Seer and seen the magic Nic or Misha cast, either in the past or the future. But what I do know is that three witches did this to kill the twins—Misha especially. The serpents went straight for her, not Nic. They only turned to her when she put herself between them."

"But why target us? We're one of them," I countered.

Miranda shook her head. "Not all will see it that way. Like the High Fae, there are some witches that will hate you for your heritage." Her eyes softened as she shared this brutal truth. "They'll see the combination of witch and Fae magic as an unchecked amount of power—an abomination. Witches believe strongly in the natural balance. Faeries are limited by their well of magic, hindered by rowan wood and Galorian silver. The witches can only act as a conduit for so much power at a time, and our magic is stunted by black iron and rue. Though the latter two are untested, I can only assume that you and Misha will not be as weakened by those either."

Another potential weakness. "We should test it—test them both together." After the apple, I'd be damned if I let myself be rendered helpless by poison again.

August looked appalled at the thought, and Miranda was hesitant, but they each understood. They'd both seen me at the bottom of the ice-covered lake.

"Once in Ankaa, in the safety of the castle grounds, we can try it and work on your and Misha's witch magic," Miranda said. "But until then, let's speak of it no more." She pointed to an ear, reminding us of all those who might be listening but could not see. There was still quite a way to travel until we reached the Montevallan capital.

I turned to my sister and saw her eyes open, listening—having caught all of our conversation. Her eyes reflected my same sentiment:

Never again, sister. You and I are never going to be caught so vulnerable again.

CHAPTER 12
Misha

I rode astride the great lion, braiding pink and yellow rose blossoms into his thick mane. The lionesses surrounded our party, patrolling along the road as we traveled.

After the serpents attacked, I couldn't bear to let them go just yet, lest more monsters stalk out of the woods. Luckily, the pride of Nemean lions seemed disinclined to leave, so it took very little of my magic to keep them nearby.

The birds flew overhead, scouting the path. Aetos, Celeste's golden eagle, and Eilith, Nic's hawk familiar.

My sister named the bird for an Alaran folktale Alesia would tell us before bed as children, the story of a human woman who slayed a basilisk in the Halcon Rainforest. The name was more than fitting.

When it needed to rest, the hawk's preferred place was upon Nic's shoulder or, more amusingly, riding upon Rasalas's back. The jaguar showed no irritation with this, and instead seemed to form a quick kinship with the other familiar and Ker, as well. The black cat split her time winding between the jaguar's paws and riding in Miranda's lap atop her horse.

Beside me, my sister rode on her blood bay mare. August and Julian led the procession, the Seraph at their side.

For the hundredth time this hour, my eyes found Julian's back as he rode ahead, even though I'd been the one to move away from him, suggesting we ride apart for a while.

Though he denied it, Julian was still angry that I hadn't used my magic to make him into the dragon again. I knew his anger was spurred by fear and hurt. He said he'd do anything to protect me, but I would give everything to keep him safe from his worst fears. I'd already made him a murderer—I wouldn't make him the monster again, even if it killed me.

The trees began to thin.

"This is the final ascent," Miranda said, sounding relieved. Like the rest of us, she was weary of traveling.

I leaned forward, stroking the lion's neck as he came to a stop. I dismounted and walked around to his front. Nic, Miranda, and Teale, riding on my other side, stopped to watch me.

The great lion lowered his head, and our foreheads met in a silent goodbye. When he walked away, each lioness came, offering the same. They brushed their foreheads against mine before they turned, heading back into the mountains behind us. The others watched silently until the last lioness pulled away.

"Why did you let them go?" Nic asked as she scooted forward in her saddle.

I mounted Luthíen behind her. "They're not tame, Nicky. They belong in the wild."

"Rasalas doesn't." Nic nodded down to him, standing beside us.

"Rasalas is a house cat." I looked down at the jaguar lovingly. "He is as tame as they get."

Nic chuckled, and I felt her warmth spread through my chest as I wrapped my arms around her. I rested my cheek on her shoulder. "Let's go, sister."

She nudged Luthíen with her heels, and our party began to travel again. I turned, finding the retreating lions one last time before they disappeared into the forest.

Atop the crest of the hill, the valley spilled out before us. Surrounded on all sides by sharp mountains dotted with snow, even in late summer, was a city.

At the far end, to the east, was the castle, a towering mammoth of dark stone and sharp spires built into the side of the tallest peak. Through its center flowed a great waterfall. The castle seemed built around it, the water spilling into a lake that separated it from the rest of the city. The water was a striking turquoise blue.

August and Julian waited for us at the pass. Nic pulled her horse alongside August's. "Your father constructed this?" She turned to August, who nodded in affirmation. "Why the lake?"

"You would think that since the man feared the watercasters so much—not that he'd ever admit it," Julian pulled Hyacinth around, coming to our other side, "that the last thing he would want to have is the source of their power so near his home. And you would be correct."

Julian reached his hand out. The two hours riding apart had been enough to make me miss him, and I could no longer stand the separation. I took it, the warmth of his palm seeping through me, blossoming all the way to my heart.

As I thought over what Julian had said, the confusion on my and Nic's faces must have been evident. August explained. "The waterfall and lake have only been here for fifteen years."

Nic quickly understood. "Since . . ."

"Yes." August nodded. "Since I killed my father. Where the lake now stands was once a sunken coliseum, a fighting pit where Fae unlucky enough to draw my father's ire were pitted against each other and all manner of beasts. Including the predecessors of your sister's lions."

"That is where you did it," Nic murmured.

The lake was where August had once challenged and dueled against his father, killing him and becoming the King of Montevalle.

"It was something to behold," Jophiel said, her blue eyes cast down into the valley. "The waterfall comes from what was once a spring-fed lake high in the mountains. Earthcasters were called in to restructure the castle, taking down the central spire and creating a clear path."

"My father's personal tower," August added, his voice pained. Nic reached for him, her fingers brushing his arm.

Jophiel continued, "When it was finished, the castle was temporarily evacuated. With a bolt of lightning, August struck the lake's rim. The water spilled out, flowing down between the remaining spires and filling the coliseum to become the lake."

Nic took in the city, silent for a moment, before returning to August. "Not afraid of any big, bad watercasters, huh?"

August laughed. "Should I be, Snow?"

"You never know," my sister teased.

I watched with rapt attention. I'd never seen my sister look at anyone like that, so enamored. In just a few weeks, August Warin had brought a light to my sister's eyes like I'd never seen.

We began to ride again, making the final descent into the valley.

Ankaa was a city of cobblestone streets surrounded by homes and businesses built of the same slate grey stone as the mountains, all with emerald-green moss and ivy clinging to the walls. Tall trees—holly, cypress, poplar, chestnut, and alder—towered between them. Water channels flowed between the buildings like streets of turquoise. Humans and faeries watched us curiously from their narrow boats as we crossed on arched stone bridges.

"The canals don't freeze in the winter?" I asked Julian.

"No." He shook his head. "This water comes from hot springs beneath the city. No matter the season, it remains warm. The lake, too, is heated by the earth beneath."

I imagined it in the winter months, steam wafting through the city in the early mornings, cloaking it in fog. How eerily beautiful it must be.

Children swam and splashed in one of the canals, stopping and waving to us excitedly as they recognized August, Julian, and the Seven.

"They're back!" they yelled, scrambling out of the water to tell their parents who they'd seen. Where the adults whispered to themselves, the children had no such qualms. "That's them! The princesses!" they said excitedly as they saw Nic and I riding on horseback together.

I smiled softly, returning their waves as we passed. I remembered how Nic and I had swum similarly in the lake in our palace gardens, along the seashore. I squeezed my sister tighter.

After passing through the city, we rode over a large stone bridge. The water of a deep moat churned beneath us and entered into the castle courtyard. Moss and flowering ivy, the blooms varying from white to yellow and red, climbed the stone walls.

We dismounted and were met by guards who would take our horses to the stables to be fed and rest.

"She'll be okay," Julian reassured me, seeing the panicked look in my eyes as they reached for Hyacinth. "They'll take care of her."

I stroked my palomino mare on the neck, kissing her once on the nose before I let them lead her away. Rasalas nudged my hand as I watched her go.

A High Fae female came quickly striding out of the castle's grand archway. Tall and slender, her skin was a rich black, and her hair was cut short to only a fine layer over her head, accentuating the rows of silver rings through her pointed ears. The priestess robes she wore were of pale blue silk, the long sleeves and skirt billowing as she walked, adding to her ethereality.

"Mother." Julian ran to Sena, lifting and spinning her around.

"You're home." Sena clutched her son tightly, a sob shuddering her breath as she leaned back to look at him. She brushed off his clothes as if she could wipe the grime away with her hands before clasping his face again.

"I'm home," Julian repeated, smiling.

"My boy." She hugged her son again, onyx eyes sparkling. "I pleaded to the Goddess Above every day for your safety, praying she'd bring you home to me. And you." She embraced August. Older than Sena by over a century, yet still, she looked at him as if he were her son. "I was so worried for you both."

As Sena hugged him, August said, "I made you a promise, Sena. I wasn't going to return without him."

"Of course not." She stepped back, wiping her eyes. "But that is the mother's curse—not a day will go by that I do not worry about you both."

Julian returned to my side, taking my hand. "Mother, there is someone I would like you to meet."

Sena's smile held a twinge of sadness as she took in my sister and me.

"But not for the first time." Sena went to Nic, kissing her on each cheek in greeting. "It's been so many years. Look how you two have grown," she said as she turned to me. The last time she'd seen us had been at our father's funeral nearly nine years ago.

Julian dropped my hand but remained at my side, giving me the chance to greet his mother.

I tried to smile but saw how unconvincingly it reflected through her eyes. The mask of the girl I had once been no longer fit.

"Oh, sweet girl." Sena hugged me tightly as I stood frozen, arms dangling lifelessly at my sides. "I heard about your aunts. They were so lovely—it's such a loss to our world. I'm so, so sorry."

Sorry.

Everyone was *sorry* for my and Nic's loss. But what could soft sentiments do to fix it? It didn't mend the chasm in my chest.

Sena ran a hand down my back, cooing softly. The mother's touch, that innate knowledge of what would calm me, only made me sob, softly at first and then forcefully all at once.

Desperate in my grief, I let her comfort me. And for a moment, I pretended that every mother I'd ever known wasn't dead and gone.

CHAPTER 13
Julian

I brushed the hair back from Misha's face, serene in sleep. She only seemed to know peace when she was dreaming, a hand clasped around the orb hanging from her bracelet. When awake, she was either inconsolable in her grief or, worse, calm—her eyes vacant, with a far-off look to them.

After our arrival, I'd brought her to my chambers, hoping the rest after traveling so long would help. In all the years I'd dreamed of Misha, this wasn't how I'd pictured having her here.

Someone who soared on highs as bright as Misha did could only feel the lows so deep they were nearly crushing. It was part of what made her so beautiful—how much she felt everything—even as I wished I could take it away, make the despair and grief easier for her to bear.

But a rift was growing between us, and the tighter I held on, the worse it seemed. A vise gripped my chest at the thought of losing her, either to the grief or to the guilt of what she thought she'd made me do.

I won't be the reason you become the thing you hate.

I reached for one of the books at my bedside, an almanac of flowering plants. In its middle was a pressed rose, pink with a golden center, still vibrant a decade later.

Brushing my fingers against the age-worn petals, I remembered the night I'd taken it.

The night I'd met *her.*

While the celebration continued inside, I stepped onto the terrace in search of fresh air—or that's what I told my mother. In truth, I was searching for the girl in pink.

All of the attendees had been told to wear a shade of purple to the wedding. It had created a lovely effect during the ceremony, the gowns, and finely-tailored suits in shades ranging from pale lavender to deep aubergine. The bride herself, Queen Adrienne of Reyna—who previously shared the throne with her brother—now Queen of Hahnaley through the marriage, wore a sparking gown of white, the dress entirely encrusted in crystals and diamonds. An unconventional color choice for a bride that the attendants couldn't stop buzzing about. Adrienne had explained it in her vows as *"until death did them part"* or something similar.

Only one other faerie stood out, seated at the front of the throne room wearing a bright, berry pink.

She was a year, maybe two, younger than I was at fourteen. Her golden-blonde hair was pinned up in a coronet around her head, and tiny flowers matching the color of her dress hung from her ears like delicate chandeliers; it wasn't fine jewelry fashioned after fuchsia buds, but real blooms that fluttered and pulsed in time with her breath.

"Dominic and Diana's daughters," my mother whispered as the ceremony went on. "My, they look just like their parents, don't they? Misha looks so much like Dominic, and Nicole—the spitting image of their mother and aunt with her black hair."

I'd hardly noticed the girl she—*Misha*—sat beside. Her twin. They did have the same features, as well as rounder eyes than most High Fae and slightly upturned noses. Their ears didn't quite come to as sharp a point. Her sister, Nicole, had also seemed to deviate from the requested color, though not quite as boldly in her pale lilac dress that shifted to silver in the faerie lights.

"Misha?" I repeated, still watching her. She whispered something to her sister. Her twin snorted with laughter, hands clasped over her mouth to make it seem like a cough, earning each of them a stern look from their aunts seated on either side.

"And Nicole." My mother nodded, but I was no longer listening.

All I saw was *her*.

Later, at the reception, after all the formal dances and introductions, my mother and I took the time to individually thank all the staff and servers who had waited on us. A kind gesture, but one not with entirely pure intentions. I knew my brother, the Montevallan King, had asked my mother to speak to those he hoped might spy for him from within the Sanserrian palace. She'd targeted the staff who had watched Adrienne with a hint of disdain, the humans and faeries the new queen had dismissed without a hint of gratitude. This included my mother.

In the line to greet the new couple and offer words of felicitation, Dominic Briar had spoken to us softly, his blue eyes kind. He was nothing at all like I'd pictured, the famous general who'd slain the High King, ending the Great War.

Adrienne hadn't looked at us at all, as if her gazes were numbered, and she wouldn't waste a single one on us.

The other attendees seemed to follow her lead. Their eyes were full of judgment for my mother, the widow of Josiah Warin. Their eyes whispered before turning away with a hint of disgust: *How could she have married* him?

I understood why they hated him—but their hate was a mere fraction of mine and my mother's. They had their assumptions, but they knew nothing. I noted the faces of those who sneered, whispering behind hands with haughty eyes. In much fewer numbers, I also noted those whose faces softened, watching us with pity, although they still did not offer a kind word lest we stain their reputation with our presence.

I couldn't discern which was worse.

All of this I kept buried, a placid smile on my face. My mother did the same. She was an expert in hiding her pain after years with my father. To anyone else, Sena was affable—amiable and easy to please. Everyone she talked to seemed to enchant and enrapture her, but only I saw the tightness at the corner of her eyes, the crack in her mask.

Adrienne Deimos ignoring her had almost been too much for me, nearly enough to make me drop the facade. She and her brother had been just as vicious in the war—worse, oftentimes—than my father. They had no right to judge my mother.

These thoughts were interrupted as Hahnaley's High Healer strode toward us in a lavender gown, the bodice threaded with gold vines and leaves. Her black, tightly-curled hair was voluminous where it brushed her shoulders.

"Sena Gale?" Eve Kamati's face was radiant, the first truly warm smile directed at my mother and me. "We haven't met, which is such a shame: I've heard wonderful things about your research on the gods and old languages."

Eve's soft brown eyes were not only kind; they were knowing. Instead of disgust for having been married to Josiah, she regarded my mother as if she somehow knew what she'd been through—like she admired her for it.

There was not a single hint of pity.

My mother's eyes lit up. "Indeed?" she asked excitedly, but her hand briefly tightened on my arm. My mother's research wasn't widely known.

"We hear many things. You know how that goes." Eve's hand waved blithely, but eyes sparked as if she had a secret—as if, while we were here to plant spies in her home, she and her mate, Alesia Sancrista, had already done so in ours.

"This is your son?" The healer smiled, acknowledging me.

"Yes." My mother's hand went to my shoulder. "Julian."

"You look so much like your mother but with your brother's eyes," Eve noted.

"Thank you." I bowed. They were my father's eyes, and while I hated having any part of them, it was one of the few features my brother and I shared. Eve acknowledged this—acknowledged who had truly been a father to me.

Alesia was the renowned warrior, but Eve was the dangerous one. Her intuition missed nothing.

"Come." Eve gestured to us. "You both must meet my mate. She may seem like a grouch at this time of night—she can only stand to be social for so long—but I swear Alesia is completely harmless."

A lie. I'd done much study on Alesia in the war. The demi-Fae was utterly frightening, deservedly so.

Eve went on, "I would introduce my nieces, but it seems both have run off. I'm sure one is upstairs, already in bed with a book. That one got her aunt's lack of social tolerance. But the other is worse. Probably rousing some sort of trouble." Eve's eyes rolled, but her expression was teasing, full of playfulness and endearment.

My mother nodded, taking Eve's offered arm. "I would love nothing more."

"If you don't mind, I would like to step outside." I held back. "Just for a breath of fresh air." Eve might not have known where her nieces had snuck off to, but I'd been watching one of them all night. Several minutes ago, she'd stepped out onto the terrace, and I was eager to follow.

Eve nodded, her smile just sly enough that I wondered if she already knew my plans. "Of course."

My mother squeezed my hand. "Careful, Julian," she whispered, low enough that Eve wouldn't overhear. "Remember what August warned you of—the other countries don't hold the North in the same esteem as they do each other. Stay mindful."

"Of course, Mother." I nodded and kissed her cheek before stepping out of the terrace doors.

The sky was the deep violet of dusk, with a spill of stars brightening the sky above. I walked the gardens, admiring their robustness for so early in spring, and came upon a small alcove. Climbing roses, blooming early for April, gave the space some privacy, but through their thorns, I could see a blur of pink.

As I grew closer, I could take her in more fully. Misha worried her lip as she paced back and forth between the blooms of the alcove: roses, wisteria, and inverted blooms of fuchsia, the same color as her tulle gown. The princess, heir to her father's earth element, spruced them where needed, pruning when necessary. She was feverish in her task, nearly obsessive.

I leaned against the trellis, hands in my pockets lest she see them shake. "Are you not keen on purple?"

My question startled her. She froze, then whipped around, looking me up and down before retorting, "I'm wearing purple."

"It's pink."

"It's *fuchsia*," she contradicted, pointing to the buds, same as the ones adorning her ears—blooming in bursting shades of pink with purple centers. "It's a shade of purple."

I chuckled, shaking my head. "I don't think your new stepmother agrees."

I'd seen the look she'd given Misha, her now stepdaughter, when Adrienne noticed her after the wedding ceremony. She hadn't been pleased with the liberties Misha had taken with the color scheme.

Misha only shrugged. "It is a bit much to demand all your guests wear the colors of your own country, though, isn't it? I mean, what about *our* country? My father is the king. He should have had some say in what they wore. At least let us don shades of green or gold for Hahnaley."

"Maybe he wants to make his new bride happy."

"*Bride.*" Misha scoffed at that, pacing again as she muttered, " . . . *stepmother.*" She said the words like they left a sour taste in her mouth, her face pinching. "If he really loved our mother, his mate, he wouldn't do this, would he? Commit to another, even for political gain?"

She looked to me for an answer, one I couldn't give. I knew nothing of love—or I hadn't.

Not until this morning when I laid eyes on her.

I'd flirted with many of the girls in my brother's court, the daughters and younger sisters of councilmen and courtiers. Even had some dalliances—all banes to my brother as he dealt with the inevitable fallout. But here, with Misha Briar, it felt like a distant memory, and I found myself wanting no one else from this point on.

I shrugged. "My father didn't love my mother, nor my brother's—his first wife. Maybe kings and rulers aren't meant to love, putting country before heart."

Misha vehemently shook her head. "No, *my* parents loved each other." She'd circled back, convincing herself of her parents' love and quickly forgetting her doubt of a moment ago. "They were a perfect match, bound to the same destiny in the stars. Their souls were crafted from the same divine essence. Everyone says so."

What an image she created: souls formed together, separated at birth, finding their way back to one another in this life, and when it was over, meeting after death among the constellations.

Who would be lucky enough to be hers—the defiant girl in pink?

"You don't like her," I said. Not a question.

"What's not to like?" Misha countered. "Adrienne Deimos is beautiful and charming and clever—" She plopped down on the stone bench, breath huffing in irritation before she grew thoughtful. "It could be

153

worse. At least she doesn't pretend she wants to be a mother to us—isn't trying to replace her. *That* would be nauseating."

Her mother, Diana, had died giving birth to her and her sister. Misha had never known her at all. But sometimes, just the idea of something, built up in your mind, made you cling to it all the more.

"I didn't ask you your name," she said, changing the subject as I sat beside her beneath the rose arch.

"Julian." I left out my surname. If she didn't yet know who I was, then maybe I could sit with her like this for a little longer. I'd be devastated if those blue eyes looked at me differently.

"Julian," she repeated. My gut tightened as she said my name, rolling the syllables over her tongue, studying it. "I'm Misha."

"I know."

A rosy blush crept along her cheeks. "I'm sorry for dumping all of this on you—you don't even know me. I just . . . there aren't many people to talk about this with except for my sister and aunts, and they've accepted the marriage, albeit begrudgingly. I think they're growing sick of me."

"I highly doubt that." It was unfathomable. "But there is no one else you can talk to? You don't seem like the kind of person who would be short on friends." Not someone who radiated with inner light like she did. We were all just moths to her flame.

Gods, please don't say you have another boy or girl you talk to like this—please don't say you're already in love.

"I'm not—I have plenty of friends." She said it with a hint of pride, maybe even arrogance. Of course, I'd already seen how well adored she was by the guests attending from the West and other countries. Misha was the sun, drawing everyone into her orbit effortlessly.

"Then why aren't you telling them this?"

Misha shook her head. "They're not . . ." She hesitated, searching for the right words. "There are just some things you can't discuss with members of your own court, even if they are your friends."

I cocked an eyebrow. "But you trust me?"

"I thought you might understand. With your brother—"

"I thought you didn't know my name."

Misha's eyes widened as she realized she'd given herself away. She flushed. "I saw you come in with your mother. The grey eyes give you away." She leaned in closer. "They're like storm clouds, heavy before rain comes pouring down."

She was so close, close enough to share breath. My heart pounded, roaring in my ears. While I'd been watching her, how had I not noticed she'd been watching me back?

"True friends can be hard to find for people like us," I admitted. Those of us in a position to be heir had to be careful in ways that others did not. She and her sister were successors to their father, and I to my brother . . . at least until he married and had little heirs of his own. Unlikely, as I'd never known him to be interested in anyone for that purpose. "But why tell *me*? Knowing who I am—who my father was?"

I had to know. Had to see if contempt or disgust or worse—pity—crept into her eyes.

She shrugged. "You looked like you could use a friend, too." Misha leaned back, and I had to stop myself from following her.

Our hands rested next to each other on the stone bench, fingertips barely brushing. Her blue eyes met mine, but if the storm was caught in my eyes, the sky was captured in hers, threaded with strands of golden sunlight. Yet, there was a loneliness in them, a touch of melancholy so different from how she let herself be seen.

A sharp voice called, breaking our trance. "Misha!" Her aunt, Alesia.

A gown of deep plum swished around her as she rounded the corner. Her black hair was pinned back, making her dark eyes all the more piercing. "There you are, mija."

Misha jumped up from the bench beside me. "Alé!" She flushed, the color descending into her neck. "I was just taking a break in the night air, and we got to talking. This is—"

"Julian Warin." Alesia smiled, not quite as warm as Eve's but not the disingenuous tight expressions of everyone else. "I've just met your mother. She is lovely." Her words rang with honesty. She looped her arm through her niece's. "But you'll have to excuse us. I've been sent to fetch this one. Her father wishes for a dance." Alesia looked as if she'd scold her niece but then softened as she met her eyes, a silent conversation drifting between them. "At least I didn't have to drag you from the library like your sister."

Misha chuckled before turning back to me. "It was nice to meet you, Julian." She inclined her head, gripping onto her aunt's arm.

I bowed and watched them walk away.

Maybe she will look back. If she looks back, I will find a way to see her—talk to her again.

My heart pounded in my chest for the long moments as I watched them go. And just before they rounded the hedge, Misha glanced over her shoulder, a soft smile on her lips. She kept looking until she and her aunt were out of view.

I didn't know if this was one of the places she liked best, but as she'd come here to settle her thoughts tonight, it seemed a good gamble. Tucked between the rose vines, I left a note, torn from the small notebook in my pocket, hoping she'd be the one to find it—hoping she'd understand who left it. But most of all, hoping she also wished to talk to me again.

If a Rose finds she needs a friend, the Rain is always eager to listen.

Inside the rolled parchment, I placed a piece of my shirt, a small part ripped from the hem that wouldn't be noticed as I re-tucked it into my trousers. Something for a raven to find me with if she did choose to write.

As I hid the note in her eye line, a few inches below mine, the petals of one of the roses brushed the back of my hand. Without thinking, I snipped it, tucking it carefully away between the pages of my notebook.

Misha had tended to it with her magic, and I wanted a piece of her to carry with me. Considering how rarely the North was invited to such events, I knew it might be years before our paths crossed again.

But cross again, we would. In only a few stolen moments, I knew I'd never wanted anything as much as I wanted *her*.

One day, our families and their history be damned, I'd make Misha Briar fall in love with me, too.

A week later, a raven had flown in through the open doors of my balcony, a piece of rolled parchment grasped in its foot.

It seems that though a flower is surrounded by lilies and busy bees, sunlight isn't all it's made out to be. A Rose very much enjoys the musings of the Rain.

Especially those lonely drops that seek to hide away from parties with me.

CHAPTER 14
Misha

J ulian's chambers looked like I'd always imagined, the furniture crafted from pale birchwood and everything in shades of sage and forest green. It smelled of him, the petrichor of damp earth and after a
spring rain. The wide double doors to the balcony were open, giving an
unimpeded view of the mountains. A morning breeze drifted around us,
cooling the room.

Vines of roses and thorns crept up the four posts of the canopy bed,
magic I'd cast since arriving that I couldn't seem to stop using. Sometimes, they wrapped around me in sleep, cocooning me from the rest of
the world.

Gemma Shaw lay opposite me on the bed; her wavy auburn hair
fanned out around her. A tray of coffee, fruit, and a variety of breakfast
cakes sat between us.

Her once generous curves had withered away. Dark hollows shadowed her hazel eyes as she stared at the etched ceiling, a painted scene of nightingales flitting about the tree canopy before a twilight sky.

After waking—I'd slept for two days straight upon arriving—she'd come to me.

We needed no words to understand.

I didn't think I could take much more suffering. The loss of my aunts and of her parents . . . it was all so much.

I sat up, reaching for the coffee, spelled to remain at the same warm temperature. The liquid heated my chest as I drank.

Gemma rolled, propping her head on her hand as she faced me. "I never thought I'd lose my family—not like this. Not so soon. Centuries from now, maybe. Some time that felt a lifetime away. I thought my parents would meet my children and then theirs. I thought we'd have generations."

That was the thing with the Fae. Because they could live for centuries—millennia even—before fading into the afterlife, you never expected their lives to be cut so short. Never expected to only have a few years with them.

"That's all I wanted. For my family to live and to grow with them forever. Why do the High Fae always have to want for more? Why do they care so much for land and power and magic that exceeds all else?" Gemma asked, growing angry, bitter resentment in her scowl.

That greed, more than anything, was what killed the High Fae—what was still trying to kill us.

"All I wanted was to be mated and have children." Tears silently streamed down Gemma's face. "To share them with my parents, watching as they laughed and smiled at them as they'd done with me. They'd have been such good grandparents." She went quiet as she thought of her parents, Orelia and Cedric Shaw, two of the kindest beings I'd ever met.

Until her brother murdered them.

Images flashed in my mind: Julian and I with a little girl—*girls*—like the twins that ran in my family. Or boys, maybe. They were harder to picture, having grown up surrounded by as many females as I did. But no matter the gender, they'd have tight curls like him, with a hair color and skin tone somewhere between his and mine. Alesia and Eve would dote on them wholeheartedly as grandmothers should, showering them with gifts and stories. When we visited the North, my aunts would sit with Sena for tea or coffee, sharing stories and laughing as they passed our children between them. One would fall asleep on a shoulder, the other with their head in a lap as one of their beloved grandmothers stroked their hair.

Visions of what could have been. Memories I would never have.

Nicole and I hadn't even known our own grandparents. Marisela, our maternal grandmother, was a human who had died over a century before we were born. Our mother and Alé never knew their father, who'd deserted them before their birth. Our father had been abandoned, found alone as a newborn babe at the Temple of the Mother in Sanserria, left in a basket woven from briar stems.

Briar: the name of the foundling who had become a king.

"Sometimes," I whispered. "I wish I hadn't woken up and could live in a dream where they still lived. Where I could still have all of those things."

Gemma nodded, understanding. She laid on her stomach, chin resting on her hands. "But that wouldn't do, would it? Because then we'd be ghosts—like them. And everything they were will have gone to waste."

I thought of how Alé and Eve would scold me for such thoughts, for even considering wasting their sacrifice. "No, it wouldn't."

Gemma sat up, wiping her face before reaching for a raspberry tart. "Aren't you curious what else you could do with it?"

"What do you mean?" I shifted, crossing my legs.

"You are an animaglia. One who not only exerts influence over animals, but your magic turned Julian into a *dragon*. Are you honestly going to lie here and pretend like you haven't been imagining what—or *who*—else you could transform? What *you* might become?"

I looked at my hands and imagined the fingers turning dark, transforming into talons. I stared at them so long, seeing them so vividly in my imagination, that I didn't know if it had become real.

"Misha?"

My hands were once again slender fingers, never having changed at all. "No, I haven't," I lied.

Gemma, sensing my sharp tone, dropped the subject. "The council meeting is beginning soon. Nic said the Northern courtiers are all complete assholes." She chuckled.

I smiled, trying to hide behind it as my heart began racing. The thought of dealing with and being scrutinized by more strangers . . . I looked down at myself, the ragged mess I was.

Gemma went on, "She said they want to get to know us, especially as they are giving us refuge." She rolled her eyes. "They aren't giving us shit. And they only want to stare and pick us apart with their own eyes." She stood, brushing the crumbs off her skirts and onto the stone floor.

Wincing, she called to the wind, and a breeze blew the crumbs out and off the balcony.

What would the Montevallan courtiers see when they looked at me? Admittedly, I was vain. I'd always cared how I presented myself. My father said my mother believed that appearances could be armor.

I looked down at myself. It was nearly midday, and I was still in Julian's dressing robe and night clothes. I also needed to bathe—my hair was starting to oil at the roots and the ends were alarmingly dry, but I didn't have the energy. A change of dress would have to do.

I couldn't find the will to care anymore. The courtiers could pick away, like vultures at a feast. I was nearly a corpse anyway.

Draining my coffee, I set down the empty mug and stood. "I'll meet you there."

CHAPTER 15
Julian

I stood on my mother's balcony, gazing upon the city below. When my father's tower was destroyed, she'd chosen this room for herself. August had given her the pick: any chamber, any tower Sena wanted, and it was hers.

She'd chosen this one. The room was small but had more than enough space, she always said. She'd chosen it not for the size but the view.

Stone steps descended from the balcony, leading into the courtyard for The Temple of the Above, where my mother prayed thrice daily. Where, after ten years of study and service, she'd been anointed Priestess.

"What do you see, darling?" My mother joined me at the rail, placing her hands on the stone, delicately folding one atop the other. Her silver rings glinted in the midday light.

"The city. Our people," I answered evasively. True, but not all of it. My mother had enough pain in her past. There was no need to bother her with the pain of my present.

She clicked her tongue. "You silver-tongued liar."

I chuckled. "Never could slip one past you."

"No," she sighed. "Once, my entire world was lies. It was a castle of glass, gleaming and enchanting. But it could not withstand any pressure or questions, and with one blow, it all came crashing down. Now, I only see truth."

My mother loved her studies, always had. It's how she'd fallen for my father. He would find her in the city library, unable to talk to her due to the strict rules, but would still seek her out. He'd pretended it was a coincidence, yet always seemed to choose the table or chair beside hers. Sena was young, only thirty, but knew of his reputation as the king—knew he held tournaments in his coliseum, forcing beings to fight to the death. She'd heard of his cruelty in wars past.

Yet, she couldn't reconcile that with the man in the library, holding the aging books so delicately, so careful and considerate with everything he touched. My mother was a kind soul but one who loved to challenge. She wanted to confront the rumors she'd heard of him and form her own opinions. Finally, she'd worked up the nerve to ask him, the King of Montevalle, why he spent so much time in the library when he hardly seemed to read much. Sena said he'd laughed, and the sound was the most beautiful thing she'd ever heard, deep and melodic. And he was so handsome. Sun-tanned pale skin that set apart gleaming silver eyes and hair as black as the night, almost blue in some lights.

"I come to be near you."

After that, Josiah Warin wooed her, sweeping Sena Gale entirely off her feet. They'd talked for hours, him listening assiduously to her knowledge and discoveries. He'd listened with rapt attention, asking all the right questions. Every day, they did this—they couldn't get enough of the other's time. When the temple confirmed they weren't mates, it didn't matter. Josiah promised her the world. Begged her to share it with him. They were married two months after their first words to each other.

It had taken half that time for him to show his true nature, but by then, she was already pregnant with me.

"You know why I love this room?" my mother asked, still looking into the city.

I nodded. Not long after their marriage, my father hadn't allowed her to leave the castle, not even to visit her small library in the city. He'd hidden his controlling nature initially and built her a beautiful library here instead, which had overjoyed her. At least, until she'd realized none of the books were of value, filled only with frivolous things that did not challenge her mind or world. All the things she loved to study were withheld. The betrayal cut deep once she realized Josiah had only feigned interest in her words.

It was then the truth came out. My father *had* come to the library to see her. Not because he'd loved her but because Sena was one of the few female stormcasters left. And nothing mattered to my father more than that.

Josiah had studied her long enough to know what would make her fall in love, then wielded it against her.

"I love watching the people of this city. I love that I can go down those steps, past the courtyard, through the gate, and be with them. There is no one to stop me, no one to question me. They are the people of my heart—they are survivors. After what they endured, the people of this city found a way to heal. To thrive."

"You knew the way my father treated his citizens and yet fell in love with him." Sometimes, it was difficult not to be angry with her for it. I didn't blame my mother, but I couldn't always understand.

"I was so young. So naive." My mother's face dimmed. "And Josiah—" She never called him my father, never referred to him as her late husband. "—had this way of making everything right seem wrong. He weaved the most beautiful lies, ones that always held a thread of truth. It was what made them so convincing. I was madly in love, and love can be the greatest solvent, concealing the worst poisons."

"If you could do it over, would you? Save yourself and deny him?"

Save herself the pain of the night she'd demanded to go into the city, sick of being deprived of her freedom. Save herself from being thrown into the stone wall by my father's lightning, shattering her ribs and femur.

She couldn't leave if she were bedbound in the infirmary, he'd said.

My mother never told me that. Damian had. He was only a child then, watching as his parents worked to heal Sena, to save her child.

That was the first time he'd attacked her. My mother was only two months pregnant and had nearly lost me. Sena had underestimated Josiah's brutality, that he wouldn't harm her in that state. It didn't matter. He had still blamed her, swearing if she lost the baby—the boy he could name heir in lieu of the son who hated him—he would kill her.

She couldn't fight back; my mother's power was only a tenth of my father's.

So she never challenged him again.

"Never," my mother said adamantly, turning away from the city to face me. "That would be to deny myself *you*."

"You could have had another son with a man who loved you, one who would treat you the way you deserve to be treated."

She shook her head. "The past makes us what we are. The girl that would have chosen such a path does not exist." Her palm gently brushed my cheek. "I know what you struggle with, my son. You think the blood on your hands stains you. That it defines you. It doesn't. It was simply a choice."

"My choice," I hissed, "was violence. My choice was death. What does that make me?"

She hesitated, reading my face. "You're not him, Jules. You could never be him. The fact that you care is proof enough."

I shook my head, her hand falling away.

"What do you see, darling?" she repeated, casting out a line. Hoping I would take it and let her convince me otherwise.

My throat tightened, unable to answer. Because no matter how my mother tried, no matter what words she used, when I looked in the mirror, I only saw my father.

We sat at the large, round table of my brother's war room, the center marked with a silver, eight-pointed star—a symbol of the celestial body our capital city was named for. Misha sat to my left, Simon on her other side, while the space to my right was empty—for now. When he arrived, August would take up the unremarkable chair, the same as all the others.

Misha sat in a daze, seeing nothing as her eyes were settled on the star. She was in fresh clothing—a forest green dress my mother had procured for her—but her blonde hair was lank, duller than I'd ever seen it. The tresses were pulled back when she normally preferred to let it hang loose around her shoulders.

Misha was still the most beautiful thing I'd ever seen.

My hand ached to reach for her, to twine my fingers with hers.

Each of the Seven were present, spread out in a way that was never pure coincidence. The seats were never assigned, but by breaking themselves up, they were staggered between the few remaining remnants of my father's court.

Josiah had not had a council he trusted as my brother did, only a court to appease and worship him. These lords and ladies didn't hold the sway of the Seven. Their appearance here was mostly to placate the High Fae aristocracy of the old North. Each who remained had sworn allegiance to my brother, yet they hadn't contested any of my father's doings before his demise.

I hoped that one day, August would tell them all to fuck off, and I'm sure he wished he could, too. But even though it had been years, the Fae were too long-lived. August's fifteen-year reign was the blink of an eye to them. He still partially relied on their allegiance to keep the North firmly in his grip. And these were the most tolerable of the old court's High Fae—barely.

August came through the door minutes before the bell tolled three, punctual as always. The rest of us were already gathered, save the courtiers. Nic walked in behind him in an embroidered black gown. Her eyes met Gemma's—seated between Teale and Shai—looking over her gaunt form.

Gemma hadn't regained the weight she'd lost since the Blood Treaty celebrations, and her face was more angular than I'd seen it. The round cheeks and curves she'd shared with her mother had withered away as she dealt with the repercussions of her two elder siblings' abuse and betrayal. Still, she was faring better than Misha, at least visibly.

The youngest Shaw shifted in her seat, returning Nic's gaze with a weak smile. She pulled her thick red hair forward as if she could hide behind it. Her haunted eyes turned to Shai, silently requesting the assistance of his magic to stabilize her emotions. The mindcaster seemed to debate within himself before acquiescing.

Gemma's posture relaxed, her hazel eyes warming as the magic drifted over her.

When it was done, Shai's eyes met mine, having felt my gaze upon them. It would be too easy for a grieving person to latch onto his magic, numbing their pain instead of bearing it. He'd need to be careful of how often he did this for her.

Shai gave a quick nod in acknowledgment before turning away, his arm still slung over the back of Gemma's chair.

When Nic's gaze lifted to her sister, her steps stuttered. Were it not for the slight dilating of her pupils, the pain would've been hidden from her face.

She's getting worse, her eyes noted.

I nodded, but I didn't know how to help Misha.

My hand reached out, sliding under Misha's. Our fingers threaded together, knitting the abyss in my chest when I was without her. The motion startled Misha, shaking her from her reverie. Her fingers gripped mine tighter.

Nic continued her steps as if our exchange hadn't happened, not wanting her sister to see her worry. Misha gave her a weak smile, her shoulders dropping infinitesimally as she relaxed in her sister's presence.

My brother pulled out the empty chair on his right-hand side, between him and Miranda. Nic's eyes softened as she took her seat, fingertips grazing his. August pushed the chair in for her before taking his own.

For all his warnings about love and pretty faces before the Blood Treaty celebrations, he'd fallen hard.

August's eyes met mine, my raised brow giving my thoughts away. To my brother's credit, he only smirked. He recognized he was in deep and didn't seem to mind at all.

Finally, the four courtiers of the Old North arrived. Late, though this meeting was supposed to be to appease them. August was dangling a hint of influence so they would feel included. As they entered and scattered between the remaining chairs, they looked over the twins and Gemma curiously but said nothing.

"Thank you all for coming," August said, initiating the meeting. "As you are well aware, the Continent has been thrown into chaos with the breaking of the Blood Treaty."

One of the lords spoke up, a broad High Fae male with overly coiffed blonde hair. "Excuse me, but—" interrupted Mannix, the least palatable of Josiah's remaining nobles. "—the princesses of a foreign country shouldn't be sitting in on matters of the North." His violet eyes flicked to Gemma and Misha before landing on Nic directly across from him. His expression grew hard as he took her in: the high-necked onyx gown covered in a subtle geometric pattern of emerald and silver crystals.

I stilled, confused. Mannix was the one who'd requested they be present.

"Adrienne Deimos has broken the Blood Treaty, something which affects all of us," August rebutted. "The heirs to Hahnaley and Desdemon will not only be privy to these discussions, but we will make all henceforth decisions as a united front."

"I don't see how their familial spats affect *us*. Adrienne Deimos and Evander Shaw took their thrones via violence, as is the old way." Mannix pointed a finger at my brother. "As *you* did. Let them argue over the succession of their own countries and leave us be."

"This is no spat." Nic gripped the armrests of her chair tightly. "Adrienne used manipulation and poison to steal mine and my sister's thrones. This was no sanctioned duel for power. She used subterfuge to murder my family, the Shaws, and nearly Julian—"

Mannix cut her off with a flippant wave of the hand. "I was not speaking to you."

August's silver eyes flickered with his magic. A threat. "When my Queen speaks, you will show her the respect she is due."

Zahra, another High Fae noble, cleared her throat. "I don't mean to be forward, my Liege, but . . . Queen?"

"Because of the nature of Adrienne Deimos and Evander Shaw's coup, I—and all of Montevalle—will recognize Nicole and Misha Briar as the rightful Queens of Hahnaley and Gemma Shaw as the Queen of Desdemon. As our allies, we will give them our full support."

"I should have clarified my question." Zahra leaned forward, pushing her long black hair over an exposed bronze shoulder. Her beaded pink gown tinkled softly as she moved. "You didn't say '*the* queen' but '*my* queen.' Is there something else we should know?"

August hadn't misspoken. "When this war is over, because I am sure it will come to that, Nicole and I will be formally mated. In addition to the West, she will be Queen of Montevalle."

Mannix's lips tightened. His alabaster skin began to redden, holding back what I was sure were choice words. I wondered if he would be wise enough to keep them in.

Everyone tensed, anticipating how this would play out.

Mannix, unsurprisingly, showed himself to be unwise. "The North has always been governed by stormcasters. Josiah's two wives were each gifted with lightning, as were all of the Northern Governors and their wives during the High King's reign."

"Never did I agree to do the same." My brother's voice evoked a challenge.

"So, you would ruin that legacy by joining with this—" Mannix's gaze roamed up and down Nic, eyes blaring with hatred. "—this half-breed from the West?" He scoffed.

Nic's eyes blazed as she stared him down.

Misha went utterly still.

Mannix had always seemed one comment away from banishment, but I was taken aback at the sheer stupidity of his vitriol. A quiet tension had filled the room. The Seven sat rigidly, ready to move at a moment's notice, but that was nothing compared to the violence in my brother's still gaze.

I leaned forward. "And what do you mean by that, Mannix? Please, I'm all ears." I kept my grip on Misha's hand, ready to pull her behind me if need be.

"You will mind your next words carefully." August's voice was low, quiet. Dangerous.

"Or what? You'll banish me?" Mannix laughed. "I've served the North for over three hundred years, before even you were born. Mine is one of the oldest stormcasting lineages."

"The most inbred," Damian mumbled under his breath.

Mannix's eyes flamed in outrage. A ghost of a smile crossed Misha's face, the first I'd seen in weeks.

"It may be, but your line is not the most powerful." Silver sparks danced in my brother's irises. "Nicole *will* be your queen. You will respect her." August spoke softly.

Only a fool wouldn't recognize the cold threat.

"*Respect?*" Mannix spat. Though he was a stormcaster, he seemed unable to sense the mounting electricity in the air radiating from my brother—or was foolishly ignoring it. "Her mother and aunt were bred and born in the gutter like rats."

Silence spread across the room, thick and cold as ice.

Misha slowly raised her eyes from the table, locked them on Mannix, and whispered, "What the fuck did you just say?"

I could have sworn that when she narrowed her eyes, the blue irises shifted, flashing serpentine, but then it was gone.

"I said that you and that bitch are no more than the offspring of half-breed gutter filth," Mannix spat at Misha, then turned back to August, pointing at Nic, "and I will not bow to her just because you like to fuck—"

August stood so abruptly his chair toppled back. Lightning flashed in his eyes, a boom echoing from outside the window. "You—"

Mannix's words were cut off as he clutched his throat. Smoke poured from his nose and mouth. He tried to cough, to scream, but only ash and flaming sparks emerged from between his lips. Where his tongue once laid was only scorched flesh.

"You should have minded your tongue in front of my sister," Nicole said from where she still sat, hard and unyielding—a pillar of ice. Calmly, she stood, chin held high. "That gutter filth—our *family* you have so egregiously insulted—had more power than you could ever dream of. Every time you open your mouth to speak and nothing comes forth, every time you try to scream and realize you cannot, you will think of this—of them. Of their daughter who took your voice."

August inclined his head, his face impassive except for the hard glint of approval in his eyes as he watched Nic. Without looking away from her, he said, "Damian, notify the healers." A brief flash of relief flitted over Mannix's face before my brother went on. "Tell them no one touches him. No one heals him."

Damian nodded, only too happy to comply. Mannix, the dense idiot, had not realized he'd also offended the High Healer's mate with his words. Miranda's fingers were white-knuckled on the arms of her chair. Damian reached for her, brushing his hand down her arm.

"Escort him from the city. He is not to return," August commanded as guards entered the war room and led Mannix out, his wrists wrapped in rowan wood.

Before he passed through the carved door, Mannix looked back, unadulterated hatred flashing through his violet eyes, directed at both my brother and Nic.

Dread settled in my gut. Execution should have been a last resort, exile being more appropriate in this instance. But Mannix might just be stupid and prideful enough to do something rash.

I leaned over Misha to Simon. "Keep eyes on him."

The spymaster nodded. "Consider it already done."

Before settling back in my own chair, I searched Misha's face. She was watching her sister; the two were engaged in silent conversation.

When she finally turned to me, I asked quietly, "Are you okay?"

She nodded, but I remained unconvinced. Her magic was roiling beneath my touch, flickering along the edges of mine. Misha pulled away, tightly clasping her hands in her lap as she looked away.

"So now we are clear." August leaned forward, recalling our attention as he and Nic's fingers threaded together. My brother lifted them, kissing the back of her hand. "Nicole does not require my adamance that you respect her and her sister. The Briars and Gemma Shaw, as queens, have diplomatic immunity. If you offend them, I will do nothing to interfere with what comes of it."

Zahra and the remaining two nobles, Carmen and her husband, Mateus, nodded. The former seemed most intrigued, eyeing Nic with new-found regard. The latter two did not seem to care as long as their position in my brother's court was unaffected.

"Jophiel." August nodded to his commander across the table. "Debrief."

The Seraph wasted no time. "Based on what we've gathered from Simon's spies and Celeste's eagles, the Desdemonian army is gathered outside of Valora but has made no move to march westward. Evander Shaw is there with them."

"Why not?" Gemma's brow furrowed. "That's the point of it all, right? My brother killed my parents so he and Adrienne could unite."

Jophiel's wings rustled, her chair the only one without a back to accommodate them. "From a tactical standpoint, Valora is the better base from which to launch a campaign against Montevalle. If I am right—"

176

"And she almost always is," Celeste cut in, spinning one of her knives between her fingers.

"I always am—no almost," Jophiel said seriously, drawing a chuckle from half the room, "Adrienne's forces will leave Sanserria and station north of Chiaran. The area is clear of the Redwood and just south of our border at the base of the mountains. That way, no matter how our army chooses to march, either force can quickly adjust to meet us head-on."

"So, we keep our movements quiet," I said. "If they don't know where to find us, they cannot combine."

"Easier said than done." Celeste's knife settled. "Shai might have weeded out Adrienne's spies, but I can't account for every animaglia that may have eyes on us, especially once we leave the city. There are too many animals to account for."

I glanced at Misha and wondered if her power would be enough to change that after what she'd done during the serpent attack. But she kept quiet, listening to the others go on.

"What if we we hinder Desdemon? Deplete their forces so they have no choice but to join now?" Nic proposed.

"And how do we do that?" Jophiel asked, eyes alight with intrigue.

"The same way we did in Sanserria: rumors. Have Simon's spies in Valora spread stories of what happened in our capital during the Solstice and the rescue—especially that my sister and I are alive after Adrienne's failed murder attempt. Mention Gemma as well, and that we three have denounced Adrienne and Evander's claims." Nic leaned forward, resting on her elbows. "We spread the truth."

Relief coursed through me. I much preferred this to going directly to the East and trying to convince anyone to flip sides. Too many variables could go poorly, and the situation could devolve into violence before we were ready. Not to mention that though Gemma was doing better, she was in no state to rouse an army, much less turn one from her brother.

"We should also mention that one Briar now controls two elements, one being fire," Teale offered. "And that the other has reincarnated dragons. They should know what they'll be up against should they remain with Evander."

"But not to fear us," Nic corrected. "They should know Montevalle is a haven for them like it is for the Hahnaleyans." She looked to August to confirm.

"Of course." My brother squeezed her hand. "We will give shelter to anyone who comes in good faith."

More refugees emerged from the Redwood daily, housed along the border and cared for by Montevallan guards. Our country had the resources to care for them until this was over, and they could safely return home or stay, should they choose.

"We should also spread that Adrienne has been stealing magic by carving out hearts," Miranda added. "That she's been seen wielding Orelia's air magic, and Evander has stolen Cedric's, which is why he's suddenly so powerful. The Desdemonians—especially their more powerful commanders and generals—should be wary that they may be sacrificed similarly."

"That's a rumor that will be easily confirmed by those closest to him," Nic agreed. "Twenty-two is the year in which the High Fae peak in magic. Evander is well past that."

"And just arrogant enough to flaunt his might with the stolen magic," August said. "His own actions will flame the whispers."

"He already has," Gemma whispered, her eyes glassy as she recalled the newly returned memories. "My brother has been using the magic constantly since the Solstice." She raised her head, arms wrapped tightly around herself as she started to tremble.

Misha stood, going to Gemma. She knelt, hugging her friend just as the tears began to fall, gently brushing them away with soft hands. "He won't get away with it, Gem."

Gemma turned, pressing her face into Misha's shoulder, embracing her as her body began to heave with sobs.

Nic joined them, smoothing a hand down Gemma's auburn hair. She didn't offer any words of solace, knowing they wouldn't dull the pain of missing her parents.

Nic only said, "Evander is going to pay."

CHAPTER 16
Misha

Sitting on the balcony beneath an overcast sky, a cool breeze blew through my hair, prickling my skin. I watched the humans and faeries far below, weaving through the streets of Ankaa.

I wondered if this was a normal day for them, uneventful and destined to be lost in the blur of their life. Were they picking up their children from school? It was the right time of day. Maybe they were purchasing groceries from the market that they'd cook with their family tonight. Perhaps they were simply enjoying the chill of the first days of fall.

Or maybe it was a day that would change everything, one that would be seared into their memory forever. One they would think upon with a smile and a flutter through their heart or reminisce upon with a laugh they couldn't keep in. Or it could be one of tragedy they'd try to forget, only for it to come roaring into their mind to steal their joy away.

I wondered if any of them would see their loved ones for the last time today. I wondered if they knew it. And if they did, I wondered if they knew how valuable it was—the chance to say goodbye.

A chance I would never get.

Celeste sat beside me, feet propped on the balcony ledge. My current chaperone.

Julian slept beside me every night, and Nic spent hours with me each day. But I could see the worry in their faces. Even Gemma was faring better in her grief.

While I . . . I was still locked in that tower.

I didn't mind Celeste. She, at least, knew how to be quiet. She did not force me into small talk I had no interest in, and if she did speak, her words weren't probing.

Watching the Montevallan citizens and imagining all the possibilities made me weary, so my eyes drifted downward. From here, we could see the training area directly below, separated from the city by a thick wall.

Across the ring from August, Nic held a sword in one hand—a practice blade to avoid actual harm—and a shield in the other. I recognized the make, though I'd only seen it in pictures. The perfect circle was etched in fine lines: a sun surrounded by tiny stars. A Seraphim shield.

Jophiel stood at the edge, instructing my sister. The edges of this shield were dull, but they'd be sharpened to rival any blade before actual battle. The Seraph must have been teaching Nic how to wield it. How to use the shield as both a protectant and a weapon.

Others watched on. Some of the Seraphim were wary, likely the older ones who didn't appreciate a non-Seraph learning their techniques. Others observed with clear surprise—at how well Nic handled the shield, spinning it about her forearm—that morphed into awe the longer they watched.

Nic had that effect. She was as graceful as a dancer as she fought. The movements were natural. They sang to her—a call in her blood.

She moved like Alesia.

"He is holding back," Celeste noted, nodding to August. "He can't let himself hurt her, even to make her stronger."

I watched my sister duck beneath his sword, shield knocking into his thigh. August stumbled but managed to keep his feet beneath him. She could have launched up then, slamming the sword's hilt into his chin, but didn't.

"*She* is holding back." Nic held that move intentionally. If I saw the opening, so had she.

Their sparring was like a dance, winding and weaving. August was stronger, all brute force, but Nic was faster, gliding and bending out of his path like a river around stone.

But they *were* holding back, both of them. From what I knew of my sister and what I'd seen of August on the plain in Sanserria, if either used their full potential, it would be disastrous.

Wings fluttered above, drawing my attention.

Eagles flew overhead in shades of gold, brown, black, and white against the grey sky, circling between the castle and the nearby mountain peak. The North had an aviary full of them somewhere among its cliffs.

"Do you feel them?" Celeste asked quietly, following my gaze.

"I do."

The animals felt like the plants and earth, little threads connecting each one to me. Like the strings of a harp, I could pluck on them if I chose. With the plants, I could call on them to grow or shrivel, bloom or decay—or I could expel my magic, creating something new.

The animals were different but similar. If I pulled on our connection, I could call them to me, compel them to act, or catch glimpses into their sight and mind.

. . . Or I could turn them into something else.

"I didn't realize the eagles here were so large," I said, watching them. Their bodies ranged from the size of hounds to ponies, large enough to be ridden should they allow it.

I looked to Aetos, Celeste's nearly constant companion. The golden eagle sat perched on the stone ledge, fussing with his feathers. So much smaller than the others.

"As a chick, he was dropped from his mother's nest," Celeste explained. "He was abandoned and forced to fend for himself for a few days until I found him. Chicks at that age are helpless, relying on their parents for everything. The time apart stunted his growth."

"An accident?"

"No." She shook her head, her black box braids shifting. She took one into her hand, curling the strand around her finger. "The mother had too many eggs and realized she could not feed them all effectively. Instead of allowing all the chicks to starve, she chose the smallest—the weakest—and shoved him out."

"Vicious," I murmured.

"Or pragmatic," Celeste countered. "Animals do not have the same morality we do."

"How did you find him?"

"I was out riding, working with my grandmother's horses, when I felt a pull to him, stronger than I'd felt to any other creature. When I found him, he was beneath a bramble bush, covered in ants and barely hanging on to life. The corpse of a rat was nearby. It was what he'd been surviving on."

"Wouldn't they have been about the same size?"

"No, the rat was bigger," she said, lips pulling up in a fond smile. "Though Aetos is small for his kind, he is a fighter, one of the fiercest among the eagles. They fight each other in training, sometimes to the death, to wean out the weakest, and in every bout, Aetos has proven himself to be the most clever and ruthless."

Another pair of eagles soared by. I tugged on their threads, watching the city and castle spread out upon the earth through their eyes. A dropping sensation pulsed through my gut.

So, this is what it is to fly.

"They love you," I said, voice soft. Indeed, the eagles turned their heads to Celeste as they passed, always seeming to search for her.

Celeste shrugged. "There aren't many animaglia in the north. There is little competition for their allegiance."

"It's more than that," I countered. "You've raised them since birth. It's not just the magic. It's the respect." As I said it, Rasalas stood, paws extended in a long stretch before he prowled over. He nudged my hand with his large head.

The eagles looked to Celeste like one would a mother. Yes, her magic allowed her to commune with them, but she did not lord it over them. The birds wanted to serve her with unwavering devotion, the same as she'd shown them all their lives.

Some things were stronger than magic.

"I know how it feels," Celeste said, her voice grave. "My parents were killed in the war against the High King."

I brought my knees up, hugging them to my chest. My arm wrapped around them, the other hand still scratching Ras behind the ear. I was unsure if I could handle speaking about it, but I was curious. "Did you fight?"

She shook her head. "No, I was only a girl, just turned eight when the war began. My parents left me in the care of my grandparents on their farm in Sossulla."

"They left you to join the rebels?"

She shook her head, shocking me. "No. My parents were also animaglia. They cared for the High King's dragons—trained them. It was . . . not entirely of their own will."

"Are you Etherii?" I wracked my brain, trying to remember if any of the High King's familial line had survived the war. We were always taught that they hadn't.

"No. My family is of a different line: the Arnelle. That was the Etherii's most guarded secret, that as their power faded, they weren't strong enough to hold their dragons' loyalty on their own. They enslaved other animaglia to help them, forcing them into blood oaths of secrecy."

"If they were bound to secrecy, how do you know that?"

"There are more ways than words to convey something." Celeste dropped her braid, pushing her hair over her shoulder. "My parents wanted to rebel, but they were so deep within the High King's court, they didn't know who to trust. Your father and Orelia had already left when my parents were summoned back to the capital, along with the soldiers who had turned rebel with them. Anyone thought to be a sympathizer or spy was hung or crucified by the Etherii and their loyalists. My parents desperately wanted to leave but were terrified to make me an orphan. Midway through the war, they finally found someone they thought would help them, someone they could trust." Pain sliced across her face.

"But they chose wrong," I whispered.

"They were betrayed." Celeste swallowed, eyes unseeing. Likely remembering the last time she'd seen them. Eight years old and much too young to be without both parents.

"They were caught?"

Celeste nodded, throat bobbing. "They were—and crucified for all to see."

She turned away and would say no more about it. I knew better than to push. Celeste hadn't told this story to get me to open up to her. She only wanted me to know that she understood. A spark of thankfulness, of camaraderie, lit in my chest for her.

I remembered the last time I saw my father, sick and wasting away in his bed, looking like little more than a shell of the man I'd always known, his beaming smile morphed into a wan pulling of his dry lips. It made me sick to remember.

Adrienne had been crying at his bedside with all the sincerity of a snake.

The clouds parted, the sun peeking through to brush my hair and legs in unwelcome warmth. It was too much—it was all too much.

As I stood, Celeste turned to me, the grief in her eyes only slightly dimmed. "Done with the fresh air so soon?"

I nodded, shielding my eyes as I walked, retreating to the space behind green velvet curtains, the dark escape of the bed that smelled like the damp earth after a rainstorm.

You never healed from losses like the ones Celeste and I had suffered; you only learned to tread the water better. But now, all I wanted was to let myself sink.

My feet padded onto the cool stone floor of Julian's chambers, nearly overrun by rose vines and thorns. More grew each day, spreading from the bed and up the walls. Julian had said he didn't care, and, Mother bless him, he meant it. I could have doused the entire room in oil and ignited it with a match, and he wouldn't mind save for if my hands were burned.

My fingers clenched. I wished they were—burned and blackened as Nic's had been during that morning in the Redwood.

Instead of bare, clean hands, I wished that blood covered them. I wished I'd killed my aunts' murderers myself in a raging inferno and had the marks to prove it. But even if I had the will to go after the conspirators that remained, I didn't have the way nor the energy.

The grief drained it all from me.

So, instead, I crawled beneath the silken sheets, lying down and touching my bracelet. I spun the moonstone orb thrice—the last gift of my aunts—and lost myself in the memories of those I'd lost. In the visions, I told my parents and aunts how much I loved and missed them and how much I still needed them.

But they didn't say it back. Because they were just memories.

And my family was dead.

When the memories paused, I opened my eyes. All the blossoms and leaves had withered.

All that was left were thorns.

I awoke to screaming.

The images from the dream assaulted my mind: my sister, slain by Adrienne over a field blanketed in snow. The only family I had, my twin sister, dead and bleeding out over the white as Adrienne held her heart in one hand.

It was what might have happened that day on the lake had Adrienne gotten through my sister's magic. A fate that had come so close to passing.

It was what would have happened had the poison been more effective.

Magic roiled beneath my skin, swarming, begging to be released.

"Misha!" Julian shouted, holding me as I shook and sobbed. I pushed him away, curling in on myself.

No.

I couldn't touch him—not now. Not when my magic was so close to blowing out of control. I felt it surging at the edges of my skin, so close to breaking free.

I couldn't do that again, selfishly turning him into something he never wanted to be.

Hurt melted his expression as I moved away from him, slicing open my chest. "I'm sorry," I wheezed. "I'm so sorry."

I wanted to tell him it wasn't true, that this wasn't what I wanted. I wanted to be in his arms—I'd never wanted anything more than him.

But more than that, I didn't want to hurt him.

I forced the magic to spill out of me another way; vines of briars and thorns shot up from the ground, covering the walls and spilling out of the doors and balcony.

"Misha!" my sister shouted. Fire blazed from her palms as she pushed through the vines, fighting to reach me. The thorns fell away, turning to ash.

"*Nicky.*" Her name was no more than a breath.

My sister reached me, fire extinguishing as she wrapped her arms around me. I was shaking as she held me, as if the snow and ice from the dream lingered beneath my skin.

I was so cold.

Nic's arms warmed with her magic as she held me, and slowly, I calmed as I pressed my face into my sister's neck.

Behind her back, a vine curled around my finger, and the thorn pricked the tip. A hazy sort of calm flooded me, and the roaring in my head lessened.

Real, this is real. My sister is not dead.

"I'm here, Misha." Nic's arms squeezed tighter around me. "And nothing is going to tear us apart again."

I pricked my finger once more, the haze dulling.

No, it wouldn't.

CHAPTER 17
Julian

I sat in the Atrium, every faerie light extinguished, with my head in my hands. The trees and plants cast long, dark shadows in the moonlight.

I only saw Misha moving—no, *pushing* away from me. The fear in her eyes, unable to bear my touch. She'd finally seen it—that she had never made me into a beast, but that I'd already been one.

"Good. This is good," I muttered.

She should be away from me. Misha deserved more than a male with blood on his hands.

Her magic had been writhing out of control beneath her skin. I'd let my own barriers down, ready to share with her. To take whatever I could, easing the burden from her.

She hadn't wanted it—hadn't wanted me.

"Good. She deserves better."

As much as I tried to convince myself of it, there was still a tiny, golden thread winding down the hall, up the stairs, and into the bed where she slept.

I would only ever want her, even if she didn't want me back.

CHAPTER 18
Nic

"I miss the cabin." Miranda sighed as she worked, plucking leaves from herbs.

Her workroom in the castle was much bigger and more opulent than the one she had in the Redwood. But I knew what she meant; this wasn't her home.

I sat across the table from Miranda, stroking a hand down Ker's back, watching as she worked. Eilith sat on the windowsill, the cool breeze ruffling her feathers.

"Can you warm the water?"

It would have been so easy to reach inside myself to the depth of Fae magic that resided within my heart, casting fire beneath the small cauldron, but that wasn't what Miranda asked for.

So, instead of following my Fae instincts, I reached out with the tendrils of witch magic. I grasped at the energy in the water and of the fire roaring on the hearth. Using all my concentration, I focused on the tinder beneath the pot, urging it to combust with the energy already within, until a tiny wisp of flame appeared.

And sputtered out.

I groaned, laying my forehead on the table. I was a terrible witch.

I hadn't slept since just after midnight when I'd been awoken by Misha's screams and magic calling to me. That was new, feeling her magic reaching out to me without touch. It terrified me.

When I felt it, I'd run, tearing out of August's chambers. All I could imagine was that someone had gotten to her—that my twin must have somehow been poisoned again. Relief filled me when I found her, thrashing and sobbing, but alive.

"You need to practice calling to the magic around you. You won't always be able to rely on the core within your heart."

This I knew better than anyone, recalling how it had drained away with the poison in the apple. I needed to master both.

"I know." I sighed, slowly lifting my head. "But I don't want to do it without Misha."

My sister and I barely knew how to control the witch part of ourselves, seemingly only able to do it when in dire need. But Misha was in no state to practice.

"How's she feeling?" Miranda asked. The look in my eyes must have said it all. "Still that bad?"

I nodded.

It had been four weeks since she'd awoken in the tower, and she was withdrawing into herself more with each passing day. Misha had been rising later, spending more and more of her time in sleep. She was rarely eating, and bathing and caring for herself even less frequently.

I was watching my sister wither away.

I felt powerless to help, a rift forming between us. Misha was building a wall around herself that I didn't know how to tear down. I didn't know how to get through to her.

The divide between her and Julian was even worse. I didn't know what had come between them. They'd been inseparable during that week in Sanserria, adamant in their letter writing in the years before. But when she'd pushed him away last night, I'd watched Julian's heart break across his face.

"There was a tonic my sister used to take daily," I said, casting fire under the pot with a flick of the wrist. "No more than a couple of ounces with breakfast. It helped her regulate her mood—the depression."

Misha had begun to take it after our Father's death when the grief hadn't abated on its own.

My sight went hazy as I remembered my sister's depression following our father's death. She'd fallen into despair and then—desperate to escape her pain—began self-medicating. Anything that would let her escape was fair: faerie wine and liquors, parties and revelry, and everything in between. And it worked . . . until the crash came. The regret and self-loathing.

Then she'd start all over again, an endless cycle of trying to escape her own mind.

Finally, Misha had come out of it. Finally, she'd had enough. That's when Eve gave her the tonic she'd been working on, unsure but optimistic that it would help—and it did. The tonic couldn't be taken with any other substances, especially not liquor. But it had helped immensely until Misha siphoned off it a few years ago. She hadn't touched wine or other spirits since.

194

"I'm familiar with those types of tonics." Miranda stirred the potion, slowly adding different herbs, oils, flower petals, and a powder that looked like ground bone. "They are usually crafted specifically for the person, unique to them alone. Do you remember how to make hers?"

I nodded as I stood, pulling several stems of roseroot and lavender from the herb planters along the wall. "Do you have saffron?"

"In the Atrium."

Miranda took the pot off the fire, setting it aside to cool before smothering the fire. She gestured at the door. I fell into step beside her as we walked.

Miranda's eyes softened in empathy, linking her arm with mine. "You and I can make the tonic, but she has to *want* to take it."

"I know." I sighed. That would be the difficult part. Deep down, unaware of it, Misha believed that if she didn't feel the agony and hurt of losing our aunts, it would mean she hadn't loved them as much as they deserved.

Oftentimes for Misha, it was soaring joy or utter despair. All-encompassing love or overwhelming grief.

I knew she didn't want to rely on the tonic again, but Misha's grief was more than her moods—it was physiological. Eve had explained as much when she'd first created it. The tonic would help her neural system rebalance, giving her a chance to return to a functional level of grief instead of . . . this.

The Atrium was only a short walk down the hall, the entrance framed by etched glass doors. The entire structure was made of glass as well, spelled against breaking and suspended on a bridge before the waterfall. The falling water pounded against the clear wall on one side, and a silvery mist obscured our view of the lake and city below. On the opposite side, midmorning light tunneled in through the glass prisms, casting small rainbows before our feet. Everything about it gave the effect of walking among the clouds.

In the center was a rounded dome, the ceiling stained to depict the sun in the center. Surrounding it was a night sky of azure blue, flecked with yellow stars that peeked out beneath swirling storm clouds, silver lightning glittering across them.

Gardens unfurled before us. The Atrium held all types of blooming flowers and fruitful trees, thriving in the controlled temperature and humidity maintained by the air and watercasters.

Rounding a corner, we came upon Julian, seated on a bench beneath a flowering tulip tree, his face pressed into his palms. He looked up as we approached, dropping his hands. The shadows beneath his eyes were dark, as if he'd been here all night.

"I'll collect the saffron," Miranda said, giving us a moment.

I sat beside Julian, leaning back against the bench. "Gemma is with her."

"Is she awake?" he asked, his gaze trained back down upon his hands. The brown skin was tinged red, as if he'd scrubbed them raw.

"No." I sighed. "She woke for long enough to eat, then curled back into bed. The thorns cover almost everything now." When I went to her last night, I'd been shocked by how much they'd grown—by how much she was losing control of her own magic.

"Misha won't let me touch her anymore," Julian admitted, his voice soft.

"She thinks she made you into a monster, Julian. She's scared of everything right now, but mostly of herself."

Finally, he looked up at me. His silver eyes, so like his brother's, were clouded with pain. "She didn't make me into a monster. I already was one."

"What?" My head pulled back, shocked. "How could you think that of yourself?"

Julian stared into nothing, trying to find the words. "The guards were coming for her, sent to take her to Adrienne. They spoke of hurting her—of the things they might do to her as she slept . . ."

Fire bubbled under my skin. The same fury reflected on Julian's face.

His jaw clenched as he gutted out the words. "I've never felt such rage. I wanted to slaughter them—tear them apart with my own hands. So, I did."

Good. I bit back the word. I wasn't what he needed to hear right now. Even if the memory of those corpses I'd walked past—and what Julian had done to them—settled something within me. I should have spat on them.

"That doesn't make you a monster. You did what you had to, Julian."

"I know that. I—" He took a deep breath. "I just wish it had all gone differently."

"Protecting her, no matter the method, doesn't make you a monster," I said, remembering Alesia's words. "They chose violence when they came for Misha—when they spoke of hurting her. You only gave them what they sought."

My hand reached for his, squeezing softly. "Thank you for protecting her when I couldn't. Thank you for saving my sister."

Julian only nodded. I couldn't read if he believed me or not. Slowly, he turned to me. "I cannot rid myself of the sick feeling that this is only the beginning."

We sat in silence for a moment, knowing it was the truth.

"I can't stand watching her break," he whispered. "I thought I knew . . . in her letters. I had no idea how bad it was."

I wanted to respond, but the words got choked up in my throat, so I only nodded.

"I don't know how to help her." Julian turned to me. "And it's killing me."

My eyes met his, and the same desperate helplessness reflected back.

"Me, too."

Returning to Miranda's study, Julian with us, we mixed together the herbs with zinc, then strained the tonic into a flask. Damian arrived, casting part of his healing magic into the liquid.

The tonic swirled and pulsed lavender in the soft light.

"The Misha you've met, it isn't—" I stopped myself from saying the normal her or her usual self. Because the depression was a part of her, one of the darker parts, but still *her*. My sister was a being of beautiful highs and lows, and the lows should not be marked as abnormal or apologized for. They just were.

"—this is only one part of her," I finished.

Miranda stood beside me, resting her head on my shoulder in silent comfort.

"We know," Damian said, inclining his head toward Julian. "This one wouldn't shut up about her for years."

A ghost of a smile graced Julian's lips. "Do you want me to go with you?" he asked me.

"No, I don't want to overwhelm her," I said. "I'll try to convince her, but she may not want the tonic, no matter how much she needs it. If we both go, she'll feel pressured."

Julian nodded, understanding.

I clutched the glass vial to my chest and prayed it would be enough.

CHAPTER 19
Misha

Vines of roses and thorns grew up the walls, furniture, floors. They slashed across the windows, until only small slivers of early morning light cut between the gaps in the leaves.

My heart raced, and, for a moment, I didn't know where I was. With the vines covering everything, it looked too much like the tower.

I couldn't move, frozen with the fear of finding out it wasn't real. The vines around me began to shift and twist. I lifted my hand, pressing a fingertip to the nearest thorn.

A prick, followed by pain. Blood welled on my fingertip.

Real.

My head swam, nearly delirious with relief. Another prick and the sensation persisted but dulled, not completely wiping it away. Not yet.

I sat up, drinking the cool water left on the end table for me.

The vines around me shifted once more, notifying me of her presence as they made way, despite her wraith-like footsteps being nearly too silent to hear. I stuffed my hand under the pillow so she wouldn't see the blood and bruises on my fingertips.

Nic set a tray on the bedside table. "You need to eat, sister."

I couldn't stand the thought of eating, never mind even lifting my head. My sister sat on the edge of the bed, running a hand through my sweat-dampened hair. My scalp ached, having gone so long unwashed.

"I went to Miranda," Nic said. "We made a vial of Eve's tonic for you."

Eve. The sound of her name constricted my throat, but I mustered the energy to force the words out. "I don't need it."

I couldn't take the tonic—but I couldn't tell my sister why.

Beneath the pillow, I stung my finger upon the thorn once more, poison flooding my system. *Prick.* I held back a gasp as my magic ebbed away, just like it had that night with the comb.

Prick. A different thorn and an antidote followed, my magic returning with it—mostly. It wasn't perfect yet; the antidote didn't clear the symptoms entirely, but it was improving.

At the very least, with the mithridatism, I would build up a tolerance to the mixture I'd grown within the thorns: rowan wood berries, rue, nightshade, and arsenic—things to affect both the Fae and witch parts of me—all so I could never be poisoned again.

It also seemed to keep the magic in check, especially when I woke from a nightmare. I couldn't let my magic turn Julian into a dragon again, all because I was in a panic.

But the constant poison flowing in my veins made me weaker by the day, and Nic would never approve if she knew what I was doing. Eve's tonic might interact with the poison, causing worse damage than my body could stand. I couldn't risk it.

"No, Nic." I shook my head, rolling away from her

"Misha, please take it." Nic reached for my hands, stopping me. Her eyes narrowed on my fingertips, the bruises. I yanked them away, but it was too late. She'd seen.

"Misha . . ." She pulled back her hands, thankfully not reaching for mine again. "Please. I don't know how else to help you." My sister's voice was desperate.

"I don't need your help, Nicky."

I just needed a little longer. A bit more time and the antidote would be perfect. I will have completed Eve's goal—creating the Panacea.

And no one would be able to poison my sister or me again.

"You're drowning, sister. You're being swallowed by all *this*." Nic waved at the thorny vines. "If you won't take the tonic, then fine, but just tell me what to do, and I'll do it. Tell me how to make this easier for you."

Anger swept through me, pushing me to rise. "Easy? How the fuck is any of this supposed to be easy, Nic?" I lashed out.

I needed her to feel the pain with me, to show me she was hurting, too. Nic felt everything so deeply. She tortured herself with it, alone, not wanting to bother anyone else with her grief. She'd done it after Father died, wanting to be strong for me. And she had been—she was one of the pillars I so desperately clung to all those years ago—but sometimes, I just wanted her to scream, too.

But Nic kept her feelings so locked up, holding onto them so tightly that sometimes, not even I could see them. Right now, looking at her, I couldn't tell if she was mourning our family anymore.

Maybe she wasn't. Maybe my sister had healed, and I was the only one left here—all at once empty and full of rage and grief.

"Misha, I didn't mean—"

I cut her off, unable to stop myself. "Well, maybe it is *easy* for you, sister, because you don't *feel*. You aren't even upset. You went to the North and made new friends and fell in love, and all that time, I was rotting away! And now you're whole and healed. Sometimes, you look like you don't even miss them, like it doesn't matter that Alesia and Eve are dead!"

As soon as I said the words, I wished I could take them back. They were the most hateful things I'd ever said.

And with them, I watched my sister's pillar crumble.

Nic stepped back as if I'd struck her, her hip hitting the tray and sending it crashing to the ground. The dishes shattered upon the stone floor. The tea spilled onto her dress, staining the mauve skirt a deep brown.

Nic was devastated, one hand clawing into the dresser to keep her upright.

I might as well have put a dagger through my twin sister's heart. That would have caused her less pain than I saw across her face.

My hateful words did what I'd intended them to, and my sister left without another word.

I returned to the bed, putting my face into the pillow, choking and sobbing. The self-hatred climbed up my spine, wrapping around my throat until I couldn't breathe.

Nic was the only family I had left, and I couldn't stop myself from hurting even her.

Before long, I'd drive away Julian as well. There was only so long he'd tolerate my pulling away and my inability to touch him without making him into a monster.

Soon, I'd be all alone.

Pricking my finger once more, I felt the poison flood my veins, but this time, no antidote followed. And I drifted back into dark oblivion.

When I awoke, my eyes were aching and so puffy it was hard to open them. When I did, I saw I wasn't alone.

"Why are you here?"

August shifted in the chair next to the bed. His movements weren't stiff enough to suggest he'd been here long, though I knew by the darkness seeping through the curtains and the candlelight that hours had passed and we were now well into dusk.

"Your sister . . . needed a moment."

Regret for what I'd done felt like a festering wound in my gut, its rot climbing up and constricting around my heart.

"Did she tell you?" I whispered.

August chuckled humorlessly. "Of course not. You know better than I how your sister hides what upsets her. She will let it stifle, repressing it until it erupts."

August stood, going to the small table and pouring a cup of tea. He added a half spoonful of sugar before putting it to his lips.

"Maybe now you know her better than I do." The thought was like a knife to the chest. "You even take your tea like her."

August hesitated before admitting, "I used to watch her during the Blood Treaty celebrations."

This I already knew. August had watched Nic, and I had watched him, fascinated by their dynamic.

August returned to the chair. "Your sister is incredibly peculiar about certain things, especially her tea. And after the way we met, she was so guarded. I just . . . it's easy to see what she hates, and I wanted to know what she liked." His fingers flexed around the mug.

My chest clenched. This was the love my sister deserved. Not mine—not after what I'd said to her.

August went on. "Nicole has this . . . *fire* in her eyes. I saw it from the moment I met her, saw how the brightness disappeared after your aunts were murdered. After everything happened, she became a shell. She has nightmares, and even now, they come to her. In her dreams, she watches your aunts die over and over again, powerless to stop it. Powerless to keep the same thing from happening to *you*. That light came back into her eyes only recently."

"In the North?" I asked.

"Only glimpses," August said. "It didn't fully return until she got you back. It went away again this morning."

My sister's devastated face flashed through my mind. It felt like a punch to the gut, knocking all the wind and air from me.

"How did you find out about the nightmares?" I asked. Nic always put silencing wards around her room. Alé only discovered it when Nic forgot to put them up one night. The entire West Wing woke to her screaming.

"She burned down her room."

I gasped, sitting up quickly. My head spun, and I had to steady myself. The poison still lingered in my system. "Was she—"

"Nicole was okay. Firecasters cannot burn. But it was an inferno: swirling flames with her at the center, clawing at herself." August's eyes went hazy as he remembered, watching it all over again in his mind. His knuckles went white against the chair. Not for himself, I knew, but for her—the moment he'd realized how much my sister had been hurting and hiding it.

"Thank you . . . for getting her out." For helping her when I couldn't, asleep and useless in the tower. *For helping her now, when I am the reason she is hurting.*

"I won't ask what happened between you," August said, grey eyes intense on mine. "That is for you and her to work out, but I understand the lashing out at those you care about most. I did the same after my mother died. The decade that followed was the worst of my life. I did many things I regret—many things I can never take back. There's a reason so many believe Adrienne's lies—believe that I am capable of murdering your sister and the Shaws."

I had never seen August like this, so unsure of himself..

"In my worst moments, I fear I am still that person. That I am no more than the murderer my father made me into. I lie awake, watching Nicole sleep, worried that she will realize this and leave."

"She won't," I said. I saw the way she looked at him, like August had given her the moon and all the stars.

"Nor will she leave you. No matter what you've done or said, you will never lose her, Misha."

Tears streamed down my face. "Maybe."

When I awoke again, it was night. A slender arm was wrapped around me, a cheek pressed against my shoulder blade. I was surrounded by the scent of winter nights: amber and fallen snow.

My voice was soft, barely a whisper floating through the darkness. "I didn't mean it, Nicky. I could never blame you, could never truly think you aren't hurting too."

My sister was still for a moment, her breaths so quiet I wasn't sure if she was awake. Eventually, in a small voice, she said, "I know."

"Do you hate me?"

Nic's arms wrapped tighter around me, holding me as tears began to stream down my face. "There are things you never have to ask, Meesh. I could never hate you."

I turned, clasping our hands together between us. How we used to sleep as children.

"You don't always have to hide, Nic. You can scream and cry and shatter something. Be angry with me for what I said—with the world for what it has taken from us—it doesn't matter. You can hurt, too. Your pain isn't a burden."

Then Nic began to cry, tears so heavy it was like they were conjured from the sea itself.

"I can't stop seeing it, Misha. I can't stop watching them die in front of me. And it's all my fault." Nic's breath heaved. "Because I couldn't stop it."

"It wasn't your fault, Nicky. Please don't think I blame you—Alesia and Eve wouldn't."

Nic was crying so hard she couldn't answer. As my sister shook with her sobs, I held her tighter. I clung onto my twin with the strength of the sun and moon, locked in their endless dance—one never whole without the other.

When Nic's breaths finally slowed, her shaking eased, I whispered, "I think I saw it."

"Saw what?"

"I think I watched them die." I could hardly choke the word out. "It was a dream, but also not, like when you were attacked by the shadowhounds. From high above, like a bird in the canopy, I watched the arrow fly into Alesia's chest, the dagger carve across Eve's throat. I watched you burn them all to ash."

My sister's brow wrinkled. "How?"

"The magic?" It came out as a guess, but I knew. "My body was stuck, but my mind yearned for you all."

Unbeknownst to us all then, I'd gone into the minds of the animals, searching for my family, desperate to know where they were and if they were safe.

The loss of our aunts felt like a weight strapped to my chest, constricting and growing heavier each day.

"Will it ever go away?" I asked her. "This crushing weight?"

Nic shook her head. "I don't think it ever goes away. I think we just get strong enough to bear it." She brushed my hair back from my face. With her thumb, she wiped away my tears. "We'll get through this, sister. Together."

I wanted to, but I couldn't bear it just yet: the weight of a world where we had no parents, no aunts. Only each other.

So, I held on tighter to my sister, clinging to her for dear life, and drifted back into sleep.

CHAPTER 20
Misha

M isha," Julian whispered my name like a dream. Too good to be real.

My eyes fluttered open as his hand caressed down my arm. I made to pull away, but he clasped my hand between both of his.

"Please, love. Don't. I stayed away as long as I can, but I—I can't bear it anymore."

I froze, stilled by the pain in his eyes.

"You shouldn't want to be here with me," I whispered. "Not after what I did."

His brow furrowed, confused. Then, his stormcloud eyes lightened with some sort of understanding. "If it's what you want—what you truly want—tell me to go, and I will."

It'd be best for him to leave. I was only good for hurting people. My family. My sister.

Him.

"I want you to go," I whispered, the words coming out more like *stay*. Julian's grey eyes flickered. With despair or hope, I couldn't tell. He moved closer, leaning over me.

"Tell me you don't love me, and I will."

I took a shuddering breath, sitting up to face him. My fingers traced his jaw, the short stubble of his beard.

"I don't love you." *I am going to love you forever.*

Julian's hands threaded into my hair, his breath hot on my mouth. I leaned closer as if I could breathe him in.

"*Liar.*"

Our lips met, and my resistance crumbled. The taste of him was a balm to my soul, my ragged heart.

Julian slowed the kiss, softly brushing my lips with his once, twice. He murmured against my mouth, "Come with me, Misha."

I didn't have the will to resist him when he looked at me like that—when he said my name like it was meant for him alone. I took a deep breath, willing the magic to know that I was safe, that it wouldn't hurt him to protect me.

I sat up, hands winding around his neck. Julian's arms came under me, lifting until I was floating, cradled against his warm chest. My body nearly sighed with relief from missing him.

Julian carried me into the attached bathing room. My feet touched softly to the floor as he reached for the hem of my nightgown. I couldn't remember the last time I'd changed it.

"Arms up, love."

He pulled the dress over my head, leaving me bare before he shed his own clothes. He held my hand as I stepped into the large tub, already filled with warm water.

The water was soft, enhanced with rose oil that turned it a cloudy pink. But there was something else, too—honey, maybe. Bubbles and tiny buds of lavender drifted on the surface, clinging to my skin.

I couldn't remember the last time I'd bathed. I couldn't remember the last time I'd cared to. The nights and days blurred together, the dreams and nightmares overtaking reality. My fingers had grown bruised and sore from the constant pricking.

What a godsdamned mess.

Julian sat behind me. He gently ran a soaped washcloth down my arms and legs, then my torso. There was no sensuality in the motion, and with the lack of such, it was all the more intimate. This wasn't an action born of desire, but love. He was caring for me, my body, in a way I couldn't, so consumed by my failures and grief.

Unconditional love, I didn't deserve.

"What day is it?" I whispered.

"September twentieth."

We'd been in Ankaa for thirteen days—I hadn't bathed in nearly two weeks.

"Lean your head back." If Julian noted my embarrassment, he didn't show it.

I followed his direction, arching my neck back before he poured the water into my hair. Once it was doused, he lathered shampoo into his palms. I ran my hands along his thighs on each side of me, corded with lean muscle, as his fingers scrubbed at my tender scalp, needing to be as close to him as possible. Julian rinsed again before coating my hair in conditioner, thicker than the kind I'd used in Sanserria, to soften my strands in the harsh, dry air of the north. Twisting it atop my head, he clipped the hair so the conditioner could sit.

Julian pulled me into him, my back to his chest, as he took my hand, using tiny scissors to trim the nails that had grown too long.

"Do you want to tell me what this is about, love?" Julian flipped my palm, showing the bruises along each fingertip.

"I don't always know when I'm awake or—" I let the word drift. A truth and a lie. I kept the secret of the poison close to my chest, holding it tight. I didn't know how he would react, and I wasn't ready to face the possibility of letting it go.

Julian nodded, not pushing. He lifted my hands to his mouth, kissing each fingertip gently. "I kills me to watch you hurt yourself."

I pulled my hands back, nodding. "I'll try to find...other methods."

Sinking my hands beneath the water, I wondered how much longer I could stand to lie to him.

Julian unclipped my hair, letting it fall down my back. I cupped the pink bubbles, smelling as he ran a large-toothed comb through my wet hair, detangling it. "Why these oils?"

"Because they smell like you." Julian dipped a pitcher into the water again, pouring it over my hair to rinse it for the final time. "Roses and freshly-tilled earth, like sunshine—I don't know how you've stolen that from the sun, but it's true." Another dip and more warm water cascaded over me.

Setting the pitcher down, his hands wrapped around me, gently gripping my waist as he leaned in. Julian's nose brushed the back of my neck as he breathed me in. "And some kind of musk. Something feral—wild." He planted a kiss there, sending shivers down my back. "*You.*"

I wrinkled my nose, shifting to put space between us. "You're too kind. I know what I must smell like."

Julian's arms tightened around me, keeping me pressed against him. "Maybe a bit more of the musk as of late."

A laugh burst from my mouth before I could stop it. But the laugh caught in my throat, congealing until it stuck. And then I was heaving, my breaths unable to come fast enough as sobs wracked my body.

"Shh." Julian pulled me into his chest. "Let it out, love. I've still got you."

Turning, I wrapped my arms around him and tucked my face into his neck. "Why are you doing this?" I choked out. "I made you into a monster."

"You did no such thing, love." Julian grasped my face. "Your magic did what it did to protect me."

"I made you a killer." I shook my head, trying to pull away, but Julian's arms held me fast. "You never wanted to harm anyone, and I took that choice away from you. I won't do it again."

I pulled my hands back, clasping them together as I drew them against my chest. I'd clung to Julian so desperately as he carried me on the Solstice, trying to get me to Eve. I'd been frantic, terrified that he'd been poisoned as well, and had wanted nothing more than to save him.

Julian's fingertips went to my chin, lifting my gaze back to his. "Misha . . ," His eyes were alight, tortured. "You didn't make me kill anyone, love. You didn't make me into a monster." His hands clasped my face. "All I ever dreamed of was a life of peace—with you. But *Adrienne* brought us this violence. *She* killed your family and mine, killed your aunts who I wanted so desperately to call mothers-in-oath one day."

The tears came harder, hearing him speak about Alesia and Eve with such sorrow—knowing he saw them as his family, too.

"But in your letters, you swore you never wanted to be like your father," I whispered. "You never wanted to kill like him."

Julian had broken that vow for me.

"Because what kind of child hopes that his father will die? When August killed him, I was *grateful*." Julian let out a ragged breath, chest shuddering. "I was grateful when I should have been sad or—I don't know—anything but fucking *happy* that my father was dead. I thought if I could swear to never take another life, if I could prevent any more bloodshed, then I could atone for the hatred of my childhood and for tricking my brother into doing what he did."

"But if it weren't for me, you—"

Julian's lips met mine, cutting me off. I felt every ounce of devotion through the kiss, how utterly he loved me. After a few moments, he eased back, his lips brushing against mine.

"Misha, if it weren't for you, my life would be like a sunless sky. If I must kill, there is no one I would rather defend with bloodshed than you. If anyone tries to steal your heart from me again, I will tear them apart—dragon or no."

I thought of how wretched I'd been since I'd awoken. How I'd hurt him every time I pulled away, unable to explain why. "I don't deserve it."

Julian kissed one eye, then the other, casting away my tears.

"You deserve everything."

I wanted to believe him so badly, so much so that I desperately convinced myself that I could deserve him. I could stamp down the darkness and only shine.

I could make myself better. For him.

214

I leaned into Julian, pressing my head to his chest, feeling his heart beat in time with mine. Julian's arms wrapped tighter around me, and for a moment, I felt a piece of my heart slide back into place.

CHAPTER 21
Nic

T he rumors weren't working. No one had emerged across the border from Desdemon. Not a single soul.

In the map room off the library, I stood over the large wooden table carved to depict the continent. The sun had set hours ago, and my eyes had gone bleary as I looked over the reports from Simon and Shai in the dim light.

Taking a deep breath, I ran my fingers over the carved trees of the Halcon Rainforest, then the star that marked the city of Alara.

August's lips pressed against the spot between my neck and shoulder.

"Come to bed, sweetheart. Worry changes nothing." One hand encircled my waist, his palm pressing against my stomach as he pulled me into him. I sighed as my back hit his chest. His other hand came around my neck, lifting my chin. August's lips caressed my forehead, my cheek. "The rumors need time to fester. Patience."

I closed my eyes, reveling in the feel of him. "What if no one comes?"

"Our army still outnumbers them."

"Barely," I hissed.

"Our forces are better trained, better prepared. North of the city, the Seraphim are prepping them now, readying the few soldiers that have not seen battle."

August's words soothed my anxiety if only a little. *We will be okay.*

I turned, wrapping my arms around him. He was so solid and sure against me, the one steady thing I could hold on to.

"She's better," I said softly, as if speaking it too loudly would make it untrue. "She looked so much better today."

Misha's hair had been clean and her skin less dull when she joined us for breakfast in the dining room. It was the first time she'd left Julian's chambers since the council meeting. My sister had been quiet, her eyes more unfocused than not, but she'd been there. She'd come.

Even Julian appeared better—brighter—as they sat side by side, so close their arms brushed with every movement.

August mumbled his agreement, hands stroking up and down my sides, as his mouth grazed my temple.

"That reminds me," I snapped, pushing him back. "It wasn't supposed to be *you* who watched her."

I'd never been so angry with him as when I'd seen August coming from Misha's room.

"Nicole—"

"What is said or happens between Misha and me is between *us*."

Ire flared in August's eyes. "You couldn't *breathe*, Nicole. You couldn't walk. I've never seen you like that. *Never*."

To say this was no little thing for him, I knew. Not after he had held me in the cabin night after night as I broke apart. Not after he'd watched me go up in flames.

I poked a finger into his chest. "It is still not your place—"

"I know, Nicole. I know," he said, clasping my hand mid-poke. "I wanted to say something, to defend you, but that's not an excuse. When I saw her . . ." August shook his head, cringing. "She was just as bad as you were. Worse. And I couldn't say anything." August stepped closer again. Hesitant, as if cornering a feral animal.

I stood unmoving, letting him approach.

Seeing that I was no longer on the attack, he lifted me onto the table, stepping between my legs. "Forgive me, Snow." August's lips cascaded down my neck, lingering at the spot on my pulse that gave me chills.

My breath caught, and I knew he'd noticed, his soft groan buzzing against my skin.

"You are only forgiven because whatever you said helped. But next time, you will stay the hell out of it." My words had lost all their bite.

"I will . . . try," August conceded, his hands gliding beneath my shirt to rest against my bare skin. "But when it comes to you, I am rarely reasonable."

I replayed that night in my mind, stiffening as I heard the words once more, the venom with which my sister spat them. *Sometimes, you look like you don't even miss them.*

August felt it, his hands tightening as he pulled me closer, our chests flush. He spoke as if he'd heard my thoughts. "It wasn't true, Nicole—whatever she said. You can have happiness and still mourn them. You don't have to suffer to prove your love."

"No," I admitted. "But it feels like I'm both. I'm the happiest I've ever been and the most miserable." In August's arms, I felt whole—and yet utterly empty as I thought of my family. "Tell me how it makes sense."

"It doesn't—it won't. You just have to live it day by day, Nicole."

August leaned in, his lips brushing mine. I sighed, deepening the kiss, opening to him. As his tongue met mine, I reveled in the taste of him. I wanted to lose myself in this moment—in him—until I felt no pain.

Hushed murmurs came from the library, interrupting us. "You know you shouldn't be down here," a voice said.

"Papa Simon, I'm just getting a book. And I could before. It's unfair!"

August and I righted our disheveled clothes and stepped into the hall. Our heads whipped around to the sound of a gasp coming from within a reading nook. We walked closer to see Simon standing with a twelve-year-old girl, tall and lanky.

Her brown eyes went wide when she saw us.

August smiled. "Jessa." The girl ran to him, jumping as he caught her in his arms. "Are you causing trouble for your fathers?"

"No!" Jessa huffed dramatically. "I was out of books," she said as he set her down.

August cocked a brow, looking to Simon.

"She has *hundreds* of books in her room." Simon countered, sounding extremely put-upon.

"But I didn't want to read any of *those*," Jessa said, holding up the novel she'd claimed. A fox and an archer gilded in gold graced the cover.

I chuckled, stepping out from behind August. "I know the sentiment."

Jessa's eyes went wide as she noticed me. She was tall for her age, only a few inches shorter than I was. She scanned me, taking in every detail.

"I'm sure that's the partial truth." Simon sighed exasperatedly. "But she's also been begging to come to this part of the castle to see you." He inclined his head to August and, to my surprise, me. "I told her it wasn't the time." His eyes softened in apology.

Jessa flushed, looking away.

"I think this is the quietest she's ever been," August said, teasing as he nudged her with an elbow. "She's usually a little terror."

Jessa turned to him, gaping. "I am not!" She nudged him back, then broke into a wicked smile. Mischievous indeed.

August smiled, then pulled me forward. "Jessa, this is Nicole. From Hahnaley."

Jessa curtsied, suddenly the picture of poise. Simon's eyebrows shot up as if this was a new occurrence. "It seems she wants to make a good impression," he murmured to August.

Jessa either didn't hear or chose to ignore her father. She stepped closer, whispering. "Can you really cast fire?"

Simon sighed. "Jessie, you can't—"

"It's okay." I smiled and turned to Jessa. I lifted my hand, calling a single wisp of flame into my palm. The fire writhed and glowed, entrancing her. The tendril transformed into a dancer, spinning and twirling in the soft light. "Your father said you like to dance."

Jessa nodded eagerly, eyes fixated upon the flame.

"Jessa!" Another man rounded the corner. His brown skin looked bronze in the dim faerie lights and the glow of the fire in the hearth. His dark eyes narrowed as he approached the girl. "I turn around for one minute, and this is where you sneak off to? I've been running all over the castle."

"She's quick, this one." Simon ruffled her curly hair. "How did she sneak past you this time?"

"She asked me to make her peppermint tea. I returned with the tray to find her room empty."

"That will do it." Simon chuckled, his arm going around the man who was several inches shorter than him, nearly my height. He immediately softened at Simon's touch. "Nicole, this is my husband, Ezra," Simon said, introducing him.

The man smiled politely, though he was clearly exhausted from searching for his daughter. He pushed back a sweep of brown hair that had fallen across his forehead. "It's so nice to meet you finally," he said, clasping my outstretched hand in each of his.

"Likewise. I've heard wonderful things from Simon."

My eyes snagged on the tattoos lining each of Ezra's arms, various types of flora and fauna wrought in simple but elegant fine lines. Each image was separate but patched together they complimented each other perfectly. The ink was remarkable, a gold that shimmered as he moved.

"Ezra is a masterful artist. Drawing, painting, and, of course, tattoos." Simon smiled. "Miranda creates the ink."

Ezra flushed, the more shy of the pair, but his modesty did little to temper how pleased he seemed to be by his husband's compliment.

"I just came to get a new book, Papa Ezra," Jessa said, the picture of innocence as she hugged her newly arrived father.

Ezra immediately melted, looking down into his daughter's wide doe eyes. "You have to tell us where you're going, honey. You can't just run off, especially not this late." His reprimand was gentle but firm.

I felt a pang through my chest as it reminded me of my own father. Misha and I hadn't been much older than Jessa when we'd hugged him for the last time.

"Okay," Jessa agreed, genuinely remorseful that she'd upset her father. She planted a kiss on his cheek, and all was right again.

"This is why she gets everything she wants," August whispered in my ear, chuckling.

"As she should," I murmured back.

Ezra kept one arm wrapped around Jessa's shoulders as she turned, facing us again. "Papa Ezra and I have been planning my birthday party. It's coming up soon."

"Three months away is soon?" August teased.

"December thirtieth." Simon chuckled. "Every year, she begins planning the day after it's over."

Jessa's attention remained on August. "Will you and Julian come?"

"Have we ever missed one?"

Jessa beamed and turned to me, her smile faltering just a notch. "Will you and your sister come?"

"Of course, I'll be there, but—" Jessa's smile dropped a fraction at my hesitation. "—but Misha *loves* being asked to attend parties. I wouldn't take that opportunity from you."

Jessa's smile returned in full force, nearly bouncing with excitement. "When can I ask her?"

Simon took her hand. "When she's feeling better, darling." Over Jessa's head, he gave me a look of apology.

It's fine, I conveyed with a soft smile. "I'll let you know as soon as you can ask."

Jessa leaned forward, looking like she wanted to say more, but Ezra cut her off. "Oh no, it's time for bed. She'll keep us talking all night if given the chance."

"But I'm not even tired," Jessa said unconvincingly, her last word cut off by a yawn.

"Sure, honey." Ezra put his hands on her shoulders, spinning her toward the library's exit. Simon followed closely behind. They waved to August and me as they went.

Jessa turned back, waving as they left the library. "Bye, Nicole!"

I returned the gesture, smiling at her exuberance—and of how much she reminded me of Misha when we'd been that age.

When we were alone, I faced August, my hands going to his chest as his arms wrapped around my waist.

"Why are you looking at me like that, sweetheart?" he asked, his voice deep—almost purring. The sound coiled a wonderful tension low in my core.

My eyes lifted, meeting his. The silver irises were molten, searing with an intensity that took my breath away. Beautiful.

"You're good with children," I said. If he kept staring at me like that, I was going to combust on the spot. I looked back down, toying with the buttons of his shirt. "You'll be a great father one day."

It shouldn't have surprised me, and I wasn't—not entirely. August was an incredible brother, friend, and king. He devoted himself entirely to those he cared about, and a child would be the epitome of that. He'd been more a father to Julian than their own, after all.

August went utterly still, arms tightening. "Is that what you want, Nicole?" A hesitant hope laced his every word.

223

We hadn't talked about our future outside of the immediate happenings, but yes. Once this war was over, I wanted everything this life had to offer, including children, with him.

My mate—this love who would never abandon me. Who knew me to the very depths of my soul.

"One day." I slowly met his gaze, peeking up at him through my lashes. "With you . . . yes. I want everything with you."

August lifted me so abruptly that I squealed, my arms wrapping around his neck to keep from falling. The next moment, he had me pinned on my back on the rug before the fireplace hearth.

"August!" I laughed breathlessly. "What are you doing?"

His answering grin was feral, hands already ripping open my shirt. Buttons be damned.

"Practicing."

CHAPTER 22
Adrienne

S oldiers were abandoning the Desdemonian army in waves.

"Track down every deserter and kill them. They're better dead than crossing the border to the North," I demanded.

The generals left to follow my orders, leaving General Zarr and me alone in the new throne room, built from the bones of one of the many terraces.

The throne was iridescent white opalite, shimmering in the early morning light. Vines of dead thorns snaked up the back, the leaves and blooms shriveled and withered. I could grow many things with the stolen earth magic but hadn't yet mastered breathing life into them. Still, the vines were thick, strong. I didn't need them to live in order for them to thrive.

My head pulsed from the weight of the minds I kept tethered to me. There were more and more each day. The constant, dull ache was maddening.

With the deserters—soon to be corpses—gone, the Montevallan army and Hahnaleyan defectors outnumbered our Reynians, remaining Hahnaleyans, and Desdemonians by several thousand.

I stood, Zarr trailing behind.

"I should go with them," he said, fingers flexing on the hilt of his sword.

"No." I kept walking, headed toward my chambers. "You are needed with me."

"And where are we going?"

Zarr had been growing restless, unsatisfied with the scraps of information I'd given him. Pleased as he was with the newfound magic he'd been gifted, it wasn't enough.

"To shatter the Montevallan forces in their own capital."

We reached my personal chambers, the door slamming behind us.

Zarr stood rigid. "To attack the heart of Montevalle is impossible. Josiah moved the city, hiding it in the mountains after the war to make it more difficult to strike, and the north is vast. It will take months of flying over the ranges to find it with as few Seraphim as we have here."

Few had joined us—several dozen at most—the vast majority living in their northern homeland. The few who lived south of the border were those who'd defied Jophiel's command and were banished after the Great War, which, blessedly, made them impeccably loyal to Zarr and very eager for retribution.

Zarr went on, "And once found, the unwinged would take months to reach them over the mountainous terrain. There is no feasible way to launch an attack on Montevalle. We need to draw them here."

"We are going to do both." I beckoned him to follow. We stepped into my closet, coming to the tall mirror at the far end. The glass rippled under my touch, allowing us to step through.

Zarr was still as he took in the dark room, the seven mirrors of various shapes and sizes. "What is this place?"

"My Hall of Mirrors."

I ran my hands over the table in the center, the wood grain stained red from the stripping of hearts. In the center rested an ivory casket fashioned from High Fae bone. It was adorned with glinting gold and diamonds in the sigil of House Deimos: an eagle with its wings spread, crowned by the sun's rays.

"When Nicole Briar escaped into the Redwood, I had my guards follow after her. But something else tracked her as well." I lifted the box and stepped toward the largest mirror—the one with obsidian inlaid with stardust and moonstones in the shape of every constellation. "You said we need more winged hunters. Here is where we will get them."

Zarr stood behind me, close enough to feel his heat against my back.

"Mirror of Sight, I request to speak to our master."

The glass went dark, coiling black smoke filling it to the brim. The mirror pulsed as a deep voice, infinite and vast a starless sky, spoke. "Have you come bearing my request?"

"I have not. The hearts evade me still."

"Surely, you have not come to ask another favor after all I have granted you: use of my mirrors, as well as the knowledge to take magic and bend it to your will." The mirror's voice rose. "All that had to be done was for you to bring me one of the hearts of the rising after the sun sets on the longest day. You were free to keep the other's magic for yourself."

"The Briars possess magic unknown. It protected them when they should have been dead."

"Why do you think I want them?" The glass shuddered, the dark tendrils thrashing behind the glass. The voice turned irate. "And yet you stand here, making *excuses*?"

"No, my liege." I lowered my head in reverence. "I beg your forgiveness. Give me another chance, and I will not fail you."

The Mirror remained quiet for a few moments as my heart pounded. I released a shaky breath when it spoke again.

"The stars whisper it is still possible," the voice said. "But a heart must be taken before the longest night is over."

"It will be done," I swore as I stood, straightening my shoulders.

"It must," the voice commanded. "For there are many ways to steal a heart. Now, tell me what you have come to acquire?"

"I need the shadows to track Nicole Briar again."

My Mirror to Spy hadn't seen any of the Briars' companions in weeks. Someone with them had put a ward on the reflections, protecting them from its sight.

"Such a request requires sacrifice."

I pressed the ivory casket to my chest, cradling the box like an infant, my skin warming its ivory exterior. Then I knelt, presenting it to the Mirror. "I offer this."

The smoky tendrils escaped from the Mirror, darting as they swept across the box to sense what was inside.

The voice sighed, pleased. "An acceptable sacrifice. Take the blackened dagger and pierce the heart of the one you love most. Let me drink of him."

Carefully, I opened the ivory box. My brother's heart rested on the once white velvet, soaked burgundy with his blood. Tendrils of his magic brushed against my fingers, begging me not to do this.

I pulled the dagger from my side. The blade glinted darkly in the light, Galorian silver alloyed with black iron. Another gift from the Mirror's master.

Zarr went still as he watched the blade pierce the heart, struggling to keep his horror in check.

My brother's magic, the remaining shred of his soul, screamed. The Mirror's dark tendrils snapped out, catching and drawing it beneath the writhing surface.

Silent tears slid down my face. *It will be worth it*, I told myself.

The revenge would make everything worth it.

The voice spoke again, giving me hope. "Tomorrow, at midnight on the Autumnal Equinox, when the veil is thinnest, the life seekers will rise. By dawn, they will find her."

CHAPTER 23
Misha

J ulian's arms were wrapped around me, his breath soft against my
neck as he slept.

I brought my hand to my chest, watching the moonlight flicker across
the orb of my bracelet.

Spinning it thrice, I watched the memories again: Nic and I with
Alesia and Eve on our twenty-first birthday, cuddled in our aunts' bed
for breakfast and laughing like we had all the time in the world.

Another spin: Our mother, Diana, sitting in a large chair, gazing
lovingly down at her expanded belly, singing us a lullaby.

Estrellita, ¿dónde estás? Me pregunto qué serás.
En el cielo y en el mar, un diamante de verdad.
Estrellita, ¿dónde estás? Me pregunto qué serás.

Our father stood over her as he planted a kiss softly on her head.

Another spin: Our father practicing magic with Nic and me as children, sprouting flowers for us—pink roses and white lilies—as we squealed in delight.

I kept the orb spinning, watching over and over until I finally fell asleep—a sleep where I was plunged into the past.

I was tiny, so small that only when my father knelt were we eye to eye.

He gently cradled my hand, turning my palm to face the sky. "Call it to you, darling."

I tried, calling upon my magic, but the earth around us only shifted. The grass grew taller, flowers sprouting where there previously had been none.

My father, ever patient, only urged me to try again. It took many more times until I could do as he'd asked.

Nic, five years old, sat cross-legged beside us, watching, playing with the flowers I'd grown. She'd begun to fashion them into tiny crowns of colorful blooms, one each for the three of us. By the time I'd finally cast a small pink rosebud into my palm, she'd finished.

Beaming, she placed one on her head—the lilies—and then mine—pink roses. Then, upon father's, a mixture of both.

"So pretty," she said, looking down at the bud in my palm with awe.

I smiled back at her, my cheeks almost hurting from the force of it. As my sister stroked her finger along the blossom, it unfurled, showing a golden yellow center amidst the pink petals.

"You two are stronger together," my father praised. "Though differing in your elements, earth and water were always meant to be together. You enhance each other."

"Like you and Mamá?" I asked as the bud twirled in my hand.

Father's eyes grew wistful, a mixture of joy and melancholy. "Yes, like me and your Mamá. Together, we were unstoppable, just as you and Nicole shall be. As you will need to be one day, when you lead this country together. When I am long gone."

Nic's little brow furrowed. "But you won't be, Papá. The Fae live forever—"

"Millennia," I contradicted. "Tutor Natalia says the High Fae can live for millennia."

Nic rolled her eyes. "That is the same as forever."

"Girls," our father gently chided. Nic and I blushed at our bickering, but our father's face was kind. "While that is true, it is also true that I may not live forever—or even for a millennium." He gave my hand a soft squeeze. "Something may happen to me, and I need to know that you two will be safe. It is why we practice so much with your magic and with your aunts Alé and Eve, too."

"Yes, Papa," my sister and I said in unison.

"We do this so you can protect yourselves and each other, and so that you can continue when we are gone."

Nic's young face grew worried. "But you promise that won't be until a millennium, right Papa?"

Our father kissed her brow, then mine. "I cannot make any promise except that it would take an act of the gods to tear me from you both, my precious ones."

Then the memory changed, ripped away.

"You need to get up, Misha." Eve knelt by my bedside, where I was curled under the covers. The curtains were drawn tight to prevent any sunlight from scalding my eyes.

My head pounded against my skull, and my throat was dry. I cursed, feeling as if the wine sloshing in my stomach would reemerge at any moment—especially if I sat up.

"I can't."

My aunt shook her head. "Yes, you can, darling. That thought is only in your head."

I shook my head, pain racketing off the inside of my skull with each movement. "Please," I whispered the words. "I feel terrible. I need you to heal it away."

"I know you do." Her hand reached for mine, her voice somehow far away. "I know you've been in pain for so long." She wasn't talking about the hangover I'd given myself.

Again.

It had been a year and a month since our father had died. He'd promised it would take an act of the gods for him to leave us, but then he'd been killed by a blood disease. An illness that had evaded even Eve's skill—something I knew she still blamed herself for. It all seemed so unfair. And the anniversary of it had been too painful, too fresh a slash in a wound that hadn't yet fully healed. So, I'd broken my sobriety.

This time was different. Instead of becoming a ghost haunted by her grief, I'd sought people—anyone who could distract me. I sought dances and revelry and every good feeling that came with them. The parties kept my mind thoroughly distracted, with the games and gambling and laughing—until I woke up like this again.

I'd stopped writing Julian. I couldn't tell him who I'd become. He had never hinted at wanting to be more than friends in our letters, but I still couldn't tell him of the hands and lips I'd let touch me. Even if, in my haze, I imagined they were his.

"It was a mistake," I groaned. "I'll never overdo it again."

I saw it in her eyes. Eve didn't believe me.

I didn't believe myself.

For a month, this went on. I would seek pleasure, trying everything to keep the grief at bay and to feel something but that all-consuming pain. Then, I'd feel horrible from the overuse—from whatever regrettable choices I'd made or hurtful words I'd said—and swear it off. Last night, Nic had been the target of my hurtful words about how she didn't even seem to be sad about the loss of our Father.

I knew it wasn't fair. We didn't process our feelings in the same way: Nic hid them, suffering alone. I just wished she would let it out once in a while, let herself rage over the unfairness of it all. That'd she'd do something to make me feel less alone in the utter devastation I felt.

I regretted what I'd said, but before long, the grief and anger and emptiness set back in, and I was looking for another escape.

"I can't anymore, Misha." Eve pushed a strand of blonde hair away from my face. "I thought I was helping you, but—"

"You are." I reached for her hand, clutching it to my chest. "I need you. I'll never not need you, Auntie."

Eve shook her head. "No, you don't." She stroked her nails along my scalp. "Only you can heal yourself of this, darling. As much as I want to help, only *you* can be what saves you."

My aunt pressed a gentle kiss to my forehead and stood, pulling her hand from mine. She walked away, wiping away her tears as she went, her silhouette dark against the golden candlelight cascading through the open door.

I called after her, begged her to come back, as her form disappeared through the arch.

Get up.

Standing on shaky limbs, I followed. As I passed through the door and tripped, falling hard onto the ground. The rug in my chambers was no longer beneath me, my hands clawing into the dirt. Scrapes and cuts marred my skin and the long sleeves of the training leathers I now wore.

"Get up, mija."

I lifted my head. Alesia was standing over me, looking as she always did, her fierce, dark eyes burning. A vengeful, warrior goddess.

"You're stronger—better—than this." Her voice was firm, unyielding, yet thick with encouragement. Never disdain.

Alé's voice was filled with love—always with love.

I pushed up from the ground, hardly on my feet, before she lunged again.

"Faster. *Harder*," Alesia urged as my arm shook with the force of blocking her strikes. "You are strong enough to beat me, Misha. Muéstrame. *Fight* for it."

She lunged again. I barely blocked her in time.

"A true battle is not over when you yield—only when you or your opponent is dead. And you must *refuse* to give up. Yielding is not an option."

Even as my muscles screamed to rest, for a break, I pushed forward, spurred on by Alesia's words.

I had to strike harder, faster, and where she wasn't expecting. I feinted right, and Alé countered, expecting me to counter back left. Except I didn't.

Rolling to the right, I struck her in the side with my practice sword. My aunt hissed, the only sign of the magicked pain she let show, and moved to retaliate, but my foot was already at her ankle, knocking her off balance and to the ground. My chest heaved as I held the practice blade to her throat.

Mother bless me, I'd done it. I'd never beaten Alé in sparring before. Not once in fifteen years of training.

My aunt smiled at me from the ground, her face lighting up with pride. "See, Misha? You're so much stronger than you give yourself credit for."

Tears streamed down my face when I realized. This was a memory, too.

Alesia's grin faltered as she pushed up to her feet. "What's wrong, mi vida?"

I dropped my sword. My arms opened to embrace her, to pull her into me. I wanted to hold the mother who had raised me one more time.

I wanted to say goodbye.

Alesia held me, stoking a soothing hand down my back. "Oh, Misha. You never have to say goodbye—not to me. I will always be with you."

It felt so real. *She* felt so real. The solid, unbreakable feel of her combined with her scent of freesia and the sea.

Slowly, Alesia disappeared, her body crumbling in my hold as she became ash in the wind. I fell to my knees, my arms empty once more.

I woke with a start, still wrapped in the sweat-soaked sheets on Julian's bed—bells clanging violently—and Alé wasn't there, nor was Eve or my father.

Because they were dead.

I looked around for Julian, but he was gone. The ringing of the bells—alarm bells, I realized—jolted through me, reverberating through the stone walls.

We were being attacked.

Magic flooded my veins, pulsing with every beat of my heart. My bones ached, and my skin itched with the fury of it.

Get up.

Because my aunts were dead. Because my father was dead. Because Adrienne had killed them all.

And I'd be godsdamned if I let her take one more person.

Get up.

I pushed myself from the bed. One foot touched the carpet. Then the other.

And I stood.

CHAPTER 24
Julian

The warning bells rang out through the city, rattling through the castle's stone as I ran.

I hated having to leave Misha, still sleeping as she clasped her bracelet, but this was dire. Ankaa had annual drills with the bells, but never in the hundred years since this city was built had they been used for a legitimate threat.

Until now.

August was already with the Seven on the main turret, gathering information from the guards who had set off the alarm. Nic stood with him, listening to every word. Everyone wore Galorian steel-plated leather armor crafted to hold off a direct magical hit.

All three of the familiars were here, all the guards giving them a wide berth. Rasalas and Ker paced restlessly in their jaguar and cat forms while Eilith sat perched on the wall, her hawk eyes on the mountains past the city.

"Something tripped the wards ten miles out to the north," the guard said before he went silent, listening to a voice we couldn't hear: a mindcaster at one of the outposts. "Only eight miles now, coming in fast."

"What is it?" August demanded.

The guard went still, connecting to the other mindcaster. The blood drained from his face, leaving him ashen. "They're gone."

"*Who* is gone?" Jophiel demanded.

"The guards at the outposts." The guard grew somehow paler. "Everyone."

"What is coming?" The Seraph demanded. "Did they share what it was?"

"I—" The guard stuttered. "I—"

Shai moved forward and took the guard's face in his hands. His black eyes were piercing as he sifted through the guard's thoughts. Then Shai, for the first time since I'd met him, went just as white. "Gods above, it—"

August snarled. "What?"

"Moroi," Shai said, letting the guard go as he turned to my brother. "A pack of them."

"That isn't possible," I said. Everyone turned to me, just noticing my arrival.

"It's what the outpost guard last saw before—" Shai held his tongue. We all knew what the guard's last sight had been. A gaping maw of fangs and soulless black eyes.

"No." August shook his head. "The Moroi are solitary creatures. They do not . . . group."

As soon as my brother said it, something hit the wards surrounding the city, impacting the shield that protected us from harm. And we saw them: winged creatures of darkness with leathery wings and bat-like faces. Twice the size as a human or Fae, their fangs protruding from their mouths were used to rip into the throats of their prey to drink down their blood: the sustenance Moroi required to survive.

There were hundreds of them.

"Well, they fucking are now," Jophiel snapped as we watched them.

The Moroi struck at the wards with their talons, scraping against the invisible shield.

"Can they get through the wards?" Nic asked, watching in horror. In the West, she would have heard of the creatures but never seen one. They didn't live that far south, even in the Redwood.

"Not at first," Miranda said. She'd been one of the ward crafters: her, August, and my mother. "The wards will hold for a while, but not indefinitely."

"How did this happen?" August looked to the witch, hoping she might have some explanation, but Miranda was at a loss.

"Adrienne," Nic whispered. She turned to August. "It has to be her, like with the skinwalkers."

"But *how*?" I growled. None of this nightmare should have been possible. As my brother had said, the Moroi did not attack in groups—and sure as hell not by the hundreds.

The solitary beings lived in the western part of the range and hunted alone—mostly livestock and the occasional unfortunate human or faerie caught unawares at night—unable to tolerate sunlight. The Moroi were territorial, just as likely to rip into each other as their prey.

Until tonight.

"That's a question for later," Jophiel snapped. "We don't have time for whys right now. But the barracks—the guards we've called in from the reserves . . ."

Dread dropped into my stomach. They were stationed outside the wards.

"Fuck," August cursed. "Shai, tell me you have sight on them."

Shai was already reaching out with his mind. "They're sequestered in the barracks, but it won't hold for long. The Moroi are clawing at the doors and shutters."

"How many are stationed out there?" I asked, afraid to know.

Jophiel went rigid. "More than half of our total forces."

Thousands—*thousands* of our army were out there at the mercy of the Moroi. "Do they have enough arrows?" A rowan wood arrow or Galorian silver through the heart could kill the Moroi, that or beheading them. Little else would stop them.

August shook his head. " If they do, they'd be in the armory, and for that—"

"They'd have to leave the barracks," I finished. "*Fuck.*"

I glanced back at the edges of the city, where buildings met mountainside. The translucent wards were cracking, distorting as the monsters tore at them. They were close to breaking through.

The familiars shifted in preparation to fight, each donning their true, menacing forms. Many of the guards paled, eyes going wide.

Jophiel turned, yelling to the other guards. "Ready the archers!"

"They won't reach them from here," Nic said, facing August, "and neither can you."

My brother had already begun to gather storm clouds above the city, but we were too far away for August to be as precise as he needed to be to strike with lightning. Without perfect accuracy, he could hit the Moroi *or* the barracks below.

"We have to go to them." Nic moved closer to the wall, flame beginning to lick down her arms. Turning the creatures to ash, with either flame or lightning, would also kill them.

"That may be what they want—what Adrienne wants if she is indeed behind this: to draw you out," Jophiel said, taking Nic's arm to pull her back, undeterred by the fire. "You expose yourself if you leave this castle. That might not even be all of them, and gods know what they have waiting to ambush you in the forest. You can't—"

Piercing screams reached us. The Moroi had broken into the barracks.

The winged monsters swooped down, carrying humans and faeries upward. The soldiers shrieked, unable to defend themselves. The few elementals among them tried using water and air to push them back, some creating earthen shields, but it only delayed the inevitable. The Moroi either severed a limb that would cause them to bleed out in minutes, ripped out their throats, or simply ripped them apart. This wasn't a feeding—it was a massacre.

"We're going," August overruled Jophiel. "We can't stay here while—"

"No."

All of our gazes snapped to the watch tower door.

Misha stood on the threshold of the open doors, golden hair billowing around her face, wrapped in her pink dressing gown. Rasalas had moved to her side, standing a head above her in his true form.

"Misha." I went to her, not knowing how long she'd been standing there, what she'd heard, or how she'd react to the bloodshed.

She held out a hand, stalling me, and went to her sister. "You're not going, Nicky."

"Misha, we have to. There's no other way."

"*No*," Misha said again. She stood straighter, firmer than she had in weeks. Misha turned to me. "We can go."

Her blue eyes pleaded with mine, asking permission to let her make me into the beast again—one capable of ending this. I thought of the blood on my hands from the last time I'd become the dragon and looked out over the city once more.

This wasn't the same.

I cupped Misha's face in my hands as I spoke to the others. "Make a small break in the wards and bottleneck the Moroi as they come through. I will herd them to you." I looked up, meeting Nic's eyes. "You aren't the only one capable of breathing fire."

Jophiel's eyes flared excitedly. "That would work, and the scales would protect him better than any armor."

"Brother." August came to my side. I turned, meeting his gaze. "Are you sure?"

I hesitated, but Misha slid her hands into mine. "He'll be safe. I'm going with him."

I began to argue, to say it wouldn't be safe for her, but when I stared down at Misha, searching her face, I saw her eyes flash—what she planned to do—and smiled.

"No. It's not safe. What if they pluck you off his back?" Nic seethed, coming around to face her sister, pulling her away from me. "How are you to defend yourself against monsters like that?" She pointed to where the Moroi continued thrashing against the wards with fingers that ended in inches-long talons.

Misha let go of my hand to squeeze her sister's. "Trust me, Nicky."

Nic stayed silent for a moment, warring with herself, as she examined her twin's face. "Okay," she whispered, letting go of Misha's hand.

Her other hand still grasped in mine, Misha and I walked to the edge of the turret. Clasping her waist, I lifted her, setting her on the edge of the stone railing. I climbed up after her.

Misha turned, blue eyes piercing as they met mine. *I love you.*

We stepped off the ledge.

CHAPTER 25
Misha

S ince I'd awoken, I had been calling forth my magic.

All of the grief, guilt, and rage that had been drowning me bubbled until it was overflowing, feeding me and the darkness within.

I gave myself over to it as the magic burned through every part of me, hitting its peak as Julian and I fell.

I no longer tried to stop it.

The magic shifted, transforming him—transforming *me*.

And darkness I became.

CHAPTER 26
Nic

M isha and Julian fell.

A moment later, Julian rose in his dragon form, pale silver in the moonlight. He flew above the turret and hesitated, great wings beating.

Misha wasn't on his back.

I rushed to the edge to peer over but was knocked back by a gust of wind. August caught me by the shoulders, halting my fall.

Spiraling toward the night sky flew another dragon, black as the darkness between stars—her eyes blazing the same furious blue I'd spent an entire life beside.

"*Gods.*"

Misha banked, letting out a roar and wave of fire that swept above us, bright as a rising sun. She sailed around the turret before she and Julian rejoined, flying wingtip to wingtip toward the Moroi.

I took a moment, just one second, to admire my sister.

She hadn't let the darkness break her.

Breaking everyone's stunned awe, Jophiel shouted, "Get into position!"

Pulled from my amazement, I squeezed August's hand. The others moved away from us, putting distance between themselves and the magic we would need to cast.

Archers knocked rowan arrows into their bows on the levels above. Miranda chanted, arms raised as she worked to open a hole in the wards.

Moments later, it opened. Moroi flooded through in a black mass of leathery wings and fangs.

The two dragons split to come at them from each side. Both Misha and Julian roared, billowing flame pulsing from their throats. The Moroi that tried to dive into the city were extinguished. The remaining were herded by the dragons, chased by trails of fire, straight for us.

"On my signal!" Jophiel commanded.

August and I raised our hands.

Their large, leathery wings beat in the air. The Moroi flew closer until I could see the blood dripping from their fangs and smell the blood on their breath.

I braced myself, planting my feet, and shoved down any fear. August's warmth at my back gave me strength.

"Now!"

Fire erupted from my outstretched hands, a vortex of flame. The Moroi screeched as they were hit by the inferno, tumbling back as they fell apart into ash.

From the right, August battered them with spears of lightning, striking down one after another. The archers struck true, catching any that evaded us. The bodies of dead Moroi crashed onto the streets and roofs below, pierced through the heart. Any that made it to the turret were torn apart by Ker or Rasalas. Eilith flew above, using her talons to rip into any that got close to August and me.

When it was done, ash rained down upon the city, coating it like autumn's first snow.

CHAPTER 27
Misha

Not all of the Moroi had gone through the wards into the city. A hundred or so remained outside, massacring the guards and civilians who lived beyond the wards.

I banked and dove.

Julian roared behind me, but I didn't heed his warning—I couldn't—not as I watched the Moroi rip apart innocent humans and faeries below. I soared through the gap in the wards, flying toward the barracks. As I flew closer, I held my fire, unsure if I could keep from scorching the humans and Fae along with the monsters.

Not that there were many left.

Between the survivors fighting for their lives, bodies were strewn across the ground, the soil and grass soaked red with blood as the Moroi feasted. Even the High Fae armed with rowan wood arrows did little against the onslaught.

I landed in a clearing in the thickest of them. The Moroi grouped, flying toward me to attack. I reared, fire lighting up the sky. Those that escaped the flames I tore apart with taloned forelegs and teeth. I ripped off their wings and heads, shredding through them and tossing the remains into the forest as I gave the remaining guards and civilians the chance to run inside the protection of the wards.

Several of the winged monsters jumped onto my back, attempting to tear through my scales with their talons. I thrashed, knocking them off as I snapped at them with my jaws.

Fire rained over us, turning them to ash as the flames skittered across my scales unharmed. Dragons could not burn.

Julian flew overhead and banked.

The Moroi surrounding me had been demolished in his sweep, and he flew after the few remaining, cutting them off before they could escape into the mountains.

Free of the monsters, I reared, beating my wings as I prepared to take off and join him—

Pain lanced through my right wing.

I roared, whipping my head around to see a spear of rowan wood, tipped in Galorian silver, lodged there.

Blood gushed from the wound as the spear sapped most of my remaining magic. I'd already used so much in Julian's and my transition. I was plunged back into my Fae form, sprawling into the dirt, the spear beside me. I clutched my arm where it bled at my triceps, trying to staunch the bleeding.

I held my breath, waiting. Listening.

Unsettling clicking came from the forest around me.

My heart thudded in panic. If one of the Moroi found me or scented me by my blood . . .

With my remaining magic, I called to the earth. Maple leaves fell from the tree above, wrapping around me as I coated myself until I was completely covered. I willed the leaves to harden, forming a sort of leafen armor. Once it was done, I scrambled, pushing off the ground with the rowan wood spear in my hand.

As swiftly as I could, I ran through the forest back toward the wards.

I was so deconditioned, each breath coming painfully, my steps slower than they'd ever been. The back of my arm was still bleeding from where my dragon's wing had been hit, healing much more gradually due to the rowan wood. Thankfully, it wasn't bleeding as profusely as if the artery had been severed. I wrapped my magic around it in a sort of tourniquet of vines as I kept running.

The trees grew thicker as I went. I dodged their trunks, leaping over fallen logs and stones in my terror. *Please let Julian be okay.*

I stopped short, skidding across the earth as I sensed it. Someone—something—was following me.

The clicking returned—the sound the Moroi used to sense vibrations. To track their prey in total darkness.

I held my breath, holding completely still except for my hand flexing on the rowan wood spear.

The brush rustled to my right, and I slowly turned my head. Twice my size and approximately ten meters away, the monster was walking on all fours, its taloned hands scraping along the ground. Its arms were winged, each nearly as long as the beast was tall. Still dripping from its fangs, the only sound was the blood splattering upon the earth.

Slowly, it turned and saw me.

The Moroi screeched, hackles rising as it lunged.

I dove out of the way as the monster crashed into the space I'd been only a second before. Dirt sprayed, its talons coming away empty. As the Moroi snarled, turning on me once more, I swung the spear. The blunt end smashed into the monster's face, spraying black blood as its head whipped back. It quickly righted itself, roaring, but I was already spinning the spear.

With all my might, I slammed the Galorian silver end into its chest, where its black, beatless heart resided.

The Moroi staggered back, bellowing in pain. The creature's body hit the ground hard, the wooden shaft protruding from between its ribs.

Dead.

My knees hit the dirt as I took deep, gulping breaths, my hands shaking.

"Impressive, princess."

I whipped around.

A Seraph male stalked toward me from between the trees. Long, silver hair braided down his back. In the darkness, his eyes were bright and gold as amber. Great white, feathered wings rose above his tan shoulders, glistening in the light of the full moon.

"You must be one of the Briars." His smile was cruel—vicious. His sword gleamed as he drew it from its scabbard, white light dancing along the blade. "You look just like your father but with your mother's face. Curious."

"And you are?"

I had no other weapon, the spear irretrievably stuck in the Moroi's chest. It would waste precious time to regain it.

I subtly sunk one palm into the dirt. I hadn't practiced the witch part of myself—a mistake, I realized, as the reserve within my chest was nearly drained—but I felt a small part of the earth, the life within, reaching out for me.

There.

The male threw his head back and laughed. "Surely you know your history, young Briar. You know who you stand before."

My memory conjured up his face but no name. Yes, I knew of him . . . in theory. He was supposed to be dead—one of the endless generals Alé had bested in the Great War, but there were so many that I had been bored to tears trying to remember all their names and titles during my tutoring.

Surely, a Seraph would stand out among the droves of those Alesia had slain. *Gods above, what was his name?*

It hit me, and I gasped. "General Carr!"

The Seraph fumed. "I am of the purest line of Seraphim, blessed directly by—"

"Harr?" I cut him off, guessing again. The magic was still forming, slower than I'd hoped, and the longer I kept him talking, the better. "Shit, that's not right . . . was it General Garr? Does it at least rhyme? Help a lady out."

"You little shit. Just like your moth—"

The *nerve.*

I held up my free hand, stopping him. "No need to be so emotional, Tarr. You can't expect everyone to remember *one* General who died over a hundred years ago."

My hand beneath the soil pulsed. Almost done.

I went on. "What if I started at the beginning of the alphabet and worked my way to it? Would you let me know when I've got it, Arr?"

The Seraph's eyes blazed with fury, his knuckles white on the hilt of his sword. To him, being forgotten was a fate worse than death.

"But you clearly know who I am," I went on, painting on a cocky smile. A mask I'd worn so many times before. "The daughter of the two most powerful Fae to exist. So please, do introduce yourself so we are on familiar footing."

The Seraph's face morphed into a snarl of rage, and all those years of practice I had baiting Nic into attacking during our training worked. He lunged.

I ducked beneath his gleaming sword. Out of time, I yanked with the witch gift, pulling the power from the earth and life around me. Death swept out in a circle: grass died and trees shriveled, their leaves dropping like fluttering husks.

The Seraph leapt into the air just in time, right before the decay hit his feet.

Shit, would have been nice if that had hit him.

The iron and carbon I had been summoning from the earth hardened in my hand, forming a steel sword whose hilt I now grasped. Above me, the male landed and struck, his sword crashing into mine. My arm shook from the impact, weak from disuse, and most of my strength had gone to slaying the Moroi.

I slid beneath him, slicing through both of the calcaneal tendons in the back of each ankle. As Fae, he would heal, but not quickly enough to stand.

Spinning around, I expected to find him knelt on the ground. The trees were too close together, their branches too low for him to use his wings effectively. But somehow, the injury only slightly hindered him. Golden light festered around his wounds, stitching the tendons back together as he stood.

It made no sense. Seraphim couldn't be healers. That was a High Fae gift.

His smile was lethal as he clasped the pendant, a golden locket, hanging from his neck. "A gift from your stepmother."

As he stalked toward me once again, Alesia's voice sounded in my mind: *Go for the wings, always the wings.*

When he lunged this time, I feinted, slicing my sword through the top bend of his wing, where the most important tendons and muscles lay.

The Seraph gave a cruel laugh. "Did your aunt teach you that, young Briar? Her training couldn't have been sufficient if she let herself be murdered so easily. An arrow through the back, wasn't it?" The wound was already healing. "How common."

"She taught me enough to kill you." I lunged again.

I needed to pierce him through the heart or decapitate him. Even a healer's magic wouldn't save him from those injuries.

The Seraph's height and bulk made him slower than I was. His sword, though gleaming with starlight, trailed behind me as I moved.

My muscles began to scream, burning with exertion. I'd gotten so damned weak from weeks of sleep under the poison, from the time after when I'd laid in bed, withering in my grief.

He brought his large sword down. I had no strength to block it, so I dove, rolling out of the way. Earth sprayed at the impact. I flicked a hand, casting the dirt back toward him and into his face.

He hissed as the dirt hit his eyes, momentarily stunning him, and I plunged my sword straight through his gut.

Snarling, he gripped the blade and yanked it, pulling the hilt from my grip. With a groan, he drew the sword out. The wound knitted together as the blade withdrew.

"That was incredibly stupid."

Using my own sword, he struck at me. I rolled away as the blade struck empty dirt. He struck again with his own on my opposite side, nearly slicing through my hand where it laid on the ground.

The Seraph made to strike again, and my muscles burned, near to giving out. I winnowed to escape the blow, but the power within me was nearly drained, and I appeared only a few feet away.

Unable to winnow again, I called to the earth, forming a shield between him and me, and prayed that it was strong enough to block him as the male brought both blades down upon me. I crouched, bracing myself for impact.

A sharp clang rang out, but the blow never came.

Peeking around my earthen shield, I saw a familiar sword, the golden hilt embedded with sapphires, blocking the Seraph's—the Iradelmar.

"Get the fuck away from my sister." Nic snarled as she pushed against his blades, aided by a blast of fire that sent the male skittering backward and thudding hard against a tree, his white wings splaying wide.

The Seraph righted himself, chuckling softly. "Both sisters. You make my job too easy."

"And who are you?" Nic asked, her slitted eyes assessing him.

I couldn't help it. A laugh bubbled up my throat as the Seraph's smile dropped, his face morphed by cold rage. Watching the warrior's face fall in wounded pride, then twist into near-mindless fury, was bliss.

Snarling, he launched himself from the tree. Their swords met again, emitting a pulsing ripple through the night.

Nic and the Seraph matched each other, blow for blow.

My sister was properly armed, but more than that, she'd been training with Jophiel for months now. She understood the Seraph's maneuvers, had taken thorough time learning, and now enacted them perfectly. She was faster than she'd ever been, yet she still moved like our aunt, fierce and unyielding.

I could have sworn the Seraph's face paled as he realized the same. This fight had thrust him back a hundred years to the battlefield where he'd been slain.

He looked as if he was fighting a ghost.

Nic had to be nearly drained from the fire blast I'd seen her cast, and yet not a single muscle quivered. She was fearfully beautiful to behold.

I knew if Alesia could see her now, she'd be incandescent with pride as she watched Nicole.

. . .But what would she have seen of me?

She'd have seen me wallowing in my grief and self-hatred, letting myself grow atrophied and frail. Alesia and Eve had dedicated their lives to ensuring Nic and I could defend ourselves, strengthened in both body and spirit. And as soon as they were gone, I'd done the opposite.

I'd let myself grow weak.

Never again would I let my aunts down. Never again would I let myself grow so vulnerable that I'd need to be saved by my sister, no matter how much I appreciated her.

I jumped at the nudge on my shoulder. Turning, I saw Rasalas, still in his familiar form.

I wrapped an arm under his leg from where I still knelt. His head loomed above me protectively as we watched my sister battle with the Seraph. If Rasalas was here, Eilith had to be close by, but it didn't look as if my sister needed her familiar's help. Nic and the male met blade for blade, strike for strike.

My sister left shallow slashes across the Seraph's body and wings, enough to maim but not kill. As they healed with his stolen magic, I saw Nic's eyes narrow in recognition. She changed her tactics.

Nic winnowed away, and he spun around, readying himself to attack when she reemerged.

When several moments passed, he laughed. "A coward, eh?" he shouted into the space where she'd disappeared. "Alesia Sancrista would be so disappointed! The only Fae who ever bested me, only to have her prodigy become a *coward*, running at the first whiff of blood."

But Nic would never run.

He whirled on me, halting at the sight of Rasalas, who was now snarling. A hawk's cry reverberated through the air.

"Go ahead," I taunted as Eilith cut through the canopy and landed, shifting from hawk to beast in a flash. "Let's see whose wings are mightier."

Eilith dove toward him. The Seraph lifted a wing wreathed in starlight, casting the familiar sprawling across the earth. She righted herself, her beak flaring in a piercing screech but withholding another charge.

All to give Nic the perfect moment.

The Seraph still had his wings splayed when she materialized above him. She brought down the Iradelmar upon the base of his wing, slicing through it entirely.

The male roared in pain as the white feathers fell to the dirt. Blood spewed from his back.

He could heal it, but he would need help to reset the wing and align the tendons and nerves just right, or risk losing the ability to fly. To do this, he would have to reach another healer within minutes.

August and Jophiel winnowed into the clearing. August called lightning into his free hand, ready to cast it toward the Seraph, but hesitated, deferring to his commander.

"Mikaela," the Seraph snarled as he saw Jophiel, his face morphed by disdain.

Jophiel stood tall. Her blue eyes blazed with matched hatred as she stared him down. "Zarr."

I snapped, pointing. "*That's* it."

The Seraph—General Zarr—looked between Jophiel and my sister, knowing he couldn't successfully strike at either, not with August's crackling bolt of lightning ready to fly from his hand. He had a choice: lose what he came for or lose his wing.

Zarr chose himself.

"I'll see you soon." The male winnowed away, the words a threat to both Jophiel and Nic.

We stared at the empty space where he'd once been. It didn't feel real. None of tonight did. That was until I felt the burning pain return to my arm.

"We need to go," August said gently, interrupting our thoughts.

I nodded, stepping forward to take Nic's hand so she could winnow me. I needed to save any remaining magic for Julian. I clasped my sister's hand as August winnowed, taking Jophiel with him back to the castle.

My palm slid into my twin's. "How did you know where I was?"

"When your dragon disappeared, I winnowed to the clearing past the wards, where I'd last seen you. Then I noticed these." She gestured behind me. Tiny pink rose buds pushed up from the ground, unfurling in the moonlight at each place my blood had fallen. "I followed them, and they led me to you."

I squeezed my sister's hand. "You always find me." Even in the depths of my own despair.

Her lips curved upward. "Always. Now, let's go. Your arm needs mending." I nodded as she said, "And we need to figure out how the hell Rainier Zarr rose from the dead."

PART II:
The Prophecy

CHAPTER 28
Misha

We winnowed to the rows of barracks as the sun began to peer out from behind the mountains—the end of a nightmare of a night.

Julian, still in his silver dragon form, was in one of the quads, covered in black blood with the bodies of the Moroi littered around him. I returned him to his Fae form, easier now that I'd done it once before. The Moroi had scratched and torn at any spots of his skin uncovered by the scales when he was the dragon, leaving behind deep gashes when he shifted.

As Damian worked to heal them, I reached for Julian, clasping his face. "I'm so sorry."

"I'm okay, love." Julian's smile fell to a grimace as he reacted to the sting of flesh knitting back together.

I looked down, unable to meet his eyes. I should have never agreed to transform him. I should have gone on my own and—

He lifted my chin, bringing my gaze back to his. "Don't, love." Grey storm clouds whirled within his irises. "Don't blame yourself."

"But—"

"No. I agreed for you to turn me. I knew the risk." He wrapped his arm around me, pulling me beneath the blanket covering him.

I brought my hands to his chest to steady myself, feeling his heartbeat beneath my palm. "But I could have—"

"Do not say go alone. That was never an option." Julian held me tighter. He kissed me softly, gently on the cheek. I could have melted into him, becoming one being.

After he was healed, Damian focused on my arm. It was quick work for the healer, and then, we dispersed back into the city.

Jophiel, Teale, and August scattered to the outposts, assessing the loss of life and searching for answers. Shai and Celeste stayed in the city, leading the search for wounded soldiers and winnowing them to the infirmary. Her eagles scouted from above—adding to the eyes Celeste had to find them as fast as possible—so she could relay locations to Shai through his mindcasting.

Many of those they found were too late to be helped.

In the infirmary, Damian and the other healers worked, saving who they could. Miranda worked beside him, cleaning and healing the gouges left by the monsters on the guards and civilians.

Nic and I helped those with minor injuries or stabilized the more brutal ones until a healer was free. We didn't have the gift of healing, but Eve had taught us that much—how to clean a wound, the measures one needed to take to save a life, and how to know when someone wasn't going to make it, healer or no.

Simon and Sena were called for the Fae and humans who wouldn't survive the day. They prayed over them, giving blessings to whichever god the injured preferred. They kneeled with them, hands clasped, and offered reassuring words to give the wounded the relief they could before they passed beyond the veil.

It was near dusk when we finally gathered in one of the now-abandoned barracks. It was the first one the Moroi had broken into, and not a single solider had survived. The bodies had been moved; they would be preserved and given to the mourning families, who would honor them passing rights, saying goodbye to their loved ones for the last time—and yet not.

I had to say goodbye to Alesia, Eve, and my father daily. Every time the wind blew their similar scents. Every time the warmth of the sun felt like the gentle pressure of their hand. With each one, each memory, I lost them again and again, so was there really ever a final goodbye?

Each of the Seven pulled up a chair in the center of the room. It was skeletal, with its long spinal rows of empty beds. Gemma was seated by Shai, shaken from the attack but demanding to be here. She had helped in whatever way she could, fetching bandages and tonic for the healers or helping Sena pray.

Every one of us was filthy and should have been starving, as we hadn't eaten in over a day. But one look around the room told me no one felt hungry, not with the unease we all felt after the attack.

Sena sat beside her son, speaking to Julian in low tones, her eyes dark with motherly concern.

I took the chair on Julian's other side but couldn't meet his eyes. Even though he was now healed, I could only see the blood that had covered him and the deep gashes marring his brown skin.

Julian reached for my chair, and I jumped. He pulled it, scraping metal across the floor until I was flush against him.

"Jul—"

He shook his head, hands sliding up my legs to my waist. Reaching my hips, he lifted, pulling me into his lap. His lips brushed my ear. "I need to hold you, love. Please." Julian's hand brushed my arm where I'd been wounded, as if he needed to feel again that it was gone.

A breath loosed out of me as I relaxed against him. After the carnage we'd seen, I couldn't blame him—I needed the reassurance of his touch just as much.

"Are you still blaming yourself?" he asked, fingers gently dancing on my skin.

I couldn't answer, the words caught in my throat. I could only hold onto him tighter.

"The scales and talons protected me, Misha. You made me into something better able to protect everything I love." Julian grasped me tighter. "The attack would have been so much worse if it weren't for you and your magic."

My magic, the ability to turn him and me into dragons. The same magic that had left a circle of death in the forest, stealing the life from the earth.

I remembered the rest of the room and reluctantly pulled away. My face burned furiously as I glanced at Sena, though her eyes were thankfully averted. I moved back to my chair, but Julian kept his arm around my waist, holding me close.

Nic and August took their seats across from us, and everyone grew quiet. The sun had set not long before, and the dimming light cast long shadows throughout the room. My sister spelled bobbing faerie lights above us, illuminating the space. Miranda and August had already warded the large room. No one would overhear us.

"Miranda, Sena, and I have reset the wards around the city," August spoke first. "We cast them farther out to cover the remaining soldiers. All civilians have been evacuated into the city itself."

"How many did we lose?" Simon asked hesitantly, afraid of the answer.

August took a deep breath. "The generals are still counting, traveling to the further outposts, but right now, the rough estimate is between four and five thousand casualties in total of both soldiers and civilians."

"Gods." Simon's skin went ashen. Celeste sat back, cursing under her breath.

"And that's just here," Jophiel said. "Word from the generals so far is that the further outposts were hit first with no warning. Many have no survivors. We were lucky to get the brief warning we did."

"So that number is only going to rise?" Simon asked.

Jophiel nodded, looking like she might retch onto the floor. The air in the room grew thick as we understood the gravity of the situation. After this strike, Adrienne and Evander's combined forces would outnumber ours—greatly.

Celeste broke the silence. "How is Rainier Zarr alive?"

"It's impossible," Shai said. "Alesia plunged her sword through his chest in the center of the battlefield. I saw it. Everyone did."

"And yet tonight we saw him. I fought him," Nic said. "Clearly *not* dead. How?" She turned to Jophiel, looking for an answer.

"After Alesia defeated him one-to-one, the rebel line charged, renewed by her victory. The area they'd fought was swarmed within seconds. We were sure he was dead—no being, even Seraphim, could survive a blow like that—so no one worried about the body. Good riddance if it had been crushed in the surge." Jophiel's eyes were distant and glazed, a ghost of the pain from her time living beneath him. "I should have checked. Been sure."

August turned to her, but his voice was tinged with the same regret. "We couldn't have known."

"Let me guess," Nic said. "The Deimos were also at this particular battle."

August indicated he, Shai, and Jophiel. "We were all there, fighting. None of us would have noticed them slipping away with the body and finding a healer to mend him."

Julian's arm tightened around me. "And Adrienne did what . . . kept him hidden in some hole in the ground so no one would know? An ace in her back pocket for just in case?"

"Seems like it," August answered.

"How many of these cards does Adrienne have left?" Julian questioned, the frustration in his clenched jaw. "How is any of it possible? Because the Moroi had to have been her work as well."

"She used the skinwalkers to track you, but what if the shadowhounds were her, too?" August turned to Nic, remembering how she'd been attacked by the beings as she fled to the North through the Redwood after our aunts' murders.

"It could have been. Bidding these beings to do her work, stealing magic, and watching us through mirrors . . ." Nic scowled. "All of this is beyond Fae magic. I want to know how she's doing it."

"There are stories," Miranda started, "among the witches. Tales our grandmothers used to keep children in line, of wicked witch sisters who defected from traditional magic, no longer calling upon nature and the celestial bodies—the remnants of the Siphon's power. They instead call upon a different god to fuel their magic. To feed him and themselves, they snatch life from humans and faeries who wander too close to their home in the dark woods. It scared the hell out of me when my abuela would tell it growing up."

"That sounds like Adrienne's magic theft, the of stealing hearts. The magic and life intertwined," I said, my brows creasing in confusion. "But how is that possible? To call upon a god?"

"It hasn't been possible for centuries," Sena said, breaking her silence. "Millennia ago, the gods often intervened in our affairs, walking among the beings of the earth and sky as corporeal as you and me."

Miranda shuddered. "But only one god would grant magic like this, and he exacts a horrible price for his . . . gifts."

"Which god?" Nic asked.

"The Void," Sena answered.

Nic's brow knitted together in confusion, a mirror to my own. Gemma looked equally as lost. "The Void?"

"Yes," Sena went on. "*L'appel du vide* is how he is spoken of in my birth language, which translates as 'the Call of the Void.' The phrase describes the thoughts that jump unbidden into your head, the ones that call to darkness or some evil. Those that tell you to take one more step off that ledge. That is of the Void."

I sat up, leaning closer. "If this is a god, then why have none of us heard of him?"

Sena's onyx eyes pierced through mine. "Because after his battle with whom you refer to as the Son—the first High Fae—he became known to the Fae as the Fallen."

I went utterly still. "The Fallen is dead."

"If Adrienne Deimos and the witches Miranda speaks of can call upon his power, then maybe not." Sena held out her hand, a scroll appearing there. "The gods' history is important for context. You, the elementals and animaglia—" She nodded to Nic, Gemma, and me, then pointed to three shrouded figures on the manuscript surrounded by symbols of the elements and different plants and animals. "—refer to these three as the Father, Mother, and Son. For simplicity, I will refer to them as I know them: the Between—the Father—god of the earth and all its elements, along with the humans, animals, and their breath of life—healing. His wife is the Made—the Mother—the human who became a goddess with the Between's magic. Their child is the Risen, who, possessing each of his father's gifts, became the first High Fae and who is the originator of the elemental, healer, and animaglia lines—or the Son."

Sena pointed to another figure higher on the scroll, one surrounded by celestial bodies and storm clouds. Great wings sprouted from her back. "The Goddess of the Above, equal in power to the Between, controlled the sky: the weather, stars, and sun. She was also the Goddess of War. She reveled in conflict but grew bored of the elemental Fae battles, so she created two new lines."

"The Stormcasters and Seraphim," I said, and she nodded.

"The Above took the two greatest warriors from each side in a human war and gifted them with a kernel of her magic: one with lightning, wind, and rain, and the other with sun and starlight. And thus, two new lines of Fae were born."

"A bit callous," I murmured.

Julian squeezed my hand, softly smiling. "When the gods yield some of their magic, they themselves become more like us, like the humans. They lose some of their heartlessness and are more capable of empathy and love. Lore says the Above fell in love with one of the soldiers she created, giving up her immortality for the female."

"Some say that she loved *both* soldiers she empowered." Sena smiled. "This is why their descendants are not enemies but allies." Sena moved her finger down the scroll to the bottom, pointing to a vast figure with darkness shrouding him, who took up most of the bottom of the page. "The Void—or the Fallen—is here. He controls shadows, death, and mental manipulation. *L'appel du vide*," she repeated.

"Originator of the mindcasters," Shai acknowledged, his jaw hard. Gemma set a hand on his arm. His eyes softened as they met hers.

Sena nodded and went on. "The Void rules death, but he cannot grant life like the Between and the Made. He can only steal it, feasting upon it to grow his own power."

"Like the skinwalkers and Moroi?" Nic pieced together.

Sena nodded. "Beings that feed upon another's life force, either by inhabiting their body or draining them of blood fall under his control. So, the shadowhounds, too, as well as other creatures of darkness."

"Which god are the witches descended from?" I asked, curious.

On Sena's other side, Miranda reached forward, indicating a figure near the bottom right corner. "The Siphon." The goddess was depicted as smaller than the others, but tendrils of her magic floated out to the edges of the page. "But witches call her the Mother."

"That is why, to avoid confusion, the priestesses refer to the Fae Mother as the Made, and the Witch Mother as the Siphon," Sena said, clarifying.

"The Siphon is a unique goddess," Miranda went on. "Beholden to none of the three realms—the sky of the Above, the earth of the Between, or the below of the Void—she has a mixture of all the gods' powers, though the diversity makes her less powerful in any particular area. What sets her apart is that she also has the ability to drain power from another god, but not like the Void can. The Void requires death to steal magic. The Siphon can simply . . . borrow it. Hence her name."

Sena leaned forward, fingers brushing the parchment. "The Void and the Siphon were once betrothed, though she was forced into it and never accepted their mating. She took steps to ensure she never produced children with him. Then, one day, she met a human man and fell in love with him. She became pregnant with his child, a daughter that would become the first witch. Terrified the Void would kill her and the unborn child for her betrayal, the Siphon fled and escaped to the earth, but not before she stole magic from each of the other gods, weakening them. Then the Siphon recanted that magic, pushing it out into the earth and sky for her descendants to forever draw upon. This made her nearly human, successfully hiding her amongst them.

"The Void, shamed and vengeful, wanted to hunt the Siphon upon the earth but could not as it was the Between's domain. When the Between refused to allow him passage, it led to war between them. The Void was more powerful since the Between's mating with the Made—his transfer of immortality and power to her—had significantly weakened him. The Void battled with them, and though the Above sided against him, he nearly won. The Void was only finally defeated by the Son. He was able to overcome the Void but perished, giving his life to end his opponent's. Afterward, the fallen god's body was cast away and sealed into a tomb, one no one has ever found. Then, the Between and the Made resurrected their son fully into a god, and he became known as the Risen . . . but such power came with a cost. Those three gods gave up their tether to this world and are now only able to watch from behind the Veil, unable to walk among us as they once had."

"So, what happened to the Above?" I asked, turning to Sena. "Why does she no longer intervene?"

"Rather than making her loves into gods like the Between, the Above cast her magic out among the sky and stars, letting her immortality fade to be with her chosen, becoming mortal like the Siphon—or as mortal as the High Fae are. She died and passed beyond the Veil as we all will one day."

Nic clicked her tongue, piecing it together. "So, if the Son—the Risen—didn't actually kill the Void and only entrapped him somehow, he would be the only god left in our realm. The Void would be able to commune with those who call upon him?"

Sena shook her head. "The other gods can still commune with those on the earth. They hear our prayers but cannot do as much as before they went behind the Veil. Their interventions would be small compared to what they once were."

"Small like turning a tribe of watercasters into the Sirens?" I asked, remembering Alesia's story. The Son had resurrected and healed them, before the Mother gifted them their deadly song, fangs, and talons.

Sena nodded. "But each expenditure further separates them from us. Now their influence only comes in whispers."

"So how is Adrienne drawing upon the Void?" Nic asked, looking between Sena and Miranda. "Because that is exactly what she is doing: using his creatures to hunt us and his tactics to steal magic from hearts."

"Mindcasters," Sena began, "were created to hunt the Siphon upon their earth and report back to the Void with their minds, so their tie to him is stronger. Just as mine and Jophiel's bond is greatest to the Above."

I glanced from the corner of my eye to Shai, tense. I told myself he wasn't Adrienne—that just because the Void created his line didn't mean he would commit such atrocities.

"But Adrienne's amount of communication with the Void seems greater than that," Sena acknowledged. "The only explanation I can think of is that she found his tomb and made some deal with him. If so, it's likely she shares the magic she steals with him, feeding his own."

"*Fuck*," Julian cursed.

"And he wants us—our hearts," Nic said, glancing up at me. "All of this began with Adrienne wanting to steal our magic."

Sena nodded. "You two are descended from both Fae and witch, possessing two gifts a piece." Something flashed in her eyes. "And not just multiple gifts, but firecasting and an animaglia with the ability to transform. These are each powers that have been gone for centuries. As the magic of this world has been slowly waning among the magic wielders, you and your sister's has done the opposite."

"Could all animaglia transform once?" Celeste asked, leaning forward to rest her elbows on her knees.

Sena nodded. "The animaglia's power, like the elementals, has faded through the generations. Before, elementals could control all—not just one element—and animaglia could transform into all manner of animals. The last documented was of the Etherii line, a predecessor of the former High King who could become a lion at will."

A lion. I felt for my magic as it slowly replenished in my chest. This morning, I'd become a dragon, but as I tugged on the magic, feeling it curl and spread around my ribs, I felt as if I could do so much more. An image of wings flickered in my vision.

"So, how do we stop Adrienne? Because an attack like last night cannot happen again." August asked Sena, his hand on Nic's back. Protective.

"I will ask around," Miranda answered instead. "See if there is a way to track down the witches from the stories. If any witches are communing with the Void, we could speak to them and see what they know. But it may come with a cost."

"Do it," August said. "Whatever resources you need, they're yours."

"I have an idea, but you're not going to like it," Miranda said, looking apologetically at August, then Nic.

"What?" my sister asked.

"I need one of the dead Moroi to use its blood to scry for the Void's influence, and—" She glanced between me and Nic. "—If I find the witches, you'll have to be the ones to go to them. If Adrienne wants your hearts for the Void, the witches will, too."

CHAPTER 29
Nic

N o," August said, voice adamant.

I turned, straightening as I faced him. "That isn't your choice to make."

He stared down at me, silver eyes blazing. "I don't care what information we might glean from them. It isn't worth the risk."

"If it could mean preventing another massacre like the one last night?" I challenged. "What then?"

August's jaw ticked, eyes blazing with the words he wouldn't say aloud. I could see it on his face—he'd let another thousand die so long as I was kept from danger, but that wasn't the answer a king was supposed to give.

He swallowed, avoiding the question. "We don't even know if Miranda can find them."

"So let her try," I said. "If she finds the witches, we can decide then."

Even then, I wasn't sure either of us would budge. If the witches were found, I would go to them for information, no matter the cost. And August would never let it happen.

He hesitated for a few moments. "Fine," August ground out.

We'd have this fight later.

"But until then," Jophiel said, unflinching as August's hard gaze met hers. "Do we retaliate?"

"Yes," Celeste snarled. The sentiment was shared by the majority of us.

"No," Shai countered. "We took a devastating blow to our forces tonight. If we retaliate out of anger, we risk exposing ourselves. Adrienne and Evander will expect it and thus will be much more prepared than we are."

"I agree," the Seraph said. "We need to regroup. They won't launch an assault on us here with their troops. So, we find out how to stop Adrienne's dark magic, preventing another attack like tonight, and we plan from there."

"And do nothing?" Celeste spat. "You would have us lick our wounds, cowering like scared animals?"

"I would have us be *wise*," Jophiel snarled. "Not run blindly into bloodthirsty revenge."

Celeste leaned forward to argue further—

"*Enough*," August commanded. "I agree with Jophiel and Shai. We need to speak to our own generals, find out exactly how much we lost tonight, and rebuild. Give Simon time with the spies to gather as much information as he can about what Adrienne and Evander might do next. And Teale—" He turned to the demi-Dryad, his face cold. "—find out why the nymphs didn't warn us of this."

The Seven took that as their dismissal, each leaving to deal with the aftermath of the attack. Gemma went with them, softly murmuring to Shai.

"Sena." I reached for her arm as she passed, halting her. "There's something else—something my sister and I have been meaning to ask you about."

From my sides, I slowly drew the swords that had once been our mother's and Alesia's.

It was time.

Misha stood, a flash of pain crossing her face as she thought of our aunt and mother, and moved to hover over the Iradelmar and Mercedelmar.

"Do you want us to stay, love?" Julian stood behind her, speaking into Misha's ear, his arm still wrapped around her. My sister nodded, her hand covering his across her stomach.

I glanced at August, still beside me. Even though I knew the witches would become a fight between us later, there was no one I wanted more at my side.

Stay, I asked with my eyes. August nodded, his hand lightly grazing the back of my neck.

I returned my attention to Sena, who was already looking over the swords.

I ran my fingers over the lines of script embedded in the blades. "We found our mother's journal. In one entry, she wrote that she had asked you to translate these."

"She did." Sena nodded. "I had just translated it when I heard about your birth—and her passing." Her eyes met mine and Misha's, full of sorrow and understanding.

Misha swallowed, pushing down her grief. "What language is it?" She leaned closer, taking in the markings that were only familiar to us from a lifetime of seeing the swords.

"The language of the gods—of the first Fae," Sena said. "For over a decade before she came to me, I'd been working on the translation, piecing together the alphabet and words from old manuscripts and codices. It was my life's passion." A dark shadow crossed her face at some memory.

This explained how Sena knew so much about them, the gods and their history, then.

"No one has managed to do it before?" I asked.

"They've tried," August said. "But Sena is an exceptional linguist. She has an innate understanding of language. I've never seen anyone able to learn them as quickly as she can."

Sena smiled at the compliment. "The airborn Fae's language evolves the fastest—the Aurae and air sprites. It's constantly changing and fluctuating. The waterborns' changes the slowest, hence their languages are closest to the old Fae—the god's language." Sena sighed. "But, because they are water-bound, that means there is very little written of their language. It has taken me years of interviews with the Naiads, Nereids, and water sprites—they rarely deign to speak to the landborn—to form the basics of their vocabulary and syntax. Casting rain for them helped, replenishing their homes with fresh water. Once I had their language decoded, I began to work on the gods'. It would have gone much faster if I could have spoken to the Sirens—their language is the eldest—but, as they are the most volatile, it was much too risky."

Misha shot me a quick glance. The Naiads and Sirens had spoken to me, several times now.

I gestured to the swords again. "So, no one else could translate these?"

"No. No one except for me and this one." Sena smiled, grasping Julian's arm. "My son has learned much of the language already. Which is good because I think it has to do with what we just discussed."

"The gods?" Misha questioned.

Sena nodded. "I think it's a prophecy tied to them." Her finger traced along the Iradelmar's blade as she read:

Born of land and sea on the longest day, the aurora arises to fulfill what was promised.

Sena lifted her hand, moving to the Mercedelmar:

The flame will return. The sea will rise. The wind will howl. The earth will break. What was once lost will return.

We stayed silent a moment, processing. Then I whispered, "Our parents: an earth and watercaster, land and sea."

"And we were born at dawn—the aurora," Misha added. "On the Summer Solstice, the longest day of the year."

"Flame has already returned," August said, his hand tightening on my nape as he looked from me to my sister. "Firecasters and dragons."

"But the rest has yet to pass," Sena said. "The wind is vague, but I think we would all notice the sea rising and earth breaking."

I puzzled over that last one—*the earth will break*—mulling it over in my mind. It was too familiar to be a coincidence.

"Our mother had a vision when she realized she was pregnant." I recited it from memory, letting Sena, August, and Julian hear it for the first time. "*Out of the fractured snow-covered ground rose a being of nightmares.*"

Misha went still. " . . . something like the Void?"

"*What was once lost will return*," Julian repeated the words on the Mercedelmar. "Gods above—Adrienne is going to try to free the fallen god."

I turned to August. "The witches, if Miranda can find them, will be more important than ever. This prophecy is only stating what *might* come to pass, but doesn't tell us how Adrienne plans to do it."

The knowledge warred in his eyes. August still didn't want to risk it. *Fine*. But if going to the witches meant preventing Adrienne from doing something horrible, I would.

I looked at Misha. She and Julian were having their own silent conversation. I wouldn't be the only one going to see the witches, and Julian looked about as inclined to see Misha go as August had me.

But then, my sister surprised me. She turned abruptly to Sena. "With Julian, is there any way for him to lead the transformation into a dragon himself if necessary? Using my magic somehow?" she asked.

August and I stood still, listening intently.

Sena went quiet, musing over it. "I'm not sure. Even if you power shared, he wouldn't be able to wield it, although that also requires touch."

"Except Adrienne found a way to wield stolen magic," Julian said. "What if the magic were—" He paused, finding the right word. "—gifted, somehow?"

Sena paused, considering. "It hasn't been done before. Not to my knowledge."

"But it has," I spoke up. "Miranda and Damian—their bond."

"Yes," Sena acknowledged. "He extended his long life to her but with the caveat that their souls are bonded. If one dies, the other will too."

Misha turned at Julian, her eyes pained. "No. I won't be the reason you die."

Julian brushed the hair from my sister's cheek. "There is no life without you, love."

Before they could argue about it further, I asked, "What if you exchanged something else besides long life? It makes sense for Miranda and Damian, since she's human. But what if you only exchanged magic? Your lives wouldn't be tied together."

Julian cocked his head, considering. "So, Misha gives me part of her magic—the ability to shift into the dragon—and I give her a piece of stormcasting magic?"

I nodded. "Yes."

Misha's eyes lit up. "I could wield lightning?"

Julian laughed, casting electricity down to his hand and holding it before her. "You are going to be a terror."

Misha turned back to Sena. "It wouldn't take too much from him, though, would it?" Her brow creased with worry.

Julian smiled, pulling her into him as he whispered in her ear, "How small do you think my well is, love?" His tone dripped with insinuation.

Misha blushed furiously. She spun around, her hand flinging out and backhanding his stomach. "In front of your *mother*?" she hissed.

"That exchange of magic could actually work," Sena said, chuckling amusedly. "But Damian and Miranda are mates, bonded by the stars. We will need to confirm your bond to do the same."

"But our lives won't be bound? Not like Miranda and Damian's?" Misha asked again.

"No," Sena answered. "Not unless you wish it."

"No," Misha said, Julian nodding his agreement.

Neither thought they'd move on if the other died, leaving this world—the devotion in their eyes was enough to dispel that thought—but that each foresaw themselves dying first, and refused to be responsible for the other's death.

Misha and Julian nodded, understanding.

"The new moon just passed," Sena said. "We will have to wait a month for the next. It's best to confirm star bonds when the sky is darkest. It is easiest to read the Above's magic then."

"The Above?" Misha asked, intrigued.

Sena smiled. "The Above is the creator of all mating bonds and threads of fate. Her power facilitated the Between and Made's transfer of magic as well as her own when she fell in love. They became the first mated pairs, bonded by more than love. Once your connection is confirmed, Miranda can perform the binding magic necessary."

"Sena," August said, and she turned to him. His hand slid into mine, warm against my palm as our fingers threaded together. My heart was in my throat as he asked, "Can you confirm one more bond?"

"Of course." She beamed, coming to hug each of us and planting a kiss on both our cheeks. "Nothing would make me happier." Sena regarded August as she did her own son, though he was older than she, and no blood was shared between them. Not a mother to replace the one he'd lost, but still family.

Sena turned to Misha and Julian, kissing them both upon each cheek before leaving to prepare in the Temple.

"Misha," I got my sister's attention, drawing her away from Julian. I handed her the Mercedelmar, our mother's sword. "It's yours. They were always meant to be wielded by sisters."

Misha clasped the hilt. Her eyes clouded with different emotions: sorrow and grief, but also hope and a spark of something I hadn't seen in a very long time.

Happiness.

"Are you tired, sister?" Misha asked, blue eyes blazing for the first time in weeks as she held our mother's sword before her.

Yes, I was exhausted after the attack. But the look in my sister's eyes renewed me. I smiled. "Why, Meesh?"

"Because I think it's time we trained again."

CHAPTER 30
Misha

I know I'm out of shape, Nicky, but the littlest one?" I teased, grabbing a practice sword.

"The fastest one, sister."

Teale, good-natured as she was, only laughed as we entered the sparring ring together. Her short, curly hair had turned from gold to red-tinted, mimicking the transition of the trees covering the mountains for autumn.

For the past three weeks, I trained every day with Nic and Julian, waking at the first light of dawn and falling into bed every night, spent, with sore and aching muscles. We began with simple things: jogging, then building to sprints while using weights to build back the muscle I'd lost. It would take many more weeks to regain it, but I already felt stronger—more myself.

I still had dreams and nightmares of my family, still found myself tearing up at the smallest things that reminded me of them. But I let myself feel the pain without letting it consume me. Every day, I found the strength to stand. To make my aunts proud. To fight for another day—and that was what mattered.

I could still grieve them, but I couldn't give up.

This was my first time sparring with someone who wasn't Nic. I had practiced with my sister for too many years and knew her methods too well. Working with her still challenged me—especially as she'd gained new tricks training with the Seven—but I needed to test myself against someone new.

Minutes later, I was out of breath.

Mother above, the demi-Dryad was fast.

Her practice sword danced around me, hitting different, vulnerable points on my arms and legs. It didn't actually slice through my skin, but I felt the pain as if it had. And that shit *stung*.

"You can always yield, Misha," Nic called out.

Like hell.

Teale was too fast to beat with speed, her dragonfly-esque wings spiriting her away before I could land a strike, so I'd have to outmaneuver her. The nymph had a pattern she liked to attack in.

I left my right arm vulnerable, hissing at the sting of her needle-like blade, knowing she'd be looking to target my ribs next. I beat her to it, thrusting my elbow outward and finally—*finally* catching her in the chest.

The force caused her to lose momentum, stumbling back. I lunged, tackling her to the ground, my blade to her throat.

"Yield," she gasped, chest shuttering as she slowly recovered her breath.

"Sorry." I winced. Standing, I held out a hand, offering to help her up.

She took it, still somehow smiling. "All part of the process. At least you went for the chest. Your sister has been known to break a few noses."

Nic smirked from where she leaned against the castle wall. "Only August's."

I saw Gemma standing off to the side with Shai. She was well trained in aircasting and shielding, yet this was the first time she was learning to defend herself without magic.

I could see why the Shaws hadn't pushed it on her. They'd put their faith in the Blood Treaty, hoping for a better world, one in which their youngest, kindest daughter would never have to be a warrior—would never have the blood on her hands that they did.

But wishful thinking wasn't reality.

It would be a while until she trained with weapons, still focusing on the basics for now. Shai showed her how to properly set her feet for optimal balance and power. Then he held up sparring pads as she took turns throwing different punches. Two jabs, a cross, an uppercut. He took the time to correct her form, gently reshaping how she formed a fist to protect her hand.

Shai corrected her stance, his hands on her hips as he helped her shift her weight. Looking away from him, pink bloomed across her cheeks. Then her eyes met mine, and Gemma's face turned the flaming red of her hair.

I looked away, saving my friend from further embarrassment over the crush she'd developed on the white-haired High Fae. Though, considering how often he worked with Gemma to unravel her memories, I couldn't fathom how he didn't see it.

I joined my sister, drinking water as we watched Julian and August spar in a different ring. They danced around each other, using one practice blade each, evenly matched.

It was an unseasonably warm October day. August's black shirt was drenched in sweat. Julian had removed his completely, and I couldn't help but admire the lithe grace of him.

I loved Julian and had never stopped for an instant, even at my darkest, but the desire I'd once felt had wasted away with my grief in the past weeks. I had felt hardly anything outside the misery and pain. Julian, gods bless him, had never pushed. He'd been content to hold me, helping me through the lowest part of my loss.

But watching him now, seeing the way he moved, trained, and sparred over the past few days had me remembering other things he'd done with his body.

I felt the heat rising into my cheeks.

Other areas, too.

Everyone else stopped to watch them, in awe of their fluid grace. Some of the observers watched with more than admiration, some of whom seemed to be having similar thoughts as me. Several of the females, especially, were watching Julian and whispering to each other, their eyes never leaving him.

Julian had told me of his . . . escapades before he met me. I was only sure he hadn't been exaggerating because of how captivating he was. More than beautiful, Julian was enchanting to look at. I couldn't fault others for being as entranced with him as I was.

But they'd better watch their damned whispers.

When they finished—a draw—Nic went to August, leaving me alone at the wall. Julian came toward me. Some of the onlookers stepped toward him, trying to draw him into conversation. He gave them polite nods of acknowledgment or a few quick words, but never slowed his pace toward me.

"Hi." I smiled, my cheeks warming as I took him in, from his bare chest down to where his training pants fit him impeccably well.

"Hi, love." Julian stole my water, taking a long drink. "Why are you smiling like that?"

My grin spread, widening across my face. "Like what?"

"Like you are thinking horribly dirty thoughts right now," he teased.

Oh, I was. Didn't hurt if the others saw it, too—saw how he hadn't looked at them once, those stormcloud eyes only for me.

Let them see he was *mine*.

"How dirty?" I teased, looking up at him from beneath my lashes, playing coy.

He chuckled, moving closer. When Julian laughed, I wished I could swallow the sound. Plant the seed within my heart, let it grow roots, and bloom through my lungs.

Julian didn't stop until I was pressed against the wall, his hips to mine, his lips grazing my ear. "*Filthy.*"

A shiver ran down my spine. I opened my mouth to say more, but my gaze snagged on Simon approaching August, his mouth set in a hard line.

Julian noticed my gaze, seeing what I had. When he turned back to me, his eyes were apologetic. "Shit, there's news."

He grabbed his shirt and slipped it on, quickly doing up the buttons and tucking in the tail. He took my hand as we walked to them.

"Numbers are coming in from Desdemon. They've lost a quarter of their army, but—" Simon hesitated.

August's brow furrowed. "But what?"

"That's it. They're lost—gone. They haven't crossed the border to us nor joined Adrienne's forces in Sanserria."

"Approximately three thousand soldiers have vanished?" Julian asked.

Simon sighed. "It appears so."

"Disappeared, or Adrienne has done something to them," Nic surmised.

A chill ran through me. Would she really kill that many people in cold blood for deserting?

Unfortunately, I already knew the answer.

"Also," Simon said, turning to Julian. "The spies have lost Mannix."

"Hell," Julian cursed. "I knew he was going to be a problem."

"Don't spend unnecessary resources searching for him. He's one person," August said. "Let him hide away somewhere and plot his misguided revenge. If he returns and tries to get past the wards, we'll know."

Nic didn't seem so sure, anxiously picking at the skin of her thumb with her index finger.

August noticed as well. His hand drifted to her hair, spooling one of the raven-black strands around a finger, his fingertips brushing her back as he did so. Nic didn't seem to notice, except that she stopped picking.

He'd settled her with a touch.

"Papa Simon!" A young girl bounded up to the spymaster, around twelve or thirteen, with a brown-haired man accompanying her. She was tall for her age, long-limbed with wild black curls. Her olive skin was tanned brown, speaking of a summer spent almost entirely outdoors. I'd seen her before with the two men—her parents—but had yet to speak to her.

The girl seemed incredibly shy, looking at me and quickly glancing away when I noticed.

"She saw you all down here training from her balcony," the man said. "It was like trying to keep a lioness caged." The girl's face flamed.

After he hugged his daughter, lifting her clear off her feet, Simon greeted his husband with a quick kiss. Then he turned to us, wrapping an arm around the girl's shoulders. "Misha, this is my daughter, Jessa, and my husband, Ezra."

The man reached for my hand. As we shook, I noticed the golden tattoos covering his arms in intricate depictions of flora and fauna. There were roses and daffodils with long lines of ivy threading past a fawn, owl, and more forest creatures.

"Those are beautiful," I said, admiring the artwork.

"Thank you," he said. "I draw them. If you are ever interested . . ."

A spark went through my mind, a hint of an idea. I returned his warm smile. "I will let you know."

The girl, Jessa, approached Nic, whispering to her, although not low enough to escape Fae ears. She snuck a quick glance at me. "Is she feeling better now?"

I looked at Julian, but he only shrugged, doing a horrible job of hiding his grin.

Nic nodded, whispering back. "You can ask her."

Jessa approached me. "Your sister promised to come." She cut a glance at Nic, who gave her an encouraging smile. For a moment, my heart panged. Nic looked so much like Eve when she used to reassure us as girls. "But she said you would like to be invited yourself." Jessa handed me a small envelope.

Smiling, I opened it. The blue card was decorated with shimmering snowflakes around the border. In the center was a watercolor dancer, seemingly entirely made from flame. I glanced up at Nic, who'd clearly had an impact on the young girl.

It read:

Jessa's Thirteenth Birthday
December 30th
The Castle Atrium

"It's beautiful," I said, taking a closer look. "What artist did you hire to make this?"

Jessa beamed, shaking her head and blushing. "*I* made it." A talent for drawing she'd honed from her father.

I gasped. "Did you really?"

I was hamming it up a bit, but the artwork was truly remarkable, and Jessa was grinning ear to ear now. Something warm blossomed within my chest, and I meant every word. "It's gorgeous." I held it to my chest. "And I would be honored to come, but . . ." I hesitated, and Jessa nodded for me to continue. I leaned closer, whispering, "May I bring a date?"

"I'm already invited, love," Julian chimed in. I held up a hand, silencing him behind me.

Jessa nodded, giving me a sly wink as she turned to Julian. "Your invitation is revoked."

As he gasped in mock outrage, she turned back to me, whispering low. "Okay, now you can invite him as your date."

I threw my head back, laughing as I hugged her. "Oh, you and I are going to be friends."

291

CHAPTER 31
Misha

Nic and I sat on the balcony, wrapped under a woolen blanket together as we watched the sun start its final descent behind the mountain peaks. My head rested on her shoulder as I felt the soft rise of her chest.

We had taken the day off from training. I hadn't been able to drag myself from bed this morning, worn down by a wave of grief. I'd awoken in my sister's arms, her lying beside me in a similar state.

Upon waking, I'd pricked my finger twice, dosing myself with the poison, followed by an antidote. It was improving, but still didn't negate the effects completely. There was some part I was still missing.

Now mid-October, the leaves had turned to various shades of gold, rust, and amber, spreading across the mountains. The spread of colors became a fiery blaze in the light of sunset.

There were no words, only my sister comforting me, and I her. Only us and the memories from this day.

The anniversary of our father's death.

On this day nine years ago, everything had been covered in downy white. Every attendee's clothes, the drapes hung from the ceilings, and the gauzy veils covering the faces of the immediate family were all pale and colorless. In mourning, we wore white, donning the color of winter—the color of death.

Nic and I—only thirteen—my aunts, and Adrienne stood at the head of the procession. My father's casket, teak and embedded with gold florals, sat before us on the bank of the lake, elevated on wooden beams that would allow it to float.

My aunts took turns speaking about Dominic Briar, giving small glimpses that could never compare to the entirety of the person we'd lost. The world couldn't know him from only a few words—they couldn't understand.

My head pounded. Everything sounded as if it were underwater.

Finally, a priestess spoke, leading the procession in a prayer to the gods. A plea to the Father to recommend his soul past the Veil where he would be joined with his mate and our mother, Diana.

When it was done, Nic and I held the torch together, touching it to the pyre decorated in chrysanthemums and marigolds. As my father's slowly blazing casket drifted away from us toward the center of the lake, we clasped hands.

At only thirteen, we'd lost both parents.

Alesia took my hand, and Eve took Nic's.

The fire billowed higher, climbing toward the sky. The wind rustled through the leaves, their colors shifting to mimic the flames of my father's funeral pyre.

Afterward, we were expected to mingle, to hold the hands of every person while they spoke of our loss or gave words of encouragement. They said how strong my sister and I were and how proud our parents would be of us. They said it with such intimacy, as if they'd known us or our father at all.

I remained silent for most of it, Nic taking the brunt of the absurdity. Shielding me, as always.

After an hour, I finally escaped, searching for solace in the gardens. I hoped no other attendees would catch me there, forcing me to smile politely as they went on again about how they were devastated over my father's loss and how he'd been such a kind and sage king. It was even worse when they then broke into tears.

I'd had enough.

It was *our* father's funeral, and my sister and I had spent the entire day comforting strangers. I wanted to be sad without an audience, to grieve without judgment, so I fled to an alcove where only my family would come looking for me.

When I saw him there, sitting on the stone bench, I froze.

Julian.

I didn't know what to say—not to him, the one person who might know what it felt like to lose a father.

I'd known he and his mother had attended as representatives from Montevalle. But I hadn't been able to bear looking at him, afraid he'd see too much.

Terrified he wouldn't see enough.

Julian looked up, seeing me. "You don't have to say anything, Misha. You don't have to pretend anymore."

His words unleashed me, like the wall of a dam breaking away. I finally began to cry as I sat beside him, my head going to his shoulder as his arm wrapped around me, and I broke apart.

After the funeral, I remembered lying in my father's bed for weeks, curled up beneath the duvet that still smelled of him, remembering how he'd taught me our land's history, how to dance, and how to create something from nothing. Even when it smelled only of stale air and must, I remained. My aunts took turns checking on me, sometimes lying beside me, hands brushing through my hair as they whispered words to give me comfort or held me silently as I cried. Other times, my sister sat with me, my head in her lap as she read me story after story from her books.

My favorite was the book of children's tales, especially the story of Snow White and Rose Red, two sisters who lived in a cottage at the edge of the wood. They befriended a monster, and he saved their life in return. One sister married the monster, the other his handsome brother. At my request, Nic told it again and again until the words seared across my brain.

The darker the shadows, the brighter the sun.

During this time, I only got up to relieve myself and eat—sometimes. Otherwise, I let my stomach go empty, the gnawing hole in my gut a reflection of my gaping heart.

The only thing that numbed the pain was the liquor in my father's sitting room cabinet. The liquid burned my throat and roiled uneasily in my empty stomach. But by the time my lips went numb, the pain had abated. The grief was still there but hidden behind a veil.

I could stand. I could leave the room.

It didn't take long for my sister and aunts to discover what I was doing, my glassy eyes and slurred words giving me away. Eve healed away the effects, taking the liquor from the rooms and common areas.

I always found more.

Liquor or wine slid down my throat first thing in the morning, and it was the last thing I sipped before bed.

I did not write Julian.

I couldn't. What would I have said? In the year since we'd met, we'd written every week, sharing funny moments from our day and asking questions to know each other better. He was someone I had thought I could say anything to, since he always understood my jokes and took in everything I said with deep consideration. I'd never felt on the same page as someone, so aligned in thought and belief.

I couldn't tell him this.

I could not tell him how wretched I was, how useless and immobile, how paralyzed I was by grief. Only the liquor drowned out the roaring in my brain, but it made his words blur on the page, too.

Julian's letters kept coming. Every week, he wrote and told me about his day, his life, and his family and friends. The ravens and hawks found me wherever I was, dropping the parchment with his inked words into my hands.

I kept waiting for them to stop. I knew one day they would. Julian would tire of receiving no response, communicating with a ghost.

They never did.

Julian even shared his darkest secrets, writing to tell me how he'd felt when his own father died. How he hated and loved the his father, revealing his guilt over the happiness he felt that he was dead but also guilt over feeling grief for a parent who had harmed him emotionally and physically.

Though it was different, he understood my grief. Julian shared the worst parts of himself, letting me know it was okay to do the same. In his trust that I would not think differently of him, I knew he would give me the same courtesy. The sentiment lit a small spark of hope within my chest.

I tucked his letters carefully into a pillow, clutching each one to my chest as I slept, and held them close to my lungs as if they could permeate them with air, ballooning my chest and swelling it with hope.

His letters evoked the feeling of the first sunny day after a grueling winter, when the sun warmed my skin all the way through my bones. Julian's letters brought new life, like sprouts formed on broken ribs. My heart bled less and beat more. With time, I was no longer a fallen tree, broken and cracked across the ground, but tall and reaching for the heavens, leaves unfurling with new life.

When morning came, I sat up, reaching for the flask I'd tucked in a secret compartment of my father's desk, one neither Nic nor my aunts had yet discovered. It had been a week since Eve had refused to cure any more of my hangovers.

As I worked the handle free, the black hawk brought Julian's letter, but this time, the bird lingered. My head pounded, needing the fix of liquor to calm my roaring mind, but for the first time in months, I hesitated.

Instead, I reached for Julian's letter, tied to the bird's leg.

Rose,

This morning, I could not sleep, so instead, I went onto my balcony. Here, there is the most beautiful view of the mountains to the east. Under the night sky above, I sat and waited for the sun to rise.

I thought of how dark the sky and earth seemed under the new moon, with only stars for illumination. How it seemed to be impenetrable—as if the sun might never rise again.

But slowly, the sky lightened, and before I knew it, I sat before the blazing aurora, dazzling all in its fiery gold.

It reminded me of you.

I know you must be suffering. I cannot imagine you are not.

But the dawn is rising, Misha, and so will you.

– Rain

The hawk, with its dark eyes, studied me. It seemed to ask me a question: *Which choice will you make today?*

I pulled open the secret compartment, taking the flask. I removed the stopper, the spiced scent hitting me, promising to take away my every woe, and to numb all my pain.

Until tomorrow.

Going into the attached bathing chamber, I poured the amber liquor down the sink.

Then, I went back to my father's desk. My hand shaking from withdrawal, I reached for a pen.

Rain,

When my father died, I felt as though I was buried under the earth beside him.

The darkness pressed me down, sinking me deeper as my lungs and organs filled with grief and sorrow.

But like a seed, the Rain coaxed me back into living. And now a small tendril of myself can peek out and see the daylight again.

If the dawn can rise after such darkness, I think I might as well.

– Rose

CHAPTER 32
Misha

I always remembered the year after my father's death with shame, drawn out by my inability to let him go.

Though dead, Alesia and Eve were still here with us. They always would be, as the mothers who raised my twin sister and me. But I couldn't let myself be buried alongside them. Not again.

"I need to say goodbye, Nicky."

Her head on my shoulder, my sister nodded, understanding.

Our aunts deserved so much more than what they'd gotten—more than what we could do—but Nic and I would give them what we could.

The next night, after dusk, I constructed a pyre at the edge of the lake in front of the castle.

Calling to my magic, I wound purple freesia and white jasmine around the posts and entangled them as they reached the pyramidal top. These were closest to our aunts' scents, reminding me the most of them.

Chrysanthemums, symbolic of bidding farewell, and marigolds, to guide the spirits, grew at the base.

Gemma stood beside me, guiding the pyre onto the lake with her aircasting, while the water held still as glass from Nic's influence. The lake's surface was a perfect reflection of the violet dusk and harvest moon in her shades of orange and red.

August, Julian, and Sena stood behind us, along with the Seven, to give support.

To honor Alesia and Eve.

As the pyre began to move away, Nic cast a small flame in the center.

It slowly snaked out, engulfing the wood but leaving the blossoms untouched until it was entirely consumed, the pyre becoming an inferno of golden light, burning as brightly as any of the stars spilled across the sky. It burned as brilliantly as Alesia and Eve's souls still burned among the heavens, looking down upon us from beyond the Veil.

Nic and I clasped hands, remembering them.

Silently, I swore I wouldn't rest until I'd reaped retribution for their murders, until this world was whole again—a reflection of the dreams they'd had.

Only when the pyre finally sank beneath the surface and the lake went dark did I tear my eyes away. I gasped, my hand coming to cover my lips. Nic lifted her head to see what I had.

All around, people had gathered. High Fae, humans, Seraphim, nymphs, and other faeries. They stood all along the bank, at the edge of each balcony, watching from every window.

A single candle was lit, and then another and another, until Ankaa was ablaze with them. Little fires dotted the city like stars fallen to earth.

Each of those gathered bowed their heads in deference, coming to pay their respects to Alesia and Eve.

Both mine and Nic's faces grew wet with tears. I squeezed my sister's hand tighter.

We stayed like that, silently connected. There were no words to convey how we felt: still broken but growing and mending more each day.

CHAPTER 33
Misha

I stood with Jophiel on the cliff's precipice. Below, Nic trained, fighting two Seraphim as they swooped and lunged for her with the practice blades. Other Seraphim had gathered, sitting along various edges of the cliff face as they watched Nic whirl and fight, her blade catching in the sunlight as she held her own.

I hadn't trained with them yet, still needing to build my strength. *Soon*, I promised myself as I watched my sister.

The winged Fae were a small, but closely knit group. The Seraphim seemed to take a community approach to life: sharing food and cooking massive meals together while many of the adults minded and played with the children, tutoring and teaching them to fly. They were a faerie race rich in the tradition of family.

When I said as much, Jophiel snorted. "They are now, but it's taken a hundred years to only begin to heal the wounds of the millennia before."

I looked at them closer, peering beneath their happy smiles. Scars adorned more bodies than not. One female had a particularly haunted look in her eyes as she watched the others train, and I wondered what horrors she'd endured.

"What was it like . . . before?" I asked hesitantly.

Jophiel's eyes gained that same distant look, and for several moments, I thought she wouldn't answer.

"The Seraphim were the prized warriors of the Etherii. We were little more than animals to them, bred to produce only the strongest and fastest. We were put through rigorous training from childhood and instructed in all manner of combat and war strategy."

My mind snagged on one horrible word. "Bred?"

Jophiel nodded. "For so long, people believed we were not capable of any emotion, only ruthless killing. Especially not love." Heartbreak flashed in her eyes. "We were banned from mating with anyone other than another Seraph. They said it would be a waste to birth unwinged Fae when our numbers were already so small."

I nodded, understanding. "My father fell in love with someone he shouldn't have, and it caused a war."

"The war had been a long time brewing." Jophiel turned to me, face stoic. "But yes, your father and mother lit the match, and we are all the better for it."

I watched the winged faeries, at least fifty in this training area alone, laughing with each other as they took breaks from the sparring and drills. They stood with an ease that only those who had known a time without freedom could revel in.

"When did the Seraphim change?"

"During the war, our people split. Half remained under our commander, Rainier Zarr." She eyed me knowingly. "Whom you have had the displeasure of meeting."

I shuddered, remembering and trying not to think of what might have happened had Nic not arrived when she did. But Nicole had held her own against him, as Alé had a century ago.

Jophiel went on. "The others—those who dreamt of more in this life—flew with me. We fought for the things we'd dreamed of but had never been granted: love, peace . . . family."

My gaze followed Jophiel's to where a young Seraphim child played in the dirt, his mother crouched over him. He had a head of light brown curls, the same warm color as his mother's. The child, approximately two years old, went from laughing joyously to sobbing as his tower of dirt was destroyed by a gust of wind. The mother picked him up, cradling him against her as she stroked down his white wings. She soothed him until he was pushing away, happy to return to the dirt.

"I had a son," Jophiel said softly, her smile pained as she watched them.

All possible replies caught in my throat at the look in her face—it hadn't ended well. The last thing I wanted to do was pry, so I remained silent, letting her continue if she wished.

When Jophiel went on, I only listened. "I became pregnant with him when I was very young, still in my early thirties and coming into myself. His father was High Fae, a single night of passion with a male that had made me laugh. For the first time in my life, he had looked at me like I was worth seeing for more than bloodshed I wrought. The elder Seraphim, our trainers, broke us of that early on—thinking that we were special."

I couldn't imagine. I'd had a father and two loving aunts who always made sure to tell us how loved my sister and I were, and how no matter what, we'd always be loved.

"I never even knew his name," Jophiel murmured. "The child was born without wings. It's why they took him from me. The un-winged—even if they were demi-Seraphim—were not allowed upon our mountain peaks." Her blue eyes went glassy, unseeing. "He was still covered in my blood, umbilical cord hanging from his stomach. I never even held him—never saw him again. I don't even know if he's still alive, or if he died soon after."

Somehow, I spoke over the tightness in my throat, terrified to ask but needing to know, compelled to understand. "What did they do to those children?"

"The Seraphim Elders told me they'd dropped him at a Temple, one where most foundlings were taken, but they never told me where, or even in which territory. I searched for decades and never found him, so I never knew if they were telling the truth. For all I know, they could've abandoned him alone and helpless in the Redwood."

A memory sparked in my mind: my father had been found and raised by priestesses. He'd become a soldier in the High King's army because he'd had no other choice. They'd seen his power and had honed him into a warrior—a warrior mighty enough to serve as a commander.

My heart thudded forcefully. "A Temple of the Mother?"

Jophiel's eyes met mine. "Yes, that's what they said."

"Gods above," Nic whispered.

Neither of us had heard her approach. My sister looked between me and Jophiel quickly. The Seraph was taller than me by a head, her arms corded in thick muscle—just like our father. Her skin was more pale than mine, but Nic saw our shared blue eyes. The same blonde hair.

Nic understood at the same moment I did. "You are his mother."

We went immediately to Miranda, none of us daring hope. Jophiel couldn't look at us, nor Nic and I her. It would be too painful to believe we had any living family only to find it was a misunderstanding—a similar story that had no real connection.

"If you indeed share blood," Miranda said, piercing my finger with the blade's tip. "The blood will join." She took Nic's, doing the same before moving to Jophiel.

We squeezed our fingers at the same time, spilling one drop of blood onto the porcelain plate. Miranda chanted the words softly, as each of our eyes fixated on the three drops of red. Slowly, they began to move.

Mine and Nic's met each other first, the most closely related as we were twins. Jophiel's gradually moved toward it, taking several long moments to travel the length of the small plate.

It, too, merged.

Jophiel's hand flew to her mouth. "All that time in the Great War, I fought near him—beside him—and I never knew. I never even spoke to him—to Dominic—my *son*." She choked.

"You couldn't have known," Nic said, her voice soft. "The High King's court would have obscured his past as a foundling of the Temple, deeming it ill-fitting for someone of his rank."

"And he was an earthcaster, as well as wingless," I said. But our father's plants *had* grown extraordinarily well . . . as if he'd produced his own sunlight—like the Seraphim.

Jophiel looked between us, Nic and me, finally taking the time to see the similarities in her own face. Mine was more obvious, but Nic shared her high cheekbones and the strong way she held her neck.

"My granddaughters."

Then we were embracing, holding onto her. Tears fell from all our eyes—tears of relief and sorrow and joy.

All of a sudden, we three weren't so alone.

CHAPTER 34
Misha

C eleste and I hiked up the cliff face, clinging to the mountainside as we ascended the narrow stone steps.

Both of us had tightly braided our hair, attempting to keep it from whipping about us as the wind lashed around the peak. A few short strands had already escaped their confinement in the northern gusts, wreaking utter havoc on my eyes and flying into my mouth.

We could have winnowed, but I'd never seen our destination before for reference. And besides, I had told myself, I needed the exercise, needed to push my body.

I was an idiot.

The fur-lined leathers we wore kept most of the mid-October cold at bay, but the wind chill was monstrous at this height. Not used to the altitude, I gulped down deep breaths, my hands clinging to the lead rope should I grow lightheaded. The eagles would catch Celeste if she fell, but I wasn't so sure about me.

If I passed out, would I still be able to shift? Would the earth rise up and catch me?

Not wanting to test it, I gripped the rope tighter, my fingers growing more numb despite the gloves.

We already knew I could shift Julian and myself with the animaglia magic, and I had called to the Nemean lions and other creatures in the woods in a burst of panic, but today, Celeste wanted to further test my ability to control animals. Specifically, how many could I control at once and for how long.

Nic stayed below with the others, spending more time with the Seraphim after the revelation of three days past.

After discovering she was our grandmother, Jophiel had taken even further passion in training my sister and me. During the day, she became even fiercer, tougher. She'd begun working with me herself, teaching me all the things she'd taught Nic during her time at the cabin and here. My body ached all over from it.

Jophiel had lost her son without ever knowing him. In the coming war against Adrienne, she was determined not to lose her granddaughters either.

During the nights, Nic and I shared stories with her. Tales of our childhood and memories of our father. My sister and I showed her our bracelets, letting her watch the memory of him. I never imagined I would see the stoic Seraph cry with such fervor, moved by a mixture of pure sorrow and joy at being able to see her son—knowing he was her son—for the first time.

Now that I watched Jophiel move more closely during training, I saw further similarities to our father, such as the way Dominic had taught us to handle our weapons when we were young. They moved with the same power, the same grace.

I was filled with a melancholic longing every time I thought of how different it could have been if we had known. She could have been a part of our lives—of his. It was the longing for something you could never have but could not stop imagining anyway.

Though the more I thought of it, the more I smiled. Nic and I had a piece of our family again.

Finally, Celeste and I reached the top of the steps. My hands and toes were numb from the cold as we walked out onto the wide platform. I flexed my stiff fingers in and out, trying to flow life back into them.

The Aerie was near the peak of the closest mountain, open to face the south to protect the birds from northern fronts and squalls. The cavern was massive, opening up into the mountain. Hundreds of nests clung to crevices along the jagged stone wall, rising over a hundred meters.

Eagles roosted in nests with their young or perched in the surrounding tree branches. They were huge, their bodies varying in size from large dogs to ponies. Celeste stalked through them, completely at ease.

I couldn't say the same for myself. The eagles cocked their heads as I passed, chittering and eyeing me warily.

Celeste approached a golden eagle in the corner. "This is Manus."

The eagle was much larger than Aetos, the greatest of all the eagles that I could see. He slowly stood from the nest where his mate sat, guarding eggs the size of melons. Flaring his wings—the long feathers ranging from brown to white and gold—he towered over me. The size of a moose, his wingspan reached nearly eight meters across.

"Do not react," Celeste whispered. "Do not flinch or step away. Slowly bow your head—*only* your head. It is a sign of respect. Manus needs to know you are not a threat but also that he cannot intimidate you."

I took deep breaths through my nose, willing my feet to merge into the earth as I slowly lowered my gaze, the motion roaring against all my instincts. Manus flapped his wings, curved beak opening as he cawed and stepped closer.

Do not move.

The great eagle cocked his head, sniffing and eyeing me more intently as he neared. Finally, determining me not a threat, his wings relaxed, tucking into his sides.

Celeste smiled. "Very good. Most don't listen the first time they meet him and run away. Then I must command him off the chase, something I hate to do—it interferes with their predatory instincts." She moved toward him, motioning me near as well. Celeste ran a hand down his neck, lovingly. "Hello, you big oaf."

The eagle lowered his head, lying it gently on her shoulder.

As I ran a hand down Manus's feathered neck, I felt a small thread going to him as my magic connected us.

The bird didn't have thoughts like ours, at least, not in any language I could understand. Instead, I felt the depth of feeling, love, and respect he had for Celeste. Images flashed of when he'd been much smaller, of Celeste towering over him as a chick and handfeeding him.

"He's loyal to you," I said, stroking his feathers.

"So, make him loyal to *you*," she said, getting straight to the point—why we'd come.

I sent magic down the thread, testing and pulling against it, trying to shift his loyalty. It felt like moving a boulder with a loop of yarn.

Expanding the magic, I imagined turning the yarn into rope, then a chain. I wrapped more loops around it, willing it to budge. The eagle's heart began to race as he panicked, fighting it.

I winced. "I can't."

Through the bird's mind, I could see how he regarded Celeste. Yes, she'd used her magic to influence him, but she'd also raised him from an egg. Their bond was more—deeper—than magic. For me to yank that loyalty away felt like a betrayal.

Celeste's eyebrow raised. "I wonder . . . but could you steal the connection if you wanted to? Pull him away if we both cast toward him?"

"I don't see why we'd need to put him through that."

"Because there are going to be other animaglia on Adrienne's side, Misha. The eagles are a valuable asset, but I need to know that you and I will be able to keep their loyalty. The enemy won't hesitate to try to steal it, no matter how it hurts them. Manus is strong. He can handle being pushed further."

I swallowed, focusing all my concentration on his loyalty. I pulled and pulled against Celeste, checking for any sign that the hold would snap or that we would hurt the eagle beyond repair.

The eagle's heart rate suddenly began to slow, plummeting. It felt wrong—all of it. I wanted to pull back, to end this.

Releasing my magic, I rocked back on my heels. "I can't do it, not without killing him."

Celeste studied me. "I guess this is a good thing. Our minds can work together to influence him, but you can't take him over entirely. That means the enemy won't be able to either."

I rolled the word over in my mind. *Together.* Celeste held influence over him, something I couldn't hope to match—but maybe I could do something else.

"What if . . ." I planted the image in the eagle's mind, seeing if he would be receptive to it. Manus began to rustle, chittering excitedly.

Taking that as permission, instead of pulling, I pushed my magic down that thread of connection. I stepped back as the eagle began to shift. The feathers along his wings disappeared. He grew, his body lengthening and bulking as scales replaced feathers. His end feathers disappeared, replaced by a slashing tail ending in sharp spikes. Manus's head was the last part to shift, horns emerging as the beak disappeared, replaced by a snarling maw of fanged teeth.

A dragon, yet not. Manus was smaller, more agile, and lacked the forelegs Julian and I had when shifted.

The dragon shifted from foot to foot, stretching out his leathery wings before cocking his head to us. Then he reared, feeling out his new body. When he made to caw, a roar emerged instead, followed by a steady stream of fire. The other eagles scrambled away, dropping from the cliff and flying out of the cavern to escape the flames.

Celeste's eyes went wide, and then she was smiling—laughing. "This is going to change everything."

I spent the rest of the day using my magic to turn eagles into dragons—the ones that were receptive to it. If the creature denied the transition, I let them be. Those with eggs or young chicks seemed least determined to shift, preferring to remain in their true forms until their young were grown.

By the time the sun set, I was exhausted, hardly able to rouse the energy to descend the mountain or winnow back to the castle. Julian came, lifting me into his arms.

I was asleep before we could make it back to his chambers.

The next day, it was the same. I winnowed to the peak with Celeste, not wanting to waste precious time hiking. By the end of the second day, we had twenty-two newly formed dragons in an array of colors ranging from brown to gold and burgundy. They flew about the peak, getting used to their new forms.

Celeste and I pushed our influence out to them, guiding and training them in their new bodies.

In the afternoon, everyone came to see. Nic and August, the Seven, Julian, Sena, and Gemma. We watched the dragons soar around the peak from the Aerie. After the devastation following the Moroi attack, we felt a spark of hope.

"One dragon is worth a hundred Fae soldiers," August mused.

Nic stood at his side, eyes wide with wonder. "You just turned the tide of this war, Misha."

I beamed, taking my sister's hand. I'd give anything to see Adrienne's face when she realized what was coming for her.

CHAPTER 35
Misha

"Good morning, love."

Lips pressed beneath my ear, then ran down my neck.

I sighed, reaching for Julian, but only grasped empty sheets. Grumbling my dissatisfaction, I peeked open an eye to see him standing beside the bed, fully clothed in the candlelight.

I turned to face him, reaching out from beneath the warm duvet into the chilled air. "What are you—"

Julian stepped back, evading my grip as a smile danced on his lips. "There's somewhere I want to show you."

"Now?" The sky outside of the windows was still black. I groaned, pulling the duvet back over my eyes. It was too cold and too early.

A moment later, arms wound around me, pulling back the sheets. I yelped like a fox yanked from its warm den but allowed Julian to haul me up until I was kneeling at the edge of the bed.

After spending the last few days working with the eagles-turned-dragons, I could have slept another several hours in blissful, dreamless sleep. But if he was going to insist I wake . . .

Julian let me tug him forward by his belt until his face was only inches from mine. His hands grasped my hips, steadying me. His skin was warm as I nuzzled into him, hands sliding up his chest. He smelled like a rain-soaked forest with a hint of something sharper, almost metallic. My lips dragged over his neck, my tongue reaching out to taste him.

His hands tightened on my hips. I whimpered at the feeling. I wanted him beneath me. I wanted him to grip me harder, to mark me with fingertip-shaped bruises as I rode—

"*Misha*," Julian groaned, stepping back to put space between us. Only a few inches, but enough to pull me from my lust-induced daze.

I wanted to jolt back, cower at the rejection. We hadn't been intimate since the Solstice. But before I could pull away, Julian's hand slid up my back, pulling me closer again. I met his eyes, reading the want on his face. His pupils were blown with desire.

Julian brought a hand to my chin, lifting as he planted a delicate kiss on my lips. "Come with me."

Not a rejection, I realized. But whatever had compelled him to wake before the sunrise, whatever he wanted to show me, was important to him.

I sighed, sitting back on my heels before sliding off the bed. I hissed as my bare feet hit the cool floor, then wrapped my arms around him again, silently urging him to carry me. Julian chuckled, obliging. My thighs wrapped around his waist as I asked, "What do I need to wear?"

The air was frigid as we walked onto the turret. Thankfully, the fur-lined leathers I'd put on—in a matte black matching Julian's—stayed the worst of the chill. The sky was black, with only a hint of violet on the eastern horizon as stars shimmered above us. Only a small sliver of the waning crescent moon remained.

"I loved to come up here as a boy, watch the sunrise over the mountains," Julian said, his breath fogging in the chill of the late October air. He came up behind me, sliding his arms around mine—already wrapped around myself in the cold—and tucked his head into the curve of my neck. "I wanted to see it with you, but—"

Leaning into him and his warmth, my head fell back against his shoulder as I peered up at him. "But?"

Julian stilled, hesitating before he said, "I thought it might be more fun to see it from the sky."

Smiling, I turned, taking both of his hands in mine. If we were to be monsters, the least we could do was enjoy it.

Considering how each time he or I shifted we shredded through our clothes, this time, when my magic flowed into Julian, he cast the clothing away, holding it elsewhere to be recalled when returning to his Fae form.

His dragon's scales gleamed in the starlight, the silvery blue of a storm cloud. I ran a hand along the scaled snout, looking into Julian's grey irises that remained unchanged. When he stepped back, he looked like part of the castle—a incandescent being that was meant to guard and protect.

I pulled at the magic within me, shifting my body until it matched his, equal in size and height. For the first time, I took the opportunity to look at myself, at the black scales and broad, leathery wings.

Something about this form felt right in some ways, more so than being Fae. I could don all the darkness that resided within me and turn it into talons and fangs and horns.

There was no more hiding behind the deception of beauty. In this form, I no longer slept. I was fully awake—free.

Julian saw it all and loved me regardless. Even with the worst, most vile parts of me on display, he saw and was not deterred. Julian's cheek met mine, brushing against me in a loving gesture. *I love you.*

When he dove off the turret, I followed, wings spreading as we fell, gliding through the air. I reveled in the cool air upon my face and the feel of my heart pounding as my wings beat to bring me higher into the sky.

The sky turned navy, then violet and pink as we flew, the mountains slowly coming to life beneath us. We dove, testing ourselves as we soared and banked through the mountains' crevices, cloaking ourselves in the silver morning mist.

As the sky lightened, the forest awoke. In this form, I could still feel the animals below as they rustled and moved. Tiny threads connected me to each of them, the life beneath me as I flew. Some birds, those too young to know fear, flew with us, dipping and gliding beneath our wings.

Julian and I flew across the mountains, reveling in the wings—the pure joy of flying—for the first time. He was magnificent as he moved—a king among beasts.

He gestured to one of the nearby mountains with his head. I followed him and we landed on one of its larger cliffs near the peak, the sun not yet risen.

I shifted back first, calling to the clothing I'd worn this morning. The top made it nearly on, with only one arm left hanging limp, and the pants appeared on but unbuttoned. The boots landed with one off and another five meters away. Not bad for a first try.

Julian lowered his head, my hands reaching for his face. He fared worse than I had as he shifted: pants on but backwards, his leather armor and undershirt missing him entirely and landing on the nearest boulder, and barefoot, his boots nowhere to be seen.

He laughed, watching me right my clothes and collect my stray boot. "We desperately need to practice that."

"I'm not the one that's completely barefoot." I chuckled as he fixed his pants before grabbing his jacket, buckling it on.

Julian took my hand, leading me to an obscured path. For several minutes, we climbed higher up the peak.

"Where are you taking me?"

"A place I've dreamed of showing you since the moment we met."

My heart melted at that, and I gripped his hand tighter.

The path finally opened up, revealing a mountainside covered in cascading pools, water flowing from one to the other as they swept down the mountain. Steam rose from them in curling wisps. Wisteria dripped alongside them, while buds of fuchsia hung from the rocks above, thriving in the humid air.

"I added the fuchsia," Julian said, pointing to it.

I thought about the night we met. "You remembered."

"I could never forget."

I didn't know if my breathlessness was from the beauty of this place or him, his brown skin nearly glowing in the soft light.

320

Julian moved behind me, wrapping his arms around me from behind as we faced east. The sun rose, bathing us in golden light. I turned to look up at him; the way the sunlight hit his skin turned it bronze, his grey irises stark against it. He was the most beautiful male I'd ever seen.

He was already looking at me.

"Beautiful," Julian said, leaning forward until our lips met. The kiss was not soft. It was a claiming—he of me, and I of him.

"Misha," he groaned against my mouth, lifting me. I wrapped my legs around his waist, needing to be flush against him.

He walked us to the nearest pool and set my feet down on the soft earth near the edge. Julian began to pull away, and a choked sound of protest escaped from me. He kissed me again, his hips pressing against mine. I groaned at the hardness waiting for me there.

"I need to get these off, love." His fingers tugged at the waistband of my pants, unbuttoning them. I nodded hastily, reaching for the buckles of his jacket, swiftly undoing them and yanking it off.

I needed him closer.

I reluctantly let him go as Julian drew the pants down my legs, stepping out of them and my boots as I shed my own jacket and undershirt, leaving me naked before him. He quickly stripped his own pants before taking my hand and leading me into the warm water.

I turned, backing away from him to the ledge, water cascading off the side and spilling into the pool beneath. I rested my elbows on the stone, breasts jutting out. Julian stalked toward me, eyes blazing with hunger as he took me in. Standing over me, he grasped my hair, tugging my head back to drag his lips against the column of my throat.

"Sit on the ledge, Misha," he commanded, "and spread those pretty legs for me."

I did as he bid. The air was frigid, sending goosebumps down my body, but Julian's hands were hot as he grasped my thighs, pushing them wider. His palms slid up to grasp my hips, keeping me steady—securely on the ledge—as he took his time making his way down my body, planting kisses upon my thighs as he went.

"*Please*," I panted, unable to take the teasing. We hadn't been together like this in the four months since the Solstice. I hadn't been ready, too lost in myself and the grief.

But now—I needed him *now*.

Julian didn't hesitate, lowering his mouth to me as he began to feast. His warm lips replaced the cold air, and I groaned as he licked and stroked, sending pleasure coiling deep within me.

"*Julian*," I pleaded. I was wound too tightly, wanted it too much.

One hand let go of my hip, stroking down my stomach. "Shh, love. Breathe." He slid a finger into me.

I clenched around it as he slowly thrust in and out. His other hand slid around my back, holding me to him as I trembled. He licked and sucked at my clit, followed by a soft graze of teeth that had me crying out. When he added a second finger, curling them into the sensitive spot inside of me, I exploded, crying his name. Julian kept moving, making love to me with his mouth and hands, extending the climax.

When I finally came down, he gently kissed my stomach before rising to stand.

"Turn around."

I obeyed, guided by his hands. He bent me over, one hand stroking down my back as the other went to my throat. "You are so fucking beautiful, Misha."

I squirmed as I felt the tip of his cock positioned at my entrance. "Julian, I need—"

My breath whooshed out as he thrust fully into me. He kept still, pulsing inside me as he pulled me up. My back met his chest, his hand still clasped around my throat.

His lips caressed the shell of my ear. "How could you ever think I could be without you, Misha?" Julian began to thrust, causing breathy moans to spill from my lips. "How could you ever think I could be without you when together, we feel like this?" His other hand circled my clit, accentuating his words.

He paused only briefly to lift my knee onto the ledge, spreading my legs wider so he could thrust deeper inside me. My head turned, seeking him. Our mouths met, his tongue softly parting my lips to seek mine. Every inch of me burned for him.

"Come for me, love."

I exploded, clenching around him.

Julian cursed, his thrusts growing faster. "*Misha*," he sighed my name like a prayer, like devotion, and then I felt him climaxing alongside me.

When he finished, he pulled out, turning me to face him and pulling me into his chest. Catching our breath, I melted into him, utterly bone-less. His hands stroked down my back, pushing the damp hair from my face.

"I love you." He kissed me softly, then again. "I will always love you. Nothing we discover tonight matters. Only this—only us."

I lifted my head, studying him. My hands traced his cheekbones, his nose, and lips. His eyes fluttered closed as my fingertips graced his long eyelashes, committing every piece of him to memory.

"Always."

CHAPTER 36
Misha

At dusk, we entered the Temple of the Above.

Sena walked ahead in her billowing priestess robes, the blue regal against her black skin.

We entered a cylindrical room with no windows, lit by only eight lanterns containing ever-burning faerie lights along the marble walls. An eight-pointed star marked the center of the floor, silver against the white. From its center rose a small pedestal on which rested a shallow bowl of lapis lazuli, its gold flecks glittering in the soft light. Two pendulums hung suspended on each side of the bowl: gold rings at the end of the silver chains.

Sena pulled a lever near the door, and the roof above split, revealing the moonless night sky. As we doused our torches, the stars seemed to sparkle brighter, almost like they were leaning closer to watch.

Sena walked to the bowl. "You will each prick your finger and place two drops of blood into the center of the basin. Then you stand on opposite sides, here—" She indicated one point of the star near the first pendulum for me and the opposite for Julian. "—And here. You will take the ring in your hand, casting a drop of magic into it, and then release it."

She handed us a small needle. I pricked my finger first and passed it to Julian, who did the same. Blood welled as I squeezed my fingertip, allowing two drops to splatter into the center of the bowl and mix with Julian's.

I took my place and clasped the gold ring in my hand, pushing a sliver of the essence of my magic into it.

Julian moved to the opposite side. "Ready, love?"

"Are you?" I cocked an eyebrow. "After this, there's no getting rid of me."

Julian only laughed. "Regardless, I could never be rid of you."

Nor I him. My soul would yearn for his for the rest of my existence.

I took a deep breath, and we released the rings over the bowl. They spun around each other in circles, crossing and interloping until—clink.

The rings locked together.

Sena's smile was overjoyed, her hands clasped together. "Mates."

Julian came around the bowl to clutch my waist in one hand while the other went for my hair. I stumbled backward as he kissed me fiercely. "I knew it from the moment I saw you in that pink dress."

"*Fuchsia*," I retorted. Julian only smiled, kissing me again.

We stepped back, his arm looping around me, keeping me close as we gave Sena space to cleanse the bowl and the rings, using magic to separate them once more. Nic and August, having watched us, already knew what to do.

Nic pricked her finger, holding it over the bowl to place her two drops of blood. Then she passed the thin needle to August. Before he did the same, he took her hand, bringing the fingertip she'd pierced to his lips and kissing it. My sister's face flamed, but she was smiling as she walked to the other side, almost giddy with love.

August pricked his own finger and held it over the bowl, their two drops apiece mixing. Then he and Nic took the rings, their eyes never leaving each other's, the gazes of two people desperately in love, and dropped them.

The rings glided through the air, spinning as they grew closer and closer together. They clinked, brushing against one another, and fell still.

Separate.

CHAPTER 37
Nic

The rings were still.

The air did not shift. The seconds did not pass. Only the stars twinkled above, laughing at us—at our hope.

At our love.

"August," Sena whispered, cracking the silence. Her voice was pained as she put a hand on his shoulder.

Neither he nor I moved, too stunned to look away from the rings.

Separate.

We were not mates.

The silence in the chamber was thick, cloying. Bands of iron seemed to have wrapped around my chest, keeping me from drawing breath.

"I don't understand," I whispered, still staring at the ring hanging there all alone.

I never saw him moving, but suddenly, August was there, clasping my face in his hands.

"I don't understand," I repeated as I met his eyes, my voice louder this time. "I feel you. I feel you everywhere." Even now, my magic pulled to him, coiling at the edges of my skin, reaching out for his. Every time we touched it was the same.

August's silver eyes glittered with unshed tears. His thumb stroked my cheek. "I always knew I couldn't deserve you."

"That's fucking bullshit," I cursed. I pulled back, pushing around him as I stepped toward the bowl, searching for that damned needle. "Do it again."

Sena shook her head apologetically. "It won't change the outcome, Nicole."

I refused to accept that. "Do it again," I growled. *Where the hell was it?*

There, gleaming tauntingly from the floor.

"Nicole." August's hand came to my arm, pulling me away as I knelt to reach for it.

I tried to yank my arm away, but his grip held firm. "It's wrong, August! It's not true. We have to do it again. We can go to a different temple. Find another priestess."

He shook his head. "*Nicole.*" He choked on my name, his voice so full of pain and sorrow.

I whirled on him, vision blurring. "Don't say my name like that." I gripped his shirt, pulling him closer.

The others had left, fleeing the temple to leave just August and me.

August's hands rested softly on my hips. "Like what, sweetheart?"

"Like you're saying goodbye." The tears spilled over, streaking down my cheeks. When he said nothing, I gripped him tighter, harder.

"*August,*" I pleaded with him.

His hands wiped away my tears. "I love you, Nicole. I will love you forever, but—"

I snarled. "*No*—no buts. We love each other, and that's it. I don't care if we're mates. I don't care if the stars don't want us together. It's my choice—*our* choice of who to love."

August leaned closer, pressing his forehead to mine. His tears ran onto my cheeks, his pain flooding me. "I am yours, Nicole. *Always*. But no matter how badly I want this—want *you*, more than anything else I've ever wanted before—I think I always knew, deep down, that you couldn't be mine. I could never deserve—"

"Stop it." I choked, pushing against him, and he let me, stepping back. The words were a stab into my heart. I wanted him to fight this—to rage like I was.

"I won't keep you from your happiness, Nicole."

"You *are*," I growled. "Because you aren't fighting this. Because you aren't choosing me. Because you aren't fighting for *us*."

"But your mate—"

"My *mate*," I sneered, the word a curse, "will die if they try to take me from you." I went to August, clasping a hand to his neck, then his cheek.

He leaned into my touch, his palms covering my hands, holding me to him.

"Do you want me to carve out their heart?" I whispered. "To prove that I love *you* and only you? I'll do it." I swore, ready to seal it in blood if he willed it. "If they try to take me from you, I'll tear it out and serve it to you as a sign of my devotion."

"Nicole," he murmured, running his hands across my shoulders. My waist. Touching me as if he wouldn't get the chance again.

"Please, don't do this, August," I whispered. "Don't pull away. Don't do this." I repeated the words over and over again until it was a chant in my blood.

I love you. Don't do this. Don't leave me.

He didn't answer me with words, his lips instead meeting mine. August's hand clasped the back of my head, nudging the kiss deeper with his mouth, his tongue. He grasped my waist and lifted me. I clung to him, my legs and arms wrapping around his waist.

August winnowed us back to his chambers. He laid me gently on the bed before making love to me, slowly and devoutly. When we finished, we began again, not wasting a single moment apart until we were utterly spent.

I tried not to fall asleep, I fought the exhaustion with everything I had, terrified of what would come next.

But eventually, I did. Splayed across August's chest, I fell asleep to the rhythm of his heart.

When I awoke, gently nudged awake by the cruel sunlight, I felt the bed cold beside me. My arm reached and found only empty sheets.

August was gone.

CHAPTER 38
Nic

All August left was a letter sitting on the pillow beside me.

I considered burning the letter without reading it but couldn't bring myself to cast the flames into my hand. My magic rebelled at the thought, abhorred. I had to read what he'd written, even as I knew it would break my heart.

Nicole,

Jophiel and I went to the border to meet with our generals in preparation for what is to come. We will return in a few days. I hope that in my absence, you can understand.

August

P.S. I will always be yours, Snow.

I crumpled the note, throwing it as far from me as I could before turning my head into the pillow and screaming until my throat was raw. The screams turned to choked sobs.

Gone—August was gone.

August wanted me to understand when *he* couldn't do the same. Otherwise, he would have known that leaving me was more devastating than anything else he could have done. I'd rather cut out my own heart and hand it to Adrienne myself. I would rather burn the damned continent to the ground before giving him up.

But he doesn't feel the same, a nagging voice said in the back of my mind. The immediate, *untrue*, that followed warred with it.

No, August loved me. He was just a damned fool who didn't think he deserved to be loved back. The thought made me furious, and I clung to it, desperately hanging on to the anger.

Anger was good.

It was much better than shattering apart.

Falling to my hands and knees, I searched for the letter, finding it moments later beneath his desk. I laid it out on the hard surface, trying and failing to smooth the creases. My hands shook, tears welling in my eyes again.

I carefully folded the note, tucking it into a book—my favorite novel. August had gotten it for me, setting it on the end table for me to find our first week here.

Half an hour later, I was running.

I sprinted as hard as I could, exhausting myself across a trail that threaded through the forest and then along a gorge. When I returned hours later, I went into the training ring, pummeling my fists against a dummy until the straw was leaking out.

No one approached me. No one asked what was wrong. They all kept their distance, glancing away when I turned toward them.

I kept going even when someone finally approached. He stood against the stone wall, watching silently.

I kept my eyes on the dummy, my knuckles raw and aching. "Say what you want to say, Julian."

He walked closer, until he stood within my eye line. "There's something you need to understand about my brother."

That gave me pause. I dropped my hands, turning to face him fully. "Don't lecture me on how I don't understand him—I love him. I know everything I need to."

Julian nodded, unphased. "But you don't know everything, specifically about who he was before. You don't know his history. August is doing this because he wants to give you what your parents had. What your aunts had."

I remembered how Alesia and Eve had looked at each other, so in love. Even when they argued, there was always the base note of their endless devotion beneath. The same was true of my parents. It was in the way my father spoke of my mother, like she was still with him even years after her passing. Even in the bracelet's shred of a memory, I could sense it—their undying love.

I remembered how August had pulled me out of the fire, how he held me as I broke apart night after night. How he'd lied, making himself a murderer and traitor all to protect me. I remembered how he made the tea.

In the months since the Summer Solstice, I'd felt nothing but cherished by him—which made his leaving all the worse.

"He *has*," I snarled.

My words were cutting, thick with jealousy. Julian and my sister were confirmed mates—as they should be. I'd known it from the moment I saw them together. They were a match made by the stars.

But I couldn't help the envy. August and I were never going to be that easy.

I removed the wrapping from my hands as I walked toward the table, hoping water would ease the tightness in my throat.

Julian followed. "You misunderstand. Your parents and aunts were mated, which means they were meant to be together in August's mind. Our father was not mated to either of our mothers. They were only married."

I spun on him. "August is *nothing* like your father."

"I know that, and you know that—but August doesn't," Julian said. "It's his greatest fear, being like him. And both his mother, Yuki, and Sena initially loved our father. They fell hard for his charms and manipulations during their courtships and married after only a few months. You know how that turned out."

I did. Josiah had murdered Yuki for daring to leave him after years of abuse, then inflicted similar traumas onto Sena as soon as they were married. Josiah had done the same to his sons before August had stopped it, finally challenging his father to a duel for the throne and ending him.

Julian went on. "I was nine when our father died, but August had nearly two hundred and fifty years as his son before then. Much of that time they were estranged, but it still took its toll. August, for the most part, has put our father behind him, but he still worries that they are too similar, as much as he tries to be otherwise."

I thought of how much he cared for his friends, his family, his country. How he was always thinking of others before himself. How August held me like I was sacred.

He would never—*never* raise a hand to me. I was never in danger with him. "August will never be like Josiah."

"No, he won't," Julian said, expressing the same sentiment. "But August doesn't know what we know. He has ghosts in his past, from the first war and before—things our father made him do. At his core, he thinks he is no better that his darkest moments, no matter how much he tries to atone."

I remained silent, ruminating over what Julian said. No matter who August had been a hundred years ago, that wasn't who he was now. And even if it was . . .

"I can't be without him," I whispered. "I can't live this life without him."

Never. In this life or the next, I would only love August Warin.

"Good," Julian said, his eyes fierce. "For once, August should be fought for."

Four mornings later, at breakfast, Miranda rushed to Misha and me, nearly pulsing with excitement.

"I found them." Miranda laid a map out before us as Misha and me jumped from our seats to see. Julian walked over, listening.

"A few spots emerged when I scryed for the witches. But this one—" She pointed to a point on the map. High in the mountains, and approximately a hundred miles north of Haldrin and the cabin, I noted painfully. "—feels right. It only landed there once, and I can't explain it, but I know they're there."

The spot she pointed to wasn't far from the road we'd traveled when coming to Ankaa. I studied the map and the lines of trees; I could almost see the dark woods and creeping mist in my mind.

I knew Miranda was right.

I looked up, my eyes meeting Misha's. "We're going."

Misha, still looking at the map, hesitated. "When?"

"Now—this morning." I pushed back from the table, ready to head to my chambers—August's chambers, I thought with a pang—to collect my weapons. He could leave, but I wasn't fucking going anywhere.

Misha straightened, crossing her arms. "Who is coming with us?"

"It should only be you two," Miranda said. "I would go, but . . ." Her words drifted away, but her hesitation made sense. If she was killed, Damian would be, too.

"You don't have to," I finished. "You are needed here."

"I'm coming," Julian said, his brow furrowed in concern, arm around my sister's waist.

Miranda shook her head. "Fae cannot go. Without a doubt, the witches' home will be spelled. It will be a death trap for your kind."

"But it's safe for us?" Misha asked, looking between me and Miranda.

Misha and I had been working on casting witch magic, drawing on the elements and natural forces flowing through everything, but we both still had much to learn.

"Not safe, exactly," Miranda answered. "But you are part witch. Any wards cast won't be able to hold you like they would the pure-blooded Fae."

"You don't have to go, Misha," I said, meeting my sister's eyes.

My sister's head jerked back as if I'd slapped her. "You aren't going alone, Nicky."

My gut twisted. If something went wrong . . . but one look at Misha said she wouldn't back down, and I wouldn't either. The witches could provide dire information about how Adrienne collected information and magic from the Void.

I nodded. "We leave in an hour."

Miranda looked hesitantly between me and Misha. "Should we notify August?"

"He left. I haven't heard from him in days," I said, looking at no one and trying my hardest to keep the emotion from my voice. "Whether I go or not is none of his concern. He's made that quite clear."

I walked away, not waiting for another reply.

CHAPTER 39
Misha

An hour later, after changing into leathers and collecting our weapons, we met at the castle's courtyard beneath a towering red maple, one as old as the stone itself. The Iradelmar hung at Nic's waist and the Mercedelmar at mine. Eve's bow was slung across my back.

I'd taken several minutes running my hands over the carvings after Nic had given it to me. Images of jasmine and freesia intertwined with moons, stars, and suns were etched into the yew. Now, I stood beneath the tree, spinning their gold mating ring around the middle finger of my right hand. I didn't know whose I had—if the band was Alesia's or Eve's—but it didn't matter. It was a part of both.

Julian clasped my face. "Be careful."

"I'm always careful." I smiled as best I could to hide the anxiety slowly flooding me. Julian didn't take the bait, his jaw clenching as he saw my diversion for what it was. My lips dropped as I swallowed. "I will try," I promised.

Julian nodded and knelt before Rasalas, eye to eye with the jaguar. He lifted a hand, rubbing behind the familiar's ear. "Guard her with your life." I could have sworn the cat nodded in response. Julian stood and kissed me one last time. "I'll be waiting for you, love."

My heart surged with warmth. With him waiting, I could come back from anything.

Nic stood a few meters away, looking out at the mountains with her own familiar, Eilith, perched on her shoulder. I wondered if she realized she was looking to the south, where August had gone.

Miranda went between Nic and me, tugging on our braids for any loose strands. "Whatever you do, do *not* allow them to have a piece of you. Your hair, a nail, even a single drop of blood. With any piece of you, they could devise a spell that could devastate you."

"Killing us?" I asked.

The witch's face grew grave. "There are worse things than death."

Unease flooded me, and one look at Nic told me she'd felt the same.

"They won't be forthcoming with any information," Miranda warned, "and if they are, know that it is a trap. Nothing comes that easy without a price."

Nic and I nodded, understanding, and joined hands.

"Ready, sister?" she asked.

I squeezed her hands. "Ready."

We winnowed, landing upon the road that had taken us to Ankaa. We would trek several miles north to approximately where Miranda had indicated on the map. Nic kept the parchment folded in her pocket.

For the first hour, we walked in silence, tense as if anything might jump out of the woods. Eilith soared above the canopy, scouting, and

Rasalas threaded through the trees ahead of us, checking back every quarter hour.

My magic reached out, latching threads to all animals within a mile radius as well as the plants and trees. I saw half through my eyes and half through theirs, monitoring for any threat. Nymphs watched from a distance, Dryads and Oreads flitting from one tree to the next. Softly glowing sprites danced in the canopy above, although the further we walked, the less inclined the faeries seemed to follow.

It was a sign we were on the right path.

I took a moment to watch my sister. The shadows beneath her eyes were dark, almost bruised, as she scanned the forest. I didn't think she'd gotten more than a few hours' sleep a night since the discovery that she and August weren't mates.

If she was sleeping at all.

Julian had talked to her, trying to give her some insight into August's mind and decision. But August shouldn't have left like he did, even if he thought it was best. And I was sure August wouldn't have if he'd known we'd be doing this today.

I strode closer to Nic, breaking the silence with my soft whisper. "We should have sent word to August. At least notified him of our plans."

Nic kept walking, silently stepping over a fallen limb covered in toadstools. "He gave up the right to know when *he* left without telling *me*."

Fair, but he'd been against us coming here and putting her into any further danger. I couldn't blame him—August had been the one to pull my sister, so close to death, from the lake. I pictured Nic, pale as the ice and snow she'd been laid upon. The thought was like a dagger to the heart.

"That's not the same, and you know it. He's going to lose his shit."

My sister shrugged, feigning indifference as her fingers brushed over the petals of a spicebush. The water on its yellow leaves turned to ice, her magic betraying her emotions beneath her stone wall countenance.

. . . Maybe August *needed* to lose his shit and realize how ridiculous he was being. He clearly wanted what was best for Nic, even if it made him utterly miserable. But my sister didn't want a perfect mate—she never had. She wanted him.

The forest grew quieter again as I slowed, giving her space.

After another half-hour of hiking through the mountains—Nic pausing once to check our progress on the map—a flash caught my eye, little more than a sliver of white between the trees.

I stopped, Rasalas halting at my side. Nic did the same, on alert but not knowing why.

I felt a thread, a tug stronger than the others. I stepped off our path, moving deeper into the forest.

"Misha," Nic hissed, watching. Eilith flew down, landing on the branch above her.

I held up a finger, quieting her as I kept my eyes on the space between the trees.

The flash of white gleamed and was gone again.

I waited, standing utterly still as I listened closely to the forest. The glimmer appeared again to my right, and my head snapped to it. Slowly, I caught sight of it weaving between the trees, wings flapping softly as it landed a few feet away.

The purely snow-white bird was the size of a hawk. It had the same hooked beak—also pale—but its tail feathers were longer, elegant as they swept across the ground. The bird was iridescent, gleaming softly of gold then silver as the sunlight shifted.

The creature was one of myth, one from old faerie tales we'd been told as children. No being I knew of had seen one for at least a hundred years. As a healer, Eve had been fascinated by them. She'd told me stories of the birds, of the time she'd been lucky enough to see one.

The Caladrius. A bird whose tears could heal any ailment.

I knelt, sitting on my heels as the Caladrius approached, rustling its downy wings.

"You have what I need, don't you?" I lifted a hand, asking permission. The bird dipped its head, allowing me to stroke its crest, the feathers there more gold than the rest. "You have what I've been searching for."

The bird cocked its head, looking at me as an opalescent tear gleamed from one onyx eye. I cupped my hand, catching it in my palm before it was wasted on the ground.

"Thank you." I called magic into my palm, studying the tear, its makeup and texture, as it absorbed into my skin.

The bird, having given me this remarkable gift, stepped back. It noticed Nic standing nearby and looked away. Bowing once more, the bird flapped its wings and took flight, leaving us.

"Was that—" Nic murmured, watching the Caladrius as it flew away.

I nodded, standing and returning to her side. I could feel the magic of the tear seeping into my blood vessels and through my bones and tissue, like a star floating through my system.

It was silent for a few moments as we began walking again.

Nic said softly, "Eve would have loved that."

I imagined our aunt's face breaking into a radiant smile as Nic and I told her the story. I took my sister's hand, squeezing it gently. "Maybe she sent the bird to us from behind the Veil."

The forest grew thicker as we walked. It felt as if no human or High Fae had dared tread here for decades. With my magic, I split a thick patch of brush, making space for Nic and me to walk through. Rasalas trailed behind as we came upon an arch of mangled vines and thorns.

The view of the forest beyond wasn't quite right, warped somehow. As Nic and I inspected it further, we realized it wasn't part of this forest at all—somehow, the trees belonged to another wood.

"I think this is it," Nic said, reaching for my hand.

I took it, turning to her. "Together?"

"Together."

We stepped through the portal.

CHAPTER 40
Misha

When we passed through, we realized Eilith and Rasalas were not with us. We turned around to see Ras pacing beyond the arch and Eilith flying and scraping at the surface with her talons. Neither familiar could pass the glimmering surface.

"Unfortunately," Nic broke the silence, her eyes filled with pain for leaving the hawk behind. "I think this means we're in the right place."

The forest here was more still, darker due to the canopy of gnarled and mangled branches knitted closely together. The sun above was obscured by thick clouds, casting everything in a bluish sheen. The trees seemed ancient, their trunks covered in emerald moss. Silver mist seeped through the trees.

We stepped further into the woods. The trees parted, revealing a lake housed within a crater. The water was a dark, impenetrable black, the surface partially obscured by fog so thick that to become lost in it would be to lose yourself.

I held my sister's hand tighter.

Mounds of jagged white stone pierced the lake's surface, spread out like graveyard mausoleums. The pieces made up larger statues: a horse drinking from the lake, a wolf mid-howl, a coiled serpent. Winding through them, a pathway of black stones rose from beneath the water, leading to a cottage on an island hardly larger than the building itself.

As we walked along the path, we neared one of the jutting mounds. The smooth white stones that were cobbled together to make up the statues were oddly shaped. Some were long with rounded ends, others flat and winglike; another was a round disk with protruding spikes—no, a chain of them.

My gut tightened. They weren't stones at all. "Is that . . .?"

Nic nodded grimly, squeezing my hand, silencing me as we passed the mound of bones, my eyes never leaving the spine that could be either faerie or human in origin.

As we neared, I took in the stone cottage, moss and lichen covering the walls and roof. A chimney puffed out white smoke, adding to the mist.

When we stepped onto the island, the door, barred with what I immediately recognized as Galorian silver, creaked open. "Come, daughters of land and sea," said a voice from within.

Nic and I glanced at each other, uneasy. Keeping each other tightly in the other's grasp, we stepped through.

The singular room was round. At the back, a circling staircase led to a level above. A counter topped with towering shelves of herbs, cursed artifacts, animal bones, and jars of things I didn't want to think too much about ran around the diameter. There were the skulls of wolves and foxes, the intricate wings of bats, and the long vertebral neck of what could only be a swan.

In the center stood three witches. As Nic and I stepped further into the cottage, they surrounded us, curious. Three cats toying with a pair of mice.

"You look just as I dreamed." A witch with dark brown skin leaned in toward Nic, sniffing. "And smell divine, like burning fires in winter." Her pale lavender eyes glowed, the irises nearly white as her hair, the color of bleached bone. She lifted a hand, not quite touching Nic, but feeling the air around her. She met my sister's eyes hungrily. "I can *feel* the power radiating off you."

"Not as much as this one." The witch with blonde hair—more yellow than gold—leaned toward me. I could almost see the veins beneath her pale skin, filled with dark blood. "*She* has a monster sleeping beneath the beauty." She leaned closer, breathing in deeply as her eyes shut, eyelashes fluttering as if in rapture. Her amber eyes snapped open. "Your essence is the thing of dreams, sunrises, and lovesick ballads. I could revel a hundred years in the youth and beauty I could siphon from you. Oh, to see the world through your eyes. But you're not so easily taken, are you? I wouldn't make it one year, much less a hundred. You'd fester, rotting me away from the inside as revenge."

My gut tightened, thinking of the piles of bones outside.

"And you—" The last one leaned toward Nic, a witch with olive skin, russet eyes, and hair the red of ripe cherries. "—Your essence would go down like starlight, tempting, only to reveal a nightmare. You'd cause a swift death, just like your fury." She reached for Nic's braid.

My sister hissed, baring her teeth as she lunged, sending the witch skittering back.

The russet-eyed witch laughed, clapping her hands together and nearly bouncing with glee. "So feisty! All fire and rage."

"Nicole," crooned the white-haired witch. I discerned her as the leader of the three—or at the very least, the most stable. She turned to me, her gaze traveling the length of my body. "And Misha. Two of witch and fae and human. We've been waiting for you."

Nic tensed. "And you are?"

The witch with yellow hair spoke first, curtsying delicately as she held the skirts of her yellow-embroidered dress. "Xantha."

"Alba," said the white-haired witch. She was perhaps the oldest, though no lines showed on her skin—on any of their cruelly beautiful faces. Her pale lavender dress fluttered around her legs as she continued circling us.

"Carmine." The red-haired witch wrapped her arms around Xantha's neck from behind.

Alba joined her sisters, leaning against the counter. "You've come with questions."

"If we have," Nic said, cutting straight to it. "What is their cost?"

"See? What did I tell you?" Carmine said in her sing-song, her lips lifting into a snake's smile. "They're clever, clever girls."

"Nothing you can't afford to lose," Xantha answered with an equally sly grin.

"That's not an answer," I refuted. The threads of my magic to the life around us were thinner here, half a tug away from snapping. I hated the feeling and wondered if Nic's tether to hers felt the same.

I wondered if we'd made a grave mistake in coming here.

"I request but a single drop of your blood," Alba said as if it were an insignificant price. "One from each of you."

Definitely a mistake. My eyes met Nic's. *No.*

"In exchange for?" Nic pressed.

Xantha smiled. "For the answers in which you seek, fair one."

"As many answers as I have questions," Nic dealt. "For two drops of blood, only to be given after you have answered them all."

"Of course." Carmine rolled her eyes dramatically as she sashayed toward Nic, reaching to run a finger along her sleeve. "*Faeries,* so particular about their bargains."

My sister's hand darted out, grasping the witch's wrist in a hard grip. "You three will answer *honestly.*" Nic thrust her back. "And never touch me."

Carmine cried out. Clutching her arm to her chest, she whimpered as she sank back against the wall. A red burn marred her skin from Nic's searing touch.

"Quiet," Alba snapped at the red witch, before turning back to Nic. "You have a deal."

"Done," Nic agreed. "But I only speak for myself. Misha will give you nothing."

Alba's eyes went to slits—she'd been had. "Clever, indeed."

"Blood is blood." Xantha clapped, her yellow sleeve drifting down to her elbow. A pale gold tattoo of a snake wrapped around her forearm, the head of which rested on the dorsal aspect of her wrist.

Carmine still murmured to herself against the wall. Quiet words about cruel, trickster faeries.

I held my tongue. Regardless if she'd kept me out of the bargain or not, Nic was smarter than this. She must have a plan to keep her from giving up her end of the bargain.

"You want to know what the Void's power is capable of," Alba said, already knowing the reason for our visit. Slowly, she began to pace around us.

"The Master of Life and Death," Carmine crooned reverently, standing straighter.

As the witches shifted, I lightly transferred my weight to keep all three in my sight. "I thought the Between was the giver of life, and the Void the giver of death."

"He is of *both*," Carmine spat, her girlish face twisting into something grotesque and vicious. In a second, it was gone, returned to its lovely state. "The Great Void can take life, making it his own. He showed us how." She picked up the skeleton of a serpent, running her finger along the ridged vertebrae.

It was as Sena had said to us after the Moroi attack—the story Miranda had told us. Witch sisters who stole the life from humans and faeries who wandered too close to their home.

"How?" Nic asked, her face like stone.

"All it takes," Xantha began. "Is a bit of—" She brought her hands to her temples. "—imagination." She fluttered her fingers.

Maybe it was because of how old they were—how sick and twisted they had become after stealing countless lives over the centuries—but these witches were fucking eerie. More than half past mad.

I was getting sick of their games. "What does that mean?"

"You must open your mind to him, lovely one," Alba said. "You call to the Void, and he will call back."

"But you have to be willing to pay the price," Carmine added, twirling as she held out her burgundy skirt. "A life for a life." I caught the flicker of a serpent's tail winding around her ankle, the tattoo ink as red as her hair.

"Is that what you promised him?" Nic asked, a hint of frustration breaking through her façade.

"Indeed," said Xantha. "A heart for a heart. A life for a life. He showed us how to call upon him. How to drain the life from others so we could live a thousand. And all we have to do is find the one that can free him."

That must have been what Adrienne had offered him as well. This is what we came for, the information that we needed. If we knew how Adrienne planned to free the Void, we could stop her.

"And what life is that?" I asked, ready to know and get the hell out of here.

"The life of the one who scorned him," Alba said, her mouth creeping into a sly smile. "The one who told the others how to bind him."

The Siphon, the blood of her child—her descendant. Another witch. Had that been why Adrienne had hunted them, forcing so many into hiding? And how many had these witches killed of their own kind, searching for the distant cousin who might free their master?

I had a sick feeling that we already knew who it was they searched for, who Adrienne seemed so determined to find and steal the heart of. We'd known it all along.

And we'd walked right into their home.

"You know what they say." Xantha leaned toward my sister. "You can't escape *fate*." Her head snapped back, laughing as if she'd told the funniest joke, one only she could understand.

Nic bristled at the words.

"You have your answers. Time to complete your end of the bargain." Alba lifted a small knife. One-half of the blade was Galorian silver, the other black iron. As she shifted, I noted the tattoo around her collar-bones, previously hidden behind her white hair. The pale ink of a serpent winding around her clavicle, encircling her neck like a pendant.

Nic tsked. "I will never have all the answers for which I have questions, and our deal has bounds on neither."

Alba's face dropped, lip curling back in a snarl. "You—"

"But answer me this," Nic walked around her, turning her back on the witches as her finger trailed along the counter lining the room. "There is something else I've been wondering: we were attacked north of the Redwood."

I understood where she was going with this, had put the pieces together as well. "That we were," I said. "It was so peculiar. There were three familiars. Three snakes."

When my sister had made a full lap, she stopped walking. "Three witches with serpent tattoos." Nic tapped her finger on the counter and fire scorched upward, blazing along the trail left behind by her hand.

Xantha yelped, jumping back toward the center of the room. Carmine only laughed, clapping her hands as if this were all some enthralling game.

My sister came to me, grabbing my arm. "Time to go." We hurried through the open door, leaving the witches trapped in a circle of fire.

Only Alba remained still, watching us. She walked forward and stuck her hand into the fire, collecting the ash and withdrawing it, unburned. "We thought you might do that, firecaster."

As Nic and I ran toward the stone steps of the lake, the witch materialized before us and blew a gust of wind strong enough to knock us onto our backs. The ash fluttered down around us.

It wasn't like the rowan wood ash. A piece of it was there, but so was rue, nightshade, and arsenic. It was a combination I knew well, but never in this dosage.

My magic flooded out of me, leaving not a single trace. The threads around me were severed, hanging slack. My breathing shallowed and my limbs went useless in paralysis. I couldn't even turn my head to look at Nic, but I knew she was in a similar state.

Not even my eyelids could blink, burning as they remained open.

"Something for the witch, the fae, *and* the human." Carmine sang as she walked out of the cottage, Xantha at her side. Taking hold of our wrists, the three witches dragged us back inside.

They laid Nic and I on the floor in the center of the room and began to draw a five-pointed star around us. My head was turned so I could glimpse Nic. Her eyes were also open but vacant. Only the slow rise and fall of her chest told me she was still alive.

"They and their little pets killed my baby," Xantha snarled, whipping out another dagger. "I want their scalps as payment."

"Patience." Alba began to cut away Nic's leathers with her small knife, working to expose the area over my sister's heart. "The hearts first."

Xantha sat back, pouting. Carmine began dancing around us, singing some mad song in a voice too lovely for the macabre verses. The words were something about making a dress of threaded black-and-gold hair, a corset of ribs, and a chime of tendons and teeth.

Desperately, I reached out to the earth around me, finding there was one single thread left of my magic, thin and fragile as spider silk. I gently tugged on it, and a small vine curled around Nic's littlest finger. None of the witches noticed.

Blood welled where the thorn pricked my sister's skin, covered in the antidote I'd been working on for months now, now twined with a hint of the gift from the Caladrius.

A tear also formed in my eye, a tiny bead of iridescence. As it fell, the liquid seeped into my skin, and the effects of the poison began to ebb away.

Nic's fingers twitched.

"She's waking." Carmine squealed giddily, kneeling beside my sister and gently brushing back her hair. "I love when they can feel it. It makes it more fun if they're awake."

"I haven't heard a good scream in *ages*," Xantha drew out the last word, moving to Carmine's side, her eyes gleaming excitedly. "And this one knows pain. Her screams will be well-deserved."

Alba clasped a hand around my sister's throat, turning her face toward her. The witch knelt, her knee on Nic's chest as she drew the knife along my sister's cheek—not cutting, only taunting.

"I don't know how you're resisting the poison, firecaster," she said. "But it doesn't matter. You have no magic to fight us with." The witch's hand tightened, cutting off Nic's air.

Wrong.

Control of my limbs seeped back into me, the threads of my magic returning thanks to the Caladrius's tear. In a few more moments, I could tear each of them apart with my thorns. Maybe even shift my hands into talons.

I hoped it wouldn't be too late.

Nic rasped a breath, and the witch's hand gripped her harder. Still, my sister managed to speak. "You've made a mistake."

Alba laughed, throwing back her head. "And what is that, my sweet?"

"I'm not only a firecaster . . . and you built your home in the middle of a lake."

Water smashed against the windows, shattering the glass.

Alba was swept off Nic in a wave of black water, the other two witches slamming with her into the far wall. The water split around me.

Finally, I could move. I turned onto all fours, then pushed myself to my knees.

I slammed my palms onto the wooden floor, and vines exploded up around me. They shot upward, then toward the witches, binding them at their waists and necks. The three would have screamed, but no sound emerged, not while water poured down their throats.

The witches fought against the vines, tearing through them. Carmine launched herself at me, her eyes red and feral.

I thought of the mounds of bones, of every life these three had taken to fuel their own miserable existences.

No more.

As Carmine reached for my neck, my hand—now tipped in long talons—found hers first. The talons sank into her skin, and I clenched my fingers as I pulled, ripping out her throat.

I dropped the pale trachea quickly, my hands beginning to shake.

Xantha screamed, launching herself at Nic. A wave of water brought Nic the skull of a stag. Without taking her eyes off the witch, my sister reached back, grabbed it, and shoved the horns into Xantha's chest.

The witch choked on a gasp, black blood pouring from her mouth.

Alba slashed through the vines with earth magic of her own, crafting sharp white branches to protect her. She fell to her knees in the receding tide, hands going to her sisters as her brown skin flushed with rage.

"You promised me blood, Nicole Briar."

Placing a hand on each body, the white witch began to chant, the words low and vicious. The corpses of the fallen witches reanimated and slowly rose.

Horrified, I reached for my sister. "We've got to *go*."

"No," Nic snarled. "Not until she's dead." She drew her sword. With a slash of the Iradelmar, she beheaded the corpse of the red witch as it lunged for her, piercing the heart of the yellow one in the same movement. The bodies dropped back to the floor only to shudder, attempting to rise again.

Alba screamed as she moved with unnatural swiftness, grabbing my sister's sword arm, nails digging in. She yanked my sister toward her with unearthly strength. Her eyes went cloudy, the irises disappearing entirely in the milky white, with a vision we could not see.

"There is *more*." Her voice was horrible, rasping. No longer her own. "Go to the place they were forged."

The white witch was finishing Nic's deal—compelled to give her more answers as she tried to take my sister's blood.

Suddenly, Alba stuttered back, hand dropping from Nic's arm. Blood poured from her chest, where my arrow had struck true, piercing her heart. The witch dropped to her knees, slumping forward like her sisters, once more utterly still in death.

Shaking, I lowered the bow.

"What did she mean by that?" I asked, looking at Nic.

"The swords," Nic whispered. "They had the prophecy on them. Maybe there is more we need to know."

"We can save it for another day." I took my sister's hand. "Let's get the hell out of here." I couldn't shake the image of those corpses rising, the unnerving power the witch had called upon to make it so. I couldn't stop thinking about my hands—covered in their blackened blood.

Nic and I ran out of the cottage. She cast fire behind us, and this time, the island remained burning.

Exhausted, we stumbled back through the portal but found only Rasalas waiting, pacing wildly.

Nic scanned the forest for Eilith, worry clouding her features. "I don't feel her nearby."

"I'm sure she's fine, Nic," I said, neither of us completely believing the words. "But we can't stay much longer."

The sun had begun to set, and it would be night soon. We weren't in any shape to search in the dark.

"She will find you," I reassured her. Nic nodded, though she still looked wary.

I grasped onto the jaguar and my sister, my body trembling as I began to realize what I'd done. The walls around our magic dropped, allowing us to share. With what we had recovered since the poison and the help of Rasalas, we winnowed back to Ankaa.

CHAPTER 41
August

J ophiel and I walked toward a meeting with the eastern generals.

The Seraph didn't look at me, still furious at what I'd done, leaving Nicole. Her loyalty had shifted from me to her granddaughter the second she'd found out their relation.

Good. Nicole deserved her devotion more than I did.

Even the thought of her name sent pain plunging into my chest. I hadn't been able to look at her when I left four days ago, otherwise, I'd never have left our room. I'd have crawled back into bed with her and plunged my face between her thighs, woken her with my tongue, and showed her how much more devoted I was to her than any mate could ever be.

I thought of challenging anyone who came to claim her and tried to take her away from me. Of skewering them through the chest with a bolt of lightning to dare claim what was mine.

But that wouldn't be fair to her. Nicole deserved better.

I'm sure Nicole was furious that I'd left, but we'd only been together a few months. With time, she would heal, and when she found her mate, the person perfectly crafted for her by the stars, she would be happy again. A male or female without so dark a past as my own. They'd be scarless and have bloodless hands.

While I—I would never heal.

I would dream of her dark eyes for an eternity. I would love Nicole Briar until the day I died, and even after, when I was only a spirit of dust among the stars.

Tomorrow, Jophiel would return to relay the news of what we'd learned these past days at the border while I stayed. If I returned now, I wouldn't be able to stop myself from going to her.

We entered the tent, the generals already gathered.

"News?" I asked, taking the chair at the head of the table.

"The Reynian and Hahnaleyan forces remain stationed outside of Sanserria, unmoved," Dario, a southern general, said. "But we still have refugees crossing over from the Redwood. It seems to be the only space safe enough for them to come through—contrary as that seems."

Not so much if he knew what I did, that Teale had somehow convinced the nymphs to help the refugees through the notoriously dangerous forest, protecting them from any guards that hunted them.

I turned to the next general.

"The Desdemonian army is gathering northwest of Bellport." Hazelle, a High Fae female with the watercasting ability—a sliver compared to Nicole's power—pointed at the map spread before us. "Half are here and half are—"

A screech cut through the air, followed by scraping upon the tent's roof. Suddenly, talons pierced the material, ripping a hole large enough for the hawk to fit through.

The black hawk landed on the center of the table. Eilith.

My heart began to pound.

There would only be one reason why Nicole's familiar was here.

"What the hell?" Another general made to shoo the bird.

Eilith turned to him, screeching, a flicker of her true form shadowing behind her. The general stumbled back in fear. The hawk turned to me again.

"Where is she?" If Nicole was in danger, nothing would keep me away.

Another screech and I knew where she'd gone. Contrary to my warning, Nicole had gone to the witches.

I held out my arm, the hawk perching on it.

"Take me to her."

The hawk familiar winnowed me to an unfamiliar part of the forest, an arch of mangled vines and thorns. The woods were quickly growing darker, the sun having set minutes ago.

The bird swooped down from my shoulder to the earth before it. She pawed at the ground furiously. Red blood had seeped into the soil.

"Nicole!" I shouted, running through the arch, ignoring the screech of the familiar behind me.

The portal drained me of all magic as I passed through, but I didn't care, desperate in my need to get to her. The arch released me in front of a misty crater lake deep in an uninhabited part of the mountains. The cottage in the lake's center was engulfed in roaring flames.

I sprinted down the path, only pausing when I reached the open door. Nothing on the inside was burning; the floor was covered in a thin layer of water.

Two bodies were strewn across the floor, one without her throat and the other had a set of antlers through the chest.

Neither body was Nicole or Misha.

Relief flooded me as I stepped out. I searched the area, finding no more trace of either sister. A sharp scratch struck the back of my neck, and I whirled, only to see nothing except the arched portal, Eilith thrashing against it in her monstrous form.

Once I was sure the twins were no longer here, I ran back through the arch, my chest easing as the magic was returned to me. Without having to ask a second time, the hawk shifted and landed on my shoulder, and we winnowed away.

CHAPTER 42
Misha

Nic and I arrived in Ankaa in the castle courtyard. My trembling had worsened as the adrenaline left me, my hands clamping onto my sister.

"Julian!" Nic shouted, holding onto me as my knees gave way.

"What happened?" He ran to us. Celeste and Shai stood back, watching.

Nic let me go so Julian could pull me into him. His arms wrapped around my waist, steadying me.

I looked back at my sister, her face creased with worry. But alive—she was alive.

"I killed them. Both of them," I murmured to Julian. "They were going to kill her, so I killed them first." I looked down at my hands. The left was clean, unmarred, but the right—

" I need to get it off." I scratched at the black blood covering my skin, left behind from when I'd torn out the witch's throat. "I need it *off*."

Julian took my hand in his, stopping me, and I panicked. Something silent passed between him and my sister, before he winnowed me into our chambers.

Julian was stripping me of the black leathers, the witches' blood blending into them. I didn't know where it ended and I began. The castle's magic already had the shower running as we stepped in, him guiding me in naked while he was still fully clothed.

I darted for the water, scrubbing at myself. It wasn't enough. Even as the blood washed away, I could still see it. I could still *feel* it.

"Misha, talk to me."

I ignored him, reaching for the knob, turning so the water was so hot it was nearly scalding.

"*Fuck*," Julian hissed, turning down the heat. "I knew I should have gone."

"*No*," I snarled. "They would have killed you. They almost—" A sob burst from my throat. "I watched them almost kill Nic. They were moments away from plunging the dagger into her chest and taking out her heart."

The chest-heaving sobs began. "They almost killed her. They almost killed my sister."

Julian took me into his arms, his white shirt plastered against his skin. "Nicole is okay, Misha. She's fine." He stroked a hand down my hair.

I pushed him away. "Because I ripped that witch's *throat* out with my bare hands!" I shouted, reaching for the scrub brush to fiercely drag it across my arms. "How can you stand to look at me?"

Julian didn't back away, but stayed silent, listening.

"And I don't regret it," I admitted, still scrubbing, leaving scratches down my right arm. "I am a monster. Because I would do it again, I would kill them all again and again and—."

"Hey." Julian took my hand, gentle but firm, and pulled it behind his back. He drew me against him, surrounding my body with his as he pressed me into the stone wall. The pressure calmed my breathing, steadying me. "Look at me, love."

I was terrified of what I would see on his face—the shame and disgust. But after a moment, I did. I couldn't deny him anything.

On Julian's face—the face of the most beautiful male I'd ever seen—I saw none of those things. Only love and understanding. He took my face in his hands. I clasped his wrists with my own, holding onto him.

"Sometimes we have to do things to protect the ones we love. It doesn't make you a monster, Misha. It doesn't make you like them."

I took a deep, shuddering breath. "Your life would be better without me in it."

Julian lifted my chin, making me meet his eyes again. "That's not true, love. You make *everything* in my life better. Brighter. Do you think me a monster for what I did in the ruins as the dragon?"

"What? No, never—"

He cut me off. "Your magic made me the dragon, Misha. But I made the choice I did to protect you. I would do it over and over again because I love you. Because you are my mate."

I shook my head. "I can't complete the bond with you."

Julian choked, going still. "What?"

"I can't let you bind yourself to me. *Look* at me!" I shouted, indicating my skin, rubbed raw, and the blood still running down the drain. Not to mention the utter burden I was in my grief. The depression would

363

come back, even if it were years from now. I couldn't shackle him with that—with me.

Julian looked down, watching me. Gently, he reached for a wayward strand of my damp hair, tucking it behind my ear. "It doesn't matter, love. This—*you*—" He held me tighter. "—are all I've ever wanted."

"You will resent me," I said, baring my deepest fear. "Because I will still be like this, still burdened by the darkness inside of me. And what happens when you come to resent the bond that ties us together?"

"*Never*, Misha. That will *never* be a possibility for us."

I swallowed. "You saw me after Alesia and Eve died. I'm better but still struggling. I think I always might in some way. I can't promise it won't happen again."

Julian's hands grasped my face. "Then struggle, love. I'll be here—I will *always* be here. You never have to do it alone."

I shook my head. He wasn't understanding. "But you shouldn't have to bear that burden—to have to bear me."

"You are not a *burden*, Misha. Never see yourself that way. You are the one I love, and struggling or not, I'd rather spend every day with you than without you. The hard days are just part of it. It's okay not to be okay, love. Whether you are in sunlight or darkness, full of joy or lost to despair, I am with you. Even when you pull away, I am with you because I cannot be without you. There is no world where I exist where you are not my center—my sun."

I remembered my sister's words, the phrase from my favorite story:
The darker the shadows, the brighter the sun.

The knot in my gut began to unravel, dissipating as I saw the fervor on his face, the love and devotion in his stormcloud eyes. "You will stay with me?"

"Always," Julian promised, bringing his forehead to mine.

"Even if I am a murderer? A monster?"

"If you are, then so am I. I told you once that there was no one I would rather defend with bloodshed than you. There is nothing I wouldn't do to keep you or our family safe, Misha. And no matter what you do—no matter how dark your mind gets, remember that you are my light, my aurora—and you will not only overcome this but become greater because of it. You shine brighter because of the darkness, and just as the dawn rises, so will you. I will never leave or resent you for it."

The fervor of his words hit me, his acceptance of all that I was. If Julian loved me, even with all my darkest parts, I couldn't be so terrible.

"I love you," he whispered, and I'd never felt so deep a truth.

"I love you, Julian." I clasped his face, looking deep into his eyes. "Know that even when the last star loses its shine, when the last flower on this earth withers and dies, my love for you still grows. My heart will be yours even after this world is ash and dust."

Julian kissed me tenderly, then deeper, utterly consuming me. When he pulled back, his breathing heavy, he said, "Complete the mating bond with me, Misha. Marry me."

I took a deep breath, my heart fluttering. "When?"

"Now. Tonight—whenever you want. Just please say yes."

I kissed him again as the barrier to my magic dropped. Julian's did as well, and we shared our magic with each other. I felt him in my soul. My entire being—*everything*—was him.

"Yes."

CHAPTER 43
Nic

I took a deep breath, attempting to steady myself and failing.

Misha and I should have been dead.

Back in August's chambers, I peeled off the ruined leather top, the neck cut down to mid-sternum. My neck was bruised from the witch's grip, my muscles barking in pain as I undressed.

All this time, Misha had been poisoning herself a little day by day, using her plant magic to create a poison and its antidote. It was the only reason we'd survived—the only reason she'd been conscious enough to act and have the ability to call to her magic. This and the gift from the Caladrius had saved us. Nothing could change my mind that it had somehow known—that it had been sent as a gift by someone looking out for us.

I couldn't discern how I felt about it: guilty that my sister had been poisoning herself for so long and I'd been none the wiser, or grateful because she'd saved our lives today.

The fire hadn't worked as I'd planned—and it had almost cost me everything.

I stripped off the boots and leather pants. In the bathing room, I stood beneath a stream of scalding water in the stone shower, scrubbing the dirt and witch blood from my hair. I was still shaking, cold to my bones.

I felt him before I saw him. The air thickened, crackling with electricity.

"Where is she?"

The words reverberated through the castle's stone, seeming to come from everywhere all at once.

I stepped out of the shower, willing the water from my body and donning a silk robe hanging beside the door. As I stepped into the bedroom, the doors blasted open, slamming into the walls beside them as August strode through.

His eyes grazed my body, searching every place. Then his silver eyes, full of relief, where replaced with thunderclouds.

"What the fuck were you thinking, going alone to somewhere like that?"

I crossed my arms, standing straighter. "I was *thinking* that we needed information only those witches could give us."

"So, you thought it would be a great idea to go *alone*?" he snarled. "To not even notify me?"

"I don't answer to you."

August was bristling with anger, but deeper than that—there was a wild panic to his eyes and disheveled hair. He'd been terrified.

A flicker of hope lit behind my ribs.

"No, but you could have died today—*again*." His jaw clenched. "You are playing with your life, Nicole, and for what?"

"I am *not* playing with my life." I turned, walking away.

August winnowed, cutting me off. He towered over me. "I pulled you from the godsdamned ice myself, Nicole. You were a whisper from death—would have been if it weren't for your mother's amulet. You think the fire magic will save you, but it won't—not always."

His words stung in their truth. I'd been too eager, too arrogant, and had almost gotten my sister killed. Shame flooded me, but I forced it down, turning it to rage.

"What do you care, August?" I screamed, stepping closer to him so we were chest to chest. If he wasn't going to back down, neither was I. "You walked away. And we—" I motioned between us. "—are nothing, right? According to you and the stars and fate. So, you don't get to come in here, throwing a godsdamned *tantrum*, because you're angry over a choice I made with my own life and body."

He rocked back as if I'd slapped him. "You could never be nothing to me," he whispered.

I took him in: the red-rimmed eyes, bruised purple beneath from lack of sleep. The days apart had taken their toll. Nearly as badly for him as it had been for me—worse, even.

This knowledge only made me angrier.

Stubborn jackass.

"You don't get to say that. Not now." My hands went to his chest, pushing him back. *When had he gotten so close?* August's heat was enveloping me, his air filling my nostrils. He surrounded me. "You don't get to say that to me, not after you left."

"Nicole—"

"Leave!" I screamed, the sound ragged. "Go back to wherever the hell you ran off to. You did it once, crept out of our bed like it was nothing. So go on—" I pushed him again. "—*go*."

August didn't budge. I stepped closer, pushing against his chest again. *"Leave!"* The word was choked, strained. My throat closed up, unable to speak another.

And then I wasn't pushing him away, my hands fisting in his shirt. *Don't go.*

I'd lost too many people I loved. I didn't care that we weren't mates, that the stars hadn't made us a pair, binding us in the ties of fate. I *loved* August. I always would—in this life and the next.

August remained silent as he read my face, my pleading eyes. Tears had begun to well there, silently streaming down my cheeks.

Stay.

His hands lifted to cradle my face. I watched him watch me. August's eyes were a mirror; everything I felt was reflected through his silver irises. Something seemed to crack inside him, the cage barring him.

"You aren't nothing, Nicole. You are everything—*everything* to me."

August's lips crashed into mine, rough and claiming as if he could hold himself back no longer. "And I will lay down my own life before I let you risk yours one more fucking time."

His hands went to my hips, lifting me in a bruising grip. I clung to him, my hands grasping tightly to his neck, fingers threaded through his black hair. Nothing felt more right. Nothing felt more sure than him solidly pressed to me.

August brought me to the bed, laying me down to hover over me—before pulling back. The warring in his eyes had returned. "Tell me, Nicole. Tell me this is what you want."

I could see it clearly, the yearning, the want—the hurt—in his eyes. August wanted this, *me*, so badly, but he would deny himself and walk away if it wasn't what I wanted.

"I want you, August. I choose you. And I don't care what the stars say. Now and forever, this—*you*—are what I want."

August shook his head, braced on his arms above me. "You shouldn't want to be with me."

"Why not?" I argued, sitting up. August had never been able to see himself clearly, how loved he was. Not by me, not by the Seven—not even by Julian. He never thought he deserved our devotion despite how he'd earned it time and time again.

"Because I'm selfish!" He gripped the sheets beside me, knuckles white. "I am not your hero, Nicole. I am your villain. Because a good male would let you go and do what's best for you, but despite this revelation that we are not meant for each other, I still *want* you. I want to hoard you away so your mate can never find and claim you. I want to keep you entirely for myself. And that's unfair to you—you should be with your perfect match. But all I can think about is how if they try to take you from me, I will rip them apart."

"You keep talking about my mate, but what about yours? What if yours comes, August, and *you* no longer want *me*?"

August's face flashed with surprise. He genuinely hadn't considered it. He'd only thought of me.

"Mate or no, it's impossible for me to love anyone like I love you, Nicole."

"Then let us be imperfectly together." I placed my hands on his cheeks, his eyes fluttering closed at the touch. "Let us fight and argue and show the stars that they are wrong—that we love each other more than anyone ever has." I lowered one hand to the skin over his heart, feeling it beat wildly in time with mine.

"Defy the stars with me."

August's hand covered mine, holding me to him. His eyes burned with lightning, warming every part of me. "When we're long gone, our bones nothing but dust, and they tell stories of the once king in the North, they may debate over the choices I've made, deem me a great ruler or the one that damned them all, but what will be unquestionable—an undeniable truth—is that I loved you."

"Then they will also know this—*you* will know this—August." My hands tightened, pulling him closer. "That I returned that love. And any being that tried to keep me from you, even my mate, became ash in the wind as they tried to stand between us."

August leaned forward—he was so fucking beautiful. His hand went to the tie of my robe, gripping the fabric as he pulled me closer, our bodies flush with each other.

"Then let nothing be between us." He pulled at the bow, the robe falling open as I was bared to him.

August ran his hands up my calves to my knees, lifting and gently nudging them apart. His lips went to my stomach, kissing the soft skin as his fingertips grazed the lacy fabric between my legs. He took a shuddering breath as he felt how badly I needed him.

I grabbed his forearms, halting his touch.

"Nicole," August pleaded, his grip on my thigh tightening before he reluctantly allowed his hand to be pulled away. His silver eyes filled with panic, thinking I'd changed my mind.

I nudged him back until we were both standing. Unbuttoning his shirt, I ran my hands from his chest down his stomach before pushing him back toward the green velvet chaise, my open robe billowing behind me. When August sat, I sank to my knees before him.

"*Mine*," I breathed.

Lightly running my nails from his knees and up his thighs, I saw how hard he already was, straining beneath the fabric. Unfastening his belt and pants, I pulled him out, stroking as I gazed up at him.

"I'm yours, Nicole. Only ever yours—" He groaned as I cut him off with a lick from base to tip, my tongue flicking beneath the head of his cock. August groaned, his hands coming to my hair, pushing it out of my face. His grip tightened as I took him deeper into my throat, and his head lolled back.

I could watch him come undone forever—and I would.

I dropped a hand to touch myself, seeking some relief.

August sat up straighter, watching. "Show me, sweetheart."

Silently acquiescing, I pushed the robe off my shoulders, spreading my knees wider so August could watch. He did this to me. He made me ache—*burn*—like this. Only him.

I continued to make love to him with my mouth, pushing us both higher. When I knew August was close, I stood.

August lifted his hips, letting me tug his pants the rest of the way off before I straddled him. I pushed his shirt off his shoulders before I leaned back, hands on his knees, and rolled myself against him, my thin undergarments the only barrier between us. He held my hips tighter, guiding me toward him. But I kept grinding, teasing, not quite letting him take control.

"*Nicole*." August's hands gripped my hips with a bruising intensity, making me gasp. Heat flooded my core.

I knew I was baiting him, testing his self-control. But I wanted August on the edge, feral, before I let him take over.

"Do you remember that first night?" I leaned forward, lips brushing against his ear. My nails gently grazed the back of his neck, leaving a trail of goosebumps. "How long had you been imagining—dreaming of me?"

"Since the alley." August pulled at the undergarments, the material biting into my skin. He tore through them as I gasped. August tossed the scraps away, his hand feeling how wet I was for him, pushing in a finger. Then two.

"Do you know how long I imagined you—wanted you?" I gasped as I rode his hand.

August stilled, hand tightening on my hip, fingers full inside me as I took his face in my hands. His eyes burned with the question his lips couldn't ask—what he so desperately wanted to know.

"Since the alley."

August didn't hesitate. His lips crashed into mine as he gripped my waist and stood, holding me against him as he flipped us. My back hit the velvet of the chaise gently. But with the gleam in his eyes, I knew what was coming next wouldn't be gentle at all.

Thank fuck.

My knees spread, eager to have him between them.

"Always in such a rush," he chided before going to his knees. "Let me take my time. Let me savor you."

His lips took their time, mouth and tongue hot over my nipples. At the sharp nip of his teeth, I squealed. He chuckled, the sound rumbling over my skin as he traveled down my stomach.

My legs spread further to make room for his shoulders. August parted me with thumbs, staring down at me admiringly. "All of this for me, sweetheart?"

"Only you."

And then his mouth was on me. Wasting no time, August devoured me until I was panting, squirming beneath him as the pressure built. As soon as I was near climaxing, he backed off, still licking but avoiding my clit, letting the pleasure recede. He did this, over and over, until I was a shaking mess.

"*August*," I snarled.

Finally, he lifted his head. Kneeling, August lifted my legs—one, then the other—so they rested on his shoulders. He lined himself up, the head of his cock resting at my entrance as his lips trailed along my calf.

"Please," I whimpered and rolled my hips, trying to push myself onto him.

He held me still. "You can tease me, sweetheart, but you don't enjoy when I tease you back?" His lips pulled into a smirk as they moved to assault the other leg with featherlight kisses.

I couldn't take anymore, edged within an inch of bursting into flames. *If he didn't push inside me right fucking now—*

August let out a dark chuckle, and in one hard thrust, he was inside me. I gasped at the fullness, but he gave me no time to adjust. One arm banded around my legs, holding them to his chest. The other thumb went to my clit, applying the perfect amount of pressure as he continuously thrust into me.

My orgasm crested, a wave of pleasure so intense I was nearly swept away, my hands gripping the edge of the chaise so hard the wood splintered. But August didn't slow, even as I screamed my release.

August dropped my legs, letting them fall to his waist. Pushing my knees wide, he gripped the hair at the base of my neck and lifted me, tilting my head down to see where we were joined. "Look at how we fuck, Nicole. Look at how you take me—how you own me completely. Only you, sweetheart. It has only ever been and will only ever be you."

I watched him thrusting into me. The way he spread me, sinking in to the hilt before pulling back again, had me mesmerized.

August loosened his hold, letting me drift back down as he leaned over me, but kept his grip on my neck. He braced himself over me with his other arm. My hands came to his face, pulling him to me. Our kiss was open and deep, a clashing that was at once violent and tender. Another climax thundered through me, hard and devastating.

August sat up, drawing me into his lap, straddling him. Lifting my hips, he pushed back into me. He soothed his hands down my back as I trembled from the remnants of the orgasm, not yet thrusting—just content to be inside me.

My hands fell upon his stomach, feathering over the scars there. The physical mark of the terrible things done to him, what he'd survived through. Deeper scars, I knew, sliced through his soul. He couldn't bear the thought of losing another person he loved—and that is exactly what the stars had done in his mind.

By not making us mates, they'd taken me from him eternally.

My palm slid over his heart, pounding and singing in a beat that called to my own. The stars, fate, none of it mattered—only this. Only him.

"Only you," I whispered, my nose brushing his.

August's hands clasped my face, holding me close. He breathed me in, releasing a shuttering exhale of relief as our foreheads met.

"Never again, Nicole. I will not—cannot—leave you again."

The truth was traced in every line of his face, the set of his full mouth, the devastation in his eyes. My magic pulsed at the edges of my skin, burning up every place August touched me.

"Let me in. Let me feel all of you," I breathed against his lips. More—I needed more of him. I would never get enough.

August hesitated only a moment before I felt the barriers to his magic lower, his power reaching for mine. I responded in kind, my magic flooding toward him in a rush as his crashed into me like violent waves breaking in a storm.

Body, heart, soul—I was completely consumed by him. His silver eyes grew lighter, flickering with the lightning of his magic, and I knew he felt the same.

I began to move. Slow at first, reveling in the feeling. August's magic hummed through my veins, making every touch more electric. Then, his thrusts began to match mine, meeting me perfectly. August's hands slid down to my hips, gripping tightly and tipping my pelvis forward so every motion ground my clit against him. I moaned, my head falling to his neck, nails digging into his shoulders. I was an incoherent mess, limp with pleasure, reciting his name like the only prayer I would ever need.

The tension that built inside me this time coiled tighter—deeper. I felt it through every part of my body, felt *him* in every breath and heartbeat. I exploded, stars wrecking my vision.

When I went over the edge this time, August came with me.

"Nicole. *Fuck.*" August's thrusts stuttered, sinking into me and stilling as I felt his warmth fill me.

As August slowed, our hearts beat furiously in sync, the magic still joined. He pressed a kiss to my damp hair. Magic cracked over our skin, a mix of his and mine. Sparks of electricity like stars mingled with embers so hot they burned a dazzling pale blue. Combined, our magic was immune to the other, dancing over our skin without harm.

"Nicole," August said my name like a promise—an oath he would die before breaking.

As I kissed him once more, my lips gently meeting his, I knew in my bones that our choice—our love—was stronger than our fate.

CHAPTER 44
Misha

T he next morning, I walked into the informal dining room on our
level, only to find Nic already there, perched in August's lap.

My heart swelled. They'd made up. At least something good had come
from yesterday.

My sister had never been one for overt physical affection. Only with
our family did she ever seem comfortable with any embrace. So, seeing
her this way, so comfortable in his arms, made me pause. They both
deserved to be this happy.

Nic and August acted as if they hadn't sensed me arrive, whispering
and nauseatingly staring into each other's eyes as my sister clutched her
cup of tea. I cleared my throat, and they didn't so much as flinch. Julian
walked in, coming to stand beside me.

He leaned down, whispering not so quietly in my ear, "Is *that* what we
looked like in Sanserria?"

This got my sister's attention.

"*Please.*" Nic turned, scoffing. "You two were the worst." She slid off August's lap onto the adjacent chair, but remained tucked into his side, leaning into him.

August's eyes finally rose, meeting ours. "Good morning."

Julian and I took the seats across from them, my eyes going back and forth between my sister and August.

The corners of Nic's mouth twitched upward. "We worked it out." She blushed.

"I see that." I was having a hard time keeping my own lips from breaking into a smile.

Most of the Seven filtered in for breakfast, along with Sena. Gemma was not long behind them. She'd begun rising earlier than before, heading to the training ring in the early morning. I knew it had something to do with the mindcaster her eyes always seemed to find.

Gemma sat beside me, her eyes going wide as she saw August and Nic. She turned to me, raising an eyebrow. *Are they?* I nodded, and she squealed. "Thank the gods."

The others reacted similarly, noting Nic and August but not mentioning it, though their smiles said enough.

The chatter in the room rose as everyone sat, filling their plates. Jophiel sat beside Nic, filling her in on Adrienne and Evander's movements—there hadn't been much—and the state of our own forces. Damian sat beside Julian. He leaned across his friend, telling stories that had me wide-eyed and gasping with laughter. Julian looked abashed, his cheeks darkening at some of them, but still he smiled at the good-natured fun.

Simon and Ezra joined. Jessa followed sleepily behind them but perked up when she saw us all gathered. She took the seat next to mine and quietly asked if I could cast magic into my palm like Nic—Ezra leaned over, scolding her for being rude.

I laughed, swearing it was fine. I cast a small pink rosebud into my palm. The petals unfurled, revealing the golden center.

Jessa's eyes went wide with amazement, and I took the briar rose and tucked it into her hair beside her ear. She grinned, fingertips drifting to the petals every so often for the rest of breakfast.

When the meal was nearing an end, some people stood to head to their different duties. Julian and I glanced at each other. Now was the time.

"We have something to tell you all." I looked at each of the Seven and Gemma, holding Julian's hand tightly. "We are going to seal the mating bond and complete the power exchange."

"Next week," Julian added, his smile wide.

Gemma gasped, hands flying to her mouth.

The room erupted into congratulations. Julian and I took turns hugging everyone, sharing in their congratulations.

Sena held onto us each especially tight, her eyes gleaming with tears of happiness. "I could not have asked for a better woman to call daughter."

At her words, I went teary-eyed, unable to find the right response to convey how much her approval meant to me. Sena's hand went to my cheek, and I realized that no answer was needed. Not everything could be expressed by words.

"We have to go." Gemma grabbed Nic's hand, dragging her away. "We have to plan a party to celebrate."

Nic seemed hesitant to leave August, craning her neck back toward him, but he only smiled, urging her to go. Miranda, Celeste, Damian, and Teale followed them, unable to tolerate missing out on anything.

When the room cleared, only Julian and I remained standing with August. He'd softly given us words of congratulations, but my gut sank, and I wondered if it had been cruel to announce our mating after his and Nic's news.

"Brother." Julian clapped August on the shoulder. "I knew you'd come around and get her back."

August's lips lifted into a smile that didn't quite reach his eyes before his gaze sank. Some of the light in them had dimmed since Nic had left the room.

"But you don't seem so sure," Julian observed, his brow furrowing as he took in August's expression. "August?"

"She's my twin," I added, hoping to reassure him. "I've been with her since birth, and I've never seen her like this. She *loves* you."

August looked up. "I still can't help but wonder if Nicole only fell in love with me because I was there after your aunt's death. Because my arms are what kept her from falling apart, and in return, she gave me her heart. But as she heals, I fear she will realize she deserves more than I can provide—because she does. She deserves so much more than I could ever give her—but I can't let her go."

I shook my head. "I watched you two dance on Solstice, August. Nic wanted you then—before. But if you don't let this go and keep making yourself miserable over it, you *will* lose her." I reached across to cover his hand with my own. August stilled but didn't pull away. "If you love Nic, then don't question hers."

August nodded. "You are wise beyond your years, little one."

I remembered how he'd called me the same thing on the Solstice, when he'd given his approval for me to be with Julian. I hugged him—he was just as stiff as he had been that night—I realized this might be what it felt like to have a brother.

Then August went to Julian, hugging him as well. He leaned back, squeezing his brother on the shoulder. "Let's get you two mated, then."

CHAPTER 45
August

A drienne was nowhere to be found.

After Simon's spies had been unable to get eyes on her, Teale and I went to the forest to speak with the nymphs, for a meeting they'd surprisingly agreed to, at the edge of the Redwood. Three of them stood before us, appearing as part tree and part ethereal being.

They relayed what had happened during the Moroi attack: how the beasts had moved in the shadow, creeping up from their dark dwellings too swiftly for any of the forest dwelling faeries to intervene.

"We thought little of it until it was too late. So much blood has been spilled recently, and it attracts the seekers of life. We did not think it was abnormal until they flew in groups, commanded by the only one who can," one of the Dryads explained, her slender limbs brown and bark-like. Her hair flowed past her hips, brushing the ground like the long branches of a willow.

In the weeks since the attack, none of them had seen Adrienne traveling nor heard whispers of her through the trees.

"The thief has been lost," another Dryad said, her long hair like vines with tiny leaves and flowering red buds; it fluttered against her green skin as if alive. "But to hear and see nothing does not mean nothing. To be out of sight and sound is to be hidden, not stagnant."

"Hidden by what?" Uneasiness settled in my gut. The skin across my chest itched and stung.

"The same one who commands." The last nymph nodded to me. She was an Oread, branches sprouting from her skull like antlers, with golden leaves at their tips. Her skin was the watercolor brown of crape myrtles. "The fireborn knows."

I understood her meaning. *Nicole.*

Teale's eyes avoided the green-skinned Dryad, one whose skin tone was only a few shades greener than her own. The red buds in the nymph's hair seemed to match the color Teale's had turned with the autumn, as well.

My half-sister. Teale spoke into my mind, sensing my curiosity.

Part of the family that had shunned her. This one at least seemed contrite, looking at Teale with a pained sort of fondness. I would guess that she was the one to convince the others to speak to us, hoping to make amends with my friend.

The willowy Dryad stepped forward. "Tell the fireborn we'll come at midnight."

I opened my mouth to ask for clarification, but then they were gone, winnowing away on the breeze. Teale's half-sister seemed to linger longer than her comrades, an apology on her face.

Only the rustle of leaves was left in their wake, not even footprints upon the soft earth.

I turned to Teale. "Is that how they always are? Half riddles and vague phrases?"

Teale sighed. She tucked a strand of red hair behind her ear. "That was quite straightforward for them, actually."

"Time to go then." We'd only gotten a small bit of information, but it had been enough. I needed to talk to both Nicole and Misha—if my brother didn't first roast me alive for being late to this party celebrating his and Misha's mating tomorrow.

Teale and I arrived back at the castle. Coming down the hallway, we heard familiar voices shouting, growing steadily more heated.

Light spilled out from the open doorway to the leisure hall. Upon entering, we stood still, observing. The others were locked in some trivial but heated argument over a game of Ships & Sirens. It was a game of strategy typically played by children, but it appeared they'd turned it into a drinking game. All were partaking except for Misha, who was whispering in her sister's ear for Nicole to then relay whatever strategy to Miranda and Damian.

Jophiel seemed to be overseeing and doing a horrible job, very clearly demonstrating her favoritism.

Julian yelled from across the table. "No secrets!"

"*You*—" Misha pointed fiercely. "—have a mindcaster on your team. If you get to share secrets, then so do we."

"You're paranoid, love. Shai hasn't used his magic once."

"Oh yeah?" Misha pinned her gaze on Gemma, hands going to her hips. "That so, Gem?" Her eyebrows raised, waiting.

"No, he's not using it." Gemma took a quick drink of her white wine, her cheeks turning ever so slightly pink.

"Aha!" Nicole pointed. "You guilty, little liar!"

Celeste shrugged, unbothered as she took a drink of ale. "We're only using our team's talents."

Jophiel waved a hand. "Not allowed. No colluding via mindcasting."

Julian, Shai, Gemma, and Celeste burst into opposition, outraged.

Celeste pointed across the table, where Misha and Nicole were already whispering again, though it seemed more giggles than words. "And what about whispering?"

"Whispering is fine." Jophiel nodded, taking another drink of wine.

They threw their hands up, grumbling about partiality and unfairness. Jophiel shrugged, utterly unphased.

Simon cleared his throat. Everyone's head whipped to the door.

Julian lifted his hands in the air, his smile wide. "Finally, brother!"

Nicole's gaze met mine, her eyes alighting with that inner fire as she took me in. Nothing else mattered or existed when she looked at me that way. Her grievances forgotten, she bounded over to me. Her team groaned at her departure.

Nicole whipped her head around, still walking toward me. "It's not even our turn. You'll be *fine*."

Not watching where she was going, she bumped into my chest. My hands gripped her waist, steadying her. "Hello, beautiful," she whispered as her hands wound around my back, so she could peer up at me with those dark eyes.

Nicole always smelled of amber and freshly fallen snow, but tonight, perhaps with the addition of a glass too many of red wine. The inner seam of her lips was a shade darker from its stain. I thought of running my tongue over it, of how much better the wine would taste mixed with her.

My gaze went lower, taking all of her in. She wore an emerald silk gown, gathered at her cinched waist with delicate straps of crystal. Nicole was beautiful in everything she wore: training clothes, armor, silk gowns, or nothing at all. But she liked these dresses best, charmed by the elegant beauty of the fabric as it clung to her and flowed around her waist and legs like water. One day, I would buy her a closet full of them, in every color she liked best.

I cupped her face in one hand, my chest tightening as she leaned into it. "Hello, Snow."

When I had first observed her at the Treaty celebrations, I'd thought Nicole hated to be touched. She avoided it whenever possible, leaning away or stepping back from courtiers who got too close—from me as well. But the more I watched her, the more I found that initial observation to be untrue. She always leaned into her sister's and aunts' embraces, even seeking it out. I realized then it wasn't all touch she hated, just the unsolicited ones. She only wanted it—craved it—from those she loved.

I would never forget the first time I'd touched her and instead of tensing, Nicole had relaxed, leaning into my hands—unconsciously seeking more.

I leaned in to kiss her quickly. Chastely. Well aware of the eyes upon us. As I pulled back, I saw it—the brief flash of panic in her eyes.

Her palms spasmed on my lower back, fisting my shirt.

Shit.

I had done this to her when I left, made her unsure of me. Though I'd declared how I felt and that I wouldn't leave again, Nicole still couldn't shake the fear that I would. The realization tore out my heart.

I tucked a wayward strand of black hair behind Nicole's ear and pulled her into me again. I kissed her, much more deeply this time. Her body melted into me, tension easing away.

The rest of the room whooped and hollered, causing Nicole's face to flame red as she tried to pull away.

I kept her clutched to me. "Miss me, sweetheart?" I murmured against her ear, too low for anyone else to hear, hoping to all the gods above that it eased her. That my words—and the tattoo I'd had Ezra ink across my ribs for her this morning—would do so.

She smiled hesitantly, gaze dropping as she took me in, running a finger down my chest. My skin rippled where she touched, but she didn't yet know about the ink. Nicole swallowed, a hint unsure. "Can you blame me?"

I was about to dip my head again when—

"Nicky!" Misha shouted from across the room. "Quit acting like a love-struck kitten and get back over here before we have to forfeit."

Nicole turned, still clutching my shirt. "We'd have won half an hour ago if any of you imbeciles had listened to me."

"Oh, don't be all 'I told you so,' Nic. It's never a good look." Misha waved her hand.

Nicole bristled at her sister's dismissal. She faced me again, irritation dancing on her features. "If she doesn't quit, I'm going to have to figure out a way to put her back to sleep," she murmured.

"I heard that!"

Nicole's answering smile was wicked. "I intended you to." Her sister shot her a middle finger. She turned back to me. "I have to go finish this. They're lost without me."

I laughed and planted a swift kiss on her lips before releasing her. "Go get them then . . . *kitten.*"

Nicole gasped. "Don't. You. Dare." She poked my chest with each word. "That's even worse than *snowflake.*"

Gods above, she was beautiful when that fire flared in her eyes. I took her by the guilty finger, bringing it to my mouth. My teeth nipped the pad.

She yelped, her eyes narrowing to slits, but amusement danced along Nicole's red-stained mouth as she half-heartedly pushed me away before walking back toward the gaming table. "I swear to the Gods, Misha, if he takes to calling me that, I'm blaming you."

Misha chuckled as if she'd love nothing more. "Sure thing, kitty cat." She bumped her hip into Nicole's who laughed, throwing her head back.

As they settled back into their game, Teale bounded over to the table, eager to join, and I went to Jophiel to debrief her. She normally would have come with us, but the nymphs were wary of the Seraphim.

Jophiel hadn't minded. She wanted to spend every moment she could with Nicole and Misha, now knowing what she did. I'd known her my entire life—for over two and a half centuries—and I'd never seen her eyes shine quite so bright as when she looked at her granddaughters.

The game fizzled, everyone who had been crowding around the table moving on to something else. Simon, after murmuring a few words to Misha and Julian, drifted out early, eager to return to his husband and daughter.

My brother, a fresh glass of wine in his hand, came toward me and Jophiel. "And why were you and Teale so late?"

I looked around at them all, their smiles and laughter. "I'm not sure this is the time."

"Brother," Julian pushed. "Tell me, or I'll imagine it to be worse than it is."

"Fine." I sighed. "Adrienne has gone missing. Even the Dryads and other nymphs haven't gotten eyes or ears on her in a week."

"Shit," he cursed.

"What's shit?" Misha appeared under Julian's arm, almost as if she'd winnowed there. "There should be no shits tonight."

"Gods above, Meesh." Nicole appeared beside me, sliding an arm around my waist. "No one wants to hear you say *shit* that many times."

Misha looked at her sister, face deadpan. "Shit, shit, shit, shit."

Both sisters remained silent for a second, locked in a standoff, then burst into a fit of giggles. I held onto Nicole as she shook with silent laughter, both amused and perplexed. I'd never seen her like this.

Gemma came over. She looked between the twins and shrugged. "You get used to it."

Once she and her sister calmed, Nicole looked up at me. "What did the nymphs say?"

I relayed the conversation, everything I'd told the others.

"Shit is right," Nicole muttered.

"So, she's using the Void's magic to hide herself." Misha deduced. "What is she planning?"

"That's what we are trying to find out," I said.

Nicole had gone still, contemplating. "The witch said something about *going to the place they were forged*. She had to have meant the swords, where they were made. What if this has something to do with it? I mean, during her vision, she said there was more."

"You want to go to the Galorian mountain?" Misha asked.

Her sister nodded.

My arm tightened around Nicole. "If you—"

"Don't worry." She peered up at me. "We won't have a repeat of the witches. If we go, we *all* go."

"When?" Julian asked.

"The day after tomorrow?" Misha suggested.

Nicole looked between her sister and Julian. "That's not too soon?"

Misha looked up at Julian, the two of them in silent conversation. My brother turned back to me. "If it gives us information on Adrienne and her secret Void magic, the sooner, the better."

Nicole switched into Alesia's native language, speaking to only her sister. "Are you sure, sister? You want to go only one day after your mating night?"

Misha flushed before answering in the same language. "We'll have that night, and plenty more after."

Miranda walked up with Damian, looking back and forth between us all. "Was that meant to be a secret? You know August and Julian understand you, right?"

Nicole went utterly still beneath my arm.

"You do?" Misha looked up at Julian, brows nearing her hairline.

My brother broke into a wide smile. "Sí, mi amor." He kissed Misha on the forehead. His accent wasn't perfect, but good enough.

Nicole gasped. "For how long?"

Miranda answered, "Always?"

She whipped around to me. "Even at the Solstice?"

I couldn't hold in my grin, remembering how Nicole had bemoaned Evander's presence to her sister. How she'd ended up in my arms instead.

Seeing my face, Misha erupted into laughter. "¡Lo sabía!"

Nicole's face went slack-jawed. I leaned into her ear. "It's not that uncommon a language, sweetheart."

"What did you hear?" she asked.

My smile grew. "Was there something you didn't want me to hear that night, Snow?"

"*No*, you prick." Nicole pushed out of my arms, looking annoyed despite the smile dancing in her eyes. She took another glass of wine from the tray and moved to hand Miranda another as well.

"Oh no, I'm not drinking that," the witch said, declining. Nicole's brows furrowed in confusion.

"She's drinking this—" Damian handed Miranda a different glass, similar to the wine Nicole held. "—because this one doesn't have alcohol." He was smiling, beaming even, as he wrapped his arms around his mate, chin resting on her shoulder.

I watched Nicole process this, slowly understanding. "Are you?" she whispered, her eyes glassing with tears. "Are you really?"

Miranda nodded, hands coming to her belly, just beginning to show. "We're having a son."

Nicole set down her glass, throwing her arms around Miranda and then Damian. "I'm so happy for you both."

As everyone else gathered around to congratulate them, I took Nicole back into my arms, wiping away the tear streaks as I saw how happy she was. My chest constricted. Never in my wildest dreams could I have imagined her, here with me, while feeling this utterly joyful—not after everything she'd been put through.

If you love her, then don't question her.

And I wouldn't—not anymore. I cast all my worries aside. Mate or no, Nicole was right where she wanted to be.

With me.

CHAPTER 46
Nic

I sat curled in August's lap before the fireplace. One arm rested on his shoulder, my nails gently running over his scalp. His arm was wrapped around me, palm cupping my hip. His other was running along my calf, nails skimming my bare skin.

Taking a drink of wine, I lowered the glass from my lips.

August snatched it from my hand.

I opened my mouth to protest, but he turned the glass, placing his lips where mine had been. His eyes never left mine as he drank. When he finished, his tongue darted out, running across the edge of the crystal over the trace remains of my lip stain.

Fucking gods.

Heat unspooled low in my core. My thighs clenched, wound impossibly tight and empty all at once. I would never stop wanting him—yearning for him.

"There is something I want to show you," he murmured, setting the glass down on the end table.

I squirmed in his lap. "Yeah?"

A low, deep laugh. "Not that, sweetheart, though it does involve the shedding of certain clothing. Speaking of—" August lifted his hand to trace the delicate strap of my dress. I could feel his gaze on the bare skin of my shoulder, tracing down my decolletage. He tugged on the strap as if sensing how much effort it would take to rip through it.

Very little. I'd worn this dress with one thought in mind—with *him* in mind.

I shifted against him, pressing my legs more tightly together as the heat between them grew, unspooling through me. For a moment, I thought I might combust just like this, only from the intensity of his gaze.

August's lips curved into a smile. He knew what he was doing. His eyes met mine, glazed and molten with heat. August's arm tightened, pressing me further against him. He leaned in, his lips brushing across the shell of my ear. A chill ran down my spine. "Nicole, if I reach—"

"Oh no, sister." Misha grabbed my hand, yanking me off his lap.

"*Misha*—" I snarled. I wanted to go back to August, hear him finish that sentence, challenge him to find out for himself.

My sister held me fast. "*No.*" She gestured between the two of us. "None of this. Not tonight. She's mine until tomorrow. You—" Misha pointed an accusatory finger at August. "—get her tomorrow and every night after."

August's fingers dug into the armrests, holding himself in place.

I turned, ready to defy my sister until I met her gaze and noted the want in her eyes—for tonight to be just the two of us. As it once had been, before the Warin brothers had shaken and reformed our worlds—for the better, but still, there was always a bittersweet tang to change.

The tension seeped out of me, and I looked apologetically to August. His face softened, nodding subtly. Understanding.

August remained seated and reached for my hand, gently kissing my knuckles. Each one, one at a time. His eyes were molten silver, burning as they met mine. *Tomorrow*, they promised.

I love you, I mouthed.

Eternally, he mouthed back.

#

An hour later, Misha and I sat on the bed in our nightclothes, a spare room for the two of us to share tonight in a different wing from Julian's and August's chambers, lest we be tempted to sneak away when the other went to sleep. A lavender duvet covered our heads, tiny faerie lights hovering around the linen as my sister and I sat cross-legged.

I took a sip of my red wine, rich with the flavor of chocolate and cherry.

"What if confirming the mating bond is a mistake?" Misha whispered, her eyes unfocused as she swirled her drink of strawberry and mint.

I nearly choked. "What?" No two people were more perfect for each other than Misha and Julian.

But my sister had her arms wrapped around her legs, distressed. "Julian will be tethered to me," Misha murmured, still in her trance, "unable to leave or escape. What if I drag him down? What if I am the thing that destroys him?" Her eyes refocused, meeting mine.

"No, Misha." I set my glass on the end table, before taking hers and doing the same. "I used to be afraid of it, but now that it's not an option—" I took a deep breath, the movement rattling my chest. "The mating bond is a gift, don't you see?"

"But the stars have forced us together. You and August get to *choose* each other. Julian and I can never have that. How can he love me, truly love me, when his choice has been taken?"

"There is always a choice, Misha. But you and Julian know you're made for each other, perfect in every way. While August and I—" My voice cracked. "I'll always have to convince August it was right. That he's not keeping me from something greater. I'm still so scared he'll talk himself into leaving again." My lower lip trembled as I held back the tears.

Misha shook her head, startling me with her laughter. "We sound like that one children's story: two bumpkin toads on a log, bemoaning our lot in life while staring at each other's pond, green and bubbling with envy."

My head tilted, incredulous. "*The Unhappy Toads*? That's what you think we are?" Misha nodded, still gasping with laughter, and I began to laugh too, shaking my head. "I don't know how you come up with this shit, sister."

Once the giggling started between us, we couldn't stop. After a minute, my sister was finally able to take a breath.

"We are ridiculous." Misha flopped onto her back, staring up at the tiny floating lights, the duvet held up by vines she'd cast. I laid beside her, little briar roses fluttering their petals at us. "I know what happened while I slept," she began, "since you've all relayed your different accounts . . . but why?"

My eyebrows puckered together. "Why what?"

Misha turned on her side, facing me. I did the same. "Why—how did you come to love him?" she clarified.

"We are the same," I said simply. When I didn't say more, she nudged my arm, urging me to continue. I took a breath, trying to determine how best to say it. "When I'm with August, it feels . . . it feels like I'm alone."

"Alone?" Misha gaped. "How can you love someone that makes you feel as if you are alone? Like being abandoned?"

I shook my head. "To you and me, being alone is not the same. You thrive on interaction, Misha. You come to life in it. I can manage it for a time, but eventually, I need space. I need to pull away to settle into myself again."

It wasn't that I didn't love time around friends or parties, because I did—for a time. But too long, and it began to feel like a façade, no more than whatever mask I was wearing. All of it drained me, and I needed space to find myself again.

Alone to Misha was abandonment. To me, it was serenity.

"And with August," I explained. "I don't feel like I have to put on a face for anyone else. I do not have to entertain or please or be strong for him. He is a refuge. With him, we are the same, so there is nothing to hide. He is a place of peace where all I have to be is who I am, and he can be all he is." A soft smile curled my lips as I pictured him and how his arms felt like home. "August is my solace. Even the worst part of me finds peace in the worst part of him."

Misha smiled, taking my hands in hers. "Yes, well," she began. "I'm very glad I stole you away then. When this is all over, and you two have proper time together, don't let it be a decade before you two emerge from your *solace*."

I chuckled, attempting to stifle a yawn as sleep called to me, my eyelids growing heavy. "Never, sister. But maybe a year."

Misha laughed again, the sound a balm to my soul, as she, too, began to yawn.

We fell asleep that way, turned toward each other with our hands clasped together—twins who'd come into this life together and would do anything to keep it that way.

CHAPTER 47
Misha

On the first day of November, Julian and I were to be mated at sunset.

Nic helped me into my dress, one of rose gold silk with a slightly lighter overlay of sheer tulle. A cape of the same material was attached to my shoulders, trailing out behind me. At the end of the train and skirt, I cast briar roses, the petals red instead of pink. They grew thickest at the hem, thinning as they traveled upward.

My sister stood before me, grasping my hands. "You're glowing, Misha. Radiant."

I felt it, too, as if a sun were bursting beneath my skin at the joy of being mated to Julian, but there was always that undercurrent of sorrow that Alesia and Eve weren't here to witness it, nor our parents.

I wanted this day to be for our mating. The first of November was when the Veil was supposedly thinnest, bringing the dead closer to us than any other day of the year.

Nic squeezed my hands tighter, knowing where my thoughts had gone. "They are, sister. They are watching from somewhere between the stars." She gently wiped away the tears that threatened to fall.

I nodded, knowing it to be true. Our family was here with us, always—in my heart and my sister's. Our family was reflected in her eyes. They were here in Jophiel, a piece of that family we'd gotten back through our grandmother.

For the ceremony, we went to the Atrium, a part of the castle I hadn't yet been to. Stepping through the doors, it stole my breath. There were tall, flowering trees of each color—reds, pinks, purples, blues, and greens—and several with leaves that looked entirely spun from gold and silver. Along our path were elegant lilies, foxglove, roses of various shades, and more. Through the glass walls, the waterfall seemed to flow golden with the light of the sunset and a rainbow was forming in its mist. In the center, nestled in the domed stained glass roof, were a multitude of faerie lights, looking like trapped stars twinkling down upon us.

And in the middle, surrounded by our friends and family, stood Julian.

His brown skin looked bronze in the light of the sunset, his formal jacket embroidered with elegant silver thread, perfectly matching his storm cloud eyes. His smile when he saw me—his smile was the thing of dreams, just as I'd imagined it in all my years of pining for him.

When I reached him, Nic let go of my hand, stepping back to join the others. All of the Seven were present, standing around us, Gemma at Shai's side and Simon with Jessa and Ezra.

Julian and I faced each other, Sena coming to one side and Miranda the other. Julian's mother kissed him once on the cheek, then turned to me, doing the same. "Never could the stars have granted me a better daughter," she said as she squeezed my hand.

My chest swelled, threatening to burst in a cascade of love.

"With the handfasting," Sena spoke louder, initiating the ceremony, "you two will be officially mated. This union is not one to be taken lightly. The mating brings a deep realization of responsibility and commitment to your mate, and though you two were deemed a perfect union by the stars above, mating does not mean your lives will be simple. Every day, you must choose to respect and love your mate above all else, in the best and worst of circumstances." Looking between us, Sena asked, "Do you each choose each other, now and every day from this moment on?"

"I do," Julian and I said simultaneously, our eyes never leaving the other's.

"Then take each other's hands."

Sena began to wind the cords around our joined hands, one made of one silver ribbon and the other gold. "With each wrap of these cords, you deepen the bond to each other. You vow to respect and support one another, grow together, offer compassion and understanding, and take each new challenge in life as one. As your hands are bound, your soul is bonded in this life and the next."

When Sena finished binding the ribbons, she stepped back, nodding to us with a soft smile. "Speak your vows as you cast a piece of your magic into the cord."

Julian went first. "Misha, I have loved you since the moment I saw you. My heart and soul have, and always will, belong to you. Whether in times of light or darkness, I am eternally yours." As he spoke, lightning crackled down his arm, flowing into the silver ribbon until it, too, was sparking with electricity.

"Julian, I have loved you since the moment I saw you and I fell deeper with each word in every letter. You are the light in my darkness, a steadfast beacon drawing me home. In a world of night, you are my sun, and I am eternally yours." I felt a sliver of my magic pull away, chipping itself from my heart. It traveled down my arm, a vine of rosebuds erupting from my skin and winding down into the gold ribbon. The silk began to glow and the blossoms unfurled slowly until they were in full bloom.

Miranda lifted her hands, murmuring the spell that would bind the pieces of our magic to the cords, severing them from us entirely. Then, slowly, the magic began to leave the ribbons. I felt the piece of Julian's magic flow from the silver one toward me, burning up my arm until it fused within my heart, replacing the part I'd given to him.

Though our exchange of magic was equal, I felt stronger—greater—for having part of him locked within me, as if together, we were more than just the sum of our parts.

One look in his eyes told me he felt the same.

At the moment the sun reached the horizon, it was done.

"By the gods above, I declare that Julian Ororo Warin and Misha Camila Sancrista Briar are now forever mated as well as husband and wife."

Sena and Miranda stepped back.

Our hands still bound, Julian pulled me forward, his lips meeting mine as the gatherers erupted into cheers. When we pulled away, I took them in, this new family of mine. Everyone was smiling, and a few were even wiping stray tears from their eyes. Jophiel was the most vocal, near sobbing with joy.

We slowly slid our hands from the cords, careful not to unravel them. To do so before the night ended was a portend of bad luck for the mating.

Nic came to my side, asking the question everyone seemed to be waiting for. "Did it work?"

Stepping back, I called to that new sliver of magic and felt it burning along my veins and skin. Lightning crackled down my arms. It was wild and erratic, but I felt with enough practice, I could form and shape it, just like the plants I casted and the animals I molded. "It worked."

My sister smiled, everyone sharing in same amazement.

"Now for the big one," August said, clapping his brother on the back.

Not wanting to destroy the Atrium accidentally, we winnowed outdoors for Julian's transition on the turret.

Julian walked away from where we were gathered in the doorway, to the edge. When he turned back toward us, his grey irises flickered with lightning as the pupils lengthened into slits. Then, the rest of the transformation began.

In a flash of cracking thunder, his body morphed, becoming the silvery blue dragon, the same height and size as when I'd transformed him. He looked the same, yet utterly different.

His wings flapped, and we watched him lift into the clouds swirling around him. Lightning danced along his wings. But this time, when he roared, his head lifting to the sky, Julian did not emit fire but a blaze of white lightning.

I ran to the cliff's edge, jumping with my arms spread wide. My body expanded, lengthening and growing. My hands and feet expelled talons and fangs lengthened in my mouth. The wings burst free as I dove and cut upward, flying to meet him.

In the waning light, we flew, dancing around each other.

CHAPTER 48
Julian

When we returned from flying, the others had gone elsewhere, giving Misha and me privacy on the night of our mating. Everyone except Ezra, who was waiting at my request.

We landed, Misha and I returning to our Fae forms, much better at keeping our clothing intact as we shifted, thanks to endless practice.

Misha shivered in the cold night air of early November. I shrugged off my jacket, slinging it over her shoulders before taking her hand and leading her inside.

Ezra smiled as we approached, sitting at a table set up with what he needed. "Ready?"

Misha looked at me, shocked. The other morning, as we laid together in bed, she had offhandedly mentioned wanting a tattoo like Ezra's—something that, more than rings, would represent our mating, forever inked upon her.

I'd always admired the way Simon and Ezra had declared their love for each other permanently on their skin. Ezra's was more evident, drawn down his arms with plants and animals that told the story of them in a language only they understood. More had been added after Jessa's addition to their lives, her favorite birds and flowers. But Simon's was more subtle: his husband's and daughter's names inked over his heart in Ezra's handwriting.

I'd only said I would consider it, wanting to keep this a surprise to her, but after breakfast, I'd gone immediately to Ezra to plan it.

Misha's eyes welled as she turned back to Ezra, nodding—a rare moment of speechlessness for her. Her fingers tightened around mine, nervous.

I chuckled. "I'll go first, love."

I sat in the chair with her—my *mate*—beside me, head resting on my shoulder as she watched him free hand what I'd asked for.

He began to ink.

Ezra tattooed a bracelet of golden vines and leaves twining around my left forearm, just above the wrist. From the stems, roses sprouted with pink petals and yellow centers so realistic they looked exactly like the flowers in life. When he was done, Misha was teary-eyed as she took in the exact recreation of her Briar roses.

We switched and, despite sitting in my lap, Misha wouldn't let me watch as Ezra tattooed her. I rested my head between her shoulder blades, breathing her in—the feral rose and musk scent of her—until it was done. Occasionally, she stiffened from the pain, and I squeezed her tighter, my lips finding her skin until she relaxed once more.

When it was done, Misha showed me the ring of silver around her left wrist, in the same location as mine. The lines were more erratic, some sharp and jagged, while others were curled and smooth, forming an image of lightning and wispy clouds winding together.

The sight awoke something deep inside me, this physical representation of the vows we'd made each other. We'd exchanged vows and magic, and every time I saw this part of me on her skin, I would remember.

My mate.

Ezra beamed at us. He'd known me as long as Simon—nearly my entire life. They were close friends of my mother's, giving her the friendship she'd so badly needed after being isolated by my father for so long.

"Thank you for letting me be a part of this day." He hugged us, kissing us each on the cheek before exiting, leaving Misha and me alone in the Atrium.

Misha walked to me, pressing herself close. She took my arm, finger gently grazing the roses, already healed. The heat in her eyes when she looked up spoke of tangling in bedsheets—*our* bedsheets—tonight and every night after.

But as much as I wanted to, I said, "There's somewhere I'd like to show you first, love."

She growled, the sound low in her throat. "If this surprise doesn't involve us naked—"

I chuckled. "I promise you'll love it, Misha."

Pouting, she took my hand, letting me lead her through the gardens. I brought her to a corner of the Atrium, one covered with dripping fuchsia blossoms and roses of various shapes and sizes, all in a different shade of pink.

It was an exact replica of her favorite place in the Sanserrian palace gardens, where she and I had met.

Misha's lips parted in awe as she took it in.

I sat upon the stone bench, pulling her into my lap as I took a small velvet box from my pocket. "We never discussed rings, but—" I opened it, and she gasped.

Inside was a round sapphire, the peach of the sky at dawn, set in gold and flanked by two roses on a diamond band, one in full bloom and the other a bud.

"The bud represents the beginning of our mating and the bloom is what it will become as we grow and flourish. The stone reminded me of you, the sunrise, and how, even after the longest, darkest night, you find the strength to rise," I whispered, placing the ring on her finger. I could have sworn the diamonds of the band sparkled brighter, as if lightning coursed through them when the ring met her skin.

Misha's eyes welled, and then she was crying.

I lifted her chin, kissing away the tears. "I love you, Misha."

"Then stop ruining my surprises," she gasped out, pulling out another velvet box from a hidden pocket of her dress.

I laughed, astonished, as she opened it, pulling out the ring. Misha smiled, the sight more beautiful than any dawn.

"You aren't the only one that came with gifts." She held the ring out to me.

It was a band of white gold, etched intricately with storm clouds and lightning on one side and the rising sun on the other. Tiny diamonds were embedded throughout, glimmering like stars.

Misha slid the ring onto my finger, her mouth meeting mine.

My wife.

Her knees settled on each side of my hips, straddling me as our kiss deepened and her skirt fell around us. Misha ground against me, where I was already hard with wanting her.

"I love you so much, Julian." Misha's hands were on my belt, unbuckling. "I need you inside me." She reached in, stroking me, pulling a sharp hiss from my lips.

"*Misha.*"

I reached my hand between her legs, making sure she was ready before I grasped my cock, pulling her silk undergarments to the side and positioning myself at her entrance. Misha whimpered as she sank onto me. I shuddered as I pushed inside her, gripping me so perfectly.

As she began to move, clinging to my shoulders, I leaned back, watching her ride me, enraptured.

I pulled her to me, devouring her with my lips and tongue. She tasted like heaven, like pure ecstasy.

Mine.

My lips cascaded down her throat, grasping her hair tightly in one hand to open her neck for me as I kissed and sucked at the skin between her neck and shoulder. My mouth moved to her ear, nipping the lobe as I whispered, "Brace yourself, love."

Misha's hands gripped my shoulder tighter as I gripped her hips, thrusting into her. The way she gasped, tightening around me, told me it wouldn't be much longer. When she climaxed, pulsing around me, I followed.

We sat together in silence, our breath slowing as we held each other. I took her beautiful face in my hands, gazing into the blue eyes that uncovered an even more stunning soul.

My wife. My mate.

Always.

CHAPTER 49
Nic

As the dawn rose, I awoke. August slept facing away from me on his side, his chest rising and falling slowly in his sleep.

Pressing myself against his back, I wrapped an arm around him, sliding my hand up his stomach to his chest. My fingertips lingered there, over the tattoo he'd gotten for me.

The choice he'd made to cover his scars.

My lips pressed to his shoulder, making my way up to the back of his neck. I was intoxicated with how his skin felt under them and his taste; the scent of smoke and rain that always felt like home.

As August woke, his hand rose, trailing up my arm. His fingers threaded through mine as he pressed my palm more tightly into his chest—against his heart.

"Snow," he whispered, his voice husky with sleep. He lifted my hand, pressing a kiss to the palm.

"Good morning, beautiful," I murmured against the back of his neck, where my lips continued their assault on his skin. Such greedy things—they could never get enough of him.

August rolled, turning toward and then on top of me, spreading my knees apart so he could nestle between them. He propped himself up on his elbows to look at me. His stormy eyes churned with emotion as I cupped his cheek. As much as I loved our passionate lovemaking, this would always be my favorite—these lazy, tender moments between us.

In a few hours, we—he and I, Julian, Misha, Jophiel, Shai, and Celeste—would go to the Galorian mountain for that last bit of information. Hopefully there'd something that could help us stop Adrienne.

Cupping my neck, he ran a thumb along my jaw. "There is something I want to do before we go today." I arched into him, unable to stop it. He chuckled. "That's not what I meant."

My thighs tightened around him. "Are you sure?"

He grunted, hardening against me. "Okay, yes," he admitted, and I gasped as his hand ran up my side, leaving a shiver in its wake. "But something else, too."

"Anything." My lips found his, soft and unhurried. "What do you want, August?"

He flipped us, pulling me on top of him. "You—always you, Snow."

I smiled, stretching out like a cat as I marveled at the feeling of him beneath me. I ground into him, reaching down and slipping him inside me. August groaned, gripping my hips. He pulled me to him, so our bodies were flush against each other.

His lips sent sparks down my throat, kissing there before traveling to my ear as he told me exactly what he wanted.

CHAPTER 50
Adrienne

I held the pendant before me, the center stone the color of fresh blood. The gold knot around it whispered a promise.

The witch had brought it to me, using the blood beneath her nails to craft this—a pendant of protection against those whose blood it housed. In exchange, I offered her protection, letting her stay in the palace as long as she lived to keep her safe.

I had stood behind her, watching her work. Once the spell was done, I'd taken the blackened dagger, slicing it across her throat. The white witch's face had frozen in shock; she'd survived this long, only for me to betray her.

In our bargain, she'd never stated how long her life would be—and her body *was* safe within the palace. I'd buried it beneath the chamber floor, where it would remain undisturbed.

It wasn't personal. I needed to atone.

The god was angry with me and with the witch and her sisters, for letting them escape . . . and he liked witch hearts best. They reminded him of the one who betrayed him, trapping him within the crystal sarcophagus. He craved their blood on his tongue, for it let him taste *her* once more.

So, I carved out her heart, black from centuries of stealing life to prolong her own, and in return, the Void gave me a gift. One greater than any he'd offered before.

The magic writhed through my fingers, up my arms.

The Call of Death.

PART III:
The Mountain

CHAPTER 51
Misha

The Galorian mountain was a peak in the southeastern part of the range. It was a small mountain compared to those around it but was unmistakable with its composition of jagged white stone. Nothing grew upon its surface. No animal trod across it. Not even snow dared fall upon its highest point—the peak was completely untouched.

This was the only place on the continent where Galorian silver could be mined and forged.

Julian winnowed with me, Shai, and Celeste. Nic and Jophiel went with August.

We emerged before a tunnel marked with black stone and inscribed with the ancient Fae language. It was midday and the sun shined above us, but the light seemed to be completely absorbed by the black rock, unsettling me.

"Are we sure this is worth it?" I murmured, unable to take my eyes off it.

"We know Adrienne promised the Void freedom in exchange for the knowledge to steal magic and use of his dark creatures," Nic said. "We know the way to free him is with our blood, but we don't know how. Maybe this will give us that last piece—the opportunity to stop her."

I nodded. My sister was right. Julian took my hand, squeezing it in reassurance.

We entered through a tunnel, lighting torches on the walls to mark our way, until we reached a large door. Nic went to reach for the bronze knocker in the center, shaped like a lion with a ring hung in its jaws.

"Only the four may pass," it spoke, and Nic's hand lurched back. "The queens and their kings."

"I guess that's us," Julian said.

I squeezed his hand. *My king.*

We hadn't discussed it yet, but he was. If I was heir to Hahnaley, their queen—though exiled by Adrienne's coup—now that we were mated, he would be King of the West in every right.

"We'll remain here," Jophiel promised.

Celeste nodded with her, Shai at her side. They, like us, were dressed in fighting leathers. Jophiel had her sword and shield slung across her back, Celeste with her bow and belt of knives at her waist, and Shai had two swords crossing his back.

The heavy door swung open, groaning as if it had been a long while since anyone had passed through.

"Any more than half an hour, Shai, and call for reinforcements," August commanded.

Shai nodded. Both Jophiel and Celeste did as well, though the former seemed more likely to tear down the door should she think we were in any danger.

I gave her, my grandmother, a small smile of reassurance.

We passed through the door, and my magic faded as if pulled behind a veil. Unreachable.

A goblin, one of the smaller faerie races, appeared through another door at the far end of the empty room. His head barely reached my waist. He nodded to my sister and me. "The peak is warded against all types of magic, Fae and witch. You, though gifted with both, can cast nothing here." A table materialized before him. "And I'll need your weapons."

No magic and no weapons. I didn't like this.

"This is new," August said, not moving to remove his swords or hidden daggers.

"The surrounding area may be yours to control, my lord—" The goblin stood firm. "—But the mountain is under no country's authority. We serve only the gods and the magic they bless us with. Remove the weapons or return to whence you came."

We looked at each other, then came to silent agreement. Slowly, we unarmed ourselves. I placed the Mercedelmar and Eve's bow and quiver upon the table. Nic did the same with the Iradelmar and a short sword. August's and Julian's swords came next, along with an assortment of knives.

"Good." The goblin gave a shallow bow. "Now, what is your reason for coming?"

Nic pointed at our mother and aunt's swords. "We were told there is more to learn about their inscriptions—the prophecy. We were told to come to the place they were forged."

The goblin leaned closer, peering at them. "Oh yes, I remember these. You must be here for their sister."

"Sister?" I asked. Alesia had told us only two were made—one for her and one for Diana. The same was written in my mother's journals.

The goblin nodded. "There was a shield crafted from the same batch of silver. One of the forgers is a Seer, a servant of the fates. When your mother and aunt left, she had a vision. She inscribed the star's words herself. Come along." He turned, not waiting to see if we joined.

Silently, we followed him down a series of tunnels, deeper into the mountain. The walls were barren earth with torches lighting the way every few meters. After several minutes of walking deeper underground, the tunnels began to lighten. The clanging of hammers upon metal met our ears, along with a deep rumbling.

We stepped into a wide cavern, the ceiling nearly a mile high. A hole was cut in the center, from which the smoke poured out. Chained in the middle was a lone dragon.

The dragon was pure white, with scales the color of snow at dawn. She was massive, slightly larger than Julian and me in our dragon forms.

We watched as a goblin struck her with a whip, the end tipped in silver. It sliced through her flank, at a soft spot not covered by scales, and she roared, blowing out fire to heat more Galorian silver for forging. Her hips and back were covered in scars from what had to be years of being struck.

"What are they doing?" I launched forward, ready to steal the whip from the goblin's hand—let him see how he liked it.

Julian wrapped an arm around my waist, holding me back.

The goblin we arrived with looked calmly on. "The fire is what feeds the forging. Dragonfire is not like natural flame. It is the gift of the gods, for to take gods-given power away, you need gods-given magic."

This was the key to forging the Galorian silver to be able to be bonded to rowan wood ash. The gods had given the Fae their magic, the dragons their fire—give and take.

"How is it alive?" Nic asked. She was holding tightly to August's arm. His face had gone pale as he looked at the whip, his eyes unseeing. As my sister gripped him harder, he looked down at her. Meeting her eyes, he seemed to come back to himself.

"Though your king killed all those in the war, not all dragons fought," the goblin answered. "This was the only youngling, and she was too small to fight for the High King. She was kept here until the war was over, until her parents returned to forge more weapons. They never did, and thus, she is the last."

Her scales were too white, the pale color of something that had not seen the sun in a very long time.

"She's been kept here for a hundred years?" I scoffed. "Forced to do this day after day?"

"Not daily, but the demand for our silver has increased as of late," the goblin answered simply. "No animaglia are here to compel her, and it would be too dangerous for anyone else to know. They may take her and put her to their own use. So, this is the solution."

"Solution?" I snarled. Julian wrapped his arm more tightly around me. I spun on him.

Let this go, Misha. Not forever, but for now, his eyes spoke to me.
Like hell.

I pulled out of his arms, making my way to where the dragon was chained. Shackles at her feet and legs kept her immobile. The muscles around her legs and back were withered, atrophied to nearly nothing. As if they hadn't been used since she was a youngling.

Everything about this was immeasurably cruel.

I moved toward the dragon, stepping softly. She seemed not to care, apathetic. Keeping my eyes on hers as I neared, I didn't see the debris on the ground and accidentally kicked a shard of metal. The dragon startled, skittering back as far as her chains would allow and roaring wildly toward me.

She hadn't seen me approach—the dragon was blind.

Had she been born this way, or had they made her so? My gut sank as I realized it was likely the latter so that she couldn't see the whips coming.

The dragon sniffed as I neared, trying to sense exactly where I was.

This was a stupid idea, but one I couldn't let go. I couldn't cast my magic here, but I could show the beast kindness.

"Misha," Nic hissed, taking my arm to pull me away just as I laid my hand on her scales.

I felt a tug, a thread forming between me and the dragon. In half of my mind, I saw nothing, only darkness, but then through me, the dragon saw through my eyes for the first time in over a hundred years.

The dragon let out a wail that could only be described as longing and amazement. She whipped her head, trying to understand, until she realized she wasn't seeing through her eyes, but mine—looking at a hand laid against white scales.

Her great horned head and onyx eyes looked unseeingly downward. I lifted my eyes so she could take herself in and see her own face. The dragon began to whine deep in her throat, a sound of sorrowful understanding.

I felt all of it, all of her. Memories of a life spent trapped here coursed through me.

When Nic's hand was pulled away and she let go of me, the connection was severed. The thread snapped.

The dragon wailed again, morosely this time. She thrashed her head and tail, searching for me to make the connection once more.

"Chione," I murmured, running a hand along her scales once more, but it seemed that my touch alone wasn't enough to respark the magic. "That's your name, isn't it?"

The dragon stilled as if she hadn't heard herself called by name in over a century. She dropped her head, snout coming level with my face. When I brushed a hand against it, she didn't pull away. Stroking across her scales, I made her a silent promise.

"It seems that with the Briars," August murmured. "No monster is safe."

The goblin cleared his throat and I stepped back reluctantly. "The shield is housed within the vault."

We followed him, crossing the cavern to its opposite side. A circular door of silver stood before us. The goblin touched it, muttering words too low for us to hear before the locks whirred and clicked. The vault door swung open.

Silver weapons of all types and sizes hung from the walls to be sold or traded to Fae or humans who could pay their price. The metal gleamed under a chandelier of sharp faerie lights in the center of the room.

The goblin walked to the far wall to open another, smaller vault. He carried out a wooden chest and set it on the table in the center of the room.

"When the shield was forged, it was locked away. Only those born on the dawn of the longest day can open it. It requires a drop of blood from each." The goblin held out a small knife.

Nic and I moved forward, piercing our fingers on the blades.

The goblin pointed to a ruby in the center of the chest's lock. "One drop here."

My sister and I laid our fingers upon it, and the blood soaked into the jewel. The lock clicked. We opened the lid, exposing the round shield beneath. The edge was rimmed in Galorian silver, sharpened as fine as a blade, with gold at the center, and embedded with sapphires and pearls. It matched the Iradelmar and Mercedelmar's hilts, along with the language of the gods engraved around its edge.

Julian moved forward, the only one of us who could translate.

"The Fallen can only rise when sun and moon join, the blood of a daughter born of three mothers cast upon the grave to break the binds. A heart taken will a heart replace."

"A solar eclipse," Nic murmured. "That's when she'll do it. Miranda will know when that is."

Daughter born of three mothers. I looked at Nic. We were born of Diana, raised by Alesia and Eve.

"*A heart taken will a heart replace,*" I repeated. "That's why she wants us—why she's been trying to take them. She needs a heart to replace the Void's—to raise him."

A slow clap came from behind us, along with a cruel and beautiful voice. "That's exactly right, Misha. Well done."

Adrienne.

CHAPTER 52
Nic

T he goblin was gone. Instead, in a gown of pure white with a gold metal breastplate, Adrienne Deimos stood blocking the door to the vault.

She was flanked by Evander—half his face still scarred from where I'd burned him—and Mannix, the courtier I'd severed the tongue of. The former was smiling cruelly. The latter only stared, hatred in his violet eyes. From behind them came Lorraine, Evander and Gemma's middle sister. She stood still, stoic as ever, although she'd grown thin since the summer, dark circles staining her undereye.

August and I moved at once, lurching to grab a weapon—any weapon—from those along the wall.

Wagging her finger, Adrienne tsked. A wave of shadow swept out, knocking us to the ground. The dark, writhing matter bound my hands and feet as well as August's. A wave of her hand, and the same happened to Misha and Julian.

It was no magic I'd ever seen or heard of before.

"Don't look so shocked, Nicky. It was a gift." Adrienne smiled, shadows twisting around her, caressing the long sleeves of her gown. "Fae and witch magic are indeed barred under the mountain, but this is loaned from a god. The same rules don't apply."

My hand slid down my leg. I wasn't silly enough to have given up every weapon upon entering. If I could just reach the swan hilt dagger in my boot—

The shadows at my wrists yanked me forward, dragging until the four of us were aligned before Adrienne. I was forced to kneel between August and Misha, with Julian on her other side.

"The Fallen knew *how* to unbind himself, but not *when*. As with all magic, there is an exception to every rule and a lock for every key. This one has three parts, one from each of the casters. His servants discovered the first two, as no prophecy can be held in one location. But this last one, the third part, evaded him . . . at least until sweet Julian so kindly read it aloud."

Adrienne walked around us, reaching for the shield. She hissed, pulling her hand back as it met the metal. It had left an angry, red burn on her palm.

I lunged for the shield but wasn't fast enough. Adrienne kicked it away.

"So, you got what you wanted. Now what?" Misha snarled. "You'll carve out our hearts and wait until there's an eclipse?"

"I could," Adrienne mused, a finger running along her bottom lip. "But I might want to have some fun first. Death is too easy for you." She stood above me, her gaze cold with hatred. "There are worse fates." Grief flickered in her piercing pale blue eyes. "There is the sorrow of losing a loved one, and my brother was the only person I've ever loved and cared for." My former stepmother kneeled down so that we were eye to eye. "And you took him from me."

"Your brother got what was coming to him," I spat, slamming my forehead directly into her nose with a sick crunch.

Adrienne's head whipped back. She fell back and barely righted in time to catch herself with her hands, stopping her from careening back into the stone floor completely. Blood gushed from her battered face, and the bridge of her nose jutted to the side at an odd angle.

Adrienne laughed, wiping the spilt blood. The sound lacked any humor. Only malice. She stood, towering above me, gold light flaring from her necklace as her nose snapped back into place. "You will get what is coming to you, Nicole. Choose."

"Choose what?" I could only imagine what she'd say. Likely how I would like to be tortured—wanting me to name the method of my own suffering.

"Choose who I will take from you in penance, dear stepdaughter." Adrienne's smile grew as the realization dawned on me. "Your sister or your lover."

She walked to Misha, running a nail down her cheek. My sister flinched back. Then Adrienne did the same to August.

He sat unmoving, still as stone. "Take me," August said.

"Always so valiant." Adrienne crooned, cupping his face.

I pulled against the shadows burning against my skin, but they didn't budge. I could have clawed her face off for touching him like that.

"But how badly would that hurt my dear Nicole? You two aren't mated after all." Adrienne turned back to me. "Speaking of mates, my mirrors told me a little secret—a juicy one. Do you want to know it?" Her wide smile was sinister.

I kept my mouth shut, not wanting to play this game.

"Come on, Nicky. Don't you want to know who your mate is? I bet August does."

He didn't react, his face solemn.

Adrienne's smile grew. "Evander," she crooned.

No, it couldn't be.

She waited several seconds. When I didn't react, she sighed, "You're no *fun*," then stood, going to him. "Evander, hand me my mirror." He obliged, stepping from the room and returning with a plain, silver oval, one small enough to be easily carried. "This is the Mirror of Truth. It sees through all deceptions, and it tells no lies."

Adrienne propped the mirror before me. "Mirror, who is Nicole Briar's mate?"

The surface rippled, and out spilled a soft, melodic voice. "Nicole Briar's mate is you, my Queen. Adrienne Deimos."

The words were a punch to my gut. "This is one of your mirror tricks," I hissed, kicking it away.

"Sadly not, Nicky." Her shadows caught it before the enchanted mirror could shatter on the ground. "But don't worry, we aren't *those* kind of mates. We could never be so mundane. No, you and I are much more special—much rarer."

And suddenly, I believed her. Looking at Adrienne, my heart festered with hate.

A mate could very well be your worst enemy instead of your one true love. A perfect adversary. I'd said those exact words to Misha months ago while we were discussing Evander during the Blood Treaty celebrations.

Maybe it would have always come down to this between Adrienne and me.

Even if she hadn't killed my father, my aunts, and the Shaws, maybe we'd always end up like this, boiling with hatred for one another, unsatisfied until the other was dead.

But I knew one thing for certain: if Adrienne didn't kill me tonight, I would find a way to get free, and I wouldn't stop hunting her until she was dead. I would make sure my hands were the ones to do it.

If we were mates, beings perfectly matched, then she wasn't the only monster.

So was I.

Adrienne saw it, that feral hatred blooming in my eyes, and rightly stepped back to hand the mirror back to Evander. "But back to the topic at hand. You have to choose one, Nic. Your sister or August." Adrienne waved a hand from one to the other.

It was a choice I could never make. Either one would split me in two, and I would never recover.

August met my eyes, the decision in them immutable. He turned to Adrienne, his voice only cold vehemence. His eyes flared with challenge. "Nicole didn't kill Alexander—I did."

Adrienne finally dropped her smile.

"August—" I began to plead.

He ignored me, continuing to speak. "Do you want to know how I did it? I grabbed him by the neck and shoved lightning down his throat until he was nothing but a charred husk. I scorched him from the inside out. And I did it all for her."

Adrienne's eyes flared with barely controlled wrath. "I was leaning toward Misha. I only need one heart after all, but maybe you will do after all."

Watching me, Adrienne knelt before August and grabbed his chin, her sharp nails digging into his skin. "Like I said, Nic, there are fates worse than death." Her eyes turned back to August. "Drop your shields."

"No—" I lunged. The shadows tossed me back. I struggled against them, fighting with every ounce of strength. As soon as I got one limb free, the shadows swarmed it again, pinning me to the floor.

August's eyes met mine, the summer storm in them churning. He murmured, "Remember what I said, Snow."

Then he looked back at Adrienne, his eyes closing for a long moment. My stepmother smiled as the magic, the mindcasting gift from the Void, poured into him.

I went still, unable to breathe, to think—

When August opened his eyes, they were a flat, still grey. All the pieces of him had been washed away, his mind shattered.

And August Warin knew nothing else.

CHAPTER 53
Julian

A ugust opened his eyes.

    Nic screamed. The sound was guttural and wretched as if something deep inside her had split in two. As if Adrienne had torn her heart out after all.

All traces of my brother were gone.

I couldn't breathe as I looked at August. I could make no sound as a vise wrapped around my chest, worse than the shadows could ever inflict.

"Oh, Nicky, don't be so dramatic," Adrienne teased. "I only erased the last hundred years or so. You are going to *love* August from the Great War. He was so cold and vicious. Well, maybe *you* won't, but *I* will." She laughed, the sound full of malice.

August stared ahead, unseeing. Unhearing. Adrienne snapped her fingers, and the shadows binding August fell away.

My brother looked around, clearly unsure of where he was. Adrienne and Mannix were the only two he'd recognize, I realized. Not even me.

He stood, standing beside her now.

"August," I whispered. I distantly felt the tears streaking down my face. My brother turned his head, studying me. No hint of recognition crossed his face—none. I swallowed, nearly retching onto the stone floor.

The pain coursing through my chest was almost too much to bear. August was my brother *and* father—the only one I would ever claim. He'd protected and raised me as his own. And now, there was not a hint of recognition flickering in his eyes. The eyes we shared.

August stayed silent, taking in his surroundings. I didn't know if his quiet was his own or if Adrienne held his tongue with her magic.

"August." Adrienne stroked a hand down his arm. "I heard about your mother, Yuki. Such a loss."

He said nothing, and only the cold calculation across his irises indicated he was listening.

Adrienne didn't seem to mind and went on. "Who killed her?"

August's lips tightened. He knew—he'd always known that our father, Josiah, had done it even if he could never prove it. But when Adrienne spoke again, I knew this truth wouldn't be one he believed for long.

"No, not your father, August. Josiah had nothing to do with it. He was stationed elsewhere. *Remember*," Adrienne urged as those black tendrils wrapped around August once more. "Who hated the High Fae more than anyone else? So much so that she turned on her own allies when she got the chance to strike them down?"

Adrienne's magic was still working, warping and twisting the memories. As August's face grew colder, darkening with rage, she broke into a wide grin.

"That's right," she said. "Alesia Sancrista."

Nic snarled. "Liar!"

Adrienne shrugged. "That's not what *he* believes, Nicky. Not anymore."

She grasped his shoulders, turning him to face us. "Look at them, August. That one—" She pointed to Nic. "—she's a bit paler, but she has Alesia's face, doesn't she? She's Diana's daughter, but Alesia raised her and her sister as her own. She loved them so much, she gave her own life to protect them."

I watched as August locked eyes with Nicole, the silver in them growing hard with hate.

Boots scraped across the floor. I turned to the open vault door to see who joined us. My heart leaped with hope when she entered. A hope that shattered just as abruptly as she calmly walked to stand beside Adrienne.

"The others are handled," Celeste said.

A snarl ripped out of me as I took in Celeste. "What the fuck did you do?"

"How did you think I knew you'd be here today, Julian?" Adrienne taunted, as if it were the most obvious thing in the world. "The witches sent you, but I didn't know *when* you'd be coming."

"No," Misha whispered, unable to believe it.

Celeste had been on August's council for nearly two decades. She'd helped harbor Nic at the cabin—except Adrienne and Evander *had* found Nicole. Everyone had assumed it had been the mirrors but—

"Twenty years with us, and this is how you repay it?" I roared at Celeste. "How could you be working with *her*?"

"How could I *not*?" Celeste snapped. "Your father took *everything* from me. And you—" Her scathing eyes cut to Nic and Misha. "—your parents, your aunts, the Shaws? They *let* him."

August's eyes had gone unseeing once more, Adrienne's magic keeping him from hearing this.

I fumed, shaking with the rage of her betrayal. "What the hell are you talking about?"

"When I was a child, my parents, both animaglia, went to war. They were keepers of the High King's dragons, but they wanted to rebel. When they finally escaped, they pled to a rebel leader who swore to house and protect them. Instead, Josiah Warin killed them—but not just that. He assaulted my mother first and made my father watch before he scorched them with his lightning, completely disregarding the rules of war."

"Our parents knew nothing of that—or he wouldn't have lived another day," Nic spat.

"They knew and did *nothing*." Celeste grabbed Nic by the hair, slamming her to the floor. She was unable to fight back, bound as she was. Celeste kicked her, sending Nic careening into the wall. Several of the swords and daggers fell, barely missing her. Nic curled around herself from the pain, gasping for air.

"I've waited a hundred years for this," Celeste went on, "crafting my magic, growing and binding myself to the eagles so finally, *finally* August Warin would notice and bring me into his circle where I waited for the perfect opportunity to bring everything Josiah Warin built crashing down."

433

"August killed our father," I rebutted.

"Before I got the chance," Celeste spat.

"Enough." Adrienne put a hand on Celeste's shoulder, pulling her back.

Something Celeste said tripped my memory, my mind stumbling over the words: the eagles. The eagles were loyal to Celeste and only her. Even Misha hadn't been able to pull them away from her influence.

The eagles that were now dragons.

CHAPTER 54
Misha

We had to kill Celeste. Because if she had control of every dragon I'd made . . .

Fuck.

August's eyes cleared as Adrienne released her mind's hold on him. He watched my sister, eyes churning with hatred.

Adrienne pulled Nic forward with her shadows, bringing her beside me. "I don't trust you hiding in the corner, Nicky. You might decide to do something stupid."

"Misha."

The voice was urgent, somehow slicing through my shields and into my mind.

"Misha," Lorraine thought again.

I glanced at her, full of hatred. She'd taken Gemma's memories and warped them to hide Evander's abuse and all the terrible things he'd done to her little sister. She was no better than Adrienne.

"Adrienne gave me a bit of magic to use in here, to assist her. But you have to tell me, is Gemma safe?" Lorraine prodded.

"Why the hell do you care?" The thought was a spear I hoped would pierce Lorraine. And it worked; she flinched infinitesimally.

"Who do you think sent her with Evander across the border to Montevalle, knowing Nic would find her—that your sister would see what was happening? Why do you think I hid all those memories?"

"You stole *her memories to protect your evil brother and to protect yourself."*

"I hid *them,"* Lorraine persisted. *"The north has a mindcaster, a well-known one. He came with you today. He unraveled them, didn't he?"*

Shai had. He'd found all of Gemma's memories, tucked in the dark recesses of her mind—or, if I believed Lorraine—hidden there by her, keeping them safe.

Lorraine went on. *"Please just tell me if she's okay. Tell me—I'll do anything. I know how to get you out of here."*

I took a second, considering, studying her. Lorraine hadn't moved. Her shoulders were back, posture rigid, and her face as stoic as it had been since she'd walked in. Her ash brown hair was styled in a perfect coronet but lank, as if she hadn't eaten properly in weeks. Lorraine's emerald-green eyes, the color she and her mother had shared, were tight—pleading as they met mine before quickly glancing away.

"Gemma is safe." I sent Lorraine images of her sister, laughing and smiling with Nic and me—training with Shai and Teale. Lorraine seemed to exhale within her mind, some of her tension releasing. *"Now help us."*

"You can get out of this, Misha. Think. You can break the bonds. I'll distract them, but you have to be ready to act when I do."

Then Lorraine was gone, stepped back from my mind. The exchange between me and her had happened within a moment, the speed of mind-casting surpassing spoken words.

August was still staring at Nic as Adrienne crooned sweetly in his ear. "You want revenge for your mother's death, to really get Alesia back? Nic's sister is right there." August's gaze slid to me, recognition in his face. "That's Dominic and Diana's other daughter. Alesia raised her, too. You only have to bring me her heart."

Think, Lorraine had urged me.

As August went to the wall, grabbing a sharp dagger with a curved blade, my mind panicked, playing the prophecy over and over again in my mind: the words on the Iradelmar, the Mercedelmar, and their sister shield. But it kept returning to that one line: *the blood of a daughter of three mothers.*

Nic and I had three mothers. Born to Diana and raised by Alesia and Eve—but there was more, a different meaning tugging at me.

A lock for every key, this one having three parts, one from each of the casters.

The three casters were the three goddesses. They had used the life of the Son to bind the Void. Nic and I were descended from each: High Fae from the Made, Witch from the Siphon, and Seraph from the Above. Our magic had grown curiously fast and had been unusually powerful since we'd turned twenty-two on the Summer Solstice.

I remembered what the goblin said when we arrived—about the drag-onfire being required to forge Galorian silver. *To take gods-given power away, you need gods-given magic.*

Because what else could unbind the chains on a tomb strong enough to hold a god . . . but a god's blood?

Adrienne could only wield magic here because she'd borrowed it from the Void, a god.

But Nic and I . . . maybe there was one last key, one thing Adrienne hadn't put together.

We couldn't break the binds on our own, otherwise, my sister would have done so already. But Nicole and I had always been two halves of the same whole. Twins, together from conception. Together, we were stronger, fiercer—unbeatable and unbreakable. Alesia, our father, Eve—everyone—had always told us so and made sure we knew it, too.

I remembered my hand grazing the dragon's scales and the thread of magic that had appeared only when my sister touched me.

As August came toward me with that dagger, I reached for my sister, grazing her skin.

Together.

Nic felt me reaching for her magic; I felt hers reach back, and I knew she understood.

Separate, we were nothing, but combined, we were the key—the power descended from the three goddesses.

In a blast of fire, the shadows binding us shattered.

CHAPTER 55
Misha

Nic pulled a dagger from her boot, swinging it up to block August's. Then she whirled, lunging for one of the fallen swords.

"No!" Adrienne screamed.

August stumbled back, taken by surprise but quick to recover. He, too, grabbed a sword from the wall, moving into a defensive position.

August and Nic stood before each other, swords drawn.

Adrienne raised her hands to recast the shadows, but Lorraine shoved her into the wall. Then she pulled a dagger from her belt, plunging it through her brother's stomach.

Evander gasped, grabbing his sister by the throat, and tossed her to the floor beside me. Hatred transformed his once handsome face into something dark and hideous. "*Bitch.*"

In the outbreak, Mannix ran, fleeing like the coward he was.

Julian dove for another sword, tore it from the wall, and went for Celeste, feigning right and left as he dodged her arrows.

I lunged for Adrienne.

"*Enough.*"

A burst of shadows blasted us back. Nic, Julian, and I slammed into the far wall. Lorraine's head cracked against the stone floor. She pushed herself up slowly, her arms buckling. Dazed.

My hand found Nic's, sharing power once more. My sister cast a shield of fire before us, pushing the shadows backward.

Adrienne laughed as the flames licked along her skin, completely unharmed. "The white witch made me something special for you, Nicky." She palmed the ruby pendant at her throat, a near match to the one my sister wore.

Our former stepmother turned to me. "You didn't really think an arrow in the chest could kill a witch who'd survived for a millennium, did you, Misha? How naive."

The shadows swirled and struck again, Nic's shield nearly buckling under their assault.

"The pendant makes me immune to your magic, Nicole. Yours and August's, who so foolishly followed you to that crater, terrified for your life. One scrape of a nail is all it took. One drop of blood from each of you."

August's eyes flickered where he stood behind Adrienne, not understanding. But the expression was quickly gone.

Adrienne might have been immune to my sister's fire, but the witches hadn't taken any of my blood that day. I pressed my hand to the floor and sent the threads of my magic outward, searching.

There.

A great groan came from the cavern, then the snapping of chains. A scream—Mannix—followed by a horrible crunching sound as he met his death at the dragon's taloned claws.

Chione, free of her bonds, couldn't see to find me, but she could feel my presence, the tug of my magic. The dragon roared as she tore through the forging equipment, claws scraping at the cavern walls in search of the vault door.

Over where fire and shadow collided, Adrienne snarled. She could stay and see if she could overpower my sister's fire before the dragon clawed her way in—but it was unlikely.

"I look forward to our next meeting, Nicole." Turning, Adrienne held out an arm. August, Evander, and Celeste placed a hand on her.

In a vortex of shadows, they winnowed away.

Nic pulled the fire back into herself, staring blankly at the place where they'd disappeared. Julian looked shellshocked as well. There were no words, nothing but raw pain tearing through all of us.

August was gone.

Chione calmed as I released my hold over her, but in the silence, something hit me—something terrible I'd forgotten.

"Jophiel and Shai."

Nic's eyes met mine, wide with terror. They'd remained outside—with Celeste.

Julian lifted Lorraine, still disoriented from the blow to her head, and carried her as Nic and I sprinted forward.

We burst from the vault into the cavern, running for the tunnel we'd come through. With our speed, it took only minutes to reach it—but every moment felt like hours.

Nic and I found Jophiel lying in the dirt before the mountain pass, the soil stained red around her. Before us, Shai fought against Rainier Zarr, barely holding him off. Another twenty or so Seraphim had come at the mindcaster's calling. They flew above, fighting the five dragons Zarr had brought with him—Celeste's dragons, the ones I'd created.

The Seraphim held them back with shields of golden sunlight, but the barriers would only hold so long. The dragons slammed into them with their fire, their talons tearing at the magic.

As soon as we stepped out of the cavern, our magic returning, the familiars arrived, sensing our distress. Rasalas went to Jophiel, snarling as she stood protectively over her. Eilith launched herself into the sky, attacking the nearest dragon.

"Misha, help her." Nic stood, drawing her sword to assist Shai. Julian set Lorraine down, stepping forward with my sister. "No, you both stay back."

He ran as he shifted, erupting into the silver dragon, more than twice the size of the others. With a deafening roar, Julian was in the air. The Seraphim pulled back, allowing him to pass. The other dragons balked as Julian flew toward them.

Zarr called to one of them. As the dragon neared, he flew to its back, clinging to the scales before flying away. The other four dragons retreated behind him, but not fast enough.

The one before Eilith tried to escape, but she clasped it around the neck. The familiar gouged her talons into the soft parts of the dragon's belly, disemboweling him before tossing the body into the ravine below.

Another dragon was disintegrated in a blast of white lightning, falling to the earth as ash. Julian caught the neck of another in his teeth. Shaking, his teeth shredded through its throat until the dragon's head was severed from its body, falling limply down the mountainside.

The remaining one—Manus, I realized with a pang—escaped with General Zarr, winnowing away.

I knelt beside Jophiel. It looked as if the dragons had attacked her. There were deep gouges through her armor. Her once-white wings were stained red with blood. One had slashed at her face, leaving her cheek open and gaping.

I wondered how long she and Shai had held them off alone before the others had arrived.

"*No.*" The word was a choked sob as I hovered over her, unsure if my grandmother was alive or dead.

Slowly, I put a hand over her chest. Faintly, it rose. There was a slight thrum in her pulse—*alive*. But it was irregular, spasming. She wouldn't be alive for much longer.

"Help me. Please," I begged, looking up at Nic, then at Julian as he landed beside us in his Fae form.

My sister's face was frozen. She couldn't process this—losing both August and the family we'd only just gotten back.

Julian was crying, shuddering as he knelt beside me. "We can't move her, Misha," Julian said, devastated. "It will cause too much damage to winnow her."

"Then call a healer!" I screamed, turning to Shai.

He shook his head in defeat. "They won't make it in time."

I shook my head. No . . . *no*. I would not lose one more family member. Jophiel could not die. My hands were still on her chest as my magic spread out from my fingertips in tiny golden threads that flooded toward her.

I can fix this. I can save her.

Just like I'd transformed Julian and myself into dragons, I imagined changing the tissue. My magic created sutures, pulling the gaping slashes back together. They filled the tears in her vessels that had caused her to bleed out and stitched back together the damaged organs.

"Misha," Nic whispered, awed as she leaned closer, taking in the golden light—no, *threads*—flowing from my hands. "Are you—"

"She's *healing* her." Julian gaped.

I imagined my threads breaking off, forming tiny cells of blood that would flow through Jophiel's veins. They went to her heart that, with a shock—a piece of the magic Julian had given me during our mating—began to beat rhythmically, no longer spasming from the blood loss.

A gasp tore from Jophiel's mouth, her eyes snapping open. I'd saved her.

A daughter born of three mothers. Three goddesses. Three magics. Earthcaster. Animaglia. Healer.

CHAPTER 56
Misha

"Celeste—" Jophiel rasped, reaching for her blade.

"Easy." Julian touched a hand to her shoulder, halting her. "We know."

Jophiel looked between us, her eyes lingering on Nic and I, assessing for injuries. "Where's—"

I shook my head, cutting her off. Julian opened his mouth, but no words came out, only a choked sob.

"August is gone." Nic stood behind us, gazing out over the mountains. Southwest—where Adrienne would have taken him. My sister was too calm, too still.

I stood, reaching for her. "Nicky—"

"We need to get back to the others," she cut me off, "and tell them what happened."

A roar sounded from inside the mountain. I turned to Julian. "I can't leave her."

"No," he agreed. "We can't. We'll remain here."

He stayed kneeling by Jophiel. Most of her wounds were healed, but they would still need to be seen by Damian when we returned. Lorraine as well. Her head was in her hands where she sat on the ground, blood slicking down her temple.

"We'll be quick." Nic and I headed back inside.

The goblins seemed to have abandoned the mountain. A wise choice, considering the magic roiling off my sister. We walked, hand in hand to keep the magic intact, lest anyone try anything. I could feel it writhing and pulsing within her. Nic was hardly keeping it contained, but you'd never know from her face. She was too collected when she should have been raging—an eerie sort of cold.

We stopped only for a moment, collecting our weapons from where we'd left them upon arriving. When we reached the cavern, the dragon was on her hind legs, clawing at the walls of the mountain as if she could reach the top. Except that she couldn't—every time she attempted to lift herself, the hard-packed dirt crumbled away. She wailed in frustration.

"Chione," I called to her, and she stopped, falling onto her forelegs as she whipped her head around, searching for me. Her nostrils flared, sniffing. "I'm here."

Nic and I stood before her, our hands still clasped. I tugged on the thread that bound me to the dragon, showing her the cavern through my eyes once more. I went to her, running a hand along her white scales.

"Come, we can't leave you here." I pushed the sentiment through our bond. A mixture of joy and dread flooded back to me. For a hundred years, this was the only place the dragon had ever known. The only home she knew, cruel as it had been.

I sent her images of the mountain range outside this one. The forests in brilliant fall colors. How the West looked in the summer, lush and green. Chione calmed, excitement overpowering the dread.

The dragon lowered herself to the ground, a leg out on which we could climb. Nic and I separated our hands only to ascend onto the dragon's back. Once there, nestled between the spines on her neck behind her head, we rejoined.

Now, Chione could see what was before her. Chittering excitedly, she began to move.

We rode through the tunnels, wide enough to accommodate the dragon, though Nic and I had to duck at some parts, flattening ourselves against her. When we emerged into the sunlight, the dragon shuddered. Though the fall air was cold, it was the first time she'd felt the heat of the sun upon her scales in over a hundred years.

"Gods above," Jophiel murmured.

Using my sight, Chione locked eyes on her, roaring at the perceived threat.

Shh. She's a friend. She's my grandmother.

Chione calmed, the feeling of contrition flowed toward me.

Then the same way I'd healed Jophiel, I sent my magic into the dragon. I targeted the atrophied muscles of her chest, back, and wings, building and strengthening them. Gilded light cascaded down her wings as she spread them, testing the new muscles.

I prodded Chione, gently asking if she remembered how to fly—if she'd ever learned. Only brief flashes returned, murky and vague from when she'd been a youngling.

I'll show you how.

Julian, Jophiel, and Lorraine joined us on the dragon's back, clinging tightly to her spines. Lorraine sat with her back to Jophiel and Julian sat in front of her. She was still dazed from the head injury and needed the support lest she be overcome with dizziness while in the sky.

I sent memories to Chione, showing her how I'd flown. Images of Julian in his dragon form as I watched him. Her memories and the muscle memory came back quickly.

The dragon beat her wings, raising us from the ground until we were flying high above the mountains and back to Ankaa.

It was an hour from midnight when we returned to Ankaa, landing on the turret. In a haze, everyone rushed us, panicked and asking what had happened.

August was gone. Celeste had betrayed us.

I explained everything to them. Julian and Nic were in no state to do so. My mate had his head in his hands, silent tremors coursing through him as he cried for his brother. Sena was by his side, murmuring softly as she hugged her son's shoulders while tears streaked down her face.

Nic just stared—she stared and stared out at the mountains. She wouldn't speak to anyone, wouldn't even acknowledge them. Not even Miranda.

Damian looked over Jophiel, healing her in the places I'd missed. Then he saw to Lorraine, golden light flowing through his hands as he worked on her concussion. Everyone was still processing, unable to speak. To leave the turret we'd landed on with the white dragon, to do anything at all, seemed an impossible task.

Julian, his eyes bloodshot and red-rimmed, eventually collected himself enough to gather everyone to head to the war room. We turned to go and—

Crack.

Everyone spun around, turning toward the sound. Lorraine was clutching her face, red from where Gemma had struck her. Teale was holding the youngest Shaw back.

"You *stole* my memories!" Gemma shouted. "All of them! You let me think Evander was—"

"*Yes*," Lorraine hissed. "I did. And you got to be happy, Gemma. You got to laugh and enjoy everything this world has to offer because of it. Because Evander *hated* that we loved each other more than we did him. The first time he struck us, you were five. You cried and cried, not leaving your room for a week. He convinced our parents you were ill, and you were too terrified to go against him."

Gemma stepped back, now leaning on Teale for support. If Gemma had been five, then Lorraine had only been ten.

Evander had been a grown Fae male.

"We should have told our parents," Gemma said. "They would have—"

"Our parents did *nothing*," Lorraine spat. "Sure, they tried at first, but he was their *son*. Evander tricked them into thinking he'd changed, but instead, he only got better at the hurting, the hiding it. Hitting us where it wouldn't leave a mark, only bruising in places they wouldn't see. So, I made a decision, that I would take it all away. That I would let you play and have a happy childhood. That you wouldn't remember so you could dote on him the way he wanted, so that he wouldn't pinch or bruise or hit you as often—so he wouldn't snap any more of your bones, Gemma! I let you love him and made you hate me. And it worked, he didn't hit you as much when we weren't together. If he did, I took away every painful memory so that you would smile, Gem. So that you wouldn't be like me."

I shuddered at what Lorraine was describing. She had kept that secret for so long, unsafe in her own home, with her own family.

"And you?" Gemma stepped forward, closer to her sister. "What happened to you, Lorraine?"

Silent tears streaked down Lorraine's face. "I couldn't make myself forget."

I thought of every moment we'd spent with her. Nic and I had never gotten along with Lorraine, had never really tried. She was always so reserved, so cold.

Remorse and guilt roiled in my chest. If we had known—

But we had. There had been signs.

At the Hunt, Lorraine had sabotaged me so Evander would win—in retrospect, a panicked moment where she'd tried to save herself and Gemma from the ire they'd have surely received if he hadn't won.

Looking at her now, at the pain in her eyes, I knew she'd suffered his anger anyway. Her actions had backfired, drawing attention from him to her, especially after I'd confronted her like I did.

I nearly vomited from the shame coiling in my gut. I should have just let it go.

There won't be any sirens in the water? Lorraine had asked Alesia that day at the beach. Not out of fear, but hope. Hope they'd sense her brother for what he was and tear him to pieces beneath the waves.

Gemma took the last step forward and wrapped her arms around her sister. "I'm sorry. I'm sorry I didn't know and didn't choose you."

Lorraine hugged her back. "I'm sorry I took your choice away."

The sisters stood quietly for a few moments, holding onto each other, before heading back to Gemma's rooms. They needed time and space to work everything out between them. A life of lost memories and lies. Devastating, but with all the best intentions.

The rest of us: Nic and me, Julian, Sena, and the Seven—Six, now—gathered in the war room.

All of the dragons and eagles were gone, the Aerie completely empty. Teale had flown there to check as we flew back, having to see it for herself. The loss of the soldiers to the Moroi, the eagles, and August . . . it was all devastating.

"You all don't understand what this means." Shai shook his head. "Only Jophiel and I have been with August since the Great War. In the past hundred years, he's—" He hesitated, trying to find the words.

"Softened," Jophiel answered. "Especially once Julian came along."

I remembered watching him battle on the plain in Sanserria and against the Moroi. August was a born warrior. His power deadly was beyond compare. I was afraid to ask, but— "How much worse was he?"

Jophiel locked eyes with my sister and me. "You had two loving parents. Even if your mother wasn't there, she was present. You heard stories of her, yes? Knew exactly how much she loved you? And you have two loving aunts—godmothers who raised you as their own. As much as you've lost, having that love and support for your formative years shaped you. Now imagine August Warin: raised by a father who prized cruelty over all else. Who tortured him into becoming the perfect weapon. The only good thing in his life was his mother, the only ray of hope that kept him good . . . and now he thinks Alesia killed her."

"So, we're fucked." I threw down the map. "They have greater numbers, the dragons, and now August Warin: death incarnate."

"Yes, they have Celeste's dragons, but they're small. Ours are greater." Julian took my hand. He meant himself, Chione, and me. "And you can always create more."

"But can we train them in time?" Jophiel questioned. "Celeste worked with those birds for decades. A dragon alone is lethal, but a trained formation?"

"We will have another army."

I jumped at my sister's voice. She stood utterly still beside me, eyes glassy as she looked down at the map carved into the table. Her gaze traveled over the rolling waves of the sea.

"We will have another army," Nic repeated and stood, grasping the Iradelmar and walking from the room without another word.

CHAPTER 57
Julian

I watched Nic walk from the room, the room utterly silent in her wake.

I'd only ever wanted a life of peace. I'd never wanted to be a warrior, never wanted the things Adrienne had forced upon all of us. But now I knew:

There would be no peace.

There would be no relenting.

There would only be war.

For my brother, I would never yield.

Not until Adrienne Deimos's head was severed from her heart.

CHAPTER 58
Nic

I heard nothing as the others spoke.

All I could see was August, our last day replaying over and over in my mind. From how we'd awoken this morning up until the moment he'd disappeared, seeing me only as his enemy.

I remembered the way he'd looked as he'd asked me to marry him.

After we made love for the last time, he and I went to Sena, asking her to perform the marriage ceremony quietly. Only Misha and Julian had been our witnesses.

As our hands were bound together with the cords—silver and red—I promised to love him for an eternity, in this life and the next. Our souls were of the same divine magic, bound in ways that fate could not decide.

August had vowed to love me past his last breath. Had said that, even in death, he would fight his way back to me. He'd said I'd given him peace in a lifetime of violence. That a moment with me was worth a thousand lifetimes without.

All of it—all of him—was gone, wiped away.

My mother had known without knowing, had told August as much. *There will come a time when you will repay the favor. When snow falls in summer and when you know nothing else.*

In her vision, she'd seen it—maybe not how August would sacrifice or who it would be for. Or even that it would be twice. But she had known.

August had realized it, too, in those moments before Adrienne had taken him.

Remember what I said, Snow.

He hadn't been talking about his profession that morning. August's mind had gone back farther, to a snow-covered lake in late summer.

Whatever divine magic compromises our souls, Nicole, know that yours and mine are made of the same. There is nowhere you could go that I wouldn't find you—no corner of this earth you could be that I wouldn't seek you out. Even if my body was broken, my mind shattered, and I lost all that I am, I would always be wandering, searching for you. Even if I knew nothing else, I will always know you.

August was not my mate.

He was the summer to my winter. The cooling rain upon my burning skin. He was every breath I took, every beat of my heart.

August Warin was *everything* to me.

My husband.

Adrienne should have killed me when she had the chance.

I ran my palm over the ring I kept in my pocket: a shimmering oval, with a pale diamond set against white gold and two tiny calla lilies along the band. August had said the color of the stone reminded him of snow in the moonlight. He said that it reminded him of me.

I read the inscription inside for the hundredth time. Vowed to make it true.

August still had his ring—a simple band of white gold hastily crafted after he'd given me mine—in his own pocket. Now, he wouldn't know what it was for.

Nor the tattoo.

My hand went to the spot between my neck and shoulder, the favorite place of August's lips. I touched the small, silver crescent moon Ezra had tattooed there this morning from a memory of a night on a rooftop. The night August's arms had held me together.

August had chosen that spot and the others, marking himself upon me eternally.

It didn't matter that he and I weren't fated by the gods and stars—our hearts and souls were one. Adrienne could change or erase every memory we'd made, but she couldn't change *him*.

I was willing to go to war with the heavens and all the gods if that was what it took to get August back.

I would start with Adrienne.

I looked to the Iradelmar again, laid out on the table before me.

The flame will return. The sea will rise. The wind will howl. The earth will break.

What was once lost will return.

My eyes went to the map, to the carved image of the sea.

I grasped my sword, sapphires burning blue in the firelight, and stood. "We will have another army."

"Sister, wait." Misha found me in the corridor.

"There is somewhere I need to go, Misha."

Her eyes were wary as she walked next to me. "Nicky, I don't think this is a good time to leave the others." Her eyes shined with sadness, not just for me, though there was plenty of concern there, but for him—August.

I stopped, turning to her. "There is someone we need to meet with."

Her brow furrowed, not understanding. "Where?"

I reached out my hand. "Somewhere far."

Misha understood my intent, taking my hand and dropping the barriers around her magic so ours fused once more, giving me the strength to make such a far leap.

Our feet touched down on the black sands of the northwestern coast. It was nearly midnight.

Misha remained on the shore as I waded into the near-freezing water, calling my flame to my skin to keep the bite away. I felt power flowing through each drop of water and called to it, sending my power out into the waves—a beacon.

It took only a few minutes for the Siren to appear. "Sister." She smiled. Her emerald hair was plastered against her scalp, bobbing in the water a few feet away.

"Niniane."

"We are much past formalities. You, sister, and you, sister—" She nodded to me, then Misha. "—can call me Nia. And what have you called me for? That was quite the beacon."

"I came to make a request to you and your sisters—*our* sisters," I amended. Each of us were children of the Mother. Nia's emerald eyes gleamed in the moonlight, intrigued. I went on, "We request your help. To aid us in our time of need."

"You've had my help," Nia said. "But war is coming, as it always has been. It won't be waged over water."

Until midnight, she'd once told me. This Siren, this Seer, had always known this moment would come.

"It will not," I confirmed. Adrienne would never be so daft. "But you once walked on land before making your home in the sea. I'm asking you to return to it."

Misha went still, her eyes going wide. *This is why you've brought us here?*

Yes, I glanced back.

Misha looked at me like I might have gone mad. Maybe I had.

The jade scales along Nia's brow furrowed. "The Sirens have ruled the seas for millennia. What makes you think we can return?"

I shrugged. "An inkling, I suppose."

The Siren Queen's eyes glimmered with something like delight. "You and your sister are masters of the elements—of water and earth. Of fire and dragons. Why do you need us?"

"Because the false one, the thief of magic, wants to awaken something long forgotten—a plague upon this earth. Not just on land but in the sea as well. She seeks to free the Void."

Nia looked out upon the waves, considering. "The currents have been shifting as of late, pulling us nearer and nearer the shore. The Mother herself guides us here." She turned back to Misha and me. "We will not refuse your call. The sea will rise."

I stepped back, returning to the sand as the Siren Queen crawled forward.

As she pulled herself onto the beach, her emerald tail split into two, forming two legs clad in green scales. The skin above followed, the gills along her ribs sealing shut until she was covered in the scaled armor from her neck to her fingertips and toes.

Behind her, the faces of other sirens emerged. A few at first, then ten. Then hundreds—then *thousands*. One by one, they moved forward, shifting forms as they walked out of the surf and onto land their ancestors hadn't stood upon for millennia.

Misha watched them emerge, eyes wide, as each siren came forth from the waves, covered in their own scaled armor.

A rustle came from the forest. Misha and I turned, seeing them at the same moment: nymphs of all kinds gathered at the forest's edge. Dryads and Oreads with their billowing tree-like limbs, now stood covered in bark-like armor. Naiads, with their grey skin, had left their freshwater dwellings in silver-scales, reflecting pale in the moonlight.

"Come." I stepped closer, the sea lapping at my feet, and took Queen Niniane of Muir's hand in mine. "We are going to war."

EPILOGUE
August

At midnight, I found myself wandering through the gardens of the Hahnaleyan Palace. I did this most nights in the weeks since we'd arrived, unsure of what I was looking for.

For the rest of them, it had been a hundred years since the war. For me, it had been a day—the memories of the last century stricken from my mind by the mindcaster, Orelia and Cedric Shaw's traitorous daughter, Lorraine. This she had done after murdering her parents in cold blood—two of the last truly good people on this continent.

I certainly wasn't one of them.

I felt nothing. My heart had been ripped from my chest the day my mother died.

The last time I'd seen her, she'd been smiling—happy, for the first time in my life. Even as war raged around us, my mother had finally found an inner peace. I'd left her alone for a handful of days, and she had been murdered.

Lightning flickered in my palms.

My father had made me into a killer, and that was what I would be. As soon as I found them—as soon as I found *her*.

I continued walking through the gardens, her face all I could see.

If I couldn't exact revenge upon Alesia Sancrista herself, I could on the one she'd raised—the one most like her.

Her daughter. My obsession.

In the corner of my eye, I caught a flash of deep red and halted, but it was gone before my eyes could find it. It had been a flicker of a skirt, a gown one might wear to a ball.

I turned down the path, towering lavender on each side of the walkway.

Don't.

I halted. The word, the female voice, had seemed spoken aloud, but no one was there.

Don't say my name like that.

A shudder of pain sliced through my chest with the words, the memory of them, and I didn't know why. Looking out over the gardens, I searched for anything—any clue.

After fleeing from the Galorian mountain, we'd arrived here. It was the first time I'd been to Sanserria, to this palace built by Dominic and Diana's magic.

But now, hearing the memory, those words, I knew it was a lie. This wasn't my first time in these gardens. I'd been here before—and I'd been with someone.

There was something Adrienne and the others weren't telling me.

I pulled the white gold band from my pocket. It was simple but elegantly wrought. On the inner band was a phrase: *A love stronger than fate.*

I had been someone's husband. Someone I couldn't remember—she'd been stolen from me. I wondered if she had been the female in red, the one I'd lost.

Or had she been taken like everything else I dared to love?

Had she been the reason for the white swan tattoo, wings spread wide, now spanning the ribs beneath my chest and covering the word my father carved? Was she the one that had left delicate scratches down my back, the claiming of her teeth upon my shoulder, each mark left by her sealed with the rowan wood ash?

My body had once been a testament to my father's cruelty, to the battles I'd fought, and the lives I'd taken.

It had become an ode to *her.*

I looked up at the stars, to Cygnus, the swan constellation, as if it could give me any sort of explanation. Any hint of what had passed in the last hundred years.

Everything was a clue, but nothing was an answer.

But I knew that for her to have seen my scars, I trusted her completely—loved her with my entire soul.

My wife.

Clenching the ring in my fist, I turned, heading back toward the palace. Adrienne was my ally. I needed her, but I didn't trust her. Not during the war and not now. I checked my mental shields, hoping to keep her mind games at bay—Adrienne had always loved those.

The flash of red again, wrapped around pale skin and night-dark hair, gone just as quickly. The Wraith moved with me through the gardens, haunting me.

As I reached the terrace, snow began to fall. It softly landed upon the white calla lilies and the blood-red roses, covering them in frost. The blooms sparkled like diamonds in the moonlight. A chill snaked down my spine, seeming to come from within.

Winter is coming.

ACKNOWLEDGMENTS

Absolutely no one was joking when they said that the second book you write will be your hardest. I'm so thankful for everyone who read Summer's Snow and loved it enough to read this book. This story means the world to me, and I'm so happy to be able to share more of these characters' stories with you.

I have such gratitude and appreciation for my incredible editors. Chris Barcellona, for helping me further develop the plot, characters, and pacing. Fall's Thorns is so much better, thanks to your touch. Chelsea Beam, for copyediting and helping me catch all those line edits. Both of you have been amazing to work with, and I will never stop recommending you.

Virginia Allyn created the phenomenal map of the Continent and is genuinely one of the kindest people I have ever met.

Laura Shallcrass did the amazing illustration for the cover. She took my inspiration board and made the perfect image, perfectly capturing the essence of this book and Julian and Misha's journey.

I'm thankful for my friends, Miranda and Darrin, the first two people I ever told about this book after I'd drunk too many glasses of wine at their house. I'm also so thankful for all my other very supportive friends and family. Your support of me has made this all worth it.

To Rachel and Kenzie and all of my amazing Booktok and Booksta social media friends. You mean the world to me.

Lastly, a big apology to everyone for that cliffhanger (insert laughing/sweating emoji). But I can promise that Winter will be worth it.